Dirk van den Boom

Rising Sun

DIRK VAN DEN BOOM

THE EMPEROR'S MEN

RISING SUN

1

Yumiko Hara tugged at her son's lapel, though everyone in the room knew that no power in the world could perfect the fit of the uniform's jacket. However, this didn't prevent the older woman from trying again and again, and her son Aritomo allowed her to do so. He knew that this activity helped her to hold back the tears that would shortly be released once he stepped out of the small house to begin his trip to Yokosuka. His mother would cry, his two sisters would cry, and the only one who would remain silent was his father, at least as long as everyone watched.

Aritomo looked out of the corner of his eye to the left and right. In the small living room, on the sofa, directly under the great portrait of the Tenno, his sisters Akemi and Beniko crouched. Akemi's wedding had been the occasion for his return home. Normally, a young officer of his age hardly got any leave, but his older sister's wedding had been occasion enough to soften the heart of a supervisor, giving him the necessary permission. Certainly, the upcoming mission was also important. As with all maiden voyages, a lot could go wrong, and this was even more true for ...

His gaze wandered, clinging to the portrait of his grandparents, two fading photographs that barely discerned anything, and then there was the small altar designed to honor his ancestors. The living room was the largest room in the small house, but when the entire family gathered, it was quite full.

Existence has always been like that. The father's rigid gaze, full of expectations and observing if everyone followed consistent rules, had determined his life. Full of discipline. The care of the mother, overwhelming when the father was not looking, the only way for her to express anything other than obedience to her husband. Full of love. The sister, intimidated, with her eyes steadily turned to the ground, flinching when the father raised her voice. Or the hand. Full of violence. The old furniture with its smell of wood, the odor of shavings and remnants from the workshop, strangely mixed with the scents of the kitchen, all put together, side by side, with only the father's chair as the only comfortable seat on which no one except him was allowed to settle. Full of hierarchies.

The pictures of the Emperor. On each wall one. Almost of it real size, framed.

Full of respect.

Maybe it was silly that Aritomo Hara had been able to free himself from this confinement by joining the fleet, a hierarchy as crushing as his father's rule over his family but promising the prospect of liberation, he hoped. Climbing up the ranks, gaining his own command, and finally able to be his own man, to stretch his neck out of the narrowness and out of submission by shouldering his own responsibility.

And now his first, the most important mission, was about to begin, and parting from the family was not bitter; he looked at it like a release from jail, warm as he was to his sisters.

Aritomo urged himself to wipe away the thought. He hadn't been allowed to tell anyone what the mission was, and he had stuck to it. His father didn't ask questions and had forbidden his family to touch the subject. He was certainly proud of his son, more than he ever expressed. He was obedient and hardworking, disciplined and honorable in what he did – and everything he had ever expected of him had always been woven into exactly the same tight corset carried by the narrow shoulders of the adolescent boy since childhood. It had been the promotion of Aritomo to *Kaigun Chui*, Second Lieutenant, which had finally allowed Akemi to bring the marriage to the son of a middle-ranking official to a successful conclusion – her liberation. She was so happy that she had begun to cry hysterically at the news. Normally, a simple artisan's daughter would have been barred from even considering this social advancement. However, when the prospective father-in-law had heard of Aritomo's admission to the Officers' Academy, it had already been suggested that the first promotion from Cadet to Lieutenant would make the Hara family worthy enough. Akemi had been very happy. Aritomo knew the husband. He was not half as rigid, immovable and domineering as her father. He would give her the freedom a girl from a humble Background could expect, and that was all Akemi needed to feel complete bliss. Beniko would surely find a husband as well, whose status was above that of a craftsman. The biggest hope for their mother Yumiko Hara, however, was, that her son, perhaps after another promotion, would himself be connected to a daughter of one of the higher officers' houses, possibly even of nobility. Successful officers were of status, everyone knew that. That was the point where his mother's hopes met his father's, a point where even he himself sometimes agreed to have a serious interest in.

Aritomo was silent on these plans. He intended to focus on the fulfillment of his duties that finally would enable such promotion. A focus which required his deepest concentration, much the same as his mother gave to the uniform jacket.

"You must look good, son."

"Yes, mother."

"Did you pack everything?"

"Yes, mother."

Yumiko Hara had checked his duffel several times. She had washed and starched all his clothes so neatly that, if one looked at them closely, they seemed to shimmer out of themselves in a strange way. Probably you could place each shirt upright on the shelf. Or hammer nails with it.

"I've packed you travel provisions, son!"

"Thank you, Mother."

The small shoulder bag had been handcrafted by Yumiko, with an artfully embroidered flag, the rising red sun, the flag of the Imperial Japanese Navy where her son served. And that should really attract everyone's attention on the long train ride to Yokosuka. The contents of the bag consisted of delicacies wrapped in oil paper, into which Yumiko Hara had put all her creative power as a cook. Her son would certainly not starve on the journey. Maybe the otherwise so perfectly fitting uniform jacket would get tight in the abdominal area. But starvation was out of the question.

7

"Mother, I have to leave. The train is leaving soon."

"Yes, yes, I know."

Yumiko's answer sounded a bit lost, and when she tugged at his lapel again one last time, Aritomo saw the soft moisture of tears in her eyes. Regardless of the fit of his jacket, he took the slender figure of his mother in his arms. He had spent a week with his family. He knew that years could pass before he met all of them again. The service of an officer was exhausting, and there was little free time. Writing letters was all that was left to him, and even that option wouldn't be available to him always because of the nature of his duties.

Yumiko Hara broke away from the embrace and looked reproachfully at her son, eyes covered with a tearful veil. "I'll wet your jacket! That is not right! You have to watch your appearance, you're an officer!"

Aritomo surrendered to his fate, allowed her to dab the barely visible damp stains off the fabric. His mother did so with the quick, precise hand movements with which she did with everything she had to do, movements all too familiar to her son.

"Leave it, it's time," her husband's growling voice said. No hug, just a grab on the forearm, a quick pressure that said everything his father wanted him to say, and there needed no further words.

Afterwards, everything went very fast, mercifully fast. They stopped at the shrine to ask the ancestors for a blessing for Aritomo and then the Tenno. Their prayers were accompanied by one of the monks, whom they motivated with a small donation to a special prayer. The ceremony was short but serious, and his family's faces had been full of pride and respect. For them, what the son had accomplished, was of extraordinary importance.

They had arrived at the train station, where, despite all their self-control and formality, at least the mother had cried silently once more, carefully hidden from the public by her relatives' bodies. Aritomo had booked second class and enjoyed the relative luxury of a neat seat. His compartment was empty when the train rolled in, but that wouldn't last for long. He waved and looked out of the window until the station had disappeared in the distance and not even the fiercely whirling white handkerchief of his mother was still visible. Only then did he sit down, filled with wistful thinking about his goodbye on one side, full of anticipation for the coming challenges on the other.

For half an hour, he enjoyed the silence, staring out of the window, as the suburbs of Kobe slowly moved past him, and the express train picked up some speed. At the next stop, more passengers climbed in, some joining his compartment, including an old man with a white beard, stock-still in his slightly scuffed suit, bowing slightly to Aritomo. This was rather embarrassing for the young man, but he told himself that the respect was for his uniform, not his plump baby-face, which he had somehow preserved despite his 26 years, and which may have contributed to the fact that he triggered more maternal reactions in women than romantic ones. There were also two other soldiers, apparently returning home from leave, both infantrymen, both older men, senior NCOs, as Aritomo recognized. They greeted each other with formal courtesy.

To avoid a conversation among comrades he didn't desire at the moment, Aritomo pulled out the newspaper he had bought at the station. He glanced at the date. It was late August in the year Taisho 3 or Koki 2574, a year that, according to the powers engaged in a great war against each other in distant Europe, was also counted as 1914. The events of the war that broke out less than two months ago dominated the headlines. Aritomo had been given instructions from his superiors before he had been granted leave to only convey Japan's official stance in conversations that their own legitimate interests – especially in Russia and China – would be duly considered, and at most some support would be given to the British allies, such as escorts. In general, however, it was believed that Japan's involvement in this war would be marginal. Aritomo had kept his relief for this attitude to himself – other officers, superiors, had been disappointed – and found nothing in the paper that changed that impression. According to the reports, ' felt that this dispute would take longer than expected, and if imperial government played its cards properly under the Emperor's wise leadership, Japan could emerge stronger from this mess than before.

Aritomo pondered for some time on the military and strategic implications while leafing through the rest of the paper, finding nothing of interest, then folded it neatly on his thighs. The rocking of the train had something reassuring. He hadn't slept much last night, for he wanted to enjoy the last evening with the family, and had talked to parents and sisters until late at night, and had waken up early in the morning so he wouldn't miss the train.

Aritomo closed his eyes and decided to go to sleep.

* * *

Fortunately, the journey was uneventful. Among the missing events he was able to avoid unpleasant and exhausting conversations with fellow travelers, the feeling of hunger and a sore back. Aritomo was very fortunate, as far as his fellow travelers was concerned, could easily satisfy himself with his mother's supplies and, moreover, knew why he had spent the money on a second-class ticket. As the train finally arrived at Yokosuka Station in the evening, the young man was maybe tired and a bit tense, but all in all in good shape.

From the station, a bus drove regularly to the Naval Arsenal, the base where Aritomo had to report on time the next morning. Yokosuka was a big city with a glorious history dating back to 1063. Here was the first modern shipyard in Japan. Here was one of the central naval bases of *Nippon Kaigun*, the navy of the Empire of Greater Japan, whose proud member Aritomo had been since the age of 17.

Just this one mission, his superiors had told him, and the promotion to *Kaigun Daii*, full lieutenant, was imminent. Aritomo's ambition was not excessive. He didn't dream of the admiral's staff, only of his own command. And he would already achieve this with the rank of a lieutenant, because the division of the fleet in which he

10

was employed offered ideal conditions for a career. Lieutenants had already been appointed commanding officers, and Aritomo himself would now serve as first officer. There were not many who could claim that at such a young age.

It was quite possible in Japan's small but ever growing submarine fleet.

His papers were thoroughly examined when he got off the bus, and that although the officer on watch was a familiar comrade of his; he exchanged a few kind words with him. It was already dark, when Aritomo had finally reached his quarters, a small room only sparsely lit by a gas lamp, spartanly furnished.

Despite the long trip, he felt a certain restlessness that wouldn't let him sleep. He stowed his luggage as far as it was necessary in view of his imminent departure. As a second lieutenant, he enjoyed the privilege of sharing a room with just one comrade, and at the moment the second bed was empty. A room for himself, that was something that irritated him. He had none at home, he had not enjoyed any during training, and he would serve on a submarine that barely gave him his own berth. Aritomo wasn't used to privacy. It made him restless.

He therefore decided to give his mind some rest by taking a walk in the calmness of the evening. As he stepped outside, he unconsciously steered his steps toward the harbor, where Navy ships were moored. He marched past the mighty units, ignoring them until he came to that guarded area where the small submarine fleet of the Empire was to be found. His face was known, yet his papers were re-examined thoroughly. Then he was let into the locked district, which was so well guarded because Aritomo's boat was stationed here.

He wandered the black shadows of the small Holland boats that still formed the backbone of the tiny fleet and where he had served at the beginning of his career. He liked to think back to that time, despite the very cramped conditions aboard the units, and the fact that these American designs were constantly struggling with all sorts of technical issues that severely affected their operational readiness and range. Aritomo had in the end served as helmsman on one of those cramped, thick-bellied boats, one of only eight crew members, and it had been a torture. But the need to build a submarine force hadn't been ignored by the Admiralty, and so they turned to the British – who built the Holland licensee – and looked around for improvements.

Aritomo's eyes fell on the very peripheral construction hall, half on land, half in the water. It was particularly secure, with additional guards, and he wouldn't gain access at this time, though he would be the first officer in the vehicle to wait for its maiden voyage tomorrow morning.

A big secret, but not one that would be kept as such for a long time. Aritomo felt a deep satisfaction that he was allowed to participate in this historic moment. If everything went well, he would make his nation and his parents proud, and if he increased his experience as a submarine officer by doing so, his own command was just a formality. His goal to train new officers at the Naval Academy would sooner or later be realized. He liked to teach and he liked to learn. A career as an instructor, in addition to his own command, was the central goal of his ambitions.

It looked good.

Everything in his life had developed wonderfully.

"Can't sleep?"

Aritomo turned to see Yuto Sarukazaki in the twilight. The *Ittoheiso* was the oldest member of his crew, the highest non-commissioned officer and at the same time the chief engineer of their boat. At almost forty, he was a formidable figure. Aritomo liked the pragmatic and effective man, and he liked to listen to his advice. This put him in sharp contrast to the captain and joint superior, Lieutenant Inugami, who insisted that the sharp line between officers and the rest couldn't be transgressed by informal behavior and exaggerated camaraderie. Why did he insist on such things in the oppressive narrowness of a submarine? Here, where a cordial cooperation between all soldiers was necessary, one didn't want to get on someone's nerves quickly. Aritomo didn't understand. For him, submarine people were a special kind, for which some of the very rigid rules prevailing in the Navy didn't apply. Locked in a metal can, threatened by a particularly cruel death, this shared destiny – the real and the potential – should make a different kind of personal connection possible.

Inugami had probably never really gotten used to this idea. But the difficult superior would remain an episode, something to endure on a path that would take Aritomo past it.

"I'm not tired yet," Aritomo replied, tilting his head toward the factory floor. "I can't wait."

"I understand you well. But it doesn't seem like everything will go as planned tomorrow."

Aritomo looked up. "What happened?"

Sarukazaki had a cigarette in his hand, its red glow well visible in the darkness.

"While you were on vacation, plans have changed. I don't know any details; so far only Inugami has been informed. But he looked so happy and pleased that an important announcement must be imminent."

Sarukazaki apparently wanted to add something, but then thought better of it and said nothing. Anyway, Aritomo guessed what he had meant to say – anything that pleased his stern commander didn't necessarily have to be positive for the rest of the crew. Inugami was far more ambitious than his first officer and ready to give anything to position himself in the right light. Aritomo knew that some of the crew members called him "Lieutenant Taisho" behind his back, hinting to the man's clear aim to rise to Admiralty rank as quickly and effectively as possible.

Aritomo always pretended he didn't hear those remarks. He didn't like the man, but to obey was his duty. After all, Inugami was only a year older, and therefore it wasn't so natural for him to beat Aritomo if he didn't quite do what the commander had asked him to. With the other crew members, perhaps with the exception of the much older boatswain, he dealt liberally with corporal punishment. Blows in the face were not uncommon. Aritomo didn't belong to the faction among Navy officers who considered this tradition to be meaningful. He didn't employ beatings, as was his freedom of choice as an officer.

But who was he to fundamentally question the traditions? That was indeed the job of an admiral.

"No rumors? Normally, lower ranks know more about everything than we do," Aritomo insisted.

Sarukazaki grinned, showing his immaculate white teeth, which Aritomo secretly envied. He took a last drag from his cigarette before dropping the shimmering rest to the floor and putting it out with the heel of his shoe. As a smoker, it was difficult for him to forgo his addiction for weeks while confined in a submarine, aside from those spells they stayed above water.

"Security measures have been stepped up, there are extra guards, and our commander is dripping with joy – I suspect we expect a really high visit to celebrate our maiden voyage. Probably someone from the highest ranks of Admiralty, if you ask me."

Aritomo nodded. This supposition did indeed fit well with his own speculations. "Then we should be ready," he said, taking in the cool evening air before turning around. "I'll try to find sleep now. I suggest you do as well, Ittoheiso Sarukazaki."

The man stood tight and saluted with a smile. "Yes, Sir." With that he turned away and disappeared in the darkness.

Aritomo paused a moment longer before following his own advice. If it was true what the man had told him – and that something was in the works there was no doubt –, he would need all his energy tomorrow in order to make the necessary preparations.

And to endure the slimy anticipation of his commander.

If he liked it or not, now was time to endure some privacy.

2

"Men, we have a great time ahead of us!"

Kaigun Daii Tako Inugami teetered on tiptoe, and almost smiled at the crew in front of him. This was unlikely – Inugami never smiled –, but he radiated such a sunny enthusiasm that no one really wanted to believe.

The thirty crew members under the command of the lieutenant had gathered in one of the classrooms. The fact that they were allowed to sit down right away spoke for the exceptional good humor of their superior. Normally, he gave a speech without worrying about the well-being of his men. Inugami himself liked to stand and endure, a passion that was not shared by everyone.

"I received the news a few days ago that the maiden voyage of our new boat will receive the utmost attention. I'm not talking about the Admiralty here – although of course they are very interested in the results –, but I mean the very highest attention." Inugami leaned forward and lowered his voice to a devotional volume. "His Imperial Highness, Prince Isamu, will accompany us on our journey."

Silence descended across the room. Inugami apparently enjoyed the awesome horror sparked by his news. Aritomo felt contradictory feelings. Of course, to be visited by the second son of the Tenno, to be able to enjoy his presence more than with a fleeting glimpse, that was more than an honor, it was an event of which they would all tell their grandchildren and grandgrandchildren. Aritomo was filled with deep reverence for the imperial family, and he was delighted to attend the military parade for the inauguration of the current Tenno two years ago. Isamu was born shortly after Hirohito, the crown prince and heir to the throne, and his mother was an imperial concubine, just as Tenno Taisho himself was the son of a concubine. There was nothing honorific about that, and their wives had quickly recognized these sons as legitimate members of the family. Isamu was thirteen years old and enthusiastic about anything to do with ships. As he knew, unlike his brother, he didn't visit the Gakushuin School, where the nobility's offspring was commonly educated, but had been enrolled at one of the preparatory cadet schools, to be able to embark on the career of an officer. One never saw the young man in public in any other attire than in the uniform of a cadet, and no one doubted that he would once become an important military leader.

Besides, he was considered reserved and reclusive, almost shy, always in the shadow of his older brother, only a few months his senior, who would most likely follow on the throne. Some said he was jealous, but that was just rumors. But the descriptions of the young man as very calm and withdrawn, rather slow and deliberate, persisted so much that Aritomo was ready to give them at least some attention.

He cleared his throat.

"But Lieutenant, is that wise? Such an illustrious person on the maiden voyage of a new submarine? Is he not putting himself in unnecessary danger?"

Inugami gave Aritomo a dismissive look before settling for an answer.

"Maiden voyage or not, we've checked the boat extensively already. It works flawlessly, as the tests have proven. The young prince has made an explicit request, and it should be our highest aspiration to fulfill it. A few hours aboard our new and big boat can't be a big risk."

Aritomo bowed his head. "I understand. Will the Imperial Highness come to us alone or with company?"

"No, of course not alone," Inugami replied in a tone that clearly expressed how stupid he considered at the question. "His personal tutor will accompany him, as well as two bodyguards. We will not travel far. It won't be a problem to accommodate four additional men for the duration of the journey."

"Of course not," Aritomo confirmed, saluting.

"I want the boat to be cleaned thoroughly today, so thoroughly that there's nothing left to clean." Inugami turned to everyone. "I

16

expect the very best effort! I will make a very, very strict inspection tomorrow morning, before the highest guest visits us! Everything must be absolutely flawless! If I recognize sloppiness, this will be severely punished! And I expect absolutely perfect behavior and one-hundred per cent discipline on board! No one fails in anything, everyone works with focus and diligence! Second Lieutenant Hara, you oversee all of this. Report to me regularly. Punish them if there are omissions. I set the highest standards!"

Certainly, there was no doubt about that, Aritomo thought to himself but otherwise only stood stock-still, making the servile impression his superior expected of him.

The briefing was somewhat lengthy, as in addition to the expiration of the maiden voyage – it should take a total of about two hours, including about an hour under water – Inugami's repeated admonishments to be aware of the particular situation and appropriate behavior took a lot of time. Even a deaf soldier with low intellectual abilities would have understood it by now and the crew of the boat really wasn't made up of fools. When the grueling session was over and Inugami left Aritomo, the very attentive observer could see relief in the faces of the men. The captain had no eye for it, because he said goodbye with an urgent appointment in mind. Aritomo had no doubt that he had much to discuss with the leadership of the base to prepare the arrival of the highest visit in full, leaving nothing to chance. On the other hand, it left him with the exhausting work that was now required – the re-examination of all equipment aboard the submarine and the detailed and very, very thorough cleaning. This was an activity no one liked, and so the mood among the men was not half as euphoric as Inugami surely expected them all to be.

But actually, that didn't matter.

Whatever the circumstances, Aritomo loved to be on the boat.

When he saw it lying in the water in front of the wharf, dragged out of the workshop for presentation, his heart pounced. The mighty body of the gray-black boat was impressive. It was a British design, the so-called E-Class. The British government had just recently given Japan the license to build this vehicle – more or less unofficially. With a length of around 54 meters, it carried eight torpedo-tubes.

Under water, it reached a maximum speed of nearly ten knots with its electric motors – something they would, officially, try on maiden voyage. It could, the British said, dive up to 30 meters deep, and that was something they hadn't done in the testing rides yet. Aritomo was sure that it could go a few meters deeper. He was eager to test the limits of the boat, though he certainly wouldn't be allowed to do so with the Prince on board.

With a total of 31 crew members, the boat was so extensively manned that, unlike the older and much smaller units, it had earned itself the presence of two officers. There were four NCOs, mostly with specializations like the experienced Sarukazaki. Thus, 25 ordinary crewmen remained. On board this boat, there would be no fresh recruits, only sailors who already were experienced. For experiments with inexperienced crewmen, this first of its kind was much too valuable. They were veterans, as far as the young submarine fleet of the Empire had any. Aritomo had had plenty of opportunity to familiarize himself with the men. They were all disciplined experts, men with great personal courage and the level of sacrifice necessary to face the dangers of traveling beneath the surface of the water in a tight metal shell. Howsoever the maiden voyage would go, the crew would do anything to make it successful, whether with a Prince as a guest or not.

Moored with bolts in front of the tower stood the second weapon of the boat next to the torpedoes, a twelve-pounder. For this cannon, they had four trained gunners on board, and everyone had at least one extensive training session with it. That was just one of the key innovations in comparison with the old boats, which had relied exclusively on their torpedoes. It was these and other design changes that were to remain hidden from Japan's enemies for the time being, and that had led to not station this new boat in the Kure fleet base, but rather here in Yokosuka. Once the boat's existence was officially admitted, it would be transferred to Kure to lay the foundations for the second submarine flotilla, which would make the old Holland boats, including their successors improved by Kawasaki, obsolete.

But before that, there were more mundane tasks, especially now, and the most important thing was to scrub and polish the No. 8

boat, so that it shone like silverware despite its dark gray color. The Prince shouldn't have any reason to complain, in this Aritomo was quite in agreement with his commander.

When the men started the work, Second Lieutenant Hara was not shy, while he supervised the joint effort, to pick up a rag himself.

It wouldn't be lack of effort from his side, he thought, if anything was found to be amiss during inspection.

Certainly not from his side.

3

There was no music and no large parade.

Prince or not, not too many people were supposed to know what a great new submarine the Japanese navy now possessed. So they kept the occasion somewhat under wraps, as far as that was possible with the attendance of a member of the imperial court. A column of four cars had pulled up, and next to the crew of the boat, a company of honor stood rigidly, fully dressed and thus in stark contrast to the submarine's men, as they wore uniforms, although clean, appropriate to the mission at hand.

Inugami had inspected the boat in the late evening, and for once had been satisfied. Despite intense scrutiny, he had noticed nothing negative, which he had acknowledged with rare praise. Everyone had noted this with relief, because Aritomo could testify that they had really made an effort.

Inugami had told them that the group of passengers would be extended by one more person. An engineer from Kawasaki would participate in the maiden voyage, officially to be available for explanations, unofficially, in order to gain additional expertise in case of problems.

That was logical and understandable, even a welcome development, as the First Officer secretly thought, despite the increasingly cramped conditions on board.

Problems could always occur. Aritomo remembered, like all his comrades, the fate of Boat No. 6, which wasn't able to surface when it stranded in depth of only ten meters due to a technical failure in a dock. The old Holland boats had provided no device by which the crew could have left their prison in submerged condition. So the men had stayed in their posts until they suffocated, only a few yards from the shore. Only the next day had it been possible to lift the boat and recover the corpses of those heroes.

The boat was now a memorial. It reminded of the dangers of this new technology.

Aritomo's gaze wandered over the hull of boat No. 8. The new design made it possible, as far as the depth allowed, for the men to leave the boat when it was beyond salvation and the surface wasn't too far away. So hopefully they would never share the fate of the deceased.

Nevertheless, the man from Kawasaki came along. He had been, it was said, involved in the construction of this boat from start to finish, and knew it even better than the good Sarukazaki, who had dealt with every nook very intensely. Aritomo didn't want to admit it, but the fact that the engineer was on board was already reassuring. And the new boat was so much bigger than the old Holland units. They would certainly be able to manage for the short trip that was planned. Orders were shouted. The honorary company presented the rifles. The submariners stood upright on the spotless hull of their boat, only Aritomo and Inugami had positioned themselves in front of the gangway over which the Prince would step.

When he left the car, suddenly there was an awe that seized all men like a paralysis. A scion of the divine Tenno was and remained something very special, and nobody could escape the charisma of the Japanese imperial house. The young man – the boy actually – looked perfect in his cadet uniform, which fitted like a glove. His illustrious father's face was recognizable on his own features, if one dared to look at it long enough. His cheeks were a bit roundish, but his gaze was as majestic and penetrating as one would expect. His companions came as announced: an elderly gentleman who had to be the tutor, two wiry soldiers clad in a plain black uniform who were undoubtedly the bodyguards armed with a pistol and a sword, a rifle on their back, as Aritomo registered, and then a man in civilian clothes, not much older than Inugami, carrying a large black briefcase. The engineer from Kawasaki.

Aritomo's eyes widened.

A *gaijin*.

The officer controlled himself. Naturally. He could have anticipated that. The boat was built based on plans of British manufacturers. There was a long tradition of cooperation between Britain and Japan, especially in the development of naval forces. And British engineers often ran around in the big yards, all under contract from the Japanese government, to help develop or transfer new technology. So it was logical, even predictable, that with this new piece of technology, the pinnacle of British boatbuilding, an engineer from distant Europe would see to it.

Aritomo scolded himself for his first, disapproving reaction.

Without the British – and other friendly European powers – the imperial fleet in its present form wouldn't exist. That might seem like a blemish, but it was also a fact. The engineer from the British Empire was a help, not a threat. He had to keep that in mind. The man was here, because the Admiralty thought it necessary.

Aritomo Hara wouldn't question that decision.

He took a deep breath. They were all complete. The big moment was imminent.

The Prince positioned himself as was expected of him but seemed strangely inconspicuous, almost shy. Instead of saying something by himself, his teacher took the floor. Aritomo only half listened to the speech. The old man greeted the soldiers and thanked them. He pointed out that the Prince was aware of the conditions aboard the boat and that careless touch or other afflictions wouldn't be construed as offensive or unruly behavior. He expressed his hope that the maiden voyage would be free of problems and praised the soldiers for their service. A little speech that should serve as general reassurance. Aritomo was astonished to find that, in spite of his superficial attention, it was effective. He felt a bit more relaxed and could recognize subtle signs of relief among his men. Everyone had been afraid of making a nasty mistake unintentionally, fatal in the immediate vicinity of such an exalted person. The visitor was obviously aware of this fear and had tried to do something about it.

Aritomo frowned involuntarily.

Why did a cadet, who lived and learned at a cadet school from morning to evening, actually need a private teacher?

22

He looked at the young Prince, who stood beside his mentor, his face uninvolved, neither approving nor rejecting, but listening just as stoically as the tight-shouldered soldiers. For a moment, however, he looked up, moving his head slightly and glancing at the men's line, stopping briefly at the eyes of Aritomo, highlighted by his position at the quayside and his officer's uniform. Their eyes didn't meet for a long time, but for the officer, that moment was rather unpleasant – and not because of a sudden reverence or some of the fear the teacher was trying to dispel.

But because he had the impression that this look of the young prince had been so terribly ... empty.

Aritomo blinked. Inugami barked an order. The boat was to made ready. All men were expected at their stations before the guests arrived. No risks. Immediate haste commenced.

Aritomo scared away the thought he had just had. He was foolish. Presumptuous. Nothing that had to occupy his brain. His duties lay elsewhere, and he gratefully accepted that insight, concentrating on making that journey of his beloved boat a great success.

For Japan.

For the Emperor.

For himself.

* * *

They gave him the tour. It was tight, it was slightly stuffy, and despite all the words of the old teacher, everyone felt a bit uncomfortable in the immediate vicinity of the Prince. The boat was a little over fifty yards long: the front-end torpedo room, the engine department with the diesel and electric motors, the close quarters of the officers – all the other crewmen slept as best they could at their stations –, the control room under the bridge, that one located on the tower, the middle torpedo room from which the boat could launch torpedoes sideways, and the small fair where heated food and tea could be cooked. After all, the boat was so wide that in some places up to three men could stand side by side.

The British engineer – Robert Lengsley was his name and he had behaved politely, friendly, even spoke some Japanese, indicating that he had been residing here for some time – stayed with Sarukazaki in the engine room.

After everything had been shown, Aritomo exhaled in relief. Lieutenant Inugami had performed like a rooster in a chicken coop, lost himself in endless explanations, almost giving the impression that he had constructed this boat on his own, built it with his two hands, and could navigate it all on his own if allowed to do so. That the young Prince had tolerated these eulogies with disciplined calmness, spoke for the young man's capacity for suffering, an ability that possibly had its roots in the strict education at court. The old teacher had asked some polite questions in the beginning, but then realized that Inugami took every other question just as a reason for a fresh speech, and it was all too obvious that the man wasn't very comfortable in the confines of the boat.

Inugami finally ordered, to everyone's relief, that the boat should proceed on its voyage. The Prince wanted to watch this process outside, from the tower, which was universally accepted, because it meant that he and his companions would not contribute to the tightness aboard the ship. The commander himself insisted on accompanying the young man outside. Amazingly, the old teacher stayed down on in the control room. He seemed to consider the finiteness of the boat to be the lesser evil than having to endure Inugami's lectures, and was visibly pleased when a cup of tea was served for him.

Aritomo bowed to the old man. "I hope the boat doesn't get too cramped for you, esteemed teacher."

"My name is Daiki Sawada, Lieutenant. I would be glad if you simply approached me as Mr. Sawada. The never-ending kowtowing is somehow misplaced in such a limited space. You bump easily into each other."

Aritomo smiled and bowed again. "Of course, Mr. Sawada. Your student seems to be very docile. He listened attentively to the lectures."

The old man's gaze faded a little, as if searching for the right answer to this claim. His distress was ended by loud orders from above. There was not much to do on the bridge. Only the helmsman relayed the commander's orders to the engine room. The soft vibration of the diesel engines filled the body of the boat as it drifted away from the quay with majestic composure – or great caution, depending on the point of view – and then slowly started up. It was not an exaggeratedly cool morning, so the wind was certainly been bearable at higher speed, and Inugami evidently linked the departure with a small harbor cruise for the Prince.

Military music was audible from the quay, and the honorary company shouted with vigor: "Banzai!"

Aritomo closed his eyes for a moment, feeling the subtle movements of the boat under his feet and the potential, still restrained, a dormant power at their command. It was an uplifting feeling and worth all of the effort.

The weather played along. The sea was calm. Aritomo looked at the instruments in front of him, the diesel engine tachometer, the compass, the speedometer. He could feel the quiet sound, the perfect position of the boat in the water. Everything went so well together. It was a marvel of technology.

"All the writing here is in English," muttered Sawada, as he studied the endless array of controls and levers and buttons that covered the wall, watching the work of the helmsmen.

"Correct. On all ships of the Japanese Navy the descriptions and signs are in English," Aritomo told him. "Most of our first ships were built by British shipbuilders, many of the consultants were British, and many of the first instructors as well. We have learned a lot from the Royal Navy, and that has been reflected in the fact that all our new ships continue to adhere to the English language. Every officer has to learn English, though many only learn the basics."

Sawada looked inquiringly at the young man. "There are enough of us who still believe it is beneath our dignity to learn a foreign language."

Aritomo nodded. "Yes, and many officers have joined this group. But we wouldn't have a fleet if we hadn't been able to absorb foreign knowledge. And we would only have enemies abroad if we refused to accept languages other than our own."

Sawada smiled. "Contracts are often temporary."

"You surely know more about these things than me. I am only a second lieutenant. I am executing the orders of those who know and guide us."

"But I suppose, Lieutenant Hara, that you took your English lessons seriously."

Aritomo nodded. "I took every one of my lessons seriously, Mr. Sawada. I come from a poor artisan's family, and the naval career was a unique opportunity for me to do something different. I was the best student in the class and received a scholarship for high school. I was third in my year at the academy. I could have gotten an assignment on one of the big cruisers. But I wanted the submarines."

Before the old man could say anything, they heard movement from above, and legs appeared on the ladder. Moments later, Inugami and the Prince had reached the bottom. They were followed by the two bodyguards who hadn't said a word the whole time.

"Get ready for diving!" the commander ordered after he himself had closed the bulkhead. "Ready to blow out!"

There was no rush. Everyone knew what to do. They had an excellent crew.

Nevertheless, Aritomo felt excitement and tension, and he wasn't the only one here.

They went down into the depth.

The boat was in its element.

And Second Lieutenant Aritomo Hara was too.

4

"We've reached a depth of 15 meters," Inugami explained in a submissive tone to a quietly muttered question by the Prince. It was the first articulated question he had asked himself, instead of nodding to emphasize his teacher's inquiries. Aritomo paid only marginal attention to the exchange. While the lieutenant was playing the tour guide, he was the first officer to oversee the boat's journey. It proved difficult to entertain the guests and at the same time run a boat. In their division of labor Inugami had therefore focused entirely on the Prince and left the rest to Aritomo.

That was quite satisfactory.

The boat worked very well. The dive had gone smoothly. As soon as the tanks had filled with seawater, the diesel engines had stopped. Completely silent, the body of the boat had slid below the ocean's surface, then the electric motors had been started.

"Does the Prince want us to resurface? Not everyone feels at home in the deep," Aritomo heard the Captain's question. The young man's answering voice was hard to understand, but with no order to end the dive, it was likely that he would endure it for a while longer. If Aritomo got it right, glancing out of the corner of his eye, the Prince was anything but sad or frightened. His movements seemed more active since the boat has started its descent, his eyes were bright. The boy was excited about this technology and glad to see it in action. Aritomo began to warm himself for the Prince, because he could understand this childlike fascination quite well.

Aritomo looked around. All crew members radiated the calm competence of experienced submariners. All of them had served on the old Holland boats. By comparison, their new home would seem like a luxury to them, as spacious as a festival hall, and even with a proper toilet that shot feces out into the water with heavy air pressure. On the Holland boats, there had been no more than a bucket filled and dumped over the side of the ship when back on the surface. That wasn't something Aritomo really liked to remember.

"We're going to periscope depth now," Inugami announced, giving Aritomo a meaningful look. But he had already taken action and whispered commands to the crew in the control room. It was barely noticeable how the boat reacted, obediently, without deviation, with a sense of elegance and security.

"Periscope depth, Captain!" Aritomo announced moments later.

Inugami pulled out the periscope and let the Prince glimpse for a while while he did nothing but look complacent. Everything went according to plan. If this trip was over, the admiralty's gaze would rest with the utmost benevolence on Lieutenant Inugami.

"I can't see much," the prince said quietly, turning the periscope a little to the left and right. "It's very foggy."

Inugami gave Aritomo a confused look. "Fog, Your Highness?"

They had left in the late morning, with bright sunshine and a calm sea. When they had looked at the horizon one last time just before diving, there was no sign of fog far and wide.

"If you allow ...?" Inugami asked, and the Prince stepped aside to make room for him. It took less than a minute, then the officer turned his eyes from the eyepiece and left it to Aritomo.

"We better return," the Captain explained. "We don't want to accidentally ram somebody. Few nautical miles away, the fog should have disappeared."

Aritomo immediately recognized the meaning of Inugami's order. In fact, the boat was surprisingly navigating in a dense soup. Where it had come from so unexpectedly and in the face of these weather conditions – that was very puzzling. Something like that had never happened to him before.

Here in relative proximity to the Japanese coast, there was a lot of busy shipping traffic. In fact, it was better to regain depth and avoid the danger of a collision. Not everyone took the regular operation of the foghorn seriously, and within the boat, one of those sounds could easily be overheard.

"Thanks for the valuable hint, Your Highness," Aritomo kindly thanked him as he had retracted the periscope. The Prince hinted a smile. With that he suddenly looked very, very young, like a child he in a way still was, after all. The first officer refrained from further comments. He had no intention of competing with his superior for the imperial favor.

There was work to do, anyway.

The boat sank cautiously back into the depths. At about twenty meters they stabilized it, and the electric motors pushed it through the waters. Five knots weren't a lot of speed but enough to keep the boat steady and slowly clear the area of the strange fog banks that had appeared so unexpectedly. Inugami had ordered to keep this course for half an hour, then reappear and observe. Although not actually dangerous, this change of plan created some tension among the men and gave the Captain the opportunity to demonstrate his leadership skills.

Aritomo frowned. There might be some tension but apparently not enough to keep the men awake. He watched as one of the helmsmen suddenly yawned and wiped his eyes. It was a bit too much for the first officer, and he gave the man a warning glance. Everyone was well-rested for this trip! But before he could say anything, Aritomo sensed that a sudden weariness overtaking him as well. Involuntarily, he ran his hands through his short-cropped hair and blinked.

Tea. He might need a strong tea. He yawned involuntarily, his gaze moving almost automatically to the carbon dioxide display. The pointer had not moved. But was the instrument correct?

He looked around. The same symptoms discernible with all men. Yawning. Blinking. The Prince was just now covering his wide-open mouth with his gloved hand.

Carbon dioxide poisoning! he thought. Inugami looked at him, the same realization in his eyes. Something had to be wrong with the air supply. The adrenaline animated him.

"Surface!" he ordered. "Immediately and hatches open!"

The boat trembled. The ballast tanks pumped the water out. Aritomo felt the bow tilt up, imperceptibly, and stared at the depth gauge. Fifteen meters. His eyes blurred. He wiped his eyes. Ten meters. He had to hold onto the wall against his will as his knees softened. So fast ... no CO_2 poisoning worked that fast.

This wasn't normal. He felt so terribly weak, very dizzy, a little sick maybe ...

He saw how Inugami swayed too. The old Sawada had already slumped to the floor, and the Prince slid down, clinging to the wall for a moment, as if to preserve some imperial dignity, uttering a soft, barely audible cry. Aritomo tried to fix his gaze on the depth gauge again. Five meters. The boat would break the water surface at any moment. If he only lasted long enough – or one of the other men – to open the hatches, at least one at the bridge ... The fresh air would ...

Aritomo's thoughts swirled, and he lost all concentration. Inugami was lying on the ground, didn't move anymore. The helmsmen sank over their instruments. With superhuman effort, he took a step toward the ladder leading up to the hatch, then clung to the rungs for a moment, forcing his eyes open, trying to ignore the dancing black veils.

He didn't succeed.

He almost felt the boat emerge with gentle sweep, but then he lost all strength and sank unconscious to the ground.

There was no one on board to open a hatch.

Aritomo came to lie next to the Prince and was as quiet as everyone else.

5

K'an Chitam looked up the temple, wondering if it was worth it. The more than 30-meter-high construction was not finished yet, but that was not necessary. The numerous workers who worked under the supervision of the great architect Chaak had time. Their ruler, the mighty Siyaj Khan K'awiil II, King of Yax Mutal and descendant of Yax Nuun Ayiin, was not only alive but continued to enjoy good health. For Chitam, that was good news on many levels: It meant that his own coronation was still quite far in the future, and it meant that he continued to live, despite his court duties, a relatively carefree life. As the eldest son of the king, he enjoyed a number of privileges, including the fact that no young woman in Mutal could avoid his advances, a circumstance that the now 25-year-old prince used extensively, wife or not. As long as he fulfilled his other duties, he was subject to no further restrictions from his father, who was always busy with other tasks. With that, Chitam enjoyed a special privilege. Usually, adultery was not a matter that his people accepted lightly. But the heir to the throne was not only the next king, he was also a man with a sunny mind, always friendly, generous, witty and lacking the arrogance of many noblemen who consistently thought they were someone better.

Of course, Chitam was someone better.

He didn't think he had to rub it in everyone's face. And the beautiful daughter of a peasant was also much more inclined to approach his overtures with a certain passion, if he didn't behave like an asshole but presented himself as a nice, good-looking, charming and powerful man who would be in charge in a few years.

One just had to put one's qualities to good use.

K'an Chitam sighed and looked at the artisans around him, who pounded the stele stones with great care and fervor. Although his father, the king, was a direct descendant of that ruler whom the conquerors of distant Teotihuacán had appointed, he was now anxious to break away from the memory of this military campaign and its consequences, and to establish a truly local dynasty. Although there were still vague references to the origin and legitimacy of their rule in the stelae commissioned by Siyaj, it was also clear that the campaign had been more than thirty years ago, and no soldier from Teotihuacán had ever returned to Yax Mutal's soil. It was therefore time to remember what was right in front of them and still very tangible. It was necessary to show the people that Siyaj and his son Chitam were rulers in their own right, chosen by the gods, and thus their mouthpiece and connection to the mortal world.

Chitam found this request of his revered father highly commendable, as he prepared the needed stability and respect for his son's rule. But just this morning, after a night of drinking, in which the Prince, together with his friends, had consumed vast amounts of holy *chi* in a very unholy way, the hammering of the artisans was almost unbearable. But since his father had told him to supervise the progress of the work himself, he had to indulge in his duty. The fact that he had drunk chi with his companions, less to gain spiritual closeness to the gods but simply to have a good time, displeased the priests at court as much as it did his father. To prove too much rebelliousness didn't pay off today. In addition, this was a good opportunity to escape Lady Tzutz, his wife, who also had little sympathy for his nocturnal activities.

Chitam knew its limits – though not in terms of alcohol consumption. It was also so damn hard to get really drunk when chi had so little power. He had to pour the stuff in liters. So it was at least helpful that the sometimes sour taste of the beverage became less obvious with increased intoxication – or he simply did perceive it that way.

The horrible feeling in his mouth this morning, however, could Chitam interpret only as punishment by the gods. The great nausea, which was additionally reinforced by the scorching heat, possibly too.

It just wasn't his day.

He shaded his eyes and looked up at the tall pyramid building. His father would find a very worthy tomb here – and hopefully many years in the future. In Chitam's opinion, it was no great joy to be king of Yax Mutal. One had to constantly participate in the rituals to ask the gods for rain and harvest, for victory in the war and for general prosperity. Only recently there had been a great ritual that Chitam had at least had to passively attend. His father had been standing on top of the temple, the priests had pierced his foreskin with a needle, and, stunned by drugs and pain, the great Siyaj Khan K'awiil II had called the gods. After that, two POWs with strong restraints, were tied together into balls and thrown down the 25-meter temple stairs. With shattered bones they had reached the bottom, and not one had complained about his suffering.

That wasn't Chitam's problem. Enemies were enemies, and prisoners of war were sometimes also victims for the gods. It had always been that way, and it always would be like that. But this tinkering, all the blood and eternal, ever-repeated rituals, that was nothing that filled the Prince with anticipation.

And so it happened that, for selfish reasons, he wished his father a long and healthy life.

"Sir?"

Chitam turned around. Behind him stood two servants, one armed with a large palm frond, with which he fanned the narrow, almost slender figure who had spoken to him. When he recognized her, a smile crossed Chitam's face, not so much because he was really pleased but rather because it was one of his duties to react in such a way.

The unattractive woman in front of him, her mouth too tight, her nose too narrow, and her shoulders too wide, was the Lady Tzutz Nik, his wife. He would never have chosen her for this position, but his mother, the most honorable Lady Ayiin, and his father, the King, who was very calculating in these matters, had insisted on this particular marriage. Tzutz Nik had all the qualities that Chitam felt were a nuisance to a woman – intelligence, a will of her own, education, and at the same time she was quite unattractive and always looked somehow sickly. Chitam had disliked most of

33

his marital duties, and although Tzutz Nik was almost six years younger than he – he in his prime age –, she had only given him two daughters, though certainly more was to be expected of her, although with his own participation somewhat forced. Something that couldn't be said of a number of other young women in Mutal.

But Tzutz Nik was his wife, and she would one day be the queen. Even now she sometimes acted as if she already held this position, at least as far as the regency over her husband was concerned. The fact that she usually had a much clearer understanding of politics and the court than himself already pointed out that she would be a queen to be reckoned with.

As has been said, Chitam wished his father a *very* long and healthy life.

The fact that his swollen eyes and strong thirst told her something about his current condition certainly didn't help make the upcoming conversation a pleasant part of the morning.

Chitam sighed.

Then he smiled as good as he could.

Because this was his duty.

Tzutz bowed respectfully; after all, there were enough spectators here. But Chitam, to whom the young daughter of a significant noble family had been married when she was sixteen years old, was able to interpret the true expression of the esteemed lady. She was not pleased.

"Sir, you skipped breakfast. Do not you feel well?" she asked with exquisite courtesy.

Chitam grimaced. Breakfast. The thought itself ... "I'm fine," he said, perhaps a little curtly, but by all the gods, he was the husband and Prince. "Thank you for your concern, my lady."

"May I remind you that we're having a banquet tonight for our good friend K'inich and his wife. We delayed this a long time, and they are in town today to pay their respects to the King."

Chitam's expression darkened. K'inich was the ruler of a small vassal settlement a few miles outside the city limits of Mutal, at least as far as one wanted to grant him the title of a "King" at all. So close to the mighty Mutal that his position was no more than that of a glorified governor. K'inich regularly came to pay his respects and to renew the bond with Yax Mutal, usually right after the first harvest. That was all well and good, but the governor's wife was an old acquaintance of the honored Lady Tzutz, and so it was customary for them to have a banquet. The "good friend" was an old-fashioned landed nobleman, and considered himself something better than the current dynasty of Yax Mutal, which was ultimately attributable only to Chitam's grandfather, who had been used by the Teotihuacán usurpers as a front. The old royal family of Yax Mutal, whose history went back much further, had been excluded from rule. One more reason for Chitam's father to establish a new, his own genealogy with a clear reference to local traditions. K'inich, of course, was not easy to wrap up. He could look back to an unbroken line of predecessors and that made him – at least in his own eyes – something special. It really had to make this man very angry that his expanded village had to pay tribute to the mighty Yax Mutal so that he could continue this tradition with his head remaining on his shoulders.

Anyway, he wasn't a good friend, and the yearly banquet a most unpleasant business. Of course, Chitam as heir apparent had to uphold etiquette. K'inich was officially a loyal vassal who always fulfilled his obligations completely and punctually. So he enjoyed the respect of such, and of course that was also for the corresponding good behavior of the Prince.

But Chitam didn't feel like good behavior today. He just wanted to sleep.

Lady Tzutz didn't seem to be prepared to liberate him from this social obligations – otherwise, she wouldn't have bothered to remind him immediately on the morning of the important day.

"I didn't think about anything else the whole day," he lied to his wife. In fact, last night he drank so much because he wanted to suppress the memory of the impending banquet. And Tzutz knew that, of course, as her fine smile signaled all too clearly.

"I'm glad, my husband," she said, bowing again, and then darting away gracefully across the paving stones of the square toward her palace. Chitam looked after her for a moment, refusing to shake his head – both because of the spectators and because of his severe pain in this area – and apparently devoted himself to the construction work again. As expected, on this front everything went very well. The tomb would become a wonderful temple, bigger than the one next to it, and a worthy addition to the acropolis. Mutal wasn't just any city, and no matter how much Chitam wished that he wouldn't become king to soon, he knew that the current expansion in both population and production would soon make it possible that tribute wouldn't only be paid by village chiefs like K'inich. No, there were more rewarding goals, and Chitam already had very precise plans.

In return, it would be worthwhile to become king.

The hammer that drove the obsidian bits into the stone really got on his nerves. He decided that he had fulfilled his duties and, with some servants in attendance, he returned to the palace where his father resided and waited for his report. Chitam was well-known in Yax Mutal, and anyone who crossed his path was respectfully keeping his distance, making the expected signs of reverence and not bothering him with unnecessary conversation. Chitam, on the other hand, was free to stop and address anyone, a privilege he used extensively in young women. He had already fathered many children in his life, and although this offspring didn't automatically lead to the mothers being promoted to a higher social rank, the royal house was also responsible for the illegitimate children, as long as legitimacy played a role. As long as the King was well, his children didn't have to suffer; the same was true for the crown prince. The population of the city grew steadily. After recovering from the invasion two generations ago, the upswing was unmistakable. Other parts of the forest constantly were cleared to make room for new fields and buildings. The city center grew more and more beautiful every year, as more and more aristocrats created grandiose structures, and the King led them all the way. Trade flourished. The upper class was covered with jewelry made of green jade, the most valuable of all gemstones, and the often magnificent presentation especially on feast days blinded the simple man. But that didn't mean that the simple peasants suffered. Farming had been refined, yields became bigger and bigger, especially with the food that formed the basis of everything: corn. The royalties paid to the ruler were enough to feed his own family. If one paid attention to all the holidays and paid homage to the King in the prescribed manner, opportunity to participate in the military campaigns arose – which in the case of Chitam's father didn't mean much, since his activities were directed more inward than outward, a circumstance his son endeavored to end in time. Everyone in Mutal lived a good life, as a citizen of one of the most powerful cities of the corn people.

Chitam stopped.

Another passerby, a man of nobility, as one could see from his retinue, had a servant hand him a cup of quill, a coffee made from roasted corn. Although the Prince did not really want to eat, he felt the need for liquid as the pleasant scent of the freshly-heated drink reached his nose. It mingled with the freshly baked corn patty, which the servant unpacked. It was certainly the privilege of the Prince to demand his own share, but at the same time it was extremely rude, because as a member of the royal family he wasn't a beggar. Chitam's eyes narrowed. The man was somehow known to him, but he was turning his face away. Had not he even bumped with him last night? At some point they had been so many, because he had lost track of everything, and some details of that merriment he could remember only vaguely anyway.

"Tell me, who is this gentleman?" Chitam quietly asked the servant closest to him. "I should know him ... By Naal, I'm getting old."

His servant bowed and made a negative gesture. "It's hot, sir. The sun obscures our thoughts. The young master there is Tek'inich, the son of the high priest of the Naal."

Chitam's memory cleared. Tek'inich was an important man. He would become high priest before Chitam became king, and that was a significant detail, for it was Tek'inich who would direct and bless the Prince's coronation ceremony.

He definitely had too much chi last night.

Tek'inich looked up, recognized Chitam and smiled at him. He beckoned to him, exactly what the Prince had hoped for.

Moments later, he drank a particularly hot quill, and he felt the warmth and strong taste spread through him, helping clear his head. He even laughed at a remarkably bad joke on Tek'inich's part. He almost even accepted the offer to try one of the corn patties.

But he didn't want to get cocky.

Chitam knew that it would be late again tonight.

They talked for a while. Tek'inich was not a man of special ambition, but he was considered wise and sensible. He would be a support to Chitam, someone whose help the young king might one day depend on. He was not a particularly likable man and was not one of Chitam's close friends, but the noble lady Tzutz pointed out to her husband every week that it would be helpful to have a nice word with him, to be friendly and polite, because you never know.

Tzutz knew a lot about all these things. She also knew Tek'inich's wife and maintained a friendly relationship with her.

That should, Chitam thought, really suffice.

When he said goodbye to the man to finally rush to his father's palace, he felt better. He developed something like optimism. Energy returned to his body.

Maybe, he thought, it would be a good day after all.

6

The dinner proved to be a test of his abilities.

Of course, this was not due to the food offered. The cooks had done their best under the supervision of Lady Tzutz. All the dishes one could imagine, made from corn, beans, pumpkin and cassava. There were three freshly roasted peccaries whose best pieces were, of course, presented to the guests and the host, the Prince. Chitam's appetite had returned, but he didn't tend to be a glutton while eating, unlike with drinking chi. His guest was less restrained and preferred to eat all the best pieces, as if it were a great shame to just eat enough and then leave the other, less worthy diners some of the specialties. Of course, there were additional guests: Some nobles who, for whatever reason, were friends with the village brush or wanted to make friends, and Tzutz had certainly selected and invited them with care and diligence. The underlying logic was female in Chitam's view, and therefore it was quite pointless to try to understand it for fundamental considerations.

The evening was absolutely predictable. The guests were of submissive politeness, but it was not by chance that the village chieftain, as Chitam still quietly called him, never missed an opportunity to spread anecdotes from the oh so glorious and, of course, endlessly long family history of his. The fact that he – very submissive and respectful – looked at Chitam and always touted a toast, didn't make things better. The message arrived and wasn't hidden from the other guests of the family. Everyone looked at Chitam, asking themselves how he'd deal with this subtle and permanent provocation. Did he stay at formal courtesy? Would he have his head cut off?

Chitam chose the former. These were the moments when he was more a Prince than an upset son, and he had a role to play. He pretended to listen attentively to his guest's monologue and made sure his wife couldn't complain about his manners. But what he had known to prevent was that the guest was served cocoa. This drink of the gods was reserved for the highest and most important occasions, the really important, the most respected and revered guests.

So there was none tonight.

Chitam was reasonably sure that this message had also come home with everyone present.

When they retired, it was already very late. Even with the exertions of the night before, Chitam felt righteously tired and was glad to be able to rest. He was now very sleepy and even ignored the nightly assessment of his lady, who couldn't fail to list to her weary husband the things that went well, and to criticize those who hadn't developed as expected. Already half-asleep, Chitam thought that Tzutz would be a good general, if he was to encounter a bad fate as king and his wife would take over Yax Mutal. At least, she had the necessary eye for detail.

In Naal's name, that she had.

Thankfully, the Prince slumbered, and with the firm intention of not getting up before noon the next day.

The night tormented him with wild dreams whose meaning he couldn't interpret. They were threatening images that scared him, and he wanted to wake up several times, but he didn't succeed. It was as if the gods sent signs to him to arm himself. Chitam didn't want to arm himself, he wanted to sleep in peace. But the dreamy images were stubborn, even when he finally awoke in between and stared into the darkness. Sleep always caught up with him quickly, almost too fast, but he immediately brought back the clear, frightening and haunting visions that filled him with greater unrest than usual.

He obviously had eaten too much. Peanut filled meat aroused this, especially if you took too much of it. His mother had already told him that. Would he listen more to his mother? But she had been dead for a year. Did she perhaps send him those dreams? Then he knew why he had always found the advice of the old woman annoying.

He found sleep again, restless though, filled with somber images, but nevertheless sleep.

When he was suddenly startled and sat upright in his bed, he was confused for a moment. Did his dream wake him up? He looked around, it was obviously early in the morning. Chitam was wide awake, and at an unusual time for him.

He listened for a moment. Silence. Touched his forehead. Fully a wake, no doubt. He wouldn't find back to sleep, no matter how hard he tried. He didn't want, anyway. He didn't look for further dreams, and he tried everything to forget the disturbing images quickly. Tzutz was still asleep, judging from her quiet face, she was not plagued by what had tormented her husband this night.

He got up cautiously, careful not to wake his wife, and left.

For a few minutes he paused in front of his father's palace, holding a stuffed cornbread in his hand, which he chewed slowly, breathing in the fresh morning air that mixed the city's scents with the pleasantly musty smell of the nearby jungle. He really enjoyed this special time at the dawn of a day, he thought. Most of the days he slept longer. Maybe he should change his rhythm a bit, earlier to bed, earlier out. The Lady Tzutz would certainly like that too.

Chitam recognized two servants approach him eagerly, but he waved a hand. The retinue was a symbol of his status, but in fact, in the city center of Yax Mutal, he needed neither protection nor servants. And since there was hardly anyone on the road at that time, he didn't need anyone, just because he felt the desire to take a morning walk.

He wandered around a bit, stretching his limbs, chasing away the shadows of the night, which fortunately, in his memory, faded more and more. The delicious cornbread with its rich filling of meat and vegetables helped him, because it revived him with new energy.

He finally stood in the great square of the acropolis, in front of the almost completed temple, which was to become his father's mausoleum, looked up the mighty structure and winked briefly.

The sky was overcast. It would rain soon.

He winked again.

These clouds were ... remarkable.

He shoved the rest of his cornbread into his mouth and squinted.

That was strange. What ...?

Then he saw the hand of the gods open the sky.

It was only a glimmer that made him wink a third time.

Then it was a bright, glistening glow, as if a knife had slipped through the sky and revealed the brightness beyond.

Chitam opened his mouth so that almost the scraps of food fell out. He stood rooted to the spot, completely absorbed and fascinated, almost paralyzed, and felt a cold terror rush into his limbs.

And he was by no means the only one.

He heard the cries of other people – fear, surprise, horror, confusion. Chitam was not distracted by that, just staring at the crack that had obviously formed directly above him.

It was ... unreal.

It was bright, glistening and something moved behind it like a glittering waterfall.

It wasn't that far away. A bird passed by, and the animal flew behind the crack.

Threateningly close, the prince felt fear. A damn deep sense of impending calamity.

The movement inside the phenomenon became clearer. The glare disappeared, was covered.

Then something black and powerful pressed itself out of the crack.

Large.

Very large.

Chitam involuntarily took a step back. But a Prince didn't run away. He conquered his instinct for flight, while others around him dropped everything and bolted screaming. Panic. Panic everywhere. Feelings like a storm, but the Prince stood like a rock, out of defiance, out of stupidity, out of dignity ... or all of that at one and the same time.

Chitam stared up.

The black thing fell like a stone, but not far, maybe ten, maybe twenty meters, straight to the top of his father's mausoleum, and as if to forcefully end the silence of the whole process, it crashed deafeningly into it. The ground shook as if a gigantic hammer had hit the ground.

And it impacted like a hammer on the half-finished building.

Now Chitam finally moved.

Stones fell down. The ominous creaking of the black thing into the temple generated a piercing sound. Chitam stumbled, almost fell, looked around, just couldn't avert his gaze, caught in a deadly fascination.

The black object wavered. It fought for its balance, as it came to rest across the dented temple, despite the swirling dust and falling debris well visible.

The crunching subsided. The screaming of the people became louder again.

The crack in the skies was gone. The heavens calm, innocent, as if nothing had happened. Birds flew. The clouds promised rain. People ran and ran.

Chitam didn't. He turned and wiped dust on his face, covered his nose, coughed several times.

He heard someone yelling instructions. One who had overcome the shock.

The Prince took a step forward, then another. The smoke spread. The big black thing rested in the middle of the pyramid and didn't move.

Chitam's eyes narrowed. That wasn't quite right. Something was spinning at one end, fast, shoveling the air and the remaining smoke around. He thought he heard a whirring sound that accompanied the strange wheel in its rush. The wheel sat right at the end of the strange apparition and did nothing but turn around completely uselessly, but it got slower and slower. It was clear to see that it came to a stop. It wasn't a wheel. There were three leaves, as if from a tree, suspended from a pole, apparently made of obsidian.

Damn, that thing was big. It looked as heavy as it had fallen, and it was … long, round, with an elevation in the middle … He had never seen anything like it and had never heard of it.

Still, it reminded Chitam of something, and he wondered a little about the image he had in mind – it looked like a fish that a man had captured with his spear from the river, a fish that had been thrown to the ground and then to be killed with a quick blow, but before its dead it twitched desperate and outside of its element.

The fact that this phenomenon reminded him of a fish was certainly due to the fact that there was water everywhere! The black thing glistened wet in the morning sun and dripped along its sides. In fact, it had emerged from the crack along with a larger amount of water, now puddling everywhere, like a rainstorm. A strange smell filled the air. It smelled ... weird.

Some of the traders – the few that traveled to the shores of the great waters to negotiate with the villages for exotic fish and crabs for the King's table – reported the specific smell of the sea. The water there was not drinkable, they had reported, and it had a different smell than that from the rivers or the big cisterns where the citizens of Yax Mutal collect the precious liquid.

Did this enigmatic object come out of the big waters?

How did that happen?

Chitam took another step forward. He saw soldiers of the palace guard appear. Officers shouted something, gave instructions, but everything was very uncoordinated, hectic.

Chitam stretched, raised his arms, and shouted, "Listen to me!"

He had a clear, far-reaching voice. Screams became quieter. Eyes turned to him, he was recognized.

"Bring the wounded away!" Chitam called loudly. "Close access to the pyramid! Bring more soldiers!"

Clear commands, a clear direction. Activity followed, this time purposefully.

Chitam breathed in the salty air, gazing at the small tower sticking out of the object, and the big sign, red on white, a radiant, rising sun.

He was pretty sure that the time of surprises was not over yet. The apparition looked as if it would come to rest after this effort. But what happened when it shook off its own confusion and awoke to new life? And no matter how dull he felt, he knew at this moment that it meant something to be the Crown Prince of Yax Mutal.

It was time to accept the duties that were involved.

But why, Chitam thought as he continued to watch the object intensely, why did he now have a very, very bad feeling?

7

Something cracked. It woke Aritomo.

He moved his head and felt a strong pain. With difficulty, his hand reached up. He touched his hair, felt moisture, felt more pain as he fingered his scalp. He opened his eyes. It was pitch dark. He couldn't actually see the hand in front of his eyes.

He found himself on the ground, and he felt ... crooked. He felt a wall on his back, and gravity pushed him slightly against it. Aritomo listened. No noise from the machine. The boat was completely still. With luck, it didn't sink but floated in the water at a certain depth or at the surface. In that case, there was hope for all of them.

He blinked. No, the darkness was real, it wasn't his eyes, as far as he could tell. He tried to ignore the throbbing pain in his skull, fought the burgeoning exhaustion, the recurring urge to close his eyelids and just have a little ...

What had happened?

Aritomo lacked any memory. Unconsciousness, probably due to carbon dioxide poisoning, he remembered. But after that? How long had he passed out? What about the boat and its crew? And why did the air smell fresh, as if it had never ...?

He felt around. The wall wasn't smooth, his hands slid over instruments, screws, then his fingertips reached a small box. In his mind, Aritomo saw what it could be ... With luck ...

He slipped sideways. Apart from the obvious head injury, he seemed to be fine, and the pain, with him giving his attention to new activity, gave way to a dull throb. It was hopefully nothing worse. But he needed light to find out – and other survivors.

He heard a moan, not far from him.

Aritomo was relieved, more than he wanted to admit. He wasn't alone.

"This is Second Lieutenant Hara!" he said aloud. "Has anyone awakened? Speak if you can!"

"Ishida here, Lieutenant," he heard a strained voice. Ishida was one of the men deployed in the control room. He was responsible for blowing and balancing the tanks. A short, stocky man with wide-set eyes, the target of good-natured mockery, which he always stuck away with a smile.

"Ishida, are you hurt?" Aritomo asked.

"No, sir, I do not think so. I was flung out of my seat and came to rest on the ground, but apart from a few bruises, I'm fine. Someone is lying on me, though. What should I do?"

"Stay where you are ... I believe ... ah!"

Aritomo had opened the box, his fingers were searching through the contents and quickly found what he was looking for: the flashlight.

It wouldn't last long. The batteries were weak. They had to act fast.

The pale light illuminated the surroundings, as he turned it on. He saw that the boat was indeed crooked sideways. The ballast was not balanced. The stern was lower than the bow. The men in the control room had slipped backwards once overwhelmed by unconsciousness.

"Ishida!"

The man moved, half buried. The man on top of him was the motionless captain.

"Free yourself carefully. To the engine room. The electric motors. We have to get them working. Raise Sarukazaki if he doesn't move yet. Take one of the other emergency lights."

"Immediately, sir."

Aritomo saw the man get up a little unsteady and shone his way to access another emergency light. Once Ishida was able to orient himself, Aritomo moved out of his lying position and struggled uphill toward the main controls. He needed to know how deep the boat was.

Other men moaned. Everyone seemed to wake up gradually. He didn't care about it anymore. His eyes fell on the Prince, who had slumped in a corner, but seemed to be unharmed. He breathed. Good news.

46

Aritomo reached the depth gauge and illuminated the numbers with the lamp. He wiped his eyes, winked. Then he tapped the instrument with his knuckle, first weaker, then a little stronger.

Nothing happened. The numbers remained unchanged. She stood at zero. The boat was therefore no longer under water, it had to be on the surface. He remembered now. Before he was unconscious, he had felt the boat breaking through the water. But why was the position of the vessel so awkward? There had to be something wrong with the ballast. But after all, they were apparently not trapped under water.

Or was the depth gauge broken?

Aritomo continued to observe the instruments, decided to try the periscope. At that moment, a sudden humming filled the ship, and the lights went on again. In the engine room, someone had obviously been successful to re-energize the electric motors. Men scrambled up everywhere. The Prince blinked as well, as one of his bodyguards bent over him with a worried expression.

Aritomo raised the periscope and looked through.

Yes, they were definitely not under water anymore. He stared into a cloudless blue sky. The weather must have improved rapidly, really in no time. It was difficult for him to turn the periscope and at the same time stay firmly on his feet, but nevertheless he began a slow 360-degree turn.

First there was only more sky.

Then there were ...

Trees.

Buildings.

Very strange buildings.

And then people. Many people who somehow looked up to him.

People with brown skin and usually dressed in very colorful robes. He had never seen anything like it.

This wasn't Japan.

The boat wasn't in the water, actually nowhere near any ocean.

This was ... nowhere.

Aritomo's head tilted back. He looked into the void for a moment, trying to sort out the impressions, to understand. No sea at all. The boat rested on something ... evidently an elevation, because the view down to the staring people went far, surely close to twenty meters. And the boat rested unevenly so the periscope's angle was tilted.

Aritomo looked again, just to be sure. No hallucination. People who mingle around excitedly. Men with spears and shields who began to instill a degree of order. Excitement. Fear.

How did that happen? Was he still unconscious, numbed by his head injury, which now caused him delusions? No.

He felt a movement beside him. The Captain had moved toward him and was apparently unhurt. He was struggling, but the fact that his first officer was already at the periscope distracted him from his own shock, reminding him of his duty.

"And? Our position?"

Aritomo turned the eyepiece of the periscope in his direction. "Please see for yourself, Captain. I can't explain."

Inugami gave his first officer a questioning look but didn't say anything further and took the periscope. He also didn't say anything when he looked through it. He remained silent as he turned away from the eyepiece. He looked pale. Then he let go and looked around, saw Sawada, the teacher. He was the man closest of being a scholar.

"Mr. Sawada, if you would just look through this? Maybe you can make sense of it," Inugami said politely. The older man, who had taken care of the somewhat confused Prince, nodded. Aritomo and his superior watched intently as the man completed his observation.

Then he took a step back and shook his head. He also looked confused and scared, but his voice was firm as he spoke.

"I ..." he began hesitantly. "I'm not sure I can really make sense of it, gentlemen, but I know pretty well what the periscope shows us."

"What?" Aritomo and Inugami asked in unison.

"It can't be. It's impossible in many ways, and I have to be deceived by my mind."

"Pyramids. Big stone buildings. Dense forests and many people, warriors with spears, all with brown skin and many full of fear and confusion," Aritomo summed his impression up.

48

Inugami nodded. "If that's a delusion, then I'm its victim, too."

Sawada looked at them both. "Me too. So I see what I see. It can't be."

"Speak, Sawada!" Inugami ordered.

"I saw drawings in an older work from our library – from the book of an American named John Lloyd Stephens. In it, he laid down his exploration of Central American jungle areas and had it illustrated by a talented draftsman. I have read this book a long time ago, but as far as I can remember, the drawings showed exactly the kind of buildings that we have here ... Anyway, the people who are staring at us must come from a long extinct civilization, from an Indian people we call the Maya."

Aritomo shook his head.

"Maya?" Inugami looked blank. "Indians?"

Sawada shrugged and wiped the sweat from his forehead.

"It can't be. Ancient kingdoms, long since overgrown by the jungle, the descendants suffering for a long time under Spanish rule," Sawada added. He scratched his head, not even believing what he was saying. "But what we see out there is not overgrown and downtrodden, and ... does not look like Central America, which I know from travelogues and photographs."

"Why Central America?" Inugami asked, still clearly struggling to see any sense in all of this. He made no progress with it, and all the others who had now straightened up, followed the discussion of the three men with utter incomprehension.

"I don't know and can't explain how we got here," Sawada. "We are on land. I guess the boat is right on one of those big temples we see everywhere. On a pyramid, it seems."

"Absurd! That's all absurd! A joke. The periscope is damaged," muttered Inugami. "That's impossible. It is inexplicable. There must be another cause for all this."

Aritomo looked at Inugami. "There is only one way to be sure, Captain."

Inugami nodded. "Hara, our pistols. Mr. Sawada, if you could ask the Prince's bodyguards? We don't have too many weapons on board, and my men are no infantrymen."

Sawada nodded, turned away. He spoke to the bodyguards, who immediately took stance and removed their rifles from their backs.

Inugami watched Aritomo take the pistols from their shared cabin. They were Nambu Type 4 guns, a 22 mm weapon with a magazine with eight bullets. They had a small box of spare magazines on board, but the normal crew didn't normally carry their own weapons. They still had two more pistols for emergencies in a gun cabinet.

The Prince's two bodyguards, however, not only wore their own Nambus, but also each carried an Arisaka Type 55 rifle that shot out of 50 mm cartridges. And they carried swords. Such were also at the disposal of the two officers, well stowed under the bunks they claimed for themselves.

That was their complete weaponry.

Aritomo hoped to impress the "Maya" sufficiently with what they had. When he checked his weapon and clicked the magazine in, he felt more secure. Whoever or whatever was out there, he wouldn't face it defenseless. The two guards also made a determined impression. They were probably a lot more qualified to fight than Aritomo. It was good that they were there.

He looked at the Captain, who hesitated a moment and then nodded.

"We're going to open the tower, Mr. Hara. We'll check it out."

8

Chitam saw his father arrive and how the Palace Guard began to clear the place. Many of the people were only too willing to gain as much distance between themselves and this apparition as possible, so that their efforts were quickly crowned with success.

Siyaj stood next to his eldest son and followed his gaze, which lay constantly cn the massive object. The King turned his broad face to the ruined temple with piercing black eyes. Chitam couldn't discern if he was particularly worried that his own tomb was now a podium for ... something that had completely crushed the half-finished point with its weight. Although his death might be imminent, it was typical of Siyaj that he was more concerned about the city as a whole than his long-term salvation.

"What's that thing made of?" the master of Mutal muttered. "Is that black obsidian?"

"Possible," Chitam replied. "But who knows? Nobody has ever seen such a construction. Look at it. It is wet."

"It came from heaven?"

"Right above the pyramid."

"Then the gods sent it."

Chitam nodded. This conclusion was indeed very obvious; in fact, it was the only possible explanation. The big picture with the bright sun painted on the black walls of the object suggested that it was a vehicle of *Hunapù* who, as sun god *Kinich Kakmó*, was watching over the Maya. His father had evidently come to this conclusion, for he had two priests armed with parchments at his side, ready to consult ancient scripture. If Chitam recognized it correctly, it was rituals for the worship of the sun god. He nodded in satisfaction. With luck, they could do everything right and prevent further destruction.

"What does Hunapù intend to do with this apparition?" the King asked one of the priests. Chitam just had to take a quick look into the man's eyes to see that he had no idea. He was an old man, familiar with all the rituals since his earliest youth, and therefore no one who was afraid of the King – except that Siyaj was considered a very mild man anyway, who in no way tended to punish others for their ignorance too harshly.

"I don't know, sir," was therefore the expected answer, which the King accepted with an approving gesture. There was nothing comparable in known history for such an event. The tales of the city didn't teach such a thing. "It is without doubt a very special blessing."

Siyaj showed confidence, relaxed.

The fear receded from Chitam's heart.

A blessing, then. Perhaps this vehicle of Hunapù was a gift designed to promote the size and power of Yax Mutal. A favor of the sun god, a strengthening, a proof of extraordinary grace. Was Yax Mutal blessed indeed? Was this a sign to signify what Chitam had dreamed of, namely, the expansion of the city, the conquest of other cities, and the establishment of a great empire with many vassals, a prayer that had been heard by Hunapù, and he now consented to these plans?

Chitam felt a positive expectancy being raised in him, almost a surge, as if he would now realize the truth, the meaning of the incident. A divine intervention, an affirmation.

He glanced sideways at his father, as he quietly conferred with the priest about the correct course of action. Would he see it that way, too? Would Hunapù accept that his father was more prudent in these matters of conquest and war? Did that even mean that the Sun God would depose Siyaj and crown him, Chitam, as the new ruler?

The Prince somehow hoped that this would happen in a way that didn't include the violent death of his father. However much he hoped that Hunapù had come to express his benevolence for the expansion of Yax Mutal's power, Chitam didn't enjoy paying for it with the untimely death of his father.

His father had always treated him well. He was not a bad king. And his son was not in such a hurry.

That should also be understood by the sun god.

Chitam hoped for the best. As far as he could remember, the sacrificial rituals for the sun god had always been carefully observed. As master of drought and heat, there was always the need to make him merciful. Regularly, the expected ceremonies had been performed to please Hunapù. The sun god could not be overly angry. A punishment was not to be expected.

The Maya of Yax Mutal, of which Chitam was sure, had done everything right.

He raised his head, looked back at the black thing.

Something had caught his attention.

Then he heard the sound.

He narrowed his eyes, and now it was easy to see that people were recognizable on the small tower that rose out of the black body of the godsend. Chitam couldn't make out too many details, but they were men, and they didn't look any different than he did. The sun god had sent emissaries to them. If these came from within the vessel, then there might be many more hidden in them, a whole army perhaps. Chitam was a little scared at the thought. It was one thing when the sun god showed his favor but quite another when he used the opportunity to send his own forces. What purpose could he follow with it?

The men stood on the tower, half-hidden by a sort of parapet, and they pointed to the assembled Maya, gesticulating, talking excitedly. Chitam hoped that everyone would remain calm.

His hope was immediately disappointed.

He spun around, as he heard the angry scream, and at that moment he recognized the voice. It was one of the men of his father's bodyguard, a head taller than the average man, a mountain of a warrior and well-versed in all weapons, not particularly intelligent, hot-blooded, easy to provoke, the ideal man in a battle.

But of little use outside any fight.

A master of the *atlatl*. Unmatched in range and force.

Before anyone could stop the man, he had stepped forward, the

53

spear-thrower in one hand, one of his javelins ready, and stretching out with his muscular limb.

"Stop!" Chitam shouted, but it was already too late. The spear rose, in perfect trajectory, and slammed with a satisfyingly loud noise against the balustrade behind which the messengers of the gods stood, seemingly unmoved, with their eyes wide open, as if they could hardly believe this crime.

The reaction came immediately. One of the messenger of the gods raised his own weapon, not unlike an atlatl, but instead of throwing it, he just aimed it at the warrior who was already preparing his second javelin, and then a *bang* sounded.

Chitam saw nothing. No visible projectile was discernible.

But the body of the warrior collapsed, and the spear sling slipped out of his powerless hand. There was blood on his chest, a wound struck by an invisible weapon, a truly divine demonstration of power.

For a moment, Chitam stared blankly at the warrior, motionless, clearly dead on the ground. Blood everywhere. No blade. No spear. No arrow. Nothing. An invisible blow, fast, deadly, something that wouldn't give you a chance to dodge, and probably no way to protect yourself from it.

The priests dropped to their knees and praised Kinich Kakmó.

Siyaj followed, raising his voice in fervor. He was scared.

Chitam, his son, did the same.

All the men, every inhabitant of Yax Mutal in sight, fell to their knees, all raising their arms. The warriors threw down their weapons and presented their breasts to the messenger of the gods, ready to make the sacrifice necessary to calm their fury.

They all sang the praises of the Lord of Drought and Heat, the conqueror of the *Xibalba* Houses, hoping that it was not yet too late.

The gods were quite moody, the Maya knew.

Chitam closed his eyes and sang. He waited and hoped. When, after a few moments, he dared to look again, the messengers of the gods were still visible, as they gesticulated and talked. Chitam watched the conversation, and it didn't feel like it ...

The ambassadors had come to a conclusion.

The men with the god-atlatls left the tower.

They climbed down to them.

And then other men followed, without visible weapons, and marched cautiously along the vessel of the sun god. Farther ahead on the object was something, a kind of pump or scaffolding that did not serve a purpose recognizable to Chitam.

More men came out of the tower. The scaffolding was turned. It was handled somehow. Something was carried from the inside of the god's vessel. Chitam saw the visitors do unintelligible things.

Then one of the men raised one arm. This gesture was familiar to the Maya. A commander thus warned the warriors in an attack before the imminent command of a storm against the ranks of the enemy was given.

A fearful murmur went through the praying Maya.

And rightly so.

A heavy bang, deafening, echoed across the square. Chitam winced. The construction, the pump was a ... a big, a very big atlatl! And when suddenly a great part was broken out of the neighboring temple, when stone and dust fountains splashed and crashed down on the praying Maya, the consequence of an invisible fist that had hit the steps of the building ... at that moment, more than reverence and devotion filled the heart of the Prince. Now panic crept up his throat, and that wasn't an emotion he'd often felt in his life.

The same was true for the others. He heard how many interrupted their singing, stood up and ran as fast as their legs carried them. Their faith had left them or their willingness to give her life for the sun god, or they had just lost their nerves.

The gods didn't punish the cowards. They didn't repeat their demonstration of power. They looked down on the remaining Maya, the brave, the faithful, the most stupid perhaps.

Chitam, on the other hand, looked up. The men up there were waiting. He couldn't interpret their behavior any different. They hoped for a reaction. They had given their lesson. Were the citizens of Yax Mutal able to understand the language of the gods? Would they ...?

Chitam felt his father rise, felt his hand on his shoulder.

"It's up to us, son."

In that sentence was all the truth that Chitam always wanted to avoid. Therein lay the downside of life in luxury and prestige. Therein lay the duty of the King and his Prince. Where others ran and prayed, they had to get up and take the next step.

Chitam didn't hesitate. He had always known it since his birth. And mastering this challenge on the side of his father, was despite his fear also his birthright as well as an obligation to his family. He couldn't turn away.

Chitam pointed to one side of the half-ruined tomb. "Father, there we can climb and meet the messenger of the gods."

The King nodded. He turned to the two priests. "You are with us."

There was fear in the eyes of the men but then pride. Who else was fit for this difficult task, if not them? Now it was time to prove that the Sun God looked with favor on the inhabitants of Yax Mutal, and if not, to find out how to restore this favor.

"Then we go."

The King said so, the Prince followed him closely, the two priests kept their distance, out of respect for their overlord as well as out of fear. Chitam sensed that this small distance would make no difference if the messengers of the gods chose to direct their invisible atlatls toward them. The realization that they were completely at the mercy of the men up there was almost liberating.

So they set off to learn the true will of the sun god.

9

Inugami waved to the two bodyguards. "Keep an eye on those four, but do not fire. We should have impressed them sufficiently."

Aritomo could only agree. The shots of the gun on the neighboring pyramid had their effect on the assembled onlookers. Many of the savages had run off after praying first. He wasn't sure if this demonstration was really necessary, but he was grateful for the clear language of the weapon. The single fighter's attack with the strange but effective spear-thrower had reminded him that if these men down there were able to overcome their awe or fear and launch an organized and massive assault on the boat, sooner or later the Japanese would have no chance of survival. Inugami's strategy of powerfully intimidating, then hopefully negotiating from a position of strength, wasn't that stupid.

If the Captain was smart enough not to overdo it.

"When I look at those four, I see jewelry and well done clothes, so I think we have to deal with high-ranking personalities," Sawada said, who had joined them on the bridge. "Maybe we are even dealing with a king or a high priest among them."

"Those two men out front gave orders earlier," Aritomo said. "They seem to be in command indeed."

"Not for long anymore," Inugami mumbled.

Something in Inugami's attitude had changed. He looked down at the city – no longer surprised or cautious but like a predator, seeing a willing prey, something to catch and use, to train, if he wanted to. He had his hands on the rail in front of him and looked calm, confident, as if he had a plan.

Inugami had never been one for whom surprise lasted for a long time, and he had never been accused of thinking on a small scale.

"What do you mean, Captain?" Aritomo asked.

The officer's body tightened. "That's obvious, Mr. Hara. I don't know what streak of fate has brought us here, and I don't know if we will ever be able to return. Maybe we will never find out. Maybe we are stranded here forever. If that's the case, we need to get set up here. And for us, given the current situation, this can only be achieved through absolute dominance. These are savages. They build very impressive buildings and certainly have their skills. But they are obviously inferior to us all, a race of natives who even consider us quite as being quite superior."

Inugami showed a joyless grin. His eyes remained cold, calculatingly staring at the four men working their way up the pyramid.

"And how right they are, among us is the divine scion of the Emperor. All of this fits so well together, as if fate has chosen us to emerge here and play an important role."

Aritomo controlled himself so as not to shake his head involuntarily. Had Inugami been hurt? Given his situation, how did he come up with such thoughts, without any clue, without any foundation? He didn't know any hard facts. And he planned ...

"Foreseen?" Aritomo echoed.

"Foreseen, yes." Inugami waved to the four men, who approached slowly and cautiously. "They want something they can worship? We will give it to them. And something worthy of it: the Prince of our divine Tenno, who also represents for us the connection to the heavenly powers. But worship will not be enough if we are forced to establish ourselves here."

"The boy is still a child," Sawada pointed out.

Inugami waved his hand with a dismissive gesture. "That shouldn't stop us. He is a symbol and represents the significance of what is about to unfold – for us who are stranded here, and those who urgently need direction and guidance."

"We know too little ..." Sawada wanted to object, but Inugami interrupted him harshly. Aritomo saw that the old man was plagued by the same doubts as himself, and they exchanged a brief, meaningful glance.

"We know enough," Inugami said. "And what we haven't yet learned doesn't change the situation we are in right now. There come the notables of this city, as I agree with Second Lieutenant Hara. If we now show weakness and willingness to compromise, sooner or later we will be at the mercy of these barbarians. If we show superiority and strength, then we have a chance."

Although there was some opposition to the Captain's premature conclusions, Aritomo recognized the logic in those words. And the risk.

"We don't even speak their language!" Sawada complained.

Inugami laughed. "Then we'll learn it. It can hardly be more complex and demanding than our own!"

Before Sawada could continue the argument, Inugami imperiously raised his hand.

"Enough of the discussion. The savages are close enough. We don't want to show any dissent, but only determined unity."

Aritomo nodded involuntarily. No matter his objections to Inugami's vision, this was neither the place nor the time. Sawada, too, finally seemed to understand this. He lowered his head and said nothing.

They watched silently as the four men approached the boat as far as the debris of the indented pyramid allowed. Inugami waved. A sailor let the prepared rope ladder slide down the edge of the tower. Inugami turned to Aritomo and Sawada.

"You come with me. The two bodyguards give us protection from here."

The soldiers nodded and raised their Arisakas. At such a short distance, they would make short work of the four savages if they were cause trouble.

Then Inugami began the descent.

When he reached the bottom, the four strangers didn't stir. They stopped waiting. Aritomo saw that they carried no weapons. That was a good sign.

He followed his commander, then came Sawada, who needed a little longer.

The two groups stood silently for a moment. Then Inugami stretched out his arms and said solemnly: "In the name of Tenno and his son, I take possession of this city for the Japanese Empire!"

Aritomo stared first at Inugami – the man couldn't seriously mean that! – and then the four savages, who made a confused impression. Of course, they didn't understand a word. Aritomo understood the words but had massive reservations in regard to their content.

Inugami pointed to the crumbling floor of the pyramid level in front of him, where they all stood. His gesture was imperious, his expression mild.

"Kneel!" he said loudly and slowly.

The four men looked at each other.

"Kneel!" Inugami said again, and now his voice got a threatening undertone.

As one of the men bowed deeply, Inugami looked pleased, nodded, encouraging him with his gestures. All four savages bowed, and the commander seemed to consider that sufficient. He had made clear who was in charge here.

Then, returning to the undivided attention of the Maya, he patted his chest and said, "Inugami!" He then pointed to Aritomo and spoke aloud: "Hara!" Finally, his finger pointed to Sawada, and he pronounced his name clearly. It was hard to misunderstand, and the savages repeated the procedure on their side.

For Aritomo, the names were barely understandable. The youngest man among the four seemed most able to express himself. Aritomo thought he had heard "Chitam." Sawada pulled out a writing pad and began to take notes and the Maya, as the teacher had called them, watched with interest.

The young man called Chitam turned his upper body to the city and made a sweeping motion with both arms. Then, very slowly and clearly articulated, he said, "Yax Mutal!"

This was undoubtedly the name of the city. Aritomo repeated the name and the gesture and seemed to find agreement with his counterparts.

"That must be enough," Inugami mumbled. "We have to discuss the way forward. We'll get back to the boat!"

He waved to Sawada and Aritomo, who immediately climbed the rope ladder. Then the commander followed. As they stood up in the tower, the ladder was pulled up and the men gradually disappeared inside the boat.

The four Maya made no move to follow them.

Inugami closed the hatch of the bridge above them, and they all stood together in the control room. The young Prince joined them, looked questioningly at Sawada, then turned his gaze to Inugami.

"Lieutenant," the Prince said slowly. "I heard what was said outside. Where are we?"

Sawada glanced at Inugami and answered instead. "Your Highness, there are two questions to answer: Where are we – and when?"

If the Prince was afraid, he didn't show it. His stoic composure was convincing, but how much of it was acting, hard training and what was his actual attitude? Aritomo looked around. On the faces of the other crew members was tense attention, a little fear but no panic. They maintained discipline.

That was reassuring.

"When?" the Prince repeated.

"The civilization of the Maya we are confronted with has not existed in this form for many centuries. It's just an assumption, but whatever brought us here took us not only through space but through time."

Everyone exchanged blank looks.

"A daring claim," Inugami said, though he seemed to have already accepted that explanation inwardly, as it offered him considerable opportunities to the extent of which he had already outlined. He felt, it was clear, as a conqueror who was chosen for great things, a man with a mission.

"A claim that explains what we've just experienced."

"How is something like this possible?, the Captain asked."

"I don't know."

"A natural phenomenon? I've never heard of it."

Sawada blinked. "Ships sometimes disappear under unclear circumstances, Lieutenant. We then assume storms or misfortune. But maybe … maybe something like this happens sometimes. It seems to have happened to us."

Inugami pressed his lips on each other. "How do we get back?"

He had to ask that question, no matter how much it drove him home or not. As the boat didn't even seem to be near the sea, it was almost rhetorical. Aritomo knew that he addressed this issue to the benefit of the crew. Nobody should think the commanding officer wouldn't try everything. That would jeopardize the loyalty of his men.

Sawada shook his head. "I don't know. Maybe never. You've already realized that, Lieutenant, right? Otherwise, you wouldn't have wanted to take possession of this city for the Empire."

"Am I a king now?" the Prince asked. Everyone looked at Inugami for an answer, until it was Sawada talking to the boy.

"If we do it right and make no stupid mistake, we may be able to achieve that goal." Then he looked up and at Inugami. "We really need to discuss what we want to do next. We can't hide in the boat forever. And we can not wait for too long. We have to keep initiative and momentum in our hands."

Sawada seemed to come to terms with Inugami's plans. Aritomo didn't mind. The primary responsibility of the teacher was the well-being of the Prince. He would do anything to ensure that.

"That's true," Inugami said. "But first we inform the crew. By now everyone should be awake. If we don't find inner strength, we can't demonstrate it to the outside."

Aritomo wasn't in any way opposed to Inugami's words.

But still.

He didn't feel easy with the turn of events. It was as if something had been set in motion whose consequences were barely foreseeable. They knew so little. How could one make grandiose plans?

It was ironic when he thought of the submarine like a fish out of water. But this also referred to him as a person, and that was a most unpleasant situation.

10

K'inich Tatb'u, whom everyone called the Jaguar Skull, looked with great satisfaction at his old enemy, the Lord of Bonampak. He was called Bird Jaguar, the once proud king of the neighboring town, situated farther to the south, where the rich forests of the lowlands gradually made way for fields on higher elevations, located on artificial terraces. Bird Jaguar was an honorable name, as Tatb'u had to admit, since his own ancestor, the third king of Yaxchilan, his great-great-grandfather, whose grandfather again had once again been the legendary Yoaat B'alam, the first king of Yaxchilan, had also carried it. A venerable rule by his family, uninterrupted for more than 70 years and, if it was for Tatb'u to decide, unbroken until the end of days.

At least the Lord of Bonampak would no longer doubt his supremacy, never challenge him anymore and present no obstacle to the rule of his city. The fight had been short and fierce, but the troops that had been led into battle by Tatb'u had at once proved to be clearly superior. Gone were the days of infamy, the stelae on which Bird Jaguar had dared to call himself and his family the superior ones, the rulers of these lands, had been shattered to pieces. Tatb'u had personally lashed out to smash the family stele of those of Bonampak with his obsidian axe – and in front of the humiliated king.

The captive now awaited death. Tatb'u had returned to his city with him and many other prisoners of war, loaded with rich prey, and had announced a great festival. Everyone was in high spirits and full of pride because of the tremendous triumph. Tatb'u had never felt so strong, and he radiated this power clearly.

"I will pay homage to the beaten king who deserves his name. No one should say I insult my own glorious ancestor by treating an enemy who calls himself that same unworthily, no matter how much he mocked me," he told the assembled notables and priests. "He and his ilk are to play against us in the ballgame. The gods may decide their fate. If they are victorious, their lives should be spared. If they lose, they are to sacrifice to Itzamnaaj, the god of our city, the Lord of Heaven. Prepare them. The beaten king is allowed to choose his own team from the prisoners. Thus speaks the gracious K'inich Tatb'u, whom everyone knows by the name Jaguar Skull."

He hadn't missed the expression of hope in the eyes of his old enemy when he announced his decision. And that was a good thing. Anyone who has hope for survival struggles. Tatb'u was aware of the outcome of the game. His players, including his own son, were unbeatable. They had been informed early on of the intentions of the ruler and had prepared accordingly. And even if it unexpectedly came to a defeat, Tatb'u would not have lost his face. He would accept the ruling of the gods and condemn the king and other prisoners of war to slave labor. For Bonampak, nothing changed anyway. He had already established a trustworthy man there as the new regent, someone who wouldn't make himself more than he was, and knew that paying tribute to his overlord once a year was an important duty that to neglect caused dire consequences.

"Pakul!"

The nobleman stepped to his King's side and bowed.

"Come with me."

The ruler and his subject left the large room that was commonly used as an audience hall. They withdrew to the King's private chambers.

Pakul was no stranger here and was politely welcomed by the servants. As a member of one of the city's most important aristocratic families, he was also the organizer of the campaign against Bonampak and thus an architect of the magnificent success he had been given to the King. And much of it had been discussed here, in relative seclusion.

"Sit down, my friend. Chi?" The King pointed to two ornate stools standing in a corner.

"Gladly, my ruler."

Tatb'u beckoned to a waiting servant. Moments later, she brought two cups of fresh chi and the men paused to enjoy the stimulating drink.

"The war against Bonampak went well, and I am grateful for it," Tatb'u began. Pakul knew that these were not empty words. Despite all the phrases and praises, the King knew very well that he couldn't have achieved anything without the loyalty of his men. "Do you have any wishes, my friend?"

"No, lord. Allow me to continue serving you."

Tatb'u grinned. "Then we're already on the subject of our conversation."

He fully appreciated the apparent modesty of his general. Pakul didn't lack wealth; he lived in a house that was surpassed only by the King's palace. There were other cravings that the man demanded, and they had much to do with killing the city's enemies and feeding on their whining as they writhed on the ground before him.

A useful pleasure, which the King gladly used for himself and whose satisfaction he gladly granted to his general.

He leaned forward. "Pakul, listen to me. When I say that our campaign was successful, you, like me, know that this is an understatement. We surprised and overpowered the idiots. We caught Bird Jaguar, as he put his cock in a servant. We have barely lost any men, as the resistance of our enemies collapsed as fast as chi flows down our throats."

To affirm this, the King emptied his cup and then turned it in his hands, pondering.

"We have time and men for a second campaign," he said.

"That's right," Pakul confirmed. He smiled eagerly. His life belonged to war. All the honors his king poured out over him meant little. He wanted to push his spear into the body of his enemies, and he wanted to plan campaigns that led to victories. There was nothing, no experience, that brought the same excitement as the ecstasy of a battle. He took every opportunity to take delight in it. "Who do we want to attack, Lord? There are a few smaller towns in the area that haven't been remembered of us for a long time and might need some assurance that we are their overlords."

"But they all pay tribute and didn't offend us. No. The gods will not be in favor of such an attack, we could be in danger of misfortune. Those who are loyal to us should remain untouched, otherwise chaos breaks out. I'm hunting for a bigger fish," the King said, smiling. "We beat the smaller cities at any time, if they should ever be rebellious, and after our last victory, it won't even come to any fight. They will throw themselves on the ground in front of us. That would be ... unsatisfactory. We don't want to waste our power and time on unworthy opponents."

"Who is our enemy?"

"Someone big. An enemy that presents a challenge. An adversary who, when defeated, brings us such riches that no one has to work for a year. And an opponent who doesn't expect our attack. Who thinks he is safe or directs his mistrust in a completely different direction."

Pakul licked his lips, not because they were wet with chi. That sounded very auspicious to him. He nodded.

"Lord, name the city, and I'll start preparing right now!"

Tatb'u smiled.

"Our destination is Yax Mutal, my friend!"

Pakul's eyes widened. First he looked almost as if he wanted to accuse his king of madness, but then he saw the scope and genius of the project.

Truly, a real challenge.

He bowed deeply.

"It shall happen as you command, my Lord!"

Tatb'u waved. "More chi."

He looked again at Pakul, behind whose eyes the military genius had already begun to work.

"Let's drink to that, my friend."

11

"We'll stay inside the boat first," Inugami said after briefing the crew on the current situation. With the exception of Lengsley, who frankly exposed all of his feelings, as one might expect, the other crew members kept tight self-control. Most of them seemed to have taken it easy, though their face showed faint traces of worry. Everyone looked indignantly at the Briton, as he let his emotions run wild, while Aritomo had kept them all in sight, as they had gathered in the open air on the foredeck of the submarine, watched by the Maya, who surely entertained their own speculation about what was happening up there.

Only two of the men, still very young, had burst into tears. Inugami had looked at this for a moment, then he had bent back and slapped them hard. The clapping sound had been heard loud and clear. The crying had turned into a painful whimper and was quickly suppressed. Inugami liked to beat, as he said, to maintain discipline. If properly angered, he wouldn't have a problem with hitting his first officer as well.

Nobody else stirred. In the men's eyes, the fear of the new situation mingled with fear of the captain. Aritomo knew that wouldn't last long. They were not in Japan anymore. The country was far, and the longer they stayed, the more this knowledge would sink in.

If Inugami overdid it, the men would eventually run away from him.

"We can endure for some time, because the air supply is secure, and we have enough food. There is no need to hurry. The savages aren't hostile and are quite impressed by us. We will explore the situation. We will, of course, always look for a way to take us home. But I admit, at the moment we are at a loss. We don't know how we got here and surely don't know how to reverse this process. But don't be afraid. This place gives us other opportunities, new chances to create something great. We should all show confidence and hope. This is a special moment in many ways, and it is our privilege to experience it. The Prince is in our care, men. That alone should give us more than enough incentive to continue to do our best."

That was the official address.

Aritomo, Sawada and Inugami, who formed something like the leadership trio who made the decisions, had some other nuances to discuss among themselves. Above all, Sawada had emphasized the need to get out of the dead end of the boat as quickly as possible and to establish itself within the city in a way that would make it possible for them to survive long-term. Inugami and Aritomo had agreed in general, but they differed on the strategy to achieve this. While the commander continued to advocate a tough approach with the establishment of clear authority, Aritomo pleaded for learning more about their new world and to try to develop a more friendly relationship with the natives in order to avoid counter-reactions, perhaps even hostility. They were so few, the Maya were so many. To be rash and ruthless was risky.

Inugami didn't want to hear about it. He thought only in the categories of ruler and ruled. Sawada also seemed to have his doubts but didn't say so, because all the time Inugami stressed that he didn't see himself as this ruler but that the young Prince as a member of the imperial family was predestined to build a new empire here if there seemed to be no option to return anymore. Anything else – a life side-by-side with these savages, probably even under a king from among them – was absolutely unacceptable to Inugami. Either they would rule, or they would die trying to gain dominance. There was no alternative for him.

Aritomo complied. He yielded with a sense of impending disaster, but the obedience to his superior had been implanted deep within him. He knew that another important condition for their survival was inner cohesion. They had to work as a unit. Otherwise, no strategy would be successful.

After a short discussion, the commander prevailed, and that was the tenor of his speech to the crew. Despite his volatile reaction to the crying men, he finally seemed to hit the right note, because the men accepted his vision. Those of them who were gifted with a great deal of imagination quickly began to think a life in luxury, with servants and willing native girls, which heightened the general mood. Those who thought a little further frowned at these reveries. The one who lived in wealth and at the expense of others should better strive for his subject's loyalty, otherwise, one morning he'd wake up with a blade in his chest. The numerical inferiority of the Japanese was something that no one could overlook, who didn't intentionally close his eyes.

Inugami then proceeded methodically, something he was quite good at.

On their first night, the two bodyguards left the boat. Of course, the savages knew of no lighting, had only a few watchfires built around the boat, and still at a respectful distance. The two men managed to sneak undetected to the ground without problems to carry out Inugami's orders. The Maya made it easy for both of them: At one of the watch fires, only one group of three men had gathered next to a single guard, two of whom had earlier joined their reception committee. Sawada was convinced to see them as notables or priests. In any case, his argument had been, they belonged to the upper class, most likely to those who could read and write.

That was sufficient for Inugami's plans. The bodyguards had been ordered to kidnap one of these men and bring him aboard. There he would be placed in the care of Sawada, with the aim of working on joint language studies. Inugami had formulated two intentions: The Japanese had to learn the savages' language – that there was no way around, he quite accepted that –, and the savages should also be taught, but not in Japanese – that should remain solely the language of the new ruler's elite – but English, which both the two officers and the two senior NCOs were quite familiar with. A barbarous language, good enough for savages of all kinds, and much easier to learn than Japanese.

Again, Aritomo agreed that this decision wasn't stupid. And again, he got a bad feeling in the matter – especially with the approach of the commander to force their first teacher and student to his lessons. That could surely be achieved in a different way.

When the two bodyguards returned, they had an unconscious man with them, limp in their arms. They had caused a bit of commotion, but Inugami had asked them not to kill anyone, and they said they had stuck to it. Aritomo helped to put the man on the bunk in the captain's cabin, as far as the glorified cabinet was to be called a cabin. It was one of the four men who had visited the boat during the day, no doubt about that. He slept peacefully.

Inugami posted guards and ordered everyone else to rest. The men made themselves comfortable at their stations, mostly on thin, roll-up mattresses. The air in the boat smelled strange. The slightly stale, metallic smell they were accustomed to now had a richer, deeper note, heavy with moisture, a bit moldy. The odor of the tropics, the jungle. He was not uncomfortable. Aritomo would get used to it.

The next morning, they looked for the abductee. He had just awakened, staring fearfully at his guards. Interestingly enough, he didn't seem to panic. Aritomo suspected that the man was a priest and responsible for all manner of cruel and demanding gods. The savages would probably offer human sacrifices and indulge in dark rituals. Such things were done only by a fearless, a cold – or a very confident man. He was scared, sure. But he was certainly not a coward, and whoever spoke to the gods expected the unexpected.

He was served a breakfast of Japanese canned food, and he regarded the food offered with astonishing pleasure, ate it with fervor and great speed. Once again, Aritomo found that the only explanation for this behavior was that this man believed he was taking the manna of his gods, a special favor, and that he might receive supernatural powers from eating it. Aritomo was reasonably sure that the standard rations could keep a healthy man alive, even if one might argue about the taste. But supernatural abilities were out of reach of dried fish.

When he had finished his breakfast, the prisoner looked at his captors with almost cheerful expectation. This was the opportunity for Sawada to begin his work. He had writing utensils with him.

70

Sawada was a fairly good draftsman, as Aritomo had discovered. This would help him in teaching the first vocabulary. The old teacher sat down next to the Maya, put the paper on his thighs and began.

Aritomo watched fascinated as the teacher proceeded. At first, they were just simple objects that Sawada apparently assumed would be known to the man. Sawada drawed these accompanied by English characters and pronounced the word. The prisoner was very docile. He picked up the pen – and it turned out that he was not afraid of this utensil, so he was familiar with the principle of writing on parchment or paper – and carefully drew strange characters and objects, until he put them in a single word. Sawada, in turn, wrote down what he had heard in Japanese script so that it corresponded to the sounds he had thought he heard. He was excited to see how, after only an hour of intense dialogue, the teacher's notebook filled with vocabulary. When they took a break and drank tea – which the prisoner also took with enthusiasm –, they had already worked out over 30 words. Aritomo took the opportunity to take a look for himself. "Ajaw" seemed to be the name of a king or ruler. The teacup was a "Ja-yi." The "Cha-ya" was the fish. There were also some verbs. "Tz'i-b'a" seemed to mean "writing," an activity the two men had been working on all the time.

After the tea break, they continued their concentrated work. Inugami, pleased with the progress, left them alone, but Aritomo remained in the entrance and watched the exchange with great interest. The men, both teachers and students, came to numbers. "Jun, cha, ox, chan, jo," the priest counted his fingers, and Sawada did the same in English.

Not much was stirring outside the boat. The warriors of the local ruler, probably a king, had sealed off the area around the crash site. There were more onlookers, many prayers and ceremonies were held. Even the abduction of the priest had caused no major reactions. Perhaps the savages thought that he would be used on board of the holy vehicle for some bloody ritual, an idea that the inhabitants of this city obviously had no problems with.

In the meantime, a complete inventory of all resources had been made on the boat itself. They still had food for about a week and drinking water would last for about that long. By then they would be dependent on food supplies by the natives. The diesel engines were able to recharge the batteries for a few weeks, providing power to the boat, but then they would fail as well, and Aritomo didn't expect to be able to provide any replenishment soon in this ... time. Inugami had therefore ordered all machines shut down. Most of the crew members were in the immediate vicinity of the boat or on the pyramid and familiarized themselves with the environment. That was a difficult process. There was some crying again. Some men seemed very apathetic and were barely responsive. The commander didn't beat anyone this time, seeming to realize that he wouldn't speed up the transition process that way. Others, however, were probably infected by the spirit of adventure. Inugami developed the vision of a kingdom in foreign times and on foreign soil, led by the crew members of the boat, and always communicated with a certain persuasiveness. Aritomo had so far never noticed this kind of charisma in the man. It was an aspect of his personality that he admired on the one hand but that made him restless on the other. Inugami went out of himself. He showed facets of a personality that had hitherto remained hidden under military discipline. Aritomo thought about it for a long time. If this was true for Inugami – what would emerge from the hidden in Aritomo Hara, here, in this new and unfamiliar situation?

That thought almost made him even more nervous.

The mutual observation of Japanese and Maya was ended by a banquet served in the early afternoon by the townspeople. Aritomo was the first to watch, alerting Inugami. The Mayan women – some of them quite pleasing to the eye, if Aritomo was permitted to say – carried large baskets or trays laden with all sorts of food. Much of it was alien to Aritomo, but he was able to identify some of the fruits, and there was a lot of fried meat. Generally, according to his impression, the natives seemed to make a lot of food from corn. In contrast to the rice he was used to, this grain seemed to be the basis of all nutrition.

"We should accept this invitation," he told Inugami, who looked a little skeptical. "For one thing, sooner or later we'll need indigenous supply anyway. On the other hand, it is necessary for us to establish a relationship with them."

"Relationship!" the commander snapped, looking half appalled at Aritomo. "Who uses such a word? We have to rule. They have to be controlled."

"That too is a relationship," Aritomo defended himself. "And they are many, many more than we are. At some point we will run out of ammunition, sir. And they have far more spears in their flings than we have bullets for our rifles. They have many warriors who can die; we only have 31 men, and every single death will cause us great pain."

Inugami stared at his first officer, as if that act would cause the awkward truth to dissipate, but neither Aritomo nor the truth were willing to relinquish so quickly. Finally, the commander lowered his head and seemed to realize that there was at least some sense in his subordinate's words. "You go," he decided. "You and two or three men, plus one of the bodyguards and Sawada. We will cover you from the tower."

"Our prisoner should join us, too."

Inugami looked at Aritomo reluctantly. "Why?"

"So people will see that we don't intend to sacrifice anyone until further notice. They should see that he is fine. The man copes well with Sawada, learns and teaches, is very enthusiastic. He should show that to the outside."

Aritomo briefly explained to Inugami his previous thoughts, and the commander agreed. Their guest had in the meantime continued his education with such intense attachment to the task and seemed so relaxed at the same time that both were quite sure to be able to continue teaching without forcing him to. Aritomo had rarely met such an eager student.

Maybe the Maya were not quite the savages he took them for. In any case, their writing and their buildings seemed to indicate that they had attained a degree of civilization that was considerable. Aritomo had looked at the city in peace with his binoculars from his elevated viewpoint. The cisterns and the terraces of the fields were impressive. The murals and the endless written representations of many buildings were elaborate and complex. In urban planning, the Maya were very advanced, careful architects, ingenious master builders, persistent and successful. Their roads were dead straight and impressive, as far as he could tell from here. He didn't even dare to compare the state of development of the current Japan of this time with that of the Maya. He assumed that his ancestor's achievements wouldn't be particularly impressive.

He doubted, however, that he would be able to warm Inugami to this comparison.

When it became clear that the food had been served and the assembled dignitaries of their hosts – including the three men left by their delegation yesterday – waited for them, Aritomo, Sawada, and a bodyguard named Tanaka listened carefully. They were accompanied by the abductee, whose renewed appearance caused a great "Hello." They knew by now that his name was Itzanami. When they were on an equal footing with the other natives and came toward them, they met many expectant looks but no great hostility.

Itzanami stepped forward and spoke. His words were received with great interest. When Aritomo heard him pronounce some English words and then, as Sawada had apparently taught him, introduced all three Japanese by name, the Maya were pleased and enthusiastic. The man was confronted with many questions, but before this threatened to become a too one-sided dialogue, one dignitary remembered his tasks as host and invited to the table.

Aritomo came to sit directly opposite the two men – on the floor, as the food had simply been placed on large mats on the ground – of which had to be the King. He knew the younger one as Chitam, because he had heard of their welcoming delegation. Now that he knew the word for King – it was called "Ajaw" – he indicated a bow and pointed to the older of the two men, then with a questioning undertone to say "Ajaw?"

The joy of their hosts knew no bounds. With the help of Sawada and Itzanami they learned that the older man was indeed the ruler of the city – which bore the name Mutal – and his younger companion was apparently the heir to the throne. Chitam was also one of the first to try to repeat the English words Itzanami used. He made a studious impression.

Aritomo noticed to his surprise that the feast, whose breadth and preparation impressed him, soon turned into a collective language lesson. It was the food that served as the basis of perception. Quickly, the words for different fruit and prepared food were exchanged, whereby Sawada didn't know in each case the appropriate English word. They were given a slightly alcoholic juice called "chi," and a bitter-tasting dark broth that surprisingly bore a name reminiscent of the English word "cocoa." Sawada assumed that this was the origin of the cocoa, although the potion burned on Aritomo's palate rather unpleasantly sour. However, the homage he received was reason enough for him not to show it. It became clear that this drink was highly regarded among the natives.

Aritomo ate and drank and learned. He liked the combination. Sawada and Tanaka, who proved to be extremely talented in expressing the Mayan words correctly, didn't hold back. And Itzanami tried constantly to identify new items he could name. Their variety of verbs and certain phrases increased in an almost exponential manner during the several-hour meal. From "eating" and "drinking" they immediately came to "give," "take" and polite formulas such as "thank you" and "please." Sawada didn't know what to do first – to write down all the new terms in his notebook, as the core of a first dictionary of words and grammar, or to taste the endless variety of food offered.

The meal already took a lot of time. Although much chi had been served, no one showed any signs of intoxication. The alcoholic content of the drink was very low. Aritomo assumed that you had to take very substantial amounts to get really drunk.

This was his consideration when he presented his gift.

He brought out a bottle of sake.

Six of these bottles were privately owned by the commander. Inugami had reluctantly separated himself from one. It would take a long time until they might be able to produce anything resembling the drink under these circumstances. And the officer liked his sake.

Aritomo quickly felt that the King of Mutal would soon share that fondness.

Expectant silence descended upon the crowd as Aritomo opened the bottle and poured the crystal-clear liquid into one of the sake cups also brought along. To demonstrate the relative harmlessness of the drink, Aritomo himself poured himself a hearty portion and poured it down his throat. The sake was good, first burned satisfactorily, then slid gently and pleasantly down the throat. Inugami had spared no expense, this was no shit, this was quality.

Then he offered a cup to the King. He didn't hesitate, took and swallowed. Then his eyes widened, he let out a gasp. Aritomo escaped neither the son's worried expression nor the fact that the ruler's bodyguards reflexively reached for the spears they had set aside.

But the King raised a hand, which immediately relaxed everyone. He stared for a moment, disoriented, at the empty sake cup, gasped again, then a smile crossed his lips, and he said a few words to Itzanami.

Sawada leaned over to Aritomo.

"I may not have understood it correctly, but I think the King spoke of sake as a drink of the gods."

Aritomo lifted the bottle, pointed it out with his finger, and said clearly, "Sake!"

The word found a lot of echo in the round.

The King held out his cup. Aritomo filled it as well as his own, which he handed to the son of the king.

Both drank. Both immediately panted. Sweat stood on their forehead. The blissful expression that followed was well known to Aritomo. This is how men looked who drank a lot and were happy when the desired effect came in earlier than expected. That made sense. The alcoholic drinks they had been given had been very mild. Strong brandy was apparently unknown to the Maya. And they liked to drink. The intoxication seemed to have a great appeal on them.

It took about twenty minutes of concentrated drinking, and the bottle was empty. The content didn't miss its effect on the two men. They had previously laid a solid foundation with plenty of chi.

Now the sake did the rest. When the two men wanted to rise, they had to be supported by their servants. The other Maya exchanged admiring and, as Aritomo thought, envious glances. The use of sake had certainly been a complete success. The drink had strengthened the visitors' godly reputation.

The problem was that only five bottles of the liquid were available for further demonstrations of its reputation. Aritomo decided to have a serious conversation with Sarukazaki. The man was very resourceful. He would find a way to produce a local alternative to sake. What was possible with rice, should also be feasible with corn, Aritomo assumed.

The rest of the meal went on without any noteworthy events, and at some point the feasting was officially ended. There was a long conversation between Itzanami and the King, and when the Japanese set out they had company – the Crown Prince joined them next to Itzanami, and also a few servants followed, heavily burdened with the countless dishes not even touched during the meal.

Everything was carried up to the boat, where the whole process had been watched with interest and astonishment. When the food had been deposited on the boat's hull by very reverent and somewhat fearful porters, they disappeared remarkably fast. Chitam stayed. He looked long and thoughtfully at the gun that had damaged the neighboring pyramid, and in his glance was both respect and curiosity. This curiosity led him and Itzanami inside the boat. They quickly understood that Chitam was eager to attend the lessons with Sawada.

Aritomo asked Inugami for permission to be a participant in the lessons as well. Even the gifted Tanaka expressed this request. Inugami agreed immediately. The lessons were to be continued intensively the very next day. Sawada was commissioned to write a textbook and was given all the paper supplies of the boat. In two weeks at the latest, so the strict command, the teacher should be able to give the entire team a first language lesson.

Aritomo admired Inugami's consequence. Many in the crew were still a bit apathetic and lamented silently. The commander maintained the discipline, inventing new tasks on a daily basis, ushered the men around and made it clear to them that they had a duty to perform. The presence of the young Prince of Japan helped. This one kept a remarkable attitude. The strict education was noticeable. And after a short while, he also wanted to attend Sawada's language lessons.

So began a great time of learning and getting to know each other.

12

Tatb'u looked at the drawings Pakul had made and again wondered how a man alone could be so talented. Of course, he roughly knew the distances to neighboring towns and knew how long it took them to walk. He himself, in his time as heir to the throne of his father as well as Yaxchilan's warlord, had traveled long distances to wage wars and to return from them – usually victorious, as he noted with a not inconsiderable degree of satisfaction.

Nobody could put this knowledge on paper as well as Pakul. The drawings he made, mostly in preparation for campaigns, were a marvel in itself, and this particular one showed not only the way to Mutal but also an approximation of their external settlement structure. Pakul had been to Mutal twice, both times as an emissary on special occasions, and his attentive, ever-seeking eye and excellent memory had served him well. No one had thought of raiding the city back then, but Pakul's almost instinctive desire to gather tactical and strategic information had led to these records, which he now submitted to his king.

And Tatb'u was very happy with all of it.

Of course, some things would've changed by now. Also in Mutal construction was going in all the time, the city expanded, everyone knew that. Their population grew, and this had consequences, above all, it aroused the greed of neighbors – and their fear of the ever-growing power of this metropolis. But everyone knew how to build a city properly, and assumptions could be based on these laws – and these assumptions, in turn, were sensibly complemented by Pakul's wonderful drawings.

"So how many men can we raise? I want everyone who can carry a weapon to march with me!" the King said. He wasn't taking any chances at the moment. The victory over Bonampak had strengthened Yaxchilan's reputation in the region. None of the smaller neighboring cities would dare question the dominance of Tatb'u and thus ask for the same fate as that of the recently vanquished. Now, indeed, was the perfect time to put all energy into the new plan without worrying too much about defending the homeland.

"I think we can count on about 3,000 warriors," his general said. Tatb'u nodded enthusiastically. This was the largest army his city had ever sent to battle. Even the great Mutal would have a hard time defending itself against a determined and unforeseen attack by so many fighters. More likely, they would be able to extract at least a considerable tribute, and they would be particularly pleased to proclaim a glorious victory over Mutal on the stelae of Yaxchilan, eternally and across all cycles connected with the name of equally glorious K'inich Tatb'u I.

The ruler enjoyed this prospect extremely well. If there were some decent victims, high-ranking prisoners who could be offered to Itzamnaaj to bless his city even more than he had done in His Grace of late, one could be more than satisfied. Everything came together wonderfully.

"When can we leave?" he asked his general.

He thought for a moment before answering. Tatb'u did not suspect for a second that the man would lie only to please him. Their relationship with each other was trusting, and Pakul always honestly said what he meant and also named any problems that might arise. If he meditated, then it was his purpose to properly correlate all facts and to consider all important aspects.

"Soon, sir. We still collect some supplies for the march. The priests are waiting for the right omen. The rituals are not finished yet."

The supplies were not a problem – after all, they had taken from Bonampak everything that had been possible to transport by human beings. But the omens had to be considered. Tatb'u had no doubt that Itzamnaaj was in favor of his plans. On the other hand – the gods were moody. It was better to make sure.

In addition, the men fought with greater zeal when they knew that their god was on their side. Such motivation was worth as much as a thousand additional warriors. That wasn't something Tatb'u wanted to do without. Despite all of his ambition, he appreciated good preparation and the use of every advantage. He was a powerful, active king, but no one had ever reproached him for being a reckless gambler.

But even better than the motivation of a thousand additional fighters were ... a thousand real additional fighters. And that was an issue that they both had to discuss now.

"Where does the road lead us?" he asked Pakul.

"I suggest we take the southern detour past the Great Lake of Peten-Itza through Tayasal and Saclemacal," Pakul said. "There are several advantages, as you know. The Lord of Tayasal is the nephew of your father. He is not one of our vassals, but his proximity to Mutal certainly makes him suspicious of becoming a victim of their quest for power – and in the not-too-distant future. If we act diplomatically, he could give us some of his men and increase our clout."

Tatb'u nodded. He had wanted to hear that.

"Besides, he'll have more up-to-date information about what's going on in Mutal. Information is important."

"What about Saclemacal?"

Pakul smiled. "The Kowoj are a proud people, my king. Saclemacal is a fairly small town, but with a history that goes way back in time – some say even farther than Mutal's, which considers itself the largest and most beautiful of all cities. Mutal is so much bigger and more powerful than Saclemacal that they have become tributary for some time – a deep thorn in the flesh of the local noble families. I am not only confident that we will be able to enlarge our army there once more, the tactical facts learned from the immediate neighborhood will be of considerable importance."

"That means you expect us to end up attacking with more than 3,000 men?"

Pakul smiled expectantly.

"If all goes well, my Emperor, we will be able to send 5000 to battle. A great alliance of three cities, led by the blessed K'inich Tatb'u. The entire lowland will speak of this campaign for hundreds of years, rest assured."

Tatb'u nodded and smiled. He liked it, as his general thought. Always the big picture in view. And all prepared in a way so that his King could send him on a campaign in whose course the fanatical warrior had the chance to bathe in the blood of his enemies. Well, the ruler of Yaxchilan was more than ready to fulfill that particular wish of the nobleman.

"Tell me once everything is prepared," he finished the conversation.

"I expect about a week before we are ready to leave," Pakul replied with a bow before retreating.

Tatb'u stepped out of his chambers and looked down from the height of his palace onto the main square of his city. There, all preparations for the great sacrificial ceremony were made. The prisoners of war from Bonampak had lost the big ballgame despite an excellent performance, whereby the pleasure of Itzamnaaj had become visible for everyone. The men were soon to be sacrificed to this god, in a lengthy and very bloody ritual in which Tatb'u had an important role to play. It was a good preparation for the coming campaign as the ritual could be used to solicit special blessings for their great plan.

About 5,000 men were available according to Pakul, and this would make a very considerable force. Mutal, even if well-prepared, would have a difficult time countering this onslaught. But Tatb'u knew that in the heat of the battle the atlatl could surprisingly strike, and the dead couldn't cherish the triumph of their companions.

No, he would make sure to instruct the priests at the upcoming sacrificial ceremony to focus all prayers on the very personal safety of the King. Tatb'u hesitated a moment, then sighed. And Pakul. He should also be named.

The bloodthirsty general was just too talented. The King of Yaxchilan would still have use for him in the future.

He should live and grow old and lead the men of the city to many more victories.

13

Aritomo and Chitam went for a walk.

In the past two weeks, the Japanese officer had learned that the roughly same-age Mayan prince was a sympathetic person with a dry sense of humor. Since he was able to express this not only through words but also through facial expressions and gestures, both of them had quickly become friendly in the course of their intensive language studies.

In general, the situation had eased during this time. There was still a certain distance, but in every sense of the word, the first exuberance of emotional stress, positive as well as negative, had passed. The ecstatic esoteric experience of the Maya, the fear and confusion of the Japanese, both leveled lower, both became manageable. Contacts became more regular, fears subsided, mutual acceptance – though not necessarily an understanding – improved rapidly. The men continued to live in the boat, but often stayed in close proximity to the confined space, lying on the foredeck, or scrambling around the half-ruined pyramid. They had learned by now that the destroyed building was actually supposed to be the tomb of the reigning king and that a new building would soon be constructed, because the ruler was – according to local standards – not the youngest anymore.

Chitam would then become the next king, such were the current rules of succession.

No one had told him that Inugami would only be ready to accept him as the vassal of a Japanese emperor, as a servant of a Japanese ruling class whose purity he sought to preserve for as long as possible. Aritomo himself was not sure how Inugami wanted to achieve "purity" when there were no Japanese women within reach. It was absolutely unavoidable – though he wisely kept that assessment to himself – that it would be Mayan women with whom the men would sooner or later get involved. None of them made vows of celibacy or had otherwise renounced carnal pleasures; they were sailors, young men who had pretty clear ideas about their leisure time activities. At some point, the inevitable would happen. Just as inevitable was everything that necessarily resulted from such bonding.

At least Aritomo had no intention of ending up as a virgin, no matter what Inugami seemed to consider as appropriate.

The language studies had progressed so far that simple content could be communicated and the rest resulted from wild hand movements. And so Aritomo approached Inugami with the idea of improving the current tactical situation through information gathering and exploring the city. Of course, the true idea behind it had been different: to leave the narrowness of the boat, to seek variety, to gather new impressions, and to enjoy the thoroughly amusing and relaxed company of the Prince, whose companionship would also ensure Aritomo's safety.

With Inugami, the military argument went better as expected. He had given his approval, albeit not enthusiastically.

And so they both left one morning, and Aritomo showed himself to Mutal, a settlement which, he was quick to discover, was far greater than had been supposed, and at least for him, the abilities of these "savages" began to shift increasingly into a different light. Yes, he still thought about the natives with a certain arrogance, but then a few days ago he had asked Sawada which year they probably had, and the teacher had speculated that they were somewhere in the fifth century AD, according to Western chronology.

"And in Japanese counting?" Aritomo had asked.

Sawada had laughed and shaken his head, knowing exactly where this conversation would take them.

"We talk about the Kofun period, young friend. The time of the kingdom of Yamato, the era of the Five Kingdoms. I don't want to say it too loud, but if we travel to Japan now – and Inugami has already philosophized about it –, we would find a society that has not progressed much further than this one here, and in many ways. Of course, there are differences – we were a seafaring nation at that time, which evolved naturally from the island situation. And you may have noticed that while the Maya know the wheel as a shape, they do not use it to accelerate means of transport. There are no carts, but otherwise ... Other tools, yes. Other raw materials, yes. But a great difference in the evolution of civilization? I say no."

Sawada had then stopped and smiled no longer.

"Do not talk about it to Inugami. He doesn't like the idea much."

Aritomo had asked many more questions, and the longer he studied the careful observations of Sawada, the less inclined he was to maintain his arrogance toward the Maya. With Inugami – and many other crew members, down to the simplest sailor – this was still the other way round. It was as if looking at one's own superiority, even that sense of being chosen, was the only way to maintain mental health in a foreign environment.

But the walk with Chitam and the content of their conversation affirmed Aritomo in his changing attitude. The architecture of the Maya was breathtaking!

The boat had landed on an unfinished structure that belonged to a group of pyramids, all therefore temples or tombs of past rulers. Directly in front of the crash site stretched a large square, which was completed at one side by the royal palace.

Chitam and Aritomo kept left and walked down the main square until they came to an artificial lake. Sawada had looked at this and another near the palace from the boat's foredeck, and had come to the conclusion that they weren't ornamental but had a very practical use: They had to be water reservoirs. In times when there was no rainfall, the supply of the population was assured, and the apparently intensive cultivation of crops could continue. He hadn't quite figured out how the water was distributed but suspected the existence of channels and ditches. Aritomo could confirm that now, for from the reservoir a web of canals, many of them underground and accessible by entrances, descended in different directions. His respect grew. This was an architectural feat, and he learned now that it was by far not the only one.

Opposite the water reservoir to the north was another square, the same size as the one in front of the palace. From here, one had a good overview of the north side of the city. The buildings lined up tightly together, and the closer they were to the central square, the bigger and more magnificent they were. Further away, they became a bit smaller, often no longer made of stone but only of wood and clay. Aritomo assumed that in the city center, the nobles lived, while the common people spread to the outer districts. There was steady traffic, goods were being transported, and the wide and well-developed roads were busy.

Where the buildings were not whitewashed, they offered colorful paintings, and these too became more numerous and impressive as one approached the city center. Aritomo regarded these sometimes very complex depictions as absolutely fascinating. They showed powerful rulers in various scenes, often courtly in nature but also successful wars, the subjugation of enemies. Religious representations were very common, especially at the temples of which he visited two with Chitam. Aritomo struggled to understand the Maya's religious beliefs, but it had become clear that they were anything but simple, even though they gave rise to bloody human sacrifices. He suspected that the Japanese were seen as emissaries of a sun god, who enjoyed the highest prestige in the city. Although apparently male, this deity reminded him of Amaterasu, the sun goddess of Japanese mythology, who was said to have founded the Imperial House. Aritomo was a man of the present – whatever that meant at the time – and had been educated with popular Buddhism shaped by the convictions of his mother. He personally couldn't connect well with the belief in a sun goddess but had to agree that the parallels were there and could be used by the Japanese for their benefit. At least, Inugami had paid close attention to Sawada's presentation on this subject.

When they left the western square, they turned to the east, walked past the palace again, and came to a third, large area, from where a mighty road led north. This too was dominated by the vast royal seat. When they finally passed the building, they came across an interesting building where they were expected. Chitam grinned and was happy as a child when he saw Aritomo's surprise. It was a sports field, big and arranged as Aritomo knew it from his time, in many ways even more splendid and spacious. A crowd of people had assembled on tribunes around a playground, a mashed field of exact dimensions, a neatly arranged quadrangle, the walls of the stands decorated with numerous representations of men playing ball.

A playing field. A sports stadium. Aritomo was totally baffled while he was led by Chitam to the seats of honor reserved for the rulers of the city. He had been invited to a sporting event! And it all looked so ... perfect and familiar that he didn't even realize the differences or the rules of the game.

Chitam apparently didn't even try to explain the game to him. Chi was served, and the Prince leaned back relaxed. Aritomo therefore decided to just watch. He could barely communicate; therefore, he wasn't capable to ask the right questions anyways.

The two teams seemed to consist of eight men each. As far as Aritomo could tell, it was a question of throwing a small ball through a stone ring embedded in the wall on the long side of the playing field. There also seemed to be something like a referee who warned players if they violated rules. So it was obviously not allowed to touch the ball with the hands. It was played with the hips, the knees and the arms. It was not a sport for the occasional exercise, nothing to shake off the wrist. Aritomo understood immediately that only real professionals would play well and effectively.

The two teams seemed to be well-trained and coordinated. The game was fast and dynamic, with rapid rallies. If the ball banged against one of the perimeter walls, it gave a hard crashing sound. He had to be very tough. Whenever he, intentionally targeted, impacted on a careless player who didn't parry or catch in time, a murmur went through the crowd. It had to be painful to handle this game if a player didn't pay attention or wasn't trained properly. The players were protected – all wore a kind of armor around their hips and wrapped shin guards –, but if a direct hit was made on the shoulder or even on the head, the risk of injury had to be great.

Not with these two teams though. These were, as Aritomo was soon able to establish, in fact real professionals, whose ball control put him in fascinated amazement. He was so taken by the rapid and perfect game play that he didn't notice the way the Prince looked at him smiling and making his own thoughts, whichever they were.

After more than half an hour – who was in the lead or not, Aritomo had not quite understood, because he hadn't managed to distinguish the two teams beyond doubt – was paused. The players were refreshing themselves, the spectators as well, as baked corn bread was served. Aritomo felt that he was hungry. Among the crowd, a friendly mood had developed, a cheerful exuberance, a general babble of voices. Undoubtedly, there was much to talk about, judging the performance of individual players and discussing the prospects for the rest of the game. Maybe even bets were made. The commencement of the game was close, for the men kept their protective gear on, wiping their sweat with damp cloths, drinking water and putting their heads together, obviously to discuss tactics for the rest of the game. Aritomo felt himself becoming impatient and excited. He wanted to know how it went and to enjoy the impressive virtuosity of the players and the acrobatic speed of their movements.

This was a lot of fun!

Add to that the colorful ambiance. The Maya hated monotonous clothing. Of course, Aritomo had to assume that everyone had dressed up especially, because the whole drama had undoubtedly been arranged by Chitam to impress the guest. But the Japanese had no problems with that. He was ready to be impressed, indeed seduced.

Not only by the spectacle of this competition. In other ways, and mindful of his previous doubts about some of Inugami's cherished plans, it quickly became clear that different seductions were on offer as well.

It had not escaped him that after the break, when the game started again and quickly picked up speed, some young girls joined them in the stands, beckoned by the Prince. The fact that they sat in the vicinity of the guest of honor and threw him quite expressive looks, usually accompanied by a magical smile, was absolutely not to be overlooked.

Aritomo still tried to maintain his dignity, answering the young women's wink with no more than a friendly nod. Whether he lived up to expectations or not, he couldn't see. For him, it was clear that women held a subordinate position to the men with the Maya, on the other hand, they talked quite freely with their male companions, and all equally offered subservient respect to Chitam. The glances with which the Prince was observed were not marked by fear. Attention, certainly also because of his authority as heir to the throne, and readiness to serve were needed, but the submissiveness to Chitam had something ... relaxed. It became clear to Aritomo, as far as he correctly interpreted this behavior, that Chitam was the son of a popular ruler who hadn't done anything that could've caused the displeasure of his subjects.

After the game was over – Aritomo still didn't know who won before Chitam rose to honor the victorious team with well-chosen words and some gifts – they left the ball court and marched back to the west, this time obviously to reach the palace. Aritomo, who had eaten plenty of the food offered during the game, found his fears confirmed: He was now invited to a meal, and not in the king's chambers, but in those of the Prince.

Aritomo considered how he could explain to the young man that he wouldn't be able to bring down another bite in the foreseeable future. But before this question could become a serious problem, he was asked to go to a larger room. It was richly decorated with colorful murals, with mats on the walls and on the floor, frugal furniture, but all in all a very appealing atmosphere. No food was served, just cups of chi, the drink that Aritomo slowly began to get used to.

He was relieved that he didn't have to stuff himself until further notice.

Here he met Lady Tzutz, the wife of Prince Chitam, and therefore, if everything went according to plan, and Aritomo had some doubts about that, the future Queen of Mutal. She was the only one present, along with Chitam and a servant, and her personality filled the room in ways Aritomo had never experienced before. Lady Tzutz wasn't beautiful. The young girls who had smiled at the Japanese on the ball court, looked much more attractive from the outside. She had no particularly attractive characteristic, and her face looked normal in an almost boring way. What made her so mesmerizing was her clear, melodic voice, which was able to conjure up an almost poetic sound even from the often harsh and choppy Mayan language. In addition, gestures and facial expressions were characterized by a dignity which was not trained and had nothing to do with her exalted status in the local society, but only with who she was.

She spoke softly, but when she did, her voice was heard everywhere. Her words had a penetrating power that was not shrill. There was strength and certainty in them. Aritomo had once known a woman who, despite a modest outward appearance, had left the same impression on other people: his grandmother, who had died long ago. When she spoke, all the men were silent too, no matter how pompous they were with their manly rights as spokespersons or decision-makers. It had been a completely automatic reaction.

And it was quite similar in this case.

The Lady Tzutz was also eager to learn and intelligent. She had obviously had her husband repeat the lessons he had shared with Sawada and the priest Itzanami at home. It certainly helped Chitam to learn at a remarkably fast pace – knowledge was best understood by explaining it to someone else, as Aritomo knew – and helped his wife develop some simple English vocabulary. Anyway, she had greeted him with a clearly articulated "Good day!" once he had been led into the room.

And their conversation, which otherwise would have been rather limited and short due to the language barrier, developed into another intense lesson, with Tzutz helping Aritomo to learn new vocabulary as well as helping her to develop her own language skills. Aritomo was amused to see how Prince Chitam was invited to participate by his wife only when it came to a correct pronunciation or discussion of a particular term. Aritomo felt the woman required more attention from him, than if Captain Inugami would've given him a difficult order. And he found himself struggling to concentrate on meeting the honorable lady's high expectations.

In addition to learning a great deal during those exchanges, there was also a second positive effect. Tzutz eventually declared the lesson ended, with a sincerely grateful smile toward Aritomo, which pleased him more than he wanted to. She clapped her hands, and servants began to serve the meal he had anticipated, and now he was feeling really hungry, which he had not thought to be possible only recently.

It was early evening when Chitam finally brought him back to the submarine. Aritomo's head was full of the impressions of the day, and he tried to draw some mental consequences. It was unmistakable that the Maya were expecting something from him. But were the expectations of this people compatible with those of Inugami? He demanded direct and unlimited power – Aritomo couldn't interpret the statements of the captain in any other way. And Inugami would never be ready to develop much understanding for those he intended to control. No matter what they might present to him, the Maya would remain savages to Inugami, good enough as subjects but only to obey and serve. Aritomo was increasingly gaining a different picture, one that was more differentiated. Would a man like Prince Chitam – or a woman like Lady Tzutz – allow someone like Inugami to tell them what to do? Despite all the divine lineage attributed to the newcomers, this bonus was quickly lost if the "rule" of the Japanese turned out to be brutal and inconsiderate, but above all a government of contempt for one's own subjects. Yes, the Maya joyfully submitted to their gods and were even willing, as they had learned from Itzanami, to sacrifice children for the grace of the heavenly masters – one of the gruesome practices in which Aritomo, in rare accord with Inugami, advocated the immediate abolition, should it ever be in their power. But the same Maya subjected these practices to a very specific understanding of nature, its environment, an eternal order. If the newcomers, the time travelers, could not fit into this nature or if they dared to destroy it, that could be fatal. And if they didn't respect those who gave everything for the preservation of this order, then the rule of someone like Inugami would also lose respect – and one day he would suddenly be very dead.

A destiny that Aritomo didn't want to share.

He said goodbye to Chitam, expressed an awkward thank-you for the day, which the Prince accepted with a majestic nod, and climbed the half-ruined pyramid to reach the boat. The guard on the bridge – as well as two sunbathing crew members on the forecastle – waved to him. When Aritomo reached the top, he saw baskets of fresh fruit standing there. The Maya had further contributed to the care of their guests. The good food would keep up the morale aboard the boat, especially for those who were still overwhelmed with disbelief.

Inugami had a fair grip on this problem, Aritomo had to give him that. He left no doubt that it was unworthy of an Imperial Japanese soldier, in the presence of a prince, to lose one's composure and let discipline falter for even a moment. And the men, who were already part of the elite of the fleet, carefully chosen for the occupation of the most important new vessel, widely accepted this view. It gave them support and orientation in a world that seemed to have lost both. And this approach forged the crew together – with each other and with the Captain. Aritomo profited as his second in command, but he wasn't sure if the long-term consequences would be so easy to handle.

He told Inugami and Sawada about his trip and the related impressions. The old teacher asked many questions. Inugami took his words in silence. Once the report was finished, Aritomo briefly considered what to do. He didn't feel tired enough to go to sleep, and he felt many doubts and fears that he simply needed to digest.

After a moment's hesitation, he realized that his way had to lead him into the engine room, where he suspected Sarukazaki to be – and Robert Lengsley, the British engineer, who was not quite involved in the discipline of the boat, a guest, an outsider and someone who, though also from an Empire of its own right, had a more relaxed view on monarchy and the divine lineage of revered rulers.

He needed someone with a relaxed view.

So he went in search of someone to talk to.

14

Robert Lengsley considered himself a man of some sophistication. Born and raised in Liverpool, he started working temporary jobs in the yards at the age of 12, and there he smelled for the first time the scent of the big, wide world. His excellent technical knowledge and desire to absorb every detail of shipbuilding like a sponge were quickly noticed. His father, an employee of the city administration with a secure but very meager income, soon gave up trying to sell his son the benefits of civil service, and then supported him in his passion as much as he could with his modest means. Lengsley had worked from bottom to top until he became one of the city's best ship engineers once he was almost 30 years old. When he moved to Vickers, he had already paid visits to many European countries and made a trip to the young United States, which also was interested in building a powerful navy. At Vickers, he was allowed to work on the development of submarines during a time that was exciting as he was allowed to do many things that had never been tried before. The urge of constant technical innovation, the race against other nations such as the German Reich, and the sometimes unrealistic wishes of the Admiralty constituted a combination of forces that only those survived who mastered not only technology but also the language of negotiation and endless meetings connected to naval politics.

And someone was ready to expand his own limits.

Robert Lengsley was such a man. After four years, he was loaned to Kawasaki in Japan for twelve months – a "loan" for which his employer got paid handsomely. Lengsley had accepted the offer with pleasure. He had always been drawn to far places. The additional benefit was that he would earn three years salary in one. Japan was a fascinating country for him, and he had learned well, even studied

Japanese intensively, although this language had been anything but easily accessible to him. The Japanese respected his knowledge and will to share it freely. Working with them had been one of the best times of his life. The crowning glory should have been the maiden voyage of the new boat. After that, Lengsley's contract expired, and he was sure he would return to his old job, with new, exciting responsibilities for the future.

Things had turned out to be a little differently now.

Still, his duties were new and exciting.

And he had definitely visited a far place. Geographically, but also in the sense of distant, a bygone era, a thought that Lengsley had neither fully intellectual nor emotionally processed until now. He had a bride at home, Edna, whom he sincerely missed and, he feared, would never see again. Most of his Japanese comrades had no problem with that. The marriage regime of the fleet was extremely strict. No one was allowed to think about a relationship without the permission of his superior, and most were arranged by the families involved. The majority on board thought of parents and siblings but not brides. Lengsley was almost envious of them but was careful not to discuss these things with anyone. He didn't know the crew well enough. Just as the boat was a foreign object in the city of Mutal, he was one inside the boat. He was treated well. He was neither avoided, nor did anyone whisper behind his back, for the latter, he surely gave no reason. Conversations were always characterized by courtesy. But the cultural distance was palpable, every day, and if anyone felt alone in this strange, exotic and incomprehensible world, it was Robert Lengsley from Liverpool. That didn't make his situation easier.

The sergeant, who was the machinist aboard the boat, was named Sarukazaki and was likable to Lengsley. Unlike most other men on board, who treated him with a relatively cool courtesy, the man sometimes joked or tried to talk about something other than their strange and frightening situation. That was certainly the reason Lengsley spent every minute in the engine room, where he had set up his nightly camp alongside Sarukazaki and another mechanic. Now and then he climbed, like the others, on the foredeck and enjoyed the sun, but even there he felt mostly lost. He was bound by the passion for technology with these two men in the engine room, a band that was also able to bridge linguistic and cultural differences. Who knew, maybe one day even a Maya could be found, who, albeit from another level, shared the same enthusiasm. Then Lengsley might eventually feel comfortable here too.

Until then, however, Lengsley realized he was one of the loneliest people of this era. He didn't really listen to many of the Japanese conversations, because his language skills were simply insufficient. At the same time, he only picked up on the Mayan language what he learned from the two-hour lesson given by the old Sawada at the captain's command – followed by the opportunity to learn another four or five hours with their Maya guests, which he subsequently did willingly. Lengsley learned as hard as he could. Feeling alone in the world awoke the urge to acquire as many things as possible that might once provide helpful protection. The ability to communicate was certainly one of them.

But everything went so agonizingly slow. And Inugami very rarely gave permission for crew members to leave the vicinity of the boat. Lengsley hadn't received any yet, and he didn't associate any hopes with each renewed request for clearance. That didn't stop him from trying again and again.

Today he had renounced the attempt.

He sat next to the diesel engine, which he had – for no reason other than occupational therapy – half dismantled, carefully cleaned, oiled and reassembled. Inugami had ordered that all machines be switched off to save gas. That brought with it certain dangers, at least in the midterm.

Lengsley and Sarukazaki had used this time to do superfluous maintenance. The boat had just been put through its paces, and the subsequent journey hadn't been too long. Much more interesting had been the inspection of the underside of the boat Lengsley had completed yesterday. The submarine had crashed into the pyramid from moderate height, and that was what the pressure hull had endured. But often the damages were hidden and not visible to the naked eye. Of course, they could only be sure if they could put the boat in a dry dock to look at it thoroughly. Lengsley was sure he could build a dry dock with local resources. But they were far from the coast, as Itzanami, the priest, had finally been able to convey. Mutal was somewhere in Central America, and the boat was literally a fish without water.

However, the inspection had been successful and satisfactory, as far as it had been feasible. The boat was, of course, very sturdy. It seemed to be in a very good condition in general, which could not be consistently claimed by the crew and by Lengsley himself.

"Mr. Lengsley? May I disturb you?"

The Briton looked up and looked into the round face of Aritomo Hara, the boat's first officer. While Lengsley secretly considered the captain of the mission as quite an asshole, he had gained a good impression of his deputy so far. Hara didn't seem quite so ... dogged. Maybe it was his full-moon face ... or the fact that when this man smiled, the joy in his eyes was also visible, while every emotion – except anger – in Inugami seemed fake.

But Lengsley reminded himself to be careful. He hadn't lived long enough with the Japanese to really read them. It was a quite different culture than his, and emotionalism was a difficult topic. There were situations in which a Japanese man could cry, while a Briton would have considered this shameful and inappropriate, even effeminate. On the other hand, a man was expected to have self-restraint and immobility, where a Brit could have shown feelings. And everything was covered over again and again by this mask of politeness, through which Lengsley couldn't always see through. What did the other really think of him? Was the praise meant seriously? And this or that remark – was that purposeful, but terribly congealed criticism, or was it just that? Lengsley was fascinated and confused by Japan. He still had much to learn.

Not to mention the culture of the Maya to add.

"Sure, Lieutenant Hara."

The full moon face smiled – and Lengsley was reasonably sure it was really smiling –, and the man squatted next to him on the floor next to the diesel engine.

"How do you feel?"

The officer's English was carefully articulated, but not always grammatically correct, possibly because Japanese generally seemed to have difficulty with this language. On the other hand, Lengsley was pretty sure that his comrades didn't laugh loudly about his attempts at Japanese, because they were far too polite and well-mannered.

"Good, thanks ... according to the circumstances. I'm running out of work, I'm starting to get bored."

Aritomo nodded. "Do not let Sarukazaki persuade you to play cards, especially real games for money."

"We played Hanafuda," Lengsley admitted with a grin. "I realized he'd let me go first to make sure I felt safe."

"That's what he does," the officer said seriously. "He's not afraid of robbing superiors, by the way. I have to warn you explicitly. He is ruthless."

Lengsley sighed playfully. "What use are my coins here? I can't buy anything anyway."

"That's true. But who knows – maybe money is one of the achievements we will give the Maya."

Lengsley said nothing. Hara certainly wanted something and hadn't initiated to him to banish his own boredom or to chat about the dangers of playing cards. The Briton became curious. Was there something coming up?

"Possibly," he replied carefully. "Or they have no need for it. What are the local people offering when they want to pay for something of value?"

"Cocoa beans, as far as I understand it. And also valuable other raw materials – obsidian, for example, if it is of very good quality, both unprocessed and in the form of blades."

"Metals?"

"Yes, they know what precious metals are. But they don't use metal for everyday use. I haven't seen any iron tools but gold jewelry. I suppose we could teach them something in this area too."

"Or the wheel. I haven't yet seen a cart," the Brit added.

Aritomo nodded. "It's a mystery if you look at the quality of their streets. Yet everything is laboriously transported by humans."

"It could be a complicated religious taboo," Lengsley said, starting to warm up for the discussion. "It seems to me that the beliefs of these people are very diverse, and we may not even know the main underlying principles."

"That was my guess at first. But I think there's a pretty simple explanation for that," Aritomo replied. He spread his arms as far as the confined space allowed. "They lack of draft animals. There are no horses, donkeys, or cattle. Most animals are small or deer that can't be domesticated to become a draft animal. Sawada says these animals didn't come into the country until they were imported by the Spaniards. But that is still far in our – current – future. Without draft animals, a cart makes less sense."

"The wheel is still useful," Lengsley said. "Even if we only have people as workers, it's possible to carry more on a good cart than by a group of porters, not to mention other areas of application. I'm talking about the waterwheel, for example, to drive a mill. There are rivers with currents. Their power does not seem to be used systematically."

"There is probably no shortage of manpower. It's like slavery. It means that technical advancement gets stuck, because the execution of all work by many available workers – at least for a time – is so cheap and simple."

Lengsley nodded. The Japanese had really thought about these things. The Briton was righteously impressed. Behind the seemingly harmless, childlike face, a keen mind was working, based on a good sense of observation. He relaxed, began to actively engage with the subject, if only because it was a welcome relief from the current monotony of his existence.

"We could also improve their warfare," he continued. "You obviously use only spear, shield, knife, and those spear throwers, which I'm pretty impressed with by the way. Apart from the King's bodyguard, the army seems to be a sort of militia into which all men are called to become warriors if the ruler wishes."

Aritomo smiled. "You talked to Sawada."

"If he has time. He is very, very busy."

"He is our teacher and at the same time the most diligent student."

"That's probably very good."

"But the subject of the war is important," Aritomo went on. "Because, of course, that's what Inugami has in mind. Establish the rule over this city and use it as the base for an empire governed by a tiny upper class – us. A thought that meets with great approval from many members of the crew."

Lengsley hesitated with the answer. He now guessed what the man wanted. He listened to him, wanted to know his opinion on certain topics. But did he do so on behalf of the captain trying to find out if the *gaijin* was trustworthy – or did he do so because he doubted Inugami's plans and saw Lengsley as a potential ally?

How should he react? He actually had to listen to Aritomo Hara first, to not make a mistake!

The conversation between the two men consequently resembled a dance of words – not one in which the partners followed each other closely entwined in a musical movement but one characterized by mutual observation, evasion, circling, without one seeking to leave the other's orbit or someone breaking off the dance. It was a dance, because it lacked the aggression of a fight, because many clever words fell, much approval was expressed, often meant seriously, and because the two dancers considered themselves not as adversaries but also not necessarily as dance partners. The dance lasted a good hour, interrupted by brief breaks in which the participants had to be clear about the next steps, the sequence of the movements, all deliberate and very focused, but without the passionate fire and the urge, striving for a satisfactory result. But once the dance was continued, it was clear that everyone was approaching each other very slowly, metaphorically groping, carefully, and cautiously. It was all about really small steps. Everyone was ready to retreat to a safe distance as if to perform the dance on a very brittle or sloping ground. When the dancers finally finished, with a degree of exhaustion, and came to the silent agreement that nothing more was to be said during this encounter, both took some basic lessons home: that they didn't think much of Inugami's plans for their future relationship with the Maya. But that they wouldn't be able to do much, as long as the majority of the crew remained loyal to the concept. That one had to try to work cautiously on Inugami to prevent the worst, that the captain overlooked how few they were, and that any mistake would mean their downfall.

And that they'd meet again, at the appropriate time, to discuss these and other topics.

As Aritomo Hara said goodbye, Lengsley paused for a few more moments sitting on the metal floor next to the diesel engine, thinking. No matter what the consequences of what had just been discussed, one thing was clear to him – and filled him with a certain satisfaction. Even if their relationship wasn't fully established, now he seemed to have found someone with whom he could talk and who had a genuine interest in making their existence bearable in this time and place so as not to end up as a human sacrifice on a Mayan altar. If Lengsley could contribute to that, then he wanted to do it as part of his certainly modest possibilities. If he found a friend in Hara, it was a positive side effect that would make his life easier here. It was a real step forward to break his isolation, escape from the mental dungeon cell he had been locked into.

Lengsley took a deep breath.

The conversation had increased his worries, raised many new questions, and painted a bleak picture of their future.

And yet, today was not such a bad day at all.

15

Tatb'u rejoiced in his army, and his army rejoiced in his brave and victorious king. The morning was beautiful, and the column of soldiers of the glorious Yaxchilan stood ready, laden with weapons and supplies, and in the most orderly fashion. Everywhere good mood could be felt, the anticipation of a campaign of epic proportions, almost palpable. The great Mutal should fall! What a fantastic outlook! Generations would speak of this war, and Tatb'u would very carefully look after it that they did, as his stonemasons were just waiting for the exact description of this special adventure, to chisel it in detail on their stelae and the walls of a new temple, which the King planned to dedicate to the great Itzamnaaj after their victory over Mutal. A temple also dedicated to this grandiose victory. It would make Tatb'u immortal – and all who were with him.

There was no doubt in the men, no hesitation, no cautious mistrust. Everywhere expectation that victory was assured, all written in the warrior's faces.

And they had every reason to feel expectant. Pakul had just received news from Tayasal last night. The local king had assured Tatb'u of his fullest support. His own warriors would be ready as soon as the army arrived from Yaxchilan, and supplies were prepared for the journey to proceed quickly. The host of Tayasal was small, but a welcome asset. In addition, the news had raised the hope that the smaller neighboring city, the ruler of Saclemacal would be inclined to support Tatb'u as well. The united army of three cities would surprise and defeat Mutal. There was just nothing that could go wrong now except Saclemacal decided otherwise and betrayed Tatb'u. At the slightest sign in that direction, the king of Yaxchilan would turn his army against the traitors and plunder the city until nothing remained. Mutal would then perhaps – for now – be saved, but booty would be distributed, and the attack would send a strong signal to the region that they had to count on Tatb'u – and above all, that he wasn't making jokes.

Even the omen of the gods were positive. The priests had confirmed the King in his plans. If there was a good time to win, then it was now. Tatb'u had not hesitated a moment to spread this highly welcome message among his own. This had contributed significantly to the increase in general morale.

Tatb'u raised both hands. It became quiet around him. He stood on the fourth step of his father's grave pyramid, and it was the symbolism that the son stood on the shoulders of his predecessor and thus emphasized the stability of his rule, which certainly didn't escape the men.

All eyes turned to him. Tatb'u said nothing. He pointed in the direction, along the big road, to the east. There the street led their way directly to the Great Lake and their allies in Tayasal. Certainly the easiest and safest part of the journey.

Then he dropped his arms and nodded.

Orders were roared. Noble officers took their places, leading the men of their clan, as has been custom ever since. Tatb'u put himself at the head of the warriors he personally selected, his family, his bodyguard. He was joined by his commander, Pakul, his face full of grim joy, his eyes full of blood-lust, holding the spear with such an energy in his hands, that there was a danger that the weapon would break by the determined grip. Pakul was ready. A good sign for them all.

Tatb'u took the first step. And his army followed him.

The road was wide and well-developed, the warriors were experienced men, after all, they had just successfully completed a campaign. They maintained an exemplary discipline, marching side by side in a long row of two, all at the same speed. Tatb'u could have been carried in a litter, no one would've had denied him this right. But he didn't lead that way. As much as his people worshiped him as the link between the earth and the heavens, so much did he value the fact that the warriors he led to battle and possibly death also respected him as warlord. He marched with them. He didn't carry his luggage himself – a little distance from the common people was expected –, but he used his own legs and not those of porters.

And he marched ahead, leading the way.

His men thanked him with a brisk step. Nobody would fall behind, nobody would falter. Not in the face of their King.

The first part of the journey lasted only two days. Then they reached the outskirts of the relatively small town of Tayasal. The peasants working on the roadside clearing the forest to create new farmland paused in their work, watching the long worm of Tatb'u's army as it moved toward their homeland. The King of Tayasal was forewarned and had informed his people accordingly. In the eyes of the observers was no fear, no one ran away. One was among allies, and Tatb'u's orders had been unequivocal. No resident of Tayasal should suffer from the approaching army. All property of the allies was to be protected, and even the smallest transgression would result in the most severe punishment.

His men obeyed. They never strayed from the path and never gave the citizens of the city more than a friendly nod, a shouted greeting. They were friends, not conquerors. Tatb'u could be proud of his warriors.

On the large main square, they were received as befitting. Tatb'u noted with great satisfaction that his ally had kept his word. His men were standing by, and since it was still early afternoon and they wanted to get on as fast as they could, they would rest for a moment, then immediately continue on their way.

There was a brief ceremony to give priority to the city's favorite deities, and then the men of Tayasal joined the growing army. The Lord of Tayasal, that was agreed, would not participate in the campaign himself and remain behind, but he sent two of his sons, whom Tatb'u allowed to march beside him.

The whole visit lasted no more than two hours, then the united army was already on the way to Saclemacal.

Tatb'u felt more and more confident with every passing day. That they enjoyed the grace of the gods was manifest in many ways. The weather was wonderful, ideal for making progress. As they rested at the Great Lake and set up camp for the night, Pakul sent a number of men to fish. They came back so loaded with booty that a big welcome was shouted and very quickly the tempting scent of roasted fish spread throughout the camp. Tatb'u made a scene of sitting close to one of the fires and tasting the catch; he not only praised the chef in charge but also pointed out that this special blessing made clear how much they were favored by the gods. This too quickly made the rounds and raised the general mood. When they set off again at dawn to cover the rest of the way to Saclemacal, it took not longer than an hour until they met emissaries from that city, who conveyed the kindest greetings and welcomed the army most warmly. Fifty porters were under the advance command sent from Saclemacal, and they all carried large containers of fresh chi. Tatb'u made sure everyone was served a cup at lunchtime, which once again positively influenced the morale of the men. The assurance of their friends from Saclemacal to stand firmly in the forged alliance and to wait eagerly to punish Mutal for its arrogance was also well-received. Tatb'u felt that this was a perfect time and basked in the prestige that fell on him as a leader due to this fact. His outwardly modest and affable manner worked particularly well in this atmosphere. His warriors would, he was sure, carry out each of his orders without hesitation and with dedication. And even Pakul's good humor showed that the General thought he was approaching a slaughter of outstanding quality that could only end with a triumphant victory.

All the wonderful joys stopped once they finally reached Saclemacal, though. The welcome was heartfelt, the warriors were ready, and they were all well looked after again. They exchanged the latest information about the conditions in Mutal, and here it was the first time that Tatb'u heard of a strange phenomenon that had haunted the city. The story was confusing and contradictory, and he wasn't sure if the story was true or a result of overindulgence of chi. Clear was, however, that something unusual had happened that claimed the attention of the King of Mutal at the moment. They would soon be able to convince themselves how much truth was in the adventurous rumors that were being delivered to Tatb'u. But the most important fact was that the inhabitants of Mutal were very,

very busy and that this occupation had nothing to do with the approaching army.

He listened to the various stories for a while. There was talk of an apparition, a boat of the gods, men who had risen from a great fish that smashed temples, invisible weapons that killed silently and without a miss. Normally this last message would have been something to worry him – but those stories were so outrageous and so absurd that the King just could not take them seriously. To develop a different strategy based on this idiocy, neither him nor Pakul found necessary.

This was a critical moment of the campaign. Saclemacal was full of spies from Mutal. No matter what the locals now knew, the army would rush ahead of the news of their advance. Mutal would be able to prepare itself, fast and inadequate, which was exactly what Pakul expected. The faster they advanced, the clearer their victory would be. Tatb'u decided to rest one night in Saclemacal and leave the next morning. Spies might have a day's march in advance, but that wasn't enough for a troubled city to take all the necessary defensive measures. One could only hastily summon your own warriors, and their morale would be bad. And since Tatb'u, through the distribution of his army and the way they camped in and around Saclemacal, cleverly disguised the true strength of his forces, the enemy would certainly expect a far smaller offensive force than those who would finally attack his lines.

Everything was wonderfully arranged, as the King of Yaxchilan observed with pleasure.

16

"Well, tell me, son."

Chitam waited until the servant had left his father's private quarters and the heavy curtains at the door had been closed both in- and outside. He looked at the cup of chi in his hand, the contents of which he hadn't touched yet, a rather unusual behavior for the Prince. Old Siyaj didn't urge his son. He knew him well enough, his weaknesses as well as his strengths. In recent years, he had to admit, he had occasionally doubted the adequacy of the designated heir to the throne for this exalted task, whether or not he was in the right frame of mind to take on the burdens of the office. Chitam drank too much and was attached to young girls, his religious zeal left much to be desired, and he liked to sleep long during daytime. In fact, his sister Une Balam was far more deliberate and, in many ways, more intelligent than Chitam, who often acted quite impulsive. But then, in the last two weeks since the arrival of the messengers of the gods, another quality had appeared in the Prince, even at the beginning of the incident itself. His determined action and eager learning, the skillful way he found access to the god's messengers and his interest in the consequences of this encounter for Mutal – all this quite impressed the old king. In addition, the highly salutary influence of his wife became apparent, who would become a very capable queen – a key reason why Siyaj had then initiated the marriage, as these positive investments had manifested in young Tzutz very early. Since Chitam was too simple to effectively avoid the manipulations of his wife unless she openly challenged his resistance, he was actually quite confident about his successor.

And the matter of the god's messengers seemed indeed to reveal unimagined abilities in his son.

Siyaj was impressed, almost against his will.

He therefore deliberately left these things to his son, especially remembering that he himself wouldn't have done it half as well. The circumstances had made Chitam more than he had been before. But this wouldn't have been possible if the potential hadn't already dwelt inside the young man.

So old Siyaj rediscovered pride for his son, and he nourished that feeling with this council of war, which he held exclusively with the Prince. There was a need to make decisions, and Chitam seemed to be able to provide the King with very valuable advice.

Although, at the moment, his son seemed to be a bit confused.

"I'm not sure, Father."

"About?"

"About some things."

"Tell me what you are sure of."

Chitam nodded and placed the cup. "The god's messengers are far ahead of us in everything. Their craftsmanship exceeds my imagination. The weapons they use are so powerful, and I don't understand how they work. They are well-organized and follow the orders of their ruler, named Inugami. They speak two different languages – not just variations of the one common in the various regions inhabited by the corn people but two really different languages, of which they teach us only one. They are not all the same despite their common origin. Some are kinder than others. Some are open to us, others hide things. There are not many. I have been near their vessel several times now and have watched it intensively. There can't be more than 30 or 40 men, Father. And I think it's important that it seems that they didn't bring any woman with them. At any rate, we never saw one."

Siyaj nodded, feeling reassured in his new confidence in his son. "What are they hiding?"

"Their intentions. Father, they are no doubt sent by the gods, nothing else can explain their appearance. But they themselves are normal people like us. They dress differently, they speak differently, they look different – though not much –, but I'm convinced that if I push my blade into the breast of one of them, I would see blood, and the man would die. They are people – special people, but no more than that."

Siyaj nodded. Chitam only confirmed his own impression.

"Go on, son. What else did you learn?"

Chitam thought for a moment. He obviously didn't want to talk too lightly to his father, must have noticed that he showed growing respect for him. He wanted to avoid mistakes that would result from hasty words. "They learn more about us than they reveal, Father. I ask questions, but I often get no real answers. Sometimes that's probably because we can exchange so few sentences meaningfully. But our mutual language skills are getting better every day. On both sides there are some who study and teach with vigor. But sometimes I think they don't want to give me an answer. That in turn may be because they lack the will to do so – for example, when it comes to the question of their origin or their mission. Or the cause is that they can't tell me because they don't know it themselves. That sometimes seems likely to me. And that makes me think the most, because if they are holy messengers ... then they should know everything. And actually, they should speak our language because it was given to us by the gods."

The King leaned forward and frowned. "They don't know why they appeared here? Is that your guess, son?"

Chitam nodded approvingly.

"That seems to be the case."

"How is that possible? If they were sent by the gods, their intentions must be clear."

"I thought so too. But ... do we know how the gods act and why they do things?"

Chitam's father sighed. A legitimate objection. Even the best priests were often embarrassed to give a clear answer to this question, which made life exciting and unpredictable.

"So what will you do, my son?"

"I don't know. But they will become more than just our guests."

"I was afraid of that."

"Many of our people have already begun to worship them. There are priests who demand to erect a temple in honor of them and their holy vessel. Their brutal power has left a strong impression. It is expected of you that you obtain their favor and use their power for the good of the city."

Siyaj looked thoughtful. "What do you think, Chitam?"

The Prince looked at the full cup of chi, touched it with his right hand, turned the vessel once around without raising it, then answered.

"The holy messengers can get rid of you, if they wish, Father. If they do it skillfully, there will be no protest. Many will rather develop hope with the prospect of great times. They will think that it is good to be touched and led by this blessing of the gods, and that having new leaders is but a small price to pay. The king is the connection of the earthly to the divine. That is his function, for which he is respected and for which he deserves obedience of everyone. But if those messengers come from heaven, can't they sustain this connection much better than the old King? I'm not of this opinion, Father. These are the conversations that I accidentally overheard. Not in the open. Not consciously in my presence. Certainly not in yours. There is just the fact that Inugami doesn't seem to make any attempt to affirm your position on the throne – or remove you."

Siyaj sighed. "If you ask me, my son, it's more because that Inugami doesn't know how easily he could eliminate me without risking a war. He's still learning our language. He is careful. The primary source of his knowledge is an old priest who has been my friend for a long time and certainly won't whisper such thoughts into that man's ear. It saves me, and it will be a while before Inugami receives hints from a different direction that make him believe he can seize control without any problem."

Chitam nodded. "Maybe a while, yes. But not for very long anymore, Father. That's why I speak a lot with the deputy of Inugami, the man named Aritomo Hara. He seems to be a sensible man and impressed by our achievements, with less arrogance and distance. He laughs and jokes with me, he learns with great eagerness, he talks to my wife with respect and without condescension."

Siyaj smiled. "Nobody ever treats Tzutz with condescension."

Chitam scratched his head before continuing. "I've also considered the fact that these strangers don't seem to have women with them, and most recently, on the ball court, I tried something. The man Hara winked at the young girl I brought close to him, not just with lust, but with real joy and sympathy. He speaks our words as well as the teacher Sawada, and he asks questions about our buildings, the architecture, the gods, our neighbors. We still can't speak fluently about all of these things, but the man learns with great obsession, and I'll keep myself close to him. Father, if we know any of the messengers who may be prepared to keep you in office and refrain from making himself ruler, it is Aritomo Hara."

The King thought for a while about the emphatic words of his son. But in his worried face it was clear to see that he was at a loss about how to proceed. He looked at Chitam, seeking help. "What's your advice, son?"

Chitam took his time. He had to know that his father was currently weighing his words unusually high, maybe too high. If he made a wrong decision, if his verdict proved erroneous, he might possibly summon the end of this dynasty. It wasn't that Mutal was alien to this kind of disaster. When the conquerors from Teotihuacán came to take the city, they swept aside the old, venerable family that had ruled the city for hundreds of years and installed Chitam's grandfather as ruler. Chitam's family history was young, young enough for them to realize that even the oldest dynasty could be blown away by the wind of events. If anyone knew that too well, then it was the current rulers of Mutal.

"We have to be very careful, Father," he said. "I'll stick to this Aritomo and double my language studies. In addition, I want to try to get in touch with other men of the god boat. I will have food and chi applied, and I will organize ball games. Young girls should be prepared to please the messengers. They are normal men. They are attracted by these charms, and I want to satisfy their needs. I want to find those with whom you can talk. Those who learn to like us, who start to find it pleasing here. Those who are willing to accept things as they are and who can see the good in them. And all this has to happen without Inugami becoming overly suspicious. Father, I don't like to say it, but in the end it will be our goal to drive a wedge between the messengers and build a bulwark between those who cooperate and those who want to go beyond our wishes."

Siyaj made a gesture of despair. "But will the people play along, Chitam?"

"That depends on the timing of the events."

Siyaj nodded mournfully. After a few moments of silent contemplation, he said, "I'll leave these things to you. They affect you the most. I am old. May they set me down and sacrifice my body to the gods, then this is my destiny. But I'm worried about you and your family, Chitam. You should get all the support I can give you. But if you're right about everything you've just said, my influence wanes with each passing day. The eyes of everyone are hopefully directed to the messengers, as they now expect wealth, fame, blessings, prosperity, and happiness from them." The King uttered a scornful snort. "What does an old king count?"

Chitam put his hand on his father's forearm in a confidential gesture. Siyaj accepted the consolation with a grateful smile. "You continue to be the connection of earth and sky, Father," Chitam said. "We have to make it clear that you alone managed to summon the messengers. Why did they come to Mutal? We are chosen – and you are the one who made this possible." He leaned forward, his pitch growing intense, urging. "We have to use this to our advantage, Father. Do not put your hands in your lap. Accept your role! Only through this strategy will we emerge unscathed and perhaps even gain an advantage."

Siyaj smiled approvingly, but his melancholy had not completely disappeared from his posture. "I like how you think, son. I have to apologize to you. My confusion was inappropriate and unworthy of a king."

"Say no more, Father. We know all these dark hours. We have to ..."

Chitam didn't get a chance to finish his sentence. The heavy curtains were pushed aside violently, and the two men looked alarmed. This was only allowed when something really important had happened – otherwise the disturber would be put to death for his insolence.

The majordomo stood in the door, and he looked visibly upset. He wrung his hands. Siyaj nodded to him, allowing him to speak openly.

"Lord, a messenger has arrived. He insisted on being admitted. You know him well, my King, it is Pax'ik."

Siyaj rose from his stool. "Pax'ik? Then let him in. Bring chi."

Chitam also got up. "Who is the man?"

"My best informer in Saclemacal. Absolutely trustworthy. Normally, he would never return here personally but send a message. Something has happened, and it is no trifle."

"I'll leave you alone."

"No, you stay. This is certainly important. You have to know."

It was not long before a small, slender man was brought in who immediately threw himself on the ground in front of Siyaj. A servant brought a tray of chi and some fruits.

"Arise, Pax'ik. Sit down. Here, have refreshments."

Moments later, they sat together. The spy was not intimidated but showed great respect and didn't take any of the refreshments offered. News were burning on his tongue. "Sir, I bring bad tidings. A large army marches on Mutal!"

Siyaj's stance stiffened. "An army? From Saclemacal? Saclemacal doesn't have enough soldiers to defeat us, even if they arm all of their women and children!"

"No, sir – not only the soldiers from Saclemacal, though they betrayed you and joined the campaign. Most of the troops come from Yaxchilan and Tayasal! It is an alliance, a united army, led by King Tatb'u personally. I don't know how many they are. Lots. They tried to hide it from my eyes, but I'm not as stupid as they think."

"Tatb'u!" Siyaj uttered the name of the ruler. "He never stops annoying me! How far are the troops?"

"One day's march, that's all. We don't have time."

"We are ill-prepared," Siyaj agreed. He turned to Chitam. "Get all the clan chiefs together immediately. Let us sound the alarm. Dispatch scouts heading for Saclemacal."

His son jumped up. "Yes, Father."

"I'm late, my lord," Pax'ik cried, lowering his face in shame. "I ran like a ghost, but I'm late."

"Pax'ik!" Siyaj said sternly. "You did what you had to do, and you did well. Your king is grateful. Take spear and shield from the armory. Thou shalt defend the city by our side and honor it!"

The man threw himself on the ground, overwhelmed with gratitude. Then he was up and running as fast as his feet carried him.

Siyaj turned back to his son. "Chitam, this is the moment that changes all our plans."

"Yes, Father. You're right. And it is the time when the messengers must prove their power." He pushed the curtain aside. "I do everything you command, and more. I'm going to the holy vessel now. I'll ask Inugami for help. Let's hope his price won't be too high."

Then the Prince disappeared. Siyaj looked after him and felt again this dark foreboding.

He sighed.

There was no doubt, regardless what kind of hopeful plans Chitam was trying to make. He had to face the facts – The gods held his fate and that of his city, there was nothing more to say.

Then he bent down, took the cup he had just served, and drank Pax'ik's chi.

The man was apparently not thirsty.

17

Inugami took a while to understand what the Mayan prince wanted him to do, but then he laughed.

What a wonderful stroke of fate!

He was filled with great joy.

He turned to Aritomo, who stood beside the commander on the bridge, where they had received Chitam and had listened to his wordy portrayal. Sawada was with them and had done his best to translate what the Prince had wanted to tell them. First they had all been a bit confused, but the excitement in Chitam's voice and his urgent undertone had by no means escaped Inugami. Now it was understandable why the man had been so hectic.

"It looks like it's now necessary to help our new friends solve a big problem, Lieutenant," he said in Japanese, so Chitam couldn't follow their conversation.

Aritomo nodded. "It's our problem too, Captain. Our boat has no wheels."

Inugami laughed again. "You see danger, I see a great opportunity. We can now finally prove how powerful we are. If we repulse this enemy, our position in this city will be unassailable." That he cast a calculating look at Chitam said a lot about what he meant by that. Aritomo just nodded. "We will fight this, Hara."

"We hardly have any weapons."

"We have the cannon, and we have time to come up with a tactical plan that will help us use it as effectively as possible. Get this chief to follow our instructions exactly. Then we should be able to offer a very impressive spectacle."

"Captain?"

Inugami licked his lips, then switched to English. Chitam, too, noticed that the messengers of the gods took his request for help very seriously.

"Second Lieutenant Hara, you will choose someone to serve as a forward observer. He should go to the top of the highest pyramid. Send someone along who can handle flag signals in his sleep. I want directions and distances for the cannon when the time comes."

"Yes, sir."

"All men who are not involved in the fighting go below deck. The bridge is staffed with our best riflemen – that is the bodyguards and two others. There is no room for more. You take over the command of the gun yourself. Every volley has to have full impact, Hara. We have to be economical with the ammunition."

"Yes, sir."

Inugami turned to Sawada. "The natives should tell us where the enemy is most likely to attack. They should stay away from this area, because there we will direct the fire of the cannon. They should attack only when I order them to. I have an idea of how to lure the enemy into a favorable killing field and would like us to discuss it together."

Sawada nodded. "I'll try to explain that."

Inugami turned back to look at Aritomo. "I gave orders, Second Lieutenant."

"I see a problem, Captain."

Inugami grimaced reluctantly but was smart enough to let his first officer speak. This was a critical situation, he needed to hear the advice of a man who had proven to have a functioning mind.

Aritomo pointed sideways at the boat down to the pyramid, whose ruin it supported.

"The recoil of the gun, fired several times, could move the boat. I don't know how massive the structure is below us and how much strain it can withstand, but if we fire more often and in high cadence, it can happen that the boat will slide. We can't control this movement. The boat could tip over, roll, or otherwise become unstable."

Inugami's eyes followed Aritomo's pointing, and a worried look crossed his face as he slowly nodded. Aritomo spoke the truth. It

115

was necessary to investigate this matter before it became a serious problem.

"That's a logical concern," he admitted. "What do you suggest?"

"We have some time before the attack commences, if I understand correctly."

Aritomo still had big problems with the way the Maya measured time. Their elaborate calendar was not straightforward. Still, he thought he had understood that Chitam predicted the enemy's attack for the next two or three "kin" or days.

"I want us to bring rocks and wood to support the boat. We can fill in the areas from which the hull protrudes and attach anchorages. That should help at least a little. In addition, not only because of the ammunition we have to shoot sparingly, but also because of the stability issues. I want to have someone on the highest pyramid not only watching the enemy but reporting a possible movement of the boat after each shot. We have to stop before things get too shaky. I don't want us to slide down or tip over, which could irreparably damage the boat. In all likelihood, there would be injured or dead people. And ..."

He looked at Inugami, hesitated, switched to Japanese.

" ... it would look very unworthy and weak if we just slid down the boulders screaming and helpless ..."

"Yes," Inugami said. The argument had great power for him. This risk had to be minimized. "I agree in everything. And we can't fire the ship's cannon any more once and if the boat comes to rest on its side," he added thoughtfully. "That would be fatal. We do it the way you suggested. Give the necessary orders."

Aritomo saluted.

He turned away and started the preparations. Chitam, looking a little lost now, looked at Sawada, who reassured him in turn. Realizing that activity ensued, the Prince had to understand that his warning had had impact. Sawada grabbed his arm and led him away. Before him laid the not so easy task of conveying the wishes of Inugami to the Prince, which would require a lot of paper and pen, and even more hitherto unknown vocabulary. Both would surely be busy for a while now.

116

Inugami left, leaving his first officer to carry out the instructions. Aritomo barely watched him go, his head already full of action now to be taken.

"Sarukazaki!" Aritomo shouted, as the chief mechanic approached him. "I need you and ten men. We have a lot of work!"

It was not long before the crew was informed and an atmosphere of excited anticipation spread among them. The time of senseless exercises in discipline was over, now purposeful activity erupted. This did more for the morale of the men than all of Inugami's efforts before. Everyone was busy doing what he was told.

Sarukazaki inspected with Aritomo the position of the boat on the pyramid. Both didn't do this for the first time. So far, they had always come to the conclusion that the boat was stable. They had thought more about how one day the steel body could be liberated from its predicament and brought back to its element, if that was ever their intention. But now it was about the boat being a gun platform and a fortress, and that required different levels of stability than before. As Lengsley joined them, an intense conversation developed immediately. The Briton had quite some knowledge of statics and gave valuable hints.

"We'll have to brace over there," he said, pointing to the areas where the boat was no longer resting on the stones and began to rise in the air. "We should do it intelligently, with logs in all directions, firmly anchored to the lower levels of the structure. Then additional stones for filling support walls, built close to tight. If we had time, I would smear mud and increase stability again. But it probably will not dry in time, and we're wasting workforce if we start now."

Aritomo nodded. "We're getting more men. You take a troop, and I tell Chitam to show you a good place for logging – probably the Maya themselves have a decent supply of logs, then they should deliver some. I take another ten men, and we start the refilling work. Where exactly do we want to attach the trunks? We should not get in each other's way at work."

It only took a moment, and then they were engrossed in a detailed plan. Half an hour later, when they had made sketches that would help them communicate their wishes for suitable building materials to Chitam, they were very satisfied with themselves. If all the work was done properly, they would stabilize the boat sufficiently to be able to fire a series of shots with the cannon without slipping the boat down the pyramid.

Finally, the intentions of the Japanese were made sufficiently clear to Chitam. Here it was again Sawada who helped them a lot. But it also became clear that the Prince's knowledge of English was quite advanced for this short time of learning. He immediately began to give his own instructions, which made implementation much easier. As Aritomo had hoped, the Maya, based on their own construction projects, had sufficient material to provide for the crew of the boat. Workers emerged, bringing massive logs that were immediately cut to size. Stones were piled up and expertly placed following the orders of Mayan architects – who, as expected, proved to be true experts in structural design. Soon, the Japanese only had to watch and give occasional instructions. The numerous workers and their unsurpassed zeal for work brought the stabilization measures to a successful conclusion already on the first day, so that Aritomo and Inugami could quickly focus on tactical issues.

The following discussion wasn't easy. Inugami apparently had the great urge to take the chance to make an example and clearly demonstrate the superiority of the time travelers. It was an opportunity to consolidate one's claim to domination and thus ultimately lay the foundation for those dynastic and imperial ideas that the commander repeatedly considered. Hara, on the other hand, was keen to be efficient, to minimize the risk to the crew while leaving a positive impression on her hosts. Both goals were by no means entirely contradictory – even Inugami wanted to avoid losses as much as possible, even though he mostly referred to his own crew, while he dismissed the potential blood toll of the citizens of Mutal with a rather nonchalant gesture of his hands.

The captain already had very precise ideas. He calculated losses of the "savages" with merciless severity.

Hara moved on brittle floor. He had to avoid any appearance of disloyalty while trying to avoid the worst excesses of Inugami's ideas.

118

It was a balancing act that required a great deal of concentration and sensitivity.

After some two hours of consultation, they had prepared a plan. It envisaged at its core that Mutal's warriors lured the attacking enemies by apparent escape movements into the city center, to place them conveniently in the field of fire covered by the cannon and the riflemen. The wide street that led from the southeast into the city, ended at the ball court and then headed west to the central squares of the city, seemed well suited. The large temple on the eastern main square, which Hara called the Jaguar temple because of its paintings and sculptures, was an excellent lookout for the observer and the provision of signals to the main square where the submarine had stranded. The greatest danger was that the enemy was primarily interested in the royal palace, which wouldn't be a very wise target to fire upon and which limited the field of fire to the southwest.

They would have to discuss these things with Chitam and his father. And that's why a balanced tactic was needed. If the Prince, who was anything but dumbfounded, had even the slightest suspicion that Inugami didn't care if Mutal's soldiers were also to become victims of Japanese weapons, his enthusiasm for the battle plan would surely be muted. The Maya had no problem dying in battle, under the guidance of their kings. They were, after all that was known, brave warriors. But a senseless slaughter without regard to losses, and then to their own people, was not something that was easy to accept.

Hara, however, wanted the King's soldiers to do the rest – to encircle and attack a demoralized and surprised opposing army in a final battle, best to force them to give up. The fact that the "messengers of the gods" didn't do everything but cooperated in the protection of the king's army would make for a much deeper bond of cooperation than humiliating enemies as well as friends, but with varying degrees of intensity.

It was hard to explain this to Inugami. When Hara pointed out that it made no sense to uselessly waste the future subjects of his dreamed-up empire he had a noticeable impact. One would need willing warriors for future campaigns – which Inugami considered inevitable. That was an argument that met with acceptance, albeit unwilling, from his superior. It was the only "rational" thought that could at least begin to change his view of these inferior natives, establishing a different perspective. Aritomo considered the Maya to be anything but inferior, and he didn't easily forgive himself for bringing this argument into play. But it helped to establish a plan, which he could submit without much pain to Chitam, as task to which he was immediately assigned by Inugami.

He felt like an ambassador between warring camps. That was exhausting.

And it was dangerous.

Aritomo wasn't sure if he liked to be the mouthpiece. He felt compelled to do so against his will, but of course he was also able to convey many of Inugami's expressions and opinions with a certain degree of self-discipline. On the other hand, he was by no means sure that an attentive observer like Chitam wouldn't begin to recognize the differences in outlook between him and the commander.

What consequences could that have?

A thought he intended to deal with later.

Darkness fell. A long, exhausting day was coming to an end. Hara sat down on the forecastle with a cup of chi and wanted to enjoy the evening sun for a few minutes. He regarded the drink in his hands with a certain regret. A few days ago, the supplies of tea had been used up. Their hosts supported them with provisions without complaint, but only with what they themselves used. Everyone had therefore necessarily developed a taste for the local food and especially the drinks. Aritomo may have already adapted better than many others, who were still reluctant to drink chi and often couldn't keep disrespectful comments to themselves. Aritomo had once been allowed to attend the production process of the drink. The raw material was from a tree Aritomo didn't know and was mixed with honey and water and brought to fermentation. The drink had, like so many things here, a religious meaning and was apparently used for ritual occasions to gain visions of the gods in a intoxicated state. The nobility, it seemed, also used it for less sacred purposes, while the common folk still had to make use of water – or what could be gained from the various fruits of non-alcoholic drink.

The use of chi was also regulated aboard the boat to set a limit on alcoholic beverages, but the tea-accustomed Japanese, far removed from any sake, needed the relaxation that this light mead offered to them. Anyway, for Aritomo the restrictions didn't apply, on the other hand, he wanted to be a role model and voluntarily – and in public – adhered to the ordered rationing.

This was his first cup today and the last one at the same time. He just wanted to take a little break. He would have a bite to eat – he found the meat-filled Maya bread pies quite appetizing – and then continue the work that could be done in the dark. If only to study Mayan vocabulary with Sawada.

"There will be a battle, won't it, Lieutenant?"

Aritomo's head jerked up as he heard the thin voice, and involuntarily his back stiffened as he realized that Isamu, the Prince, had appeared quietly beside him. The officer turned to see the towering figure of one of the two bodyguards behind the boy's narrow body and started to get up, but the Prince's hand abruptly settled on his shoulder.

Aritomo froze. He was not allowed to touch a member of the imperial family. Conversely, of course, it was something else, and in the narrowness of the boat touch could never be completely avoided, which had led to the relaxation of certain rules. But it was still an unusual, unthinkable act.

"Stay seated," the Prince said, squatting next to him.

Aritomo slowly put the cup down. Prince Isamu was old enough to take the occasional gulp – there was much and heavy drinking at the imperial court, even though the legendary Meiji had been someone who had given the sake a certain ... indifference – but both Sawada and Inugami had come to the conclusion that it wasn't yet appropriate for the Prince to partake in such merriments. The last tea had been stretched to the end only for the use of the young man, and now he was allowed to enjoy fruit juices and water.

"There will be a battle?" the Prince asked again.

Aritomo cleared his throat. The presence of the bodyguard made him restless. He knew that Inugami was fine with the two soldiers. He was afraid that they would report anything they heard, if necessary. He had to choose his words wisely for that reason alone.

"Yes, Highness, that's correct. The city is being attacked by its enemies. Captain Inugami has ordered to help the rulers of Mutal in defense. We are preparing for this right now."

"So we're not going back to Japan?"

Aritomo was silent for a moment, not sure how to answer. In the hustle and bustle of the past few weeks, this option had taken a back seat so much that he couldn't imagine anyone still holding onto it. But who wanted to blame the boy?

"We ... are far from the coast, my prince. If the boat is to be launched, we need the help of these people, otherwise we can't succeed. And if we want their help, we'll have to help them in this hour of need."

"And then we'll go back to Japan?"

In Prince Isamu's voice, self-discipline and longing fought each other. How did the boy felt on board, exempted from all the ship's work that might focus his thoughts, without function or task? Too much time to ponder, Aritomo thought.

"My prince, it will take some effort to return to Japan. But it's a different Japan from what we know. It is not even a unified country at the time, but divided into smaller kingdoms, some of which are permanently at war with each other. I'm not sure what our fate would be if we go there."

"Yes ... no ..." The Prince searched for words. "I mean ... will we go back to *our* Japan? Will I see my father and mother again? Will I go back to school?"

Aritomo sighed. Sawada had certainly told him which situation they were in. The fact that the young prince turned to him showed that he didn't believe – or didn't want to believe – the explanations of the old teacher. But the officer who had proven himself in the past few weeks as someone who handled the situation well and who was a respectful person ... and unlike Inugami, also able to say a kind word ... seemed like a more reliable source of information.

That put a heavy burden on Aritomo's shoulders, for the Prince's question didn't come up by chance. He expressed a hope – with all the self-control of a boy a desperate to show dignity in despair.

"My prince ..."

"Call me Isamu, second lieutenant. At least when we are alone. Your captain will not allow it otherwise."

Aritomo looked up at the silent figure of the bodyguard.

The Prince grinned and looked for a moment like the boy he really was.

"They don't care. As long as you don't try to kill me, and we have a reasonable conversation, my bodyguards will ignore you."

Aritomo nodded. "Isamu, then. I'm Aritomo."

The prince shook his head. "You are Second Lieutenant Hara. You are the elder. Here you are above me, no matter where I come from."

Aritomo sighed. The boy didn't make it easier for him. But maybe it was just fine in the face of the conversation they had to have now.

"To get back to the question ... Isamu ... I want to be very honest: I don't know why we fell through time and ended up in this place. It was certainly nothing that we have arranged. Maybe it was a natural phenomenon that repeats itself. We can wait and hope for that. But until further notice, we all, including you, have to deal with the prospect that we will stay here. Maybe only a few months or years – or forever. The sooner we make friends with this thought, the faster we can focus our energy on creating a new life here. The conditions are favorable. The Maya are well-disposed to us. If we succeed in helping them to defend the city, our relationship should improve even more. If we make the right choices, we can all enjoy a comfortable and safe life here and will be masters of our destiny. That's very important, Isamu. We have to face reality and begin to shape it. We can't give up. This isn't our way. Captain Inugami reminded us of our duties. We have to fulfill them in every situation."

"Your duties seem to be clearer than mine," the boy mumbled, looking pensively over the foredeck, past the cannon over the city, slowly sinking into the darkness. Both scented the smells of the evening jungle that stretched out along the edges of the city, now familiar and pleasant. The animals of the night commenced the acoustic background of the scenery.

"Anyway, I know that I have a responsibility and can't escape it through despair and distress," Aritomo replied. "Sometimes I feel weak too. I'm confused. But I'm not alone with that, and I have to be a role model for others who feel similarly. I deliberately chose this path when I volunteered for the navy, when I wanted to become an officer. It's my job, it's inseparable from this uniform and my position. Just because things have happened that I don't understand and that threaten to exceed my horizon, I mustn't shy away from this path. I would betray myself if I did."

Isamu nodded. "And what is my way, Second Lieutenant Hara? What is my duty?"

Aritomo thought that was a pretty smart question for a boy of this age, and one that should be appreciated by a suitably smart response. But the officer was faced with a dilemma: What had been communicated to the Prince as part of his previous education, and how, perhaps, had Sawada answered that question? It didn't suit him to confuse the Prince with contradictions that would only worsen his mood. Nevertheless, he couldn't get out of this situation by making general observations, as the Prince's earnest and hopeful gaze made clear.

Aritomo hesitated for a while, then said, "You are a prince, a member of the Imperial House. You are a leader. You still lack the life experience to fulfill that role, but once the day comes, you're grown and need to make decisions. For your own life and, in all likelihood, for other people as well. That is your destiny. And it has nothing to do with whether you are in Japan and in our old time or here and now. It's your destiny because you're Prince Isamu. Time and space have no meaning. It's what makes you special. That's your way. A difficult way. But you are not alone. We will all help you and stand by your side. Together we can take the necessary steps."

"That sounds really hard," Isamu muttered, still looking depressed. "I think that's a high expectation. I'm afraid I can't satisfy it." He looked up at Aritomo. "Will you really help me? I don't know what lies ahead."

"I don't know either," he replied softly. "I'd like to have a little more security and confidence too. We are all in the same position," he said with a sweeping gesture, "and sit in the same boat. All we can do is make the most of the situation and see what the next step might be. But we will help each other. It won't work out otherwise."

"What's the best? Whatever the captain orders?"

Aritomo pressed his lips on each other. Now he finally entered very, very fragile ground. No matter what he said, it was basically wrong.

"The captain is in command. We follow his orders faithfully. He listens to the advice of all of us. Whether it's always the best we advise and what he commands, no one knows. All we can hope for is that we stick together, Prince Isamu. Now everyone counts. Also you. You in a very particular way."

The boy said nothing and stared into nothingness. Aritomo felt his own words to be hollow and empty. He didn't believe in what he had just said. Inugami was an ungracious superior who was able to take advice, but rarely requested it, and often regarded it as criticism in principle, even when reasonable. If Isamu was an attentive observer, he'd already noticed that as well.

Maybe it was his good upbringing, or he didn't want to destroy the feel-good illusion of Aritomo's words – at least, the Prince was silent, and the officer was relieved not to go deeper into that subject for now.

It was only postponed, he was sure of that. Isamu was an important tool in Inugami's far-reaching plans. And in Aritomo's eyes, especially after this conversation, that already had something tragic about it.

The Prince had not been asked by anyone if he was ready to be that tool.

Aritomo sighed softly and got up. "My prince, we are facing a battle. May I withdraw myself?"

Isamu looked up at him and just nodded.

Aritomo bowed correctly and left, leaving the boy pondering and doubting.

He probably couldn't have helped him anyway.

18

Siyaj knew he was taking a big risk, but it was necessary to do so.

He looked at the worm of soldiers approaching Mutal and felt despair. The crazy king of Yaxchilan might be at least megalomaniac, but he had underpinned his megalomania with vigorous action and good planning, he had to acknowledge that. An army of this size had never been seen by Siyaj. He had heard of Teotihuacán's soldiers, numerous and powerful, as they had once conquered Mutal and appointed his father as ruler. He hadn't been born by then. He always had the feeling that the ancients inflated the story a little, especially those who wanted to give the impression that the brave inhabitants of the city simply had no chance against such a massive onslaught. That was probably a matter of pride. His father had told him the events with much drier words. But still ... Teotihuacán's troops had defeated Mutal's defenders in no time and had therefore definitely been much superior. There was no doubt about that.

Siyaj suddenly knew how his distant predecessor, the last representative of the old dynasty, must have felt shortly before his end. What had it been like to look at the mighty northern warriors, knowing that he himself was powerless to oppose this force? It must have been a devastating feeling, especially when one could look back on a long line of ancestors that was about to be eradicated and send to oblivion by the attackers. Siyaj couldn't really complain – if that hadn't happen, he wouldn't call himself King of Mutal –, but he'd never felt the need to feel like someone on the losing side of such a historic process.

But the comparison didn't quite fit.

The holy messengers were with them now.

Somehow at least.

He had thought about it for a long time, especially after talking to his son.

Siyaj took a step forward, a sign for his entourage to follow him. He had only a few dignitaries: some priests, a few men of his bodyguard, no great number. His goal wasn't to offer Tatb'u a battle, but rather to talk to him.

On the one hand.

The advance divisions of the united adversaries had long since seen him and his followers, and it took only a few minutes before Tatb'u and a number of nobles and soldiers stepped forward to march toward Siyaj. It was the first time that the two kings met, and their mutual mistrust was almost physically palpable. When they had approached within a few yards of each other, Siyaj ordered his companions to wait. He alone walked the last few meters which separated him from the confidently smiling Tatb'u.

There was an expectant silence, as they faced each other. It was as if the whole world held its breath.

The two men measured themselves briefly. Tatb'u was much younger than the Lord of Mutal, and his muscular body showed that he didn't shirk from hard work or the hardships of battle. Siyaj had heard about it and knew that this added to the respect this man enjoyed. It would be stupid to ignore or underestimate this aspect.

"You have traveled a long way, my brother," Siyaj greeted the man from Yaxchilan, indicating a bow, a greeting among equals.

Tatb'u did the same. "A quick trip, master of Mutal, and one that certainly surprised you."

Tatb'u could certainly afford a certain complacency. Siyaj didn't let that irritate him.

"I'm not as prepared as I'd like to be, yes. What exactly has challenged your indignation so much that you must wage a war against us, my brother?"

Tatb'u laughed. "In your question lingers all the arrogance of Mutal, an attitude that more than answers your query."

Siyaj nodded thoughtfully. "I understand."

"May I offer you chi?"

"But of course."

Tatb'u waved, and a servant stepped out with cups and a pitcher. He poured them both, and Siyaj drank without hesitation. Tatb'u was an honest warrior and wouldn't resort to treachery by poisoning the Lord of Mutal. He had no need of such humiliating behavior in the face of the forces at his disposal. His counterpart drank without hesitation and waited patiently for Siyaj to empty his cup. The drink had refreshed him.

"You have come to offer us your surrender, noble Siyaj?" Tatb'u then asked casually, as they had emptied the cups and put them out of their hands.

"An interesting thought, but that doesn't match our arrogance," Siyaj answered with a regretful undertone. "We at Mutal think we are invincible and supremacy is ours ... right? How can we waste a moment thinking of surrender?"

"Yes, that's to be expected. A bad trait. An instruction seems to be appropriate. Mutal is learning slowly. First came the gentlemen from Teotihuacán and chastised the city, now the successors of those disciplinarians have to learn a lesson in humility. Mutal is stubborn, isn't she?"

"So you are Mutal's new master?" Siyaj asked, showing no emotion as to whether Tatb'u's words offended him.

"And a stricter one, should the student prove to be insufficiently docile."

"Ah, I understand. I'm afraid that we have a certain amount of stubbornness that is hard to control even through the exercise of heavy beating. In that sense, your point of view is correct. We learn things very slowly because we find the lesson unnecessary."

Tatb'u grinned. "I will do my best."

"I have no doubt about that."

"We can really cut this short," Tatb'u said, looking so patronizing that Siyaj had to struggle to stop himself to start the battle by widening the king's grin with his sacrificial knife. "I'm even disposed to some mercy. You may name those whom I should exclude from the thanksgiving ceremony after our victory. I will do my utmost to fulfill this wish. Your wife or your son? I am not without magnanimity, King of Mutal."

Siyaj bowed his head, not so much out of courtesy, but more so that the man couldn't see the hatred in his eyes too clearly. He was here to provoke Tatb'u, not in a crude and direct way, but with the degree of subtlety expected of a man of his position. It was necessary to do things with a certain understanding of style, that had always been his view – even an endeavor with a fateful outcome.

"Your generosity honors you, noble Tatb'u," he said with exemplary self-control. "But I would do my son wrong if I took the pleasure away from him to lower his blade into your breast."

The king of Yaxchilan grimaced. That wasn't exactly the answer he expected.

"Mutal's arrogance is anything but a rumor," he said, and the jovial undertones were gone from his voice. "It's not a myth, but it obscures your senses like a shield that you carry before your eyes. Take a look around, master of Mutal. My army includes the men of three cities. Mutal is big and powerful, I'm always ready to admit that – that's why I'm here to feed on this wealth. But I'm prepared, and you are not. Your troops are fewer in number. You will lose this fight. I'm not afraid of this battle, but I give you the chance to avoid it. We want to be reasonable, Siyaj. You are not a fool. Overcome your arrogance, and I want to be a gracious winner. Remain stubborn, and the streets of your magnificent city will be the rivers through which the blood of your people flows."

"You said that very poetically," Siyaj said approvingly. "I'm sure you've practiced those words so many times that you can recite them in a dream."

"Arrogance!" Tatb'u snapped, and he slowly looked like he was losing his patience. He had to save face here, where all his followers were witnesses of the altercation. If he looked like a fool in this banter, that wasn't good for his image.

Siyaj steeled himself. Now came the part of which he had said nothing to Chitam. He sent a heartfelt request for forgiveness to his son, whom he would now put a burden on his shoulders that might be too much to carry. He himself had come to the conclusion that he was no longer the right person to lift that kind of weight.

He had to ignite in Tatb'u, the only one here, who radiated true arrogance, burning and blinding scorn. The Lord of Yaxchilan had to act carelessly, hurriedly, quickly, had to run into the great trap, so that the roads of Mutal would turn into rivers, just as Tatb'u had prophesied.

But it was supposed to be the blood of the attackers to flow in these channels, not that of Mutal's men.

Siyaj was an old man, and he hadn't had many battles lately. But the long obsidian knife he wielded was a carefully crafted, high-quality blade as sharp as it could be. A beautiful piece, with wonderful ornaments on the knob, worthy of a ruler of Mutal.

He wore it open at his side, for it was a weapon that suited him, and no king would refuse him to come before him without it. Siyaj had thoroughly practiced this movement, and he was sure she would not miss his target.

Everything was very fast, almost fluent. The weapon, one moment still in its sheath, carefully tied around his waist, and then suddenly in his right hand. Tatb'u's eyes widened, surprised, taken by the sudden movement. Would the Lord of Mutal humble himself in his fear, the King of …?

No, he wouldn't.

The blade jerked forward, describing a semicircle that ended in the chest of the man standing next to the King of Yaxchilan, silently following the conversation.

Siyaj had the man's likeness described in particular detail by his agents, over and over again.

He was confident that with this powerful movement that sank the obsidian blade deep within the body of the utterly surprised and defenseless nobleman, he killed the commander of Tatb'u's forces, the man named Pakul.

Siyaj let go of the blade. The falling body of the man almost tore it from his hand anyway. Tatb'u stared with terrified eyes at the corpse of his companion, his lips silently forming his name, and Siyaj read "Pakul" in it.

Satisfied, the ruler of Mutal took a step back, raised his arms, then received the spear of Tatb'u, who, guided by a sure and skilled hand, now dived into his breast.

Siyaj died without emitting a sound.

His men turned around. They were only a few confidants going with Siyaj, and no one had been forced to do so. Everyone had been informed of the King's plan. Everyone had agreed to accompany the ruler on this last journey. They ran away, conscious that their escape was futile, and the swarm of spears, powerfully fired by the opponents' *atlatls*, mowed them down in a few moments.

Many voices of rage echoed from the throats of those of Yaxchilan, and the loudest shouting was done by Tatb'u, who had lost his faithful general and adviser. Arrogance and cowardice, both shown by Mutal, and now it was no longer all about prey, glory and the will of the gods. Now just anger and the deep need for revenge filled the men of Yaxchilan.

A war cry rang out from the throat of the Tatb'u. It was picked up by thousands of throats, reinforced in many voices, repeated, and the spears and shields were raised in the air as a sign that they were all more than willing to be Mutal's stern and merciless master.

And then, slowly, but with a sure step and ever greater speed, the warriors of Tatb'u ran, led by their King, who brought them all closer to the glory of a just and absolute victory.

The streets of Mutal, of which they were sure, would become rivers of blood.

The time had come.

19

Chitam watched his father die, and he felt betrayed.

He stood on top of the roof of the palace and could only make out the details because he had been given one of the magical glasses that the messengers of the gods carried with them to make distant objects visible. He lowered the heavy glass and handed it to Lady Tzutz, who was standing next to him, taking it without hesitation and raising it to her eyes.

"He didn't tell me," Chitam muttered softly, accusing his wife, as if she were responsible for the omission. Tzutz knew what it meant, and her face reflected the sadness her husband felt at that moment.

"I'm not surprised," she replied softly as she returned the glass. "Your father was old, Chitam, and he was increasingly angry and anxious about the changes that came with the arrival of the holy messengers. He felt insecure and felt that the world he knew was threatened to get out of hand. Didn't you notice that?"

"A bit." Chitam recalled their last conversation, in which the King had already made it clear that he felt a little overwhelmed by all of it. Maybe he could have read the signs correctly, enough to talk to the father and to implant him with a little more confidence, however limited the amount was Chitam himself was able to feel. Then maybe this act could have been prevented.

Then he wouldn't feel this deep hole torn into himself as he did now, a hole that he would plunge into if he didn't take care of himself. He felt Tzutz's hand on his arm. She knew him better than anyone and knew what he felt. She would hold him as he stood on the edge, staring down into the void that had become a deadly temptation for Siyaj.

His father had died an honorable death, there was no doubt about that. It had also been a meaningful death, robbing the enemy of his general, inciting him with blind revenge, and giving the soldiers of Mutal motivation to defend the city with particular tenacity – now led by a young man ...

Oh, he was king now!

The realization came to Chitam with some delay. Adding to the sudden sadness about what had just happened, he now felt the heavy burden that had come so unexpectedly on his shoulders. He wasn't prepared for it. Or maybe he was. But he would have liked it to be a bit more ... foreseeable. Not so abrupt. And not as a result of a ...

He felt Lady Tzutz's hand in his own. She was his queen now. That was certainly a greater blessing for this city than his taking office, he thought. She would keep him from acting on uncontrolled emotions. She would probably make smarter decisions than he did. Had his father set his hopes more in her than in him?

As if she had guessed his thoughts, he heard her whispering in his ear.

"Your father doesn't want you to act like a maniac now. Stick to the plan. Let Tatb'u come to us."

Chitam nodded. She was right, as always. And no specific request was needed to hurry the King of Yaxchilan.

Tatb'u came. The shouting from his army was loud and clear, and even the naked eye saw that his men were rushing toward the city, eager to shed the blood of Mutal's men.

Chitam took a deep breath.

"Why didn't he tell me?" Again his accusatory gaze met his wife, who accepted it with equanimity.

"Because he didn't want you to stop him," she answered. "And because he wanted to be a real king for a last time, before things slipped completely from his hands."

Chitam nodded. "But that also means that I may not become a real king anymore."

Tzutz smiled. "Maybe, my husband. But you are more likely to face this new situation successfully than your father could ever be. If anyone can lead the people into this new age, it is you. Siyaj recognized that well. He has paved the way for you. Be grateful to him."

134

Chitam snorted. "I find it hard to be grateful right now."

"Make an effort. Later. Now there is something else to do. Tatb'u is coming. Let's make sure he takes the right road and follows the right steps. Your first task as a military leader is to lead. You can grieve later. Hurry up."

Chitam squeezed his wife's hand again, then turned away abruptly. He hurried down to the entrance of the palace, where the leaders of the family clans, and at the same time the officers of Mutal's army, were waiting for him. From the grim and determined faces, Chitam realized that they, too, had learned of the end of Siyaj through the numerous scouts on the rooftops of the city.

The main dignitaries came forward and threw themselves to the floor. Chitam looked down at them.

He was now ruler of Mutal.

Everyone knew it. Everyone could see it. And they all now expected him to fill the newly gained position with life.

His joy was expected to be limited. And no one cared.

He raised both arms.

"Rise!"

Everyone followed his orders, looking at him intently.

"The enemies of the city killed our King!" he intoned aloud. He saw the anger and outrage in the men's faces in front of him. "The holy messengers have shown us the way to destroy our enemies. We now want to act wisely and deliberately and not risk our victory by carelessness. My father has provoked Tatb'u in a well-calculated manner and thus created the conditions for our triumph. His sacrifice was considered. Now we have to show respect for him by accepting this sacrifice and acting just as smartly and deliberately. Let us take our anger. It should burn deeply in our hearts and purify our minds. We control it and use its power to make the right decisions at the right time."

"The men are ready!" one of the noblemen cried. "Fighting has already begun."

Chitam nodded.

"Then let us retreat at the right time, and lure the enemies into the city, so that we may prepare a feast of special kindness for the holy messengers."

He looked around, still seeing expectant faces, still seeing anger and outrage but also the willingness to do it the right way.

Chitam smiled.

It was weird that he was flooded with confidence at that very moment, but he sucked in the feeling and refreshed himself through it.

Then he extended both arms again, this time to one side, and felt his spear and shield being pressed into his hands. Chitam knew that his job was to join the fight in order to gain legitimacy. He hoped he would meet Tatb'u. He would seek the king of Yaxchilan and challenge him if time and opportunity arose.

He held the spear in the air.

"Mutal!" he shouted as loud as he could.

"Mutal!" The reply came in many voices.

Chitam felt the power of response. He smiled again, shaking his spear in the air, and left the palace to join the fighters. He looked to the side, saw the god boat on the pyramid, which should have been the tomb of Siyaj. What irony, he thought suddenly as he marched down the street. The god's messengers had destroyed the mausoleum of Siyaj with their arrival, and at the same time ...

He frowned, remembering his wife's words.

And at the same time they brought about his father's death.

Chitam grabbed the spear tighter and stepped faster.

He couldn't afford to lose his enthusiasm now.

20

Aritomo looked at Isao Imakura and nodded to him. The gunner perched on the seat of the gun, the two loaders crouched beside him, ready to reload or intervene whenever a problem arose. Aritomo didn't expect any problems, the gun was brand new and hadn't shown any malfunction in trial shooting before their maiden voyage. It was in excellent condition, and Imakura was an excellent gunner, using the deadly weapon with dreamlike confidence. Aritomo would be almost superfluous if not for having the responsibility to give the order to fire.

They had set the cannon so that it would sweep the big boulevard that led to the site in front of the palace. Thereto the men of Mutal should lure the enemy, and then suddenly, upon a given signal, run away, as if all courage had left them. That was the time when Aritomo would give the order to fire, and they would do so as fast as the cannon could. The explosive ammunition would cause a massacre in the dense mass of enemies, to the extent of which Aritomo didn't want to imagine right now.

He didn't feel well. His stomach was upset. He had never been involved in combat. His career has gone so far without the need to raise the weapon against an enemy. Of course, this possibility had always been clear to him. He wouldn't have joined the navy if he had any qualms about killing the enemy, if necessary.

Yet. The first time was bad, even veterans had told him. Some got used to it afterwards. Aritomo was not sure if he wanted to belong to that group. A submarine made it more convenient to kill. Often one didn't see the enemy, or only from a distance. You didn't have to deal with the details and the consequences. The enemy sank, that was enough.

A loud scream could be heard up to their position. Aritomo knew what that meant. The fight had begun. He fixed his binoculars on his eyes and saw the army of the King of Yaxchilan pour into the city. A thin line of defenders stood in its way, ready to retire at any moment. Mutal couldn't muster half the number of fighting men her opponent had pulled together. Under normal circumstances, the outcome of this battle would be completely predictable.

But these were not normal circumstances, as the ruler of Yaxchilan would notice shortly.

Aritomo lowered the glass and looked around. The crew's four best marksmen, including the Prince's two bodyguards, had come to the bridge and were aiming above the gunner's heads at the square in front of them. The officer regarded it as inevitable that the attackers would flee there. In addition to the salvos from the guns of the four men, they expected about 400 warriors of Mutal, all armed with atlatls, which were still hidden on the backs of the various buildings and only would come to light when Inugami ordered it.

The Maya hadn't been pleased with this tactic. To hide? To seek shelter behind the walls instead of openly fighting? Such behavior was not particularly honorable, even if the enemy was clearly superior. Every war was a holy war, and those whom the gods chose as victors should also triumph. Inugami and Aritomo were both quite in favor of divine providence but felt it could do no harm to help out a little. Good javelin throwers firing from an elevated position at a disoriented and anxious mass of enemies sounded like a good idea to win the game without putting your own forces at risk unnecessarily.

Aritomo, too, was a friend of honorable behavior. But even more he was struck by the idea that all those who belonged to their side survived this encounter as unscathed as possible. The Maya had finally bowed and abandoned their resistance. The success would speak for itself, the Japanese were sure of it.

The screaming became louder. Aritomo looked again through the binoculars and saw the defenders slowly recoil. The attackers seemed to become even more enthusiastic by this, shouting their triumph and pushing forward with increased strength, toward assured victory. Everything went according to plan. Aritomo's restlessness intensified.

138

Maybe it was because good plans had always made him nervous, including maneuvers and exercises. One quickly became too confident and made mistakes.

If the men of the submarine made a mistake, this was the last thing they would ever do. There was no second plan, no retreat position, no alternative.

Yes, Aritomo thought, that was probably the real reason for his unrest. He stood with his back to the wall, as all of them. And that wasn't a nice position to be in.

After all, it made things easy.

"Imakura?"

"We are ready, Lieutenant."

Aritomo nodded. It spoke for his feelings that he asked more than once, but the men didn't seem to mind. They all just hoped that the measures they had taken would stabilize the boat sufficiently. Lengsley had been very confident. But he was also not on the front deck and would fly to the ground if the boat slipped off. For now, they would only shoot single volleys. But later, Aritomo thought it necessary for at least a minute or two to keep up with the highest rate of 15 rounds per minute. The impression on the enemy had to be a lasting and an absolutely overwhelming one. And the inhabitants of Mutal had to be impressed, too, that was almost as important as the fight against the attackers, especially in the long term. The occasional volley might not even be noticed even by some of the warriors. Given the superiority of the attackers, it was also necessary to reach a decision quickly.

Two minutes with thirty rounds, that would put the submarine in strong vibrations. And squatting on a pyramid instead of lying in the water was a huge difference.

Aritomo continued to stare through the binoculars. The fighting toward the palace had increased. It wouldn't be long now. Chitam would dissolve the last line of defense and then give his men the order to flee, not too fast – the attackers should remain incited to persecute – but fast enough to strengthen the prospect of a near and quick victory in Tatb'u. So the enemies should be lured to the square and thus into the field of fire of the twelve-pounder.

It went along nicely.

Aritomo turned on the magnification as the mass of soldiers approached. He saw the warriors of Mutal, led by nobles who wore the characteristic headdress. He also believed that he had seen the signs of Chitam himself, in the middle of the fray, surrounded by the men of his bodyguard, on the front line. The Prince had to feel a great deal of anger, anger at those who had killed his father, and at his father, who had only known to pursue this one way. Aritomo was sure there was more to it than the willingness to make the highest sacrifice for his city. Maybe if his vocabulary allowed it one day, he would talk to Chitam about it.

He felt that it was important. Important for the future of Maya and Japanese alike and in a different way than Captain Inugami imagined.

"Stand by!" he warned. The first of Chitam's men poured into the square screaming and waving their arms, either to lure the opponents with verve by serious attempts of exaggerated acting, or because they were afraid that the metal atlatls of the holy messengers would kill them if they wouldn't make a lot of noise.

Aritomo raised an arm. "Now wait!" he exclaimed loudly. "Wait!"

Then they came.

Like a tidal wave, they streamed in, thousands of soldiers, victoriously howling, as the cowardly defenders of Mutal fled before them, past the palace, entering the square, as they broke through the feeble lines of their enemies. It had to be a joy for the men of Yaxchilan, a triumph beyond compare.

Aritomo clenched his teeth. "Wait!" he said again. "Just one moment!"

21

"The fools! We have them!"

The words left Tatb'u's mouth, as he saw the ranks Mutal's men breaking. Triumph shimmered in his eyes, the certainty of a man who was about to accomplish the greatest victory of his life, who would make history. The palace was unprotected in front of them. The occasional volley of an atlatl from the roof of the palace didn't disturb anyone. The shots were acts of desperation, hoping for a lucky hit. By now it should be clear to all, attackers and defenders, that the gods had blessed the King of Yaxchilan and would give him total victory. Already, the men were storming the King's edifice, ready to break any resistance that might still be apparent within the large building. Tatb'u had given the explicit order to renounce destruction and wild looting. Mutal was a great prize, a prey of considerable proportions. And all of it belonged to him. He would distribute what was to be distributed, but no one would carry any valuable object from the city without having first obtained Tatb'u's permission. Tatb'u intended to be very generous, but he had to exercise total control.

Riches were of value only if they were preserved.

For a moment, Chitam had met him in the battle – if one wanted to call the feeble retreat of Mutal's men a battle. The Prince showed his incompetence as a warlord and as a fighter, as he pitifully tucked his tail in every attempt by Tatb'u to meet him and sought a way out. He hadn't looked for a fight, ran around like a coward, and instead of being an example to his men, he called them to back down the moment they were particularly hard-pressed. What a miserable behavior, unworthy of a true king. This city deserved to be defeated.

Deeper and deeper, the invaders streamed into the city, conquered one building after another. The inhabitants of Mutal hid themselves in fear.

The trouble was that the blood paid by the city's warriors was not half as high as Tatb'u had hoped. No rivers of blood. Yes, men fell, but rather because they didn't run away fast enough. This wasn't a real fight. They drove Mutal's elite before them. Where did the fame of this mighty city come from? If the best proved so weak, it must have been a gigantic trick by the ruler of Mutal, who persuaded his neighbors that the big city was invincible and of significant military power. In fact, Mutal was made up of women who wore men's robes and wielded their weapons in the air just for decoration. And those loud cries and laments when they ran off! In the face of this spectacle, would all of the gods not conceal their faces in shame and crown those of Yaxchilan as victors solely because they were no longer prepared to endure this terrible tragedy?

Tatb'u was sure that the god of Yaxchilan, Itzamnaaj, would certainly not be very pleased with this war. The attackers really did what they could. But nothing more was achieved than running after Mutal's warriors. And the new king was the first to speed away! That wasn't a real pleasure at all. If only for Pakul's sake, he had to bring this to an end, and if he had the enemies executed at the end of the day instead of killing them in battle, then it should happen just so.

Nobody would praise the greatness of Mutal anymore.

For many years, embarrassing silence would reduce the fame of this city to nothing.

Then he saw what his spies had told him. From a distance, it hadn't been easy to observe, but now the shape and dimensions of the ... *thing* that rested on the unfinished structure were more clearly discernible. For a tiny moment, Tatb'u had felt awe, indeed, he wanted to admit, had considered the idea of perhaps carrying the attack with a little less force and more caution. But the thing was just sitting there, and if it served any purpose, it seemed to be nothing more than looking weird. And Mutal's men didn't expect much from it or they would fight more manly, knowing that whatever, at the right time, would come to their aid.

Silly thought.

Indeed, Tatb'u had within reach the greatest triumph of his life. He was now sure that Siyaj had sought death, realizing that his city would fall. The old man didn't want to be sacrificed in a ceremony or even taken to Yaxchilan as a prisoner, he wanted to make himself a martyr. Thus, despite his violent death, he was a bigger coward than even Tatb'u had thought possible in his contempt. Siyaj was of the same weakness as his miserable son and must have instilled this attitude early in his Chitam's cradle. A family of weaklings, without a doubt.

But the King wiped away the thought. That was the past. Now he had to make sure that nothing stood in the way of victory. And what was more appropriate than to chase after the fleeing enemy, whose lamentation was like mocking the gods, so to help as many as possible of those unworthy to go from life to death?

He ran with his bodyguards past the palace where fighting was still underway. The mass of Mutal's warriors, however, wailed back into the direction of the ... thing that still didn't do more than just ...

A crackling thunder shook him.

Did something collapse?

Then another loud thunder. Tatb'u staggered and covered his ears. Something cracked in it like when he climbed a mountain. A sudden, forceful wind blew through the streets.

The warrior before him, a second ago upright and powerful, collapsed, covered in blood. The King stared at the man who was missing an arm, gone as if by magic. Tatb'u looked around. He heard screaming, real lamentation, and he saw blood everywhere. He saw ... broken limbs, arms, legs, a torso that was lying on the ground, dismembered by many knives, its innards spread out on the pavement. It was all ... suddenly so different.

Again the thunder. And then again and again and again. Dull and dark, with lighter, crackling sounds in between, in even faster order. Tatb'u wiped blood from his eyes and realized only now that something had hit him on the head and the red brook ran down his face from his hair. He dropped to his knees, for he felt a little dizzy.

Around him, his warriors fell to the ground, and cruel wounds ripped open their bodies. They all screamed and were stunned because there was no enemy to see, no knife, no atlatl, just those noises, then bright light where ... something happened. Men fell back without a wound, as if they had run against a wall in full swing.

Tatb'u had a bad headache. He decided to sit down. A little rest might be good for him.

Everything around him was in disarray. The thunder clearly came from the black thing on the pyramid. It sounded monotonous, and with the same cadence of its occurrence the warriors of his army died around him. They died without knowing what killed them, without being able to defend themselves. Some looked almost weird in how they raised their shields. Once, Tatb'u saw a shield being torn off with the arm behind it. Then he was startled when suddenly men emerged behind the pyramids and wielded weapons he knew well: atlatls, a few hundred, fired from elevated position to a maelstrom of dying, over-challenged attackers, and they demanded a high toll of blood.

Tatb'u realized that his prophecy about the flow of blood was going to be true. Just not quite as he had imagined.

Then the thundering stopped. Everywhere people ran and fought. Everything was mixed up. Tatb'u was really not feeling well. He wanted to straighten up, but he lacked the strength.

He looked up and saw someone wearing a very beautiful headdress. Royal insignia. It had to be the son of Siyaj, the heir to the throne. Chitam. Yes, that was his name. Tatb'u realized that he was no longer able to think very quickly and clearly.

Chitam looked down at him without pity. Tatb'u understood now. It was a painful realization that stirred up in him. He had been so wrong, had been so sure of victory. What a stupidity. Yes, he couldn't expect pity. Not from the son of Siyaj, and not from Itzamnaaj, whose reputation he had disgraced, to which he had paid no honor. So close to victory, he had failed so massively. What a punishment. What a hubris. Tatb'u didn't know what he now deserved, and his mind was foggy. He would soon find out, because as soon as he took the next step, he was sure of that, he would be reproached for his transgressions.

Wiping his face faintly, he looked up at Mutal's new King, who stared at him with irony in his gaze.

It was probably time.

It was over.

Tatb'u nodded, as Chitam craned his spear backward to let the weapon sink into the chest of the King of Yaxchilan with deadly precision.

That was just right.

Death was a mercy for him. At least, Tatb'u was spared many a sight when his lifeless body finally fell to the ground, stretched out, covered in blood, in their faces surprise and grief coming from a profound humiliation that the gods had prepared for them at the last moment.

He didn't see the worst.

He didn't see hundreds of his followers, in complete panic and without guidance, leaving the streets of Mutal and running blindly into the jungle, pursued by furious peasants venturing out of their huts, struck down by sticks or knives led by untrained men. As women stepped out of the house and shouted insults after the fleeing, words filled with filth, and some brave ones took it upon themselves to thrust the occasional blade into the body of a fugitive.

He no longer saw how the seemingly disorganized crowd of Mutal's warriors turned like a man, drew arms, closed the ranks, as Prince Chitam himself took command, how orders were given and obeyed. He no longer saw Mutal's suddenly disciplined and effective force pursuing the fugitives or fighting those who sought to disappear in nooks and crannies, how the atlatls sowed death and harvested blood, how the warriors marched on, the shields lifted up against the feeble resistance of the desperate, and drove the men of Yaxchilan away from the squares, through the streets, accompanied by the shouts, insults, and mocking of the inhabitants.

He no longer witnessed the capitulation, in which the leaders of the units from Saclemacal and Tayasal threw down their weapons, laying flat on the ground, arms and legs stretched out to stop fighting for themselves and their men. Chitam had given clear instructions for this case and ordered that all those who surrendered should be spared until their fate was determined by him and the priests. Tatb'u didn't see the remaining leaders from Yaxchilan, so suddenly robbed of their allies, finally abandoning all hope and begging for mercy where no escape seemed possible. It was not long before hundreds of prisoners were rounded up by the warriors of Mutal, all in one place, bound and humiliated, often injured and shocked at the unexpected turn of events, desperate at the lack of favor by their gods.

All this Tatb'u from Yaxchilan no longer saw, and that was a good thing.

22

Inugami and Aritomo marched past the mountain of piled corpses. Although everyone around them was very busy – recovering injured and dead, repairing damage to the buildings and the ground caused by the twelve-pounder –, there was an expectant, almost reverent silence. The glances with which the two officers were considered were no longer characterized by too much shyness and fear like a few days before. They also lacked the mistrust that Aritomo often perceived, subliminal, often associated with great caution or anxiety, yet recognizable if one took a close look at the behavior of their hosts.

There were different looks, different expressions in those faces.

Aritomo recognized reverence, he enjoyed boundless respect. He saw gratitude, even worship. Aritomo read the willingness to believe and follow, he discerned a collective awareness that something out of the ordinary had happened, something with a divine purpose. Proof had been given to them, the proof that Yax Mutal was indeed chosen, that they were all among the elevated few, and that with the messengers of the gods at their side, nothing would be impossible.

What did they possibly mean with "by their side"? Why "at their side"? He saw the willingness to follow and obey, a form of loyalty that clearly bordered on worship.

Inugami certainly noticed it too.

His confident smile, complacent, with that slightly cruel expression in the corner of his mouth as he looked at the tattered bodies of the warriors of Yaxchilan, spoke volumes. Everything had happened as he had planned. The desired effect had been triggered.

The Maya would eat from their hands. They were now led by a former prince who had been known to never spurn young girls and drink, and who had never been struck by any particular ambition. A man who would stand in the shadow – in the shadow of an extraordinary victory, for which he wasn't responsible as a king, but had to be attributed directly to the miraculous, mighty work of the holy messengers.

The work, the decisions and the power of their leader Inugami.

The effects of the battle were horrible to behold. Aritomo had been trained in iron discipline, but here he was confronted, for the first time in his life, with a massacre in which he himself had no insignificant share. The Mayan warriors worked with dumb earnestness, neither shocked nor appalled. There was an almost happy mood when the bodies were taken away. If someone recognized a nobleman from one of the three enemy cities, even occasional jubilation erupted. Aritomo couldn't share that attitude. He saw the remnants of those men who had stood in the center of the explosions. They looked the worst. Then came those who were hit by shrapnel, with sometimes horrific injuries. And finally all those killed by the spears of the atlatl or the volleys of the gunmen. Their death had been almost merciful compared to the fate of her comrades. Enough of the enemies had died in the onset of panic, trampled to death, or when they had run into the spears of the suddenly not so fickle or cowardly warriors of Mutal. They didn't have a clear overview, but Aritomo would be very surprised if more than 500 men had fallen on the side of the defenders. The corpses that they gathered here, however, clearly went into the four-digit. And out of the streets and along the escape route of the panicked runners, the enraged citizens must have inflicted even more deaths, and they were still hunted down by the men of Mutal.

It was important to find all the bodies. The city and the districts were criss-crossed by canals and water reservoirs. The Maya may had no idea about bacteria and infections, but they were a warlike people and had to realize that corpses would contaminate the precious wet. This would, if not properly cleaned up, lead to a late triumph of the late Tatb'u, and nobody was interested in that. So they started collecting the dead bodies, as quickly as possible, and the focus was first on cleaning the water. Half-naked warriors waded through the reservoirs and canals, collecting corpses. The water hadn't made the deceased more attractive. The burning sun and the midday

148

heat made things worse. Chitam had ordered to set up big fires. In the evening, all fallen fighters should burn, those of the enemy in a non-ceremonial and despised manner, their own dead with the blessing of the gods and under the complaints of their loved ones in a special place. Already for the next day great services were announced, in which, as Aritomo suspected, the preparations for the second, bloody act of this war would be made. He knew that human sacrifices were not foreign to the Maya; they were even considered an important part of religion, though not part of daily practice, just a necessary ingredient to make the gods merciful. And prisoners of war, especially those of such high status, were particularly well suited as donations. There would be no slaughter of hundreds of prisoners. The Maya's practice wasn't about conscious cruelty or the incarnation of a special sense of hate. It was about spiritual needs, at least from their point of view.

Inugami and Aritomo agreed to reject this practice, albeit for different reasons. The Captain had announced his intention of talking to Chitam about it, and the fact that they made this trek through the mounds of corpses was connected, not least, with the discussion of this subject. Only the most necessary sacrifices should be allowed, only very few of their opponents should be killed. Inugami had a different use for the prisoners.

Sawada accompanied them, his face frozen into a motionless mask. The old scholar wasn't a soldier, never been one. He knew his books and his studies. For him, this sight was even harder to endure than for Aritomo, who was always confronted with this prospect as a soldier, and had prepared himself to a certain degree. But the man fared remarkably well. Still, the fixed gaze, with which he regarded only the way ahead, spoke volumes. Aritomo couldn't blame him. He would have gladly spared himself that sight, but Inugami repeatedly pointed to this or that – to the effects of the shelling, to the work of the artisans who had immediately begun to repair buildings, to some particularly maimed victims – that Aritomo couldn't afford to just look away like Sawada.

He had to glance at everything, accept Inugami's comments, answer questions, give assessments. It took a lot of effort to do all this. He mastered himself well, at least he assumed so, but eventually his lack of passion for slaughter would strike the Captain – if not in this battle, then possibly the next. Aritomo would have to consider this. Was the soldier's profession perhaps the wrong choice for him? He had never expected to be attacked by such scruples.

The Captain didn't seem to recognize Aritomo's problems, or he simply didn't care. The way he looked at the dead was more than arrogant. It was as if he didn't see the mortal remains of humans in all the casualties, but rather of animals that had just been led to slaughter. His remarks were of technical coldness, of effectiveness and efficiency, of the use of existing resources, analyzed tactical errors of enemies and allies alike.

What Inugami said wasn't stupid, and that made things even worse. Aritomo felt that his superior had adapted surprisingly quickly and had an alert mind. He was able to assess the Maya's military capabilities – he even praised the atlatl's accuracy and impact – and he had some pretty good insights into their tactical usability. But at the same time, it was as if he was talking about tokens, not real fighters who fought real battles, and in these, as they had just shown, died a very real death.

Inugami went away with a nonchalance that Aritomo couldn't understand. If Mutal was the place to spend the rest of their life – and Aritomo lost hope of a return to their own time with each passing day –, then it was necessary, not only helpful, to build a relationship with the Maya, which clearly went beyond their use as human material for military missions.

Inugami saw it differently.

Aritomo had known that, of course. But this walk across the field of death showed it once more in all clearness. It robbed him of every illusion. Everything was now clearly spread out before him, and he saw his role in all this. As a faithful paladin of a grandiose warlord, a ruler who just wouldn't bear the name of a king because a young prince was well suited to act as a puppet in front of him.

Or was he?

Aritomo was almost glad once they reached the palace. Everywhere were traces of the fight. Desperate invaders had hitherto been entrenched in the narrow spaces, and it had been particularly difficult to defeat them. The men of Tatb'u had endured to the bitter end, and none of them had been led into captivity. The bodies had already been carried out, and the worst devastation had been eliminated, yet there was still much to do. The metallic scent of blood hung in the air, and the reddish-brown spots were everywhere.

They were led by a servant into a room that was slightly larger than the others and looked like the King's private rooms. Here they found Chitam, along with the priest Itzanami. The new King of Mutal also wanted to make sure that all those who could best communicate with each other were present. In addition to them, other men were present Aritomo couldn't quite remember. However, from their posturing and clothing, he concluded that there were high noblemen, clan leaders, men Chitam had to rely on to establish his rule – or who had insisted on attending that gathering, just because the prince was not yet comfortable on his throne and the opportunity was favorable to steer him in the right direction.

Wherever they would point to.

Aritomo felt uncomfortable, despite all the accentuated friendliness, the food, the relaxed posture of everyone involved. He kept glancing sideways at his commander, who regarded Chitam with condescension, just like the dead on the way here.

That couldn't be good.

It was too difficult. They all tried, tried their best, and especially Sawada and Itzanami struggled, but in the first few minutes Aritomo realized that they were in for a very tedious conversation.

They lacked words, grammar and possibly patience.

They complimented each other on this victory, but these utterances seemed like a formality that both sides expected in some way, but which wasn't meant seriously, because they knew it would lead to consequences. And what those were would ultimately decide if they would be satisfied with this triumph.

Inugami had a better grip on this than Aritomo had expected.

Chitam showed more royal dignity than ever in his life.

Sawada and Itzanami were focused and attentive, and worked hard to find the right words. They failed more than once. Everyone groped their way to the core of the statements. It was like circling a military target and then attacking it from different locations, hoping that one of those moves would eventually produce the desired result. Aritomo felt that both sides were painfully aware of the danger of major misunderstandings and did everything they could to reach a common understanding of what they were talking about.

It was still very tedious.

And it dragged on, very tiring, because utmost care meant that many things were repeated several times to ensure that everything was well understood. Chitam's face had remained an iron mask throughout the encounter, but Aritomo had the impression that the King's mood was constantly worsening. He couldn't blame him. Inugami had come up with demands made with cold courtesy, insisting, and he wiped away all objections.

This approach couldn't make anyone happy except himself.

In the end – after a good two hours – they hadn't progressed too far. After all, Inugami had managed to get his message across, and it was one in which Aritomo had unconditionally supported him: The prisoners of war from the three hostile cities shouldn't be sacrificed in bloody rituals. Instead, they should be the basis for a new, even greater army of Mutal, an army of slaves who could earn fame and rank, and good treatment through special bravery in battle. Aritomo knew where Inugami got this idea. At the Military Academy he had chosen a historical subject for his thesis, a work that was highly valued and formally imposed upon his first officer for reading. The subject had been the Janissaries, the elite troop of the Ottoman Empire, a military unit made up of slaves, who paid for their special privileges, which they enjoyed despite their status, with extraordinary bravery and great fighting spirit. This was the concept that inspired Inugami, and he did everything to make it understandable to Chitam.

Aritomo knew what ulterior motives Inugami had. The Captain would like to take care of the training and organization of this troop. He wanted to form a force that didn't feel loyalty primarily to the King of Mutal but to himself. And he wanted to lay the foundation for the imperial plans that had driven him since their arrival in this time.

When they left the palace two hours later and set out on their way back, the Captain had achieved a great deal. Chitam's position had been weak. His counselors had wanted to fulfill every wish of Inugami. They saw in the leader of the holy messengers a kind of savior, a representative of higher powers, who would lead the city to an unprecedented position. Chitam couldn't argue against the public mood after this great victory, Aritomo had noticed. He had tried to fight a rearguard action, and not without skill. But in the end he had to agree reluctantly to the proposals, especially when the priests had agreed to rethink the ancient rituals in the face of this heavenly sign and possibly ... adapt.

The prospect of power and wealth, the smell of an empire under construction – all this produced an astounding amount of flexibility even in some narrow-minded man. Or, Aritomo mused, maybe it was simply to exchange one kind of bigotry for another.

During their discussion with Chitam, cleanup operations were intensified. The night was coming soon, and it was necessary to have at least most of the dead recovered. A smell of roasted flesh hung over the city, and Aritomo knew that this had nothing to do with a feast in honor of her victory but with the burning of corpses in full swing. The columns of smoke, which stood high in several places in the almost calm air, spoke volumes.

Along the road across the square to the submarine, there were no more dead lying. Only the craters far away from the boat were still clearly visible, wherever the cannon's fire had ripped open the floor or damaged buildings. Again, the Maya would go to work quickly. Their skills as master builders were impressive, even if Inugami was willing to express this positive assessment only sparingly.

"I'm very happy, Second Lieutenant Hara," Inugami said after leaving the palace behind. "You speak the language of these savages already very well. I'm sure the new chief will realize that our call for an end to useless human sacrifice makes great sense."

Aritomo tried a smile to show that he appreciated the praise.

"The ... King agreed," he said. "He wasn't the deciding factor personally. The priesthood is of great importance. We must now use the exuberance of our victory and the demonstration of our power to break up certain old structures. The reduction of human sacrifice is certainly one important task."

"Yes, yes," Inugami nodded. "Let's keep an eye on the priests. As long as they submit, we want to leave them alone. Whether they stop their silly rituals or spill their own blood on their altars, I'm content. But we can't allow these prisoners to be slaughtered. The men are devastated and demoralized. We will set them up, build them up, give them a new perspective, new opportunities, and respect. We will shape them, Hara, like clay in the hand of the artist. They will be very grateful to receive this second chance and be ready to fight for us with all their hearts."

Aritomo said nothing. He couldn't argue with Inugami – the likelihood that his plan would come to pass wasn't so small –, and he didn't want to start a discussion about what it would mean to "fight for us." An army wasn't created to make pointless parades, and Inugami was pragmatic. An army was created to use it.

"In the medium term, we need to think about what we can do with this Chitam," Inugami said, tearing him out of his thoughts. "I had the impression he wasn't half as enthusiastic as the others of his entourage."

Aritomo nodded. Inugami had a good ability of observation when he considered it worthwhile to use it. Of course, every waking eye had noticed in the past two hours that Chitam knew very well where the journey was going and that he was in danger of becoming King of Inugami's graces. Of course, he didn't like that prospect much.

"What do you mean exactly?" Aritomo asked, though he thought he knew pretty well what the Captain was after.

"We need to get rid of him," Inugami said with a serenity as if talking about removing a stain on his tunic. "He seems to think of himself as someone who still acts independently. But that time is over soon. We can only have one king, just one symbol of our new power. And that's Prince Isamu alone. If someone sits on this throne, then it will be him. We must do everything in our power to make this transition as smooth as possible. You know these people better than I do, Hara. I expect you to make suggestions."

154

Inugami did not even wait for his first officer to reply. They were always greeted by working Maya, very respectful, submissive, and Inugami, in a good mood, apparently wanted to appear affable. He returned the greetings, waved, smiled, nodded encouragingly. He staunchly believed that Aritomo would have no trouble developing a way to eliminate Chitam.

But Aritomo Hara pressed his lips on each other. With this order, this clear intention, things headed for a decision – a decision on Mutal's leadership and the political future, but also a decision on whether Aritomo continued to obey without complaining or whether he was seriously considering how he could shape an alternative approach.

As they came close to the boat, Aritomo remembered his conversation with Prince Isamu. He pictured the boy on the Throne of Mutal, steered, pushed forward, a puppet in the hands of others, especially Inugami's. That was what the Prince was afraid of, what gave him unquiet nights, and with that he sensed the same doom as Aritomo did. Isamu would have a secure and sheltered life, like all Japanese emperors before him. But Inugami didn't want a Meiji, the famous emperor who had begun to rule himself and was willing to leave the Imperial Palace. He wanted to be a shogun and govern in the name of the emperor, without having too much regard for his opinion.

Aritomo saw this clearly in front of his eyes.

He saw that this way would only lead through a sea of blood. In order to bring legitimacy to this new form of rule, Inugami had to prove himself in further victories, in quick succession and not too far in the future.

"One more thing, Hara," Inugami said as they stood at the foot of the pyramid where the boat rested. "These closer cities that have joined this Tatb'u … what were their names? I just can't handle this monkey language."

Aritomo took a deep breath. "Saclemacal and Tayasal."

"Yes, that's it. We have to take care of them. They are currently without defense."

Inugami paused and looked at Aritomo with a smile.

"This is the perfect time to strike. We should take advantage of the hour, Hara. We have to work out plans! We will attack!" He slapped Aritomo on the shoulder. "That will be great, Hara. Grandiose indeed!"

And then he started the ascent to the boat.

Aritomo followed him silently.

23

"There's no doubt about it," the priest said, looking Chitam straight in the eyes, and with a challenging self-confidence his father would've never allowed. It was these little gestures that showed him how shaky his position was and how little he could trust that the ancient traditions still had the same power as before.

Chitam bowed his head, avoiding being too arrogant or self-important. He couldn't afford a showdown right now. The conversation with Inugami had shown this clearly. He, too, had had to back off, being very aware of his fragile position.

The clan leaders who marched against him were too many, and only too willing to contest the throne. All of them believed that Mutal now had to do everything to serve the will of the holy messengers. As long as Chitam seemed to agree completely, that was no problem at all. But if he showed too much resistance – or only persistently pointed out possible dangers of the chosen path –, it would only be a matter of time before he was replaced by a more docile candidate.

That was kind of weird, and Chitam didn't miss the irony of the situation. Inugami wanted to fulfill his desires, which he himself had cherished for many years: a more active, military foreign policy, more campaigns, conquests, more subjugations – more fame and more victories. He differed in this request neither from the dead Tatb'u nor from the Lord of the holy messengers. But Inugami turned everything upside down. He ignored the traditions, first gently, but then surely it'd become more and more. He'd anger the gods.

He'd make a joke out of King Chitam.

There were, he was sure, enough nobles who were quite capable of bearing the heavy burden of this office and enough priests who would give such a process the necessary spiritual blessing. That worked hand in hand.

Chitam stood on brittle ground.

Certainly, the formal courtesy, the phrases and gestures of submission, all that was true. Also, the priests would continue to advance the preparations for enthronement – nobody was interested in a vacancy – and the people, well, the people ...

Funny, usually a king of Mutal didn't worry too much about the people. As long as the centuries-old contract was upheld, there was just the ruler and those who served him unconditionally. As long as the king, through his association with the gods, provided for harvest and food, as long as he performed the rituals and did everything to ensure the blessing of the heavens, he fulfilled his duty and deserved submission and servitude. Only if one day he could no longer fulfill this important function, his position would be endangered.

Or if someone showed up who gave the appearance – the very convincing, almost irrefutable appearance! – to do the job much, much better?

And that's exactly where Chitam was standing for now, and he was very much aware of it. The number of his allies was clear, and there were quite a few who felt a new wind that would carry them higher – what did all the loyalties and customs count in this situation?

Chitam was distracted by his gloomy thoughts as the music grew louder. The victory celebration was in full swing. For three days they had all toiled and cleaned up, for three days the traces of the double-edged triumph had been eliminated. Now Mutal was on his feet, serving up what was possible – and many things were possible because all the supplies of their invaders had fallen into their hands. The prisoners of war were given only the most necessary rations, and so there was enough for a glittering party that would last well into the next morning. Normally, this would have been an occasion for Chitam to join in the celebration – although, under the critical eye of his wife, who inevitably took part in the celebration, the party mood would be somewhat diminished. But today he wasn't so cheerful, because basically he wasn't happy. His father's death loomed too clear in his memory – and the end of the world in which he had grown up was imminent.

158

Chitam tried to hide, but that wouldn't help him either.

It was a lazy evening, the music sounded happy, people danced.

For the first time, all the inhabitants of the boat were crawling out of the black belly, at least that was said. Chitam assumed that some were still left behind to guard this most precious possession of the messengers. Still, he had never seen so many of the strangers in a heap before, and many of them had never been more than a few yards from their vessel since arriving. They seemed confused, overwhelmed, like many of their braver comrades in their early days.

Chitam had made sure that shyness didn't last too long. He might have no real power to strengthen his position against the holy messengers, but he had come to the conclusion that they were as much men as were his people, and that certain ... confidence-building measures would take effect as soon as the opportunity arose to apply these. He knew that Inugami was critical of this and didn't encourage the men's connections with the women of the city, that he planned to control them.

Chitam considered this a pointless endeavor, and he did his part to substantiate his argument.

The victory celebration offered the perfect opportunity.

There was no shortage of young girls who were willing to be interested in the holy messengers without the king's particular encouragement. A marriage with such a man promised, above all now, prestige and wealth, and for some farmer's daughter the rise in areas of the society that otherwise would have remained closed to her. The strange visitors had begun to abandon their initial restraint. After some cups of chi and stomach stuffed with corn patty, they began to relax. The darkness of the dawning night, dimly lit by the fires and torches on the fairground, enveloped the girls' bodies in auspicious flickering. No matter how much the messengers were of divine descent, and Chitam had developed some doubt in that regard which he wisely kept to himself, it was clear that they were also men. Men who had been trapped in their boat for weeks.

Chitam hadn't gotten the impression that physical love among men was particularly favored by the holy messengers. It wasn't uncommon among his own people and wasn't punishable as long as it was nonviolent, which in turn was subject to harsh sanctions. But the ravenous gaze with which the visitors, released from the confines of their vessel, looked at the bodies of the girls, actually said everything that Chitam wanted to know.

And he did everything to provide ample opportunities.

Even otherwise, the festival left nothing to be desired, at least according to its own standards. Chitam had ordered the best of what the kitchens gave. Mounds of cornbread filled with chili peppers, beans or meat had been prepared. Pumpkin meat was also presented in numerous variations. Peanuts, pekari and deer meat as well as many different fruits rounded off the menu. Nobody on the King's table should lack anything, and everything was replenished immediately. And the guests ate vigorously. It seemed to them to be rude to leave the table earlier than others, and they consumed as if they hadn't eaten for days.

Chitam provided what was needed, but ate and drank, contrary to his usual custom, only with great restraint. Instead of indulging in these joys, he spent his time watching the revelers and tried to draw conclusions from their behavior.

The first thing he found out was that he wasn't the only one who preferred observation. For even the one who bore the name of Aritomo Hara only made moderate use of the offerings, sitting beside the old teacher, whom the messengers had brought with them, and spoke sparingly to his table mates. Sawada himself spoke more, sitting himself next to Itzanami, and both used the time of socializing to provide each other with additional vocabulary. Chitam saw the two men taking paper into their hands to take notes, and he had to suppress a smile at this extraordinary learning, as it would have been unseemly. The other man next to Aritomo was someone whom Chitam had met during one of his visits to the boat. He looked a little different than the other holy messengers, especially in the face. Aritomo had tried to explain to him that the man with the difficult name was from a faraway nation and actually didn't belong to the people possessing the vessel. But it seemed that there was a good understanding between him and Aritomo Hara, for both kept putting their heads together and talked seriously. Worry clouded their faces, and though Chitam couldn't hear what they were talking about, he felt a strange kinship with them, as if he knew they were pondering the same issues as he did.

Maybe it wouldn't be a bad idea to start a conversation with both – on a suitable occasion. If possible so that the leader of the messengers didn't notice.

Inugami himself, on the other hand, seemed to enjoy himself royally. He drank and ate, and laughed loudly, even louder as the evening progressed. He was also devoted to female society, more than Chitam had expected of him, and looked like a real nobleman of status, with the measure of both contempt and implied dominance in regard to all the carnal pleasures expected of him. If he behaved accordingly, no one would blame him, for he was the one who had brought Mutal, with the weapons of the gods, victory over an insidious enemy.

Most of the other visitors showed no excessive restraint. However, as Chitam discovered, they had apparently been ordered to follow some general rules of behavior. Thus, even after two hours of feasting, no one who was really drunk, and though the pleasant company of willing femininity didn't fail to affect any of the men, there didn't arise any kind of forcible abuse, which was regarded with great disapproval even among the powerful of Mutal.

In short, the behavior of the guests was fully acceptable, and this fact alone was disturbing enough. Because it meant that Chitam had no arguments in his hand to shine a slightly worse light on the messengers in the future.

At an advanced hour, the first of the guests disappeared with accordingly animated accompaniment into the darkness. They would find corners where a cotton mat could be rolled out quickly and taken to action. By midnight, well over half of the messengers had bidden their goodbye from the circle of tablets to continue the rest of the night in a different way. It was remarkable that Inugami, too, had finally stood up, with each arm twisted around the waist of a bride, still somewhat insecure despite the support, walking out into the darkness. In addition to a number of guests who could finally preferred more of the chi and other drinks than the company of a woman, Aritomo Hara and the man with the strange name remained seated as well, and Sawada and Itzanami were mainly concerned with providing the names of the food items and writing them down.

Chitam's gaze wandered over the crowd of remaining revelers, whose volume was now decreasing, either from fatigue or from the effects of the drinks, or both. The new ruler of Mutal felt dearly how leaden tiredness tore at his limbs. Just a few weeks ago, the celebration would've just begun for him at this time, but now he was starting to falter. It was as if the burden of events had dumped many extra years of life on his shoulders, and these would now prematurely claim their toll. He still didn't enjoy the feast and was saddened that the dark clouds over his heart had apparently robbed him of the ability to live the day – and the night – away from all the worries. He had feared something like that. That's why he'd never hurried to follow his father. But he didn't expect it to crush him so severely.

His eyes remained on his own family, his brothers and sisters, of which he had many, for besides his official queen, Chitam's mother, Siyaj had cherished many mistresses.

He frowned when his eyes caught Une Balam's. His younger sister had been in a particularly good mood. She was originally supposed to be married to a prince of the ruler of Tayasal, a man she had never met, of course, and who was said to be considerably older than she was. His bones were reportedly burned to ashes on one of the heaps of corpses and thus used as fertilizer for the fields of Mutal. Une Balam was relieved to witness this kind of termination of a long arranged engagement. It was now up to Chitam to agree on a new, suitable connection, but the newly enthroned master of Mutal, who, like many of his siblings, was very attached to Une Balam, was in no hurry to accomplish of this task.

And given the observation he was making, the haste subsided even more. Because although Une Balam joked and laughed and showed herself relaxed and happy in the company of her family – for good reason –, Chitam noticed that her eyes were always directed to glance at Aritomo Hara, who behaved so differently from the celebrating men around them. Was it his seriousness and ability to

162

keep self-composure that interested her? Was it his exotic status as one of the leaders of the messengers of the gods? Was it his polite but certain way of rejecting the advances of the other young women who saw him as interesting and worthwhile prey?

Chitam couldn't be the judge of it, but it seemed to him that it might make sense to have a conversation with Une Balam and possibly create a suitable occasion within which she could again have the opportunity to meet Aritomo Hara. Maybe in a slightly more private, less public environment.

That should be arranged.

Over the next few hours, the audience thinned out more and more. The morning was already approaching when Chitam officially disbanded the table, signaling to the most stubborn guests that the festivity had come to an end. Some of the revelers had already fallen asleep on the edge of the food trays and were now gently woken up by their friends or servants to indicate that they should continue their night's sleep elsewhere. From the messengers, Aritomo and the man with the strange name remained until the end, as if they had been waiting for something. When Chitam got up, the two men did the same and approached him with determination. The prince narrowed his eyes and ran a hand over his face, trying to dispel the burning tiredness. If they had been waiting for something, it was obviously an opportunity to have a relatively unobserved conversation with the new Lord of Mutal. Aritomo Hara was also accompanied by the man named Sawada, who, despite his advanced age, had endured longer than Itzanami and still looked awake and interested. Whatever energized the scholar, Chitam wanted a little of it.

He sighed and struggled for self-control. He couldn't complain about his fate and make plans, while preferring the night's rest to a potentially important conversation. He was the King. He had duties.

Aritomo and his companions bowed to the Mayan ruler, showing a degree of genuine respect that the captain of the strange vessel generally lacked. Chitam decided that it would be really inappropriate to walk away too hastily now, even if his body longed for his bed. Instead, he nodded to Aritomo in a friendly manner, concentrated on his language skills, and began the difficult process of a conversation in two languages, some directly, some translated, some with intense gestures and often enough with endless repetitions.

Probably everything would make sense very quickly. He turned to the remaining messengers, earnestly trying his language skills. He was now almost accustomed to certain meanings and statements.

"I hope you enjoyed the party," Chitam said, using the most predictable of all questions.

"I'm very happy," Aritomo replied. "The food was tasty."

"I too thank you," Sawada replied, indicating a bow. The third man, whom Aritomo again introduced as "Lengsley," made a gesture of approval. He had the weakest language skills of all and could only help by using the language of the messengers. They would now all try their best to translate in every direction, and both Itzanami and Sawada seemed eager enough to try their skills in earnest.

"Let's talk for a moment," Aritomo requested. "We are worried."

"I feel so, too. Maybe our worries are the same."

They moved to one side and sat again close to one of the few still burning fires. Chitam sent the remaining servants to remove the remnants of the celebration and leave him alone in the company of the messengers. With deep respect, they rushed to comply with this request.

Somewhere outside in the darkness, they heard voices, the laughter of a woman. The celebration was obviously going on elsewhere.

Aritomo stared silently into the fire for a few moments before beginning.

"My captain wishes to embark on a campaign against Tayasal and Saclemacal."

"A wise decision. Both cities must be punished." Chitam reacted in the spirit of tradition. Of course, both areas were now on the top of a counterattack list, and even if the divine messengers wouldn't push for it, he would soon have thought about an appropriate punitive expedition himself. Their interests met here, and maybe Chitam would've been more annoyed if they'd disagreed.

"My Captain is pursuing more far-reaching plans than just punishing those who opposed Mutal," Aritomo said.

164

Chitam nodded. "That's what I expect."

"He wants to build an empire," Aritomo said simply. Chitam needed some time to understand the underlying principle of what the Japanese wanted to make clear to him. The Maya were familiar with eternal rounds of conquest and submission for centuries, but they rarely conquered anything permanently. Defeated cities were made to pay tribute and to formally recognize the suzerainty of the victor, but in fact they remained autonomous in many ways, and once the memory of the lost battle faded or leadership changed, it could very quickly come to renewed fighting – sometimes with an exactly reversed outcome. The idea of a permanent, well-organized territorial state, which encompassed many cities and spread over a wide area, was quite understandable for the Maya as a concept, but wasn't part of their historical experience in general. Many of their wars had a ritualistic character and were necessary to affirm their own view of cosmic balance. The opportunity to wage these wars was more likely to exist when there was a certain permanent selection of potential adversaries. An empire was anxious to consistently reduce this choice, as it ultimately sought absolute supremacy over everything achievable and defensible. It would necessarily transform many of the traditional behaviors and spiritual commitments of the Maya – or even deny them altogether. It would probably trigger a social shock.

Chitam mused. He may not have been able to grasp all of this, but he was intelligent. Intelligent enough to realize that change was needed and that this change would be at the expense of many established ways and structures – and that it could well be that he would be among those structures that this wind would sweep away.

"I understood him that way too," Chitam replied, quite sure that he got the idea. Aritomo had gone to great lengths to explain it, and there was not much doubt left.

"This will bring great change."

"It will bring forth many deaths and probably the indignation of the gods."

Aritomo smiled. "But you call us messengers of the gods."

Chitam made a wiping gesture with one hand. "I see more clearly than the others, but it doesn't make me more powerful." He leaned forward. Every tiredness seemed to have left him. "Inugami doesn't do anything in order to increase the glory of Mutal, but to accumulate his own. It's supposed to be *his* empire."

"Not yours," Aritomo confirmed. "And not in his name. The formal ruler will be the boy."

"Your own prince, yes." There was no contempt in Chitam's voice, more something like bitterness. He had no quarrel with the boy, only with his protector and ... spokesman.

"Our own prince, indeed."

"Is he ready?"

"Nobody asks of his opinion in the matter."

Chitam nodded. He knew the situation.

"What role do I play in the Captain's plans?"

"That of a helper to be disposed of should he begin to disturb."

"When will I be regarded a disturbance?"

"I can't say for sure."

Chitam looked at Aritomo and frowned. "You're the second behind Inugami. Why are you talking so openly about these things with me?"

"Because I don't necessarily agree with his plans."

"You don't want to found an empire?"

Aritomo hesitated, as if he didn't know a clear answer, at least not one that clearly affirmed or denied the question.

"Not like that," he said almost as expected.

"You don't want the little prince on my throne?"

"Not really."

"And I could help you to prevent it?"

Aritomo laughed. "We can't stop it. Most of my people follow Inugami. And after defeating Mutal's enemies, many of your people will follow him as well. We finally proved that we are true messengers of the gods."

Chitam looked at Aritomo with a smile. "You have nothing to do with the gods, do you?"

The man looked around involuntarily before answering the question, but then his face became very serious.

166

"Not that I know."

"Your vessel ..."

"Is craftsmanship. And absolutely out of place here. It needs the sea."

"Craftsmanship?"

"From a distant land and a distant time. Don't ask me how we got here. None of us has the slightest idea."

"You really don't know?"

"We know little. At least about these things. We're as puzzled as you are."

Chitam pressed his lips together, looking pensively into the glow of the fading fire.

"So what are we doing?"

Aritomo sighed.

"I'll try to use my little influence on Inugami to keep things under control. You should try not to be too brash and demanding toward him. At the same time, you should look for allies among your own people, as I do among mine." He nodded in the direction of Lengsley, who returned the gesture and remained silent otherwise.

Chitam followed this brief exchange with his eyes and frowned. "But that sounds like we're pondering a kind of civil war, messenger. Maybe not now but sooner or later."

Aritomo's face had a very unfortunate expression as he grasped the meaning of the word.

"No I don't want that."

"It could come that way."

"Then it will be up to you to take the risk."

"And Inugami?"

"If he sees a real chance, he'll grab it. He knows what he wants, and he calculates pragmatically. He accepts sacrifices, and he sees the possibility of success, many of them, especially considering the Maya who are ready to follow his dream. He is confident that he will prevail."

Chitam nodded slowly. That was about what he had expected. Then, slowly and articulated, he said, "And he probably will."

* * *

Aritomo was confused. He understood the man in front of him only with effort anyway. But how was he to classify the fact that if he offered Chitam a chance to win the upcoming power struggle, he probably wouldn't take it? Why did they have this conversation? To assure each other of the fact how terrible the situation was?

Aritomo knew he had to ask himself that same question as well. It had been his decision – after a long discussion with Lengsley and Sawada, who had fatherly feelings for Prince Isamu and apparently enjoyed little to see him as a puppet of Inugami's imperial interests – to approach Chitam. But what exactly he was expecting from this conversation and what the consequences would be ... Aritomo had to admit that he hadn't thought it over. Was there something like a basic trust into the omniscience of a monarch deep inside him, as he had been taught in school and academy since childhood? Had he transferred this belief in the infallibility and sanctity of the chrysanthemum throne to this ruler of Mutal, if only unconsciously?

If so, he'd made a mistake. And Chitam's answer indicated that the barrier between them was still terribly large. It consisted of a lack of knowledge of the right words but also of the fact that two different cultures, not only separated from each other by geography but also by time, met here. What this actually meant was sometimes masked by the hustle and bustle of the past few weeks, or they just didn't want to believe it. Those who acknowledged such differences had to deal with problems and hurdles that cost a lot of energy to deal with. It was so much easier to fade those things out and succumb the illusion that everything was less problematic if one didn't think too much about it. Aritomo, who considered himself more of the brooding type, wasn't allowed to take this escape. He had expected either too much or too little of their hosts.

He met Chitam's gaze, who was alert, not uncritical but also seriously curious. The young ruler was not sure about things, not even about himself. He needed advice and guidance. But was someone like Aritomo the one who gave advice to a king? Had not the officer quietly come here to seek guidance from a ruler?

168

"I confused you," Chitam said.

Aritomo winked approvingly.

"I explain it to you," Chitam said. "We will lose through a civil war. It'd make Mutal vulnerable to its enemies – and we will amass enemies, more and more of them. If we want to prevent your captain from creating an empire according to his ideas – an empire that would be nothing more than a continued foreign rule, as if the conquerors from Teotihuacán had not only occupied Mutal in the short term but permanently incorporated it into their own empire –, then this can't be undone by a civil war. But your captain wants to make us Maya the slaves of his plans, establish an army dedicated solely to his glory. He doesn't understand us."

"He doesn't want to understand anyone," Aritomo explained. "He doesn't think it necessary."

"Yes. He doesn't want to understand anyone," Chitam repeated. "But we're not fighting for glory and power alone, we're fighting because the gods sent the signs, and the stars point the way. If they do not, we won't raise our weapons. If we are not allowed to sacrifice the prisoners, then we can't be sure of the favor of the gods. What kind of life shall we lead when we just begin to pay homage to your Captain but forget whom we really should owe allegiance and respect?"

Aritomo said nothing and just listened attentively.

"There will be no civil war with me," Chitam said again. "It won't happen because it only causes damage and nobody gains from it. If it comes to the point of fighting for my throne and the future of the true Mutal, then there is only one chance of success: We seek help from outside – from others who understand the danger of Inugami's plans, the threat within these concepts, and they must rally around me to avert this danger. That alone is a promising way."

Chitam closed his eyes. He had shot his powder. Sawada translated a few things for Lengsley, so there was enough time for Aritomo to think what he could possibly reply. He hadn't even considered the matter from this side. The world outside Mutal was intangible to him. It had come to him through the attack of the Yaxchilan-coalition, but he hadn't really understood the conditions of this area. Was Inugami far enough in his understanding? Or did the other Mayan cities didn't bother him at all, their existence mere cornerstones of a campaign that would lead to something in which formerly independent cities would play only a minor role? Points on a map? Stones in a big game?

"So we'll delay what we won't be able to prevent in the long run," Lengsley muttered in Japanese and looked questioningly at Aritomo. "In that case we should prepare, Lieutenant Hara. We should prepare ourselves for the inevitable."

Aritomo nodded slowly. He didn't quite understand the extent of this kind of preparation, but Lengsley's thoughtful expression showed him that the Englishman was evidently already making quite precise plans.

Aritomo looked at Chitam as the King rose.

"We want to sleep," the ruler of Mutal said. He smiled at Aritomo. "I invite you to the palace once you have rested. Let's have a breakfast together to discuss how to get the big boat off the pyramid. I don't think it should or can stay up there forever. It was already quite shaky when the mighty fire-atlatl spoke."

Aritomo nodded. The volleys had begun to crunch their construction in spite of all supporting measures. They had all been happy when Inugami had given the order to stop. "It's a good topic," Aritomo said, not least because the captain also thought he needed a solution.

"Then come to the palace, if you can find the strength."

Aritomo rose, indicating a bow.

The celebration was over.

They had serious business to tackle.

24

Inocoyotl threw his upper body onto the floor and pressed his forehead against the carpet. He lay motionless, and like every time he humbled himself before the divine ruler, he knew he could lose his life at that moment. But Meztli was not a man who tended to punish his subordinates without cause, and his faithful servant had been summoned to the palace by the King himself. Inocoyotl didn't know if it was a good thing or a bad thing to be personally acquainted with the ruler of the great Teotihuacán, but at least his family seemed to think that this fact had served them well.

He had often met both Meztli and his father. When the predecessor on the throne had destroyed the former dynasty in a bloody palace coup, many were frightened. But the young Inocoyotl had seen a chance, and since then he might not have proven to be indispensable but quite useful, without imposing himself. Slowly he had risen in favor, and although the path had been rocky, it had been worthwhile.

Only a year or so ago, he and his family had moved from the lower district to the one closer to the palace, getting a new home adjacent to the seat of power, in a preferred location, not far from the King's residence, a sign that Inocoyotl, the former merchant and soldier, was one of the few out of the class of his birth who made it.

By making himself useful.

To this benefit, he gave his life entirely to Meztli, the King, who could take this present with a movement of his hand, without anyone taking him to account. And with another move, he made Inocoyotl a rich and respected man, to whom even high priests and warriors reacted with respect. And since both triumph and humiliation were so close together in this palace, Inocoyotl was never overjoyed to be summoned here, for he never knew exactly what those in power were considering.

But the ruler was obviously not angered by anything, and Inoco-yotl would live. On the contrary, the face of the greatest king in the world showed that he was up to something, and he was sure that he considered it a favor. Inocoyotl knew that his judgement was sometimes different, but as long as he kept his head on his shoulders, he was willing to stop arguing.

"Get up!" The King's sonorous voice reached his ears. Only a few who entered the audience chamber were allowed to glimpse the lofty figure of the mighty, and anyone who did so without permission faced instant death, even if he otherwise enjoyed the ruler's favor. Inocoyotl was one of those who were allowed, as requested, to look the King in the eye, and he did so every time with the timidity of a man who had learned such behavior from childhood, to respect the highest servant of the Great Goddess and to show absolute devotion.

Meztli didn't offer a terrible sight. He inherited his strong stature from his father, and his face was neither pleasant nor disgusting. The headdress of the King and the stately robes suited him well, and his strong, deep voice helped him to radiate authority and power. He'd been Lord of Teotihuacán for three years, ruler of the great metropolis, the center of the world, and although the end of this world was imminent – soon, or later, depending on the priests' assessment –, it was the epitome of power and influence, eternal part of the structure that the gods had created.

Inocoyotl rose but kept his head down respectfully, careful not to get too close to the throne. He didn't want to test his luck. The four men of the ceremonial guard were not to be misinterpreted as a mere decoration. Their mighty lances bore sharp obsidian blades and would cut Inocoyotl's body to pieces, if they discerned only a hint of threat to their overlord. The man stayed where he was, humble, submissive, and eager to hear an assignment from his ruler, for otherwise he wouldn't have bothered to summon him.

Inocoyotl had been sent by Meztli's father, the special envoy who had traveled around the world as the eye and ear of Teotihuacán. Growing up as the son of a lowly civil servant, he had first made a name for himself as a steward, then a soldier, and made his contribution to postponing the end of the world for a while. The fact that he stood and breathed here indicated that this contribution was significant enough to keep the gods from their great work of destruction. Then he had started trading when he was a bit too old for war, and since he enjoyed the ruler's favor, doors had opened to him that had remained closed to others of his status. So he had come to wealth and a large family, and his active life had kept him agile and strong despite his age of nearly 50 years, so that he had been consulted by Meztli again and again for advice and assignments. Now that he was standing before the ruler again to receive his tasks directly from him, and not from any of the royal administration, the importance given to the mission by the highest authorities became obvious.

Inocoyotl again bowed to this highest authority and said, "I serve you, Your Majesty. Speak and command, I will do everything faithfully."

Meztli nodded and waved. "Bring a stool for my visitor."

A servant appeared out of nowhere and brought a seat. Inocoyotl was aware of the special grace of this gesture. He sat down with a token of gratitude and looked up at the king, recognizing a friendly, even encouraging smile.

Today, the older man decided, he probably wouldn't die.

Even the four guards seemed relaxed.

Inocoyotl allowed himself to exhale in relief. These audiences made him mad. It was already too much for an old man like him. But then the curiosity outweighed any concerns, and he leaned forward a bit, signaling his attention.

And Meztli didn't let him wait long.

"When was the last time you traveled, my old friend?" the King asked his servant, and Inocoyotl tried to answer the ruler's question as accurately as possible.

"Lord, I traveled to Izapa once last year to see to it and do business," he said truthfully. Of course, Meztli knew that – because besides, Inocoyotl had had the order to observe his governor without him knowing. The mission had been unproductive in that particular aspect – the man had proven to be a loyal, though relatively unimaginative, servant to his master.

"I remember. Your report was detailed."

"I serve as well as I can."

Meztli nodded approvingly. "You do. And that's why I want to send you away again. You should travel south, deeper into the land of the corn people. I'll send you to Mutal, my younger brother."

Inocoyotl bowed humbly. Mutal was well known to him. Meztli's grandfather had once sent a military expedition there, a large army, and the city had fallen under its onslaught as had many other settlements on its way. At that time, a high nobleman had been installed as the new king, and the whole of the current dynasty was derived from that blood of Teotihuacán. It was likely that the memories were still vivid, but the bonds of submission had faded. Inocoyotl guessed what purpose his expedition would have.

"You've been to Mutal before, my friend?"

"No, my lord. I was once in B'aakal, but I never traveled further. One day I was supposed to go to Yaxchilan, but illness stopped me. This was while your honorable father was still alive."

"I understand. Well, it's time to remind our younger brothers that their older relative looks at everything in their sphere of influence with great attention. The reports that the traders bring to us point out that the wars those peoples are having with each other are increasing in violence, and that many rulers – and by the way, among them Yaxchilan's, as you just mentioned it – are thoroughly thinking of establishing a certain suzerainty."

Of course, none of these Mayan states would ever equal the great Teotihuacán; on the other hand, it was a mistake to close one's eyes to such developments. The king seemed to share that assessment, another indication that the big city had had stupider rulers in the past.

"The struggles of the corn people come and go, and the size of their cities is changing like the waves of the ocean, great King," Inocoyotl replied. "It's their disunity and inability that will cause them to never be a serious threat to the glorious Teotihuacán." He bowed his head again before continuing. "But it is wise to remind them that their doings are being assessed and they are well advised to remember the power of this city – which has made many of them what they are today. Even the ruler of B'aakal didn't like remembering that his ancestors were from here, and when I visited him, he wasn't happy. But he didn't lack respect, if I may add that."

"That's good," said Meztli. "Respect must be renewed, and you shall bear signs of it to me."

Inocoyotl bowed again. That was a matter of course.

"I will do your bidding, great lord."

"Take your own men. In addition, you will receive from me thirty soldiers under an experienced leader. I want to give you a seal so that everyone knows that you are under the protection of Meztli, and no one should come too close or endanger your journey. From the stores of the palace, take what you need for the journey. Observe everything carefully and bring the blessings of Meztli to my younger brothers. I want to give you presents that you hand over in my name. Travel to Mutal, stay there, then return to me with a thorough report."

"Everything should be done as you say, my lord," Inocoyotl said.

The King smiled pleased. Of course, he hadn't expected any other answer, but it seemed to make him happy that the order was accepted with such great readiness.

"When can you leave?"

"Allow me a moon for the preparations of my journey, my lord."

"It is granted to you. Before you leave, ask for an audience. I want the priests to bless you and your men."

Inocoyotl couldn't do enough bows. A blessing in the presence of the Divine Ruler? A direct favor of the Great Goddess, seen by the court and all the notables? In fact, Meztli seemed to consider this mission to be very important, otherwise he wouldn't shower such extraordinary mercy on his emissary.

"For that I thank you, my king."

Meztli seemed very satisfied. He waved.

"All is said then."

Inocoyotl knew that he was dismissed. He rose from his stool, felt a servant take it away, and threw himself face down on the floor again. So he remained for the prescribed seconds, before he slowly rose and turned away, with his face turned downwards, to leave the audience chamber at a quick pace.

As he was led outside by a servant through the corridors of the palace and released to the square, he breathed. The anxiety that he felt again and again in the face of these kinds of encounters left him, and he could feel relaxed.

Noon had arrived. Inocoyotl looked into the sun and enjoyed her warmth.

"Lord, you are back!"

Two of his men had waited for him in the shadows and were now approaching him, their faces filled with curiosity and awe. For them, it was hard to imagine what honor and favor it was to be called near the ruler, even to talk to him. No matter how exhausting or frightening these visits were to Inocoyotl, they increased his prestige quite considerably, and with it, his value as someone to be known in the higher circles of the city. The journey to Mutal, with the seal of the king and thirty of his men as protection, would enhance this reputation once more. It could well be that, if he was too frail to be able to continue these efforts, he would be called to the court as a royal adviser and thus experience the culmination of his career.

He hoped he would end with the mercy of a dignified death.

Inocoyotl was determined to prevent a direct post at court if it was only in his power. There was nothing that seemed more terrible to him than having to bear the presence of the ruler daily and to feel the unspoken but constant threat. Meztli was a good man. Even when he was in a bad mood, he handled his family well, they said. But it happened that kings died a sudden and utterly unexpected death. And who knew what fury a potential successor would unleash?

Inocoyotl shook at the thought. It wasn't so much about himself. He was old and replaceable. But he had a large family, and a raging king who, unlike the present ruler, didn't know how to tame his feelings, could do whatever he pleased to punish someone who had caused his indignation.

He served his Lord with fervor but hopefully never good enough to be received in the highest graces. There were rewards whose consequences were incalculable. He was much more modest in his aspirations.

Inocoyotl nodded friendly to his servants.

Then he looked to the left, toward the moon pyramid, which stretched mightily and dominant into the blue sky. He looked to his right, across the square in front of the palace, down the broad, central street that pierced all of Teotihuacán, the Road of the Dead, which ended at the Temple of the Winged and finally led out, a path that Inocoyotl was about to begin. His own house was not far from here, north of the Sun Pyramid, and thankfully often in the shadow of the magnificent structure, making life here a lot more bearable.

He took another deep breath, met the expectant gaze of his servants, who had patiently waited until he finally stirred.

There was a lot to do. A moon for preparation was generous, but it didn't make sense to unnecessarily strain the ruler's patience, even that of a well-balanced man like Meztli.

"We have work," he announced. "A great grace. Let's start quickly!"

25

They were all sweating, and not only because it was very hot.

Inugami and Aritomo wore nothing but shorts, their torsos bared, and already tinged with red from the bad sunburn they were beginning to develop. Nevertheless, Aritomo felt well, better than in a long time. He stood in front of the line of prisoners and began the next exercise, shouting loud orders that they wouldn't yet but soon understand.

Aritomo had fervently engaged himself in the task of developing a training plan for Inugami's janissaries. It was an interesting challenge and a welcome distraction from pondering the future. His plan had met with Inugami's approval and, to his surprise, the captain had ordered to take part in the exercises where possible. Well considered, this request was not so surprising. Inugami wanted to establish a personal relationship with his soldiers, make them his guard, his praetorians. And so he sweated with them, gave orders, punished and praised, established his authority.

The training program consisted essentially of four components. First there was the physical training with numerous exercises that they had taken directly from the training manual of the Imperial Navy and they just followed them. Then there were language studies in which the slave-soldiers learned English, at least enough to be able to understand and execute basic commands. The third component consisted of combat training; in addition to the spear, the blade and the atlatl, this included unarmed combat, as taught in the Japanese armed forces. Here, non-commissioned officers of the boat helped with the teaching of basic techniques. After all, the fourth unit had not started yet, because language skills had not proceeded long enough – the theoretical transfer of knowledge. This began with the introduction of Japanese ranks, albeit in simplified form, for the new army. Inugami envisaged a total of five ranks, which would have to apply to the new slave soldiers – a basic one, two NCO ranks and two officer ranks. Currently, however, the men had not yet been assigned to any. Once the three-month basic education would be completed and, above all, those that best mastered the language lessons emerged, they could take a first step in that direction.

Discipline was also taught to the slaves. It wasn't that the Mayan warriors were a wild bunch, but Aritomo and Inugami soon realized that an army in these latitudes was not a professional military force. Apart from a small core of armed men – mostly a permanent bodyguard for the ruler –, the warriors were all peasants led by their clan chiefs, the Maya nobility, and at the behest of the king, while in peacetime they tended to the land or performed other services, such as to dedicate their labor to the monumental splendors of this civilization. Many of the men had learned a lot because of the permanent military campaigns of the city-states and gained experience. They also knew how to obey and to maintain a minimum of self-organization. The classic battle wasn't the standard but rather attacks on defended cities, with a mix of street fighting and confrontation in larger squares and suburbs. Remarkable was that the Mayan cities were all but unfortified. It seemed like inviting the enemy to launch an attack, and perhaps that had something to do with the fact that religious and political motivations were indistinguishable in many of these conflicts. So far, the former had strongly determined how a war was waged, the latter rather when, and a careful consideration of star constellations also seemed to play an important role in answering the question of the right timing.

All this – this form of "superstition" –, Inugami wanted to drive out. Aritomo wasn't sure if that would work, but the eagerness with which the commander rushed for the task – and the strong support by the rest of the crew he observed – made him reluctant to criticize the plan too loudly. In the opinion of many of the crew, they saw a civilizational work here, of leading the savages into a glorious future, liberated them from archaic ideas and practices, brought progress and a new, forward-looking order. They all overlooked – or disparaged – the accomplishments of their hosts. This meant not only the wonderful and architecturally sophisticated buildings but also the elaborate system of agriculture, which made it possible to feed a growing population in a relatively small space and to allow a metropolitan lifestyle. Aritomo came from a nation in which agriculture had a traditionally very high priority and took an important place in the consciousness of the people. It was amazing that others on the boat could overlook these things without considering them, just because they thought of the Mayans as underdeveloped natives.

That, Aritomo thought, couldn't make things easy in the long run. There would inevitably be tension, and no matter how superior their weapons were, the Maya were many, many more, they weren't primitive idiots. While they certainly didn't understand how the god-messenger technology worked, they knew with confidence what they could do with their own.

The POWs, on the other hand, were demoralized and shocked, so didn't ask any of these questions. The inhabitants of Mutal, however, would someday realize how little the visitors appreciated what they had built up over the centuries with intelligence, knowledge, and skill. On the long run, they needed to be treated with respect.

And, this thought always came back to Aritomo: There were many, so many more than the handful of Japanese.

To be fair, Inugami seemed to anticipate trouble. Otherwise, he wouldn't be so committed to create an instrument that could compensate for this numerical disadvantage. And Aritomo helped him with it.

What else could he do?

"We'll take a break!" the commander shouted, as they completed another round of physical exercises that served not only as fitness building but, above all, learning collective, coordinated, and possibly identical movements, forging a community that understood itself and acted as a unit. The Mayan warriors had no choice – they were prisoners, slaves and their only alternative was to be sacrificed in some rituals or being exploited otherwise –, and they worked

180

hard. Inugami had to take care of the moment when joining in from coercion became part of conviction, yes, enthusiasm. If he dealt with it correctly and purposefully, then he would have created his janissaries, and they wouldn't run away at the first battle.

Inugami toweled the moisture on his face and upper body. He looked at the crowd of war slaves, as they squatted on the ground. Some had been assigned to water service and rushed from man to man with large vessels full of liquid to provide them with the necessary fluids. The two Japanese also brought out their metal bottles and drank.

"You're making progress, aren't you?" Inugami observed.

"Yes, sir. They are a bit confused at times, but the routine of training will take that away."

Inugami nodded. "Once they get used to this routine, we start to shape and forge them. The goal must be supreme valor and absolute submission. In parallel, they are allowed to build decent accommodations. I have identified a place where we can put up barracks. Building houses seems to be in the blood here. They should be well housed and fed. Then we will start rewarding individuals who are excellent – one day off, maybe a few women, the first promotions. Sawada is in the process of developing a system of medals and decorations with Mayan nomenclature, which we can use. We also have to think about a uniform. I propose we're going to start with a sash that everyone must wear and where we can attach badges and awards."

Aritomo nodded silently. Inugami's enthusiasm was intense and almost contagious. He had the right ideas. It didn't work any different in the Japanese forces, actually in all armies of the world. Why should the Mayans not react to such incentives in the desired form?

"We should talk to Chitam about the barracks. We need his help for that," he said quietly. Inugami stared at him a bit dumbfounded, then made a derogatory gesture.

"Yeah, talk to him. I'll show you the place afterwards. Farther outside. Ideally suited. He will agree." Inugami smiled bleakly. "He has to agree. It's not like he has a big choice. Did you hear it? Yesterday volunteers turned up!"

Aritomo looked up. "Volunteer?"

"Yes, the duty guard told me about it."

"Volunteers for what?"

Inugami pointed to the resting soldiers. "To join. The army of the divine messengers. A good dozen young men, eager to serve us. If this is a trend, we must consider building a volunteer company. Some other rules maybe. That needs to be well-considered."

"All these men are needed to tend for the fields," Aritomo reminded him. "If we build up an additional standing army, we withdraw workers. We have to think about food security."

"I've already considered that. Our slaves here need physical training. We will clear the forest and create additional fields, which we will plant and maintain regularly, for our own needs as well as for the city. Of course, everyone has to have enough to eat. Otherwise, we cannot wage war. We'll start right away once the basic training is over."

Aritomo wiped his towel over his forehead. Inugami had evidently thought about everything thoroughly. The Captain pursued his plans not only with great vigor but also with a certain circumspection. Nevertheless, Aritomo was sure ...

"I gave Lengsley and Sarukazaki another order," Inugami informed him. Aritomo looked up in alarm. The ideas just spilled out this man and each held the potential of further dangers for all of them. He could barely keep up with Inugami, who was slowly outgrowing himself.

"They're supposed to sit down with the local craftsmen – stonemasons, weapons manufacturers, and architects and builders, who seem to have some technical understanding. We have to get involved in weapon development. We need superiority in tactics, strategy, numbers, discipline of the troops – and their equipment. I want better protection, armor, so that atlatls fired from a distance no longer automatically lead to fatal wounds. The shields they use are inadequate. They are made of wood and animal skin or woven mats. And I want better offensive capabilities."

"The bow," Aritomo muttered. "There are small bows used for hunting, but the weapon of choice is the atlatl. If we could develop longbows ... The materials are available. Only for really good armor, we lack the metal. We have to find some ores, and that seems to be difficult, otherwise obsidian wouldn't be so important around here."

Inugami nodded. "I like how you think. Sit down with them, if you can. Keep an eye on the discussions. We should concentrate on a few key improvements and implement them consistently. Slipping would be a mistake. We set clear priorities and don't do everything that might be desirable."

"Yes," Aritomo replied. "And what about the wheel? I think it's a priority."

"Yes, the wheel. It doesn't help us much without a draft animal. We *need* a draft animal. Until then, however, we should construct carts drawn by six men, such as ox or horse-drawn carriages. They will be slow but with a good chassis still better and more effective than transporting goods on your back. I also want Lengsley and Sarukazaki to think about war machines. We have to impress. If we manage to build catapults – two or three are enough – and fire suitable ammunition, which is above all effective ... fire pots or something combustible is always good, and in case it rains, something with shrapnel ... bags of obsidian shards bursting open, maybe ... it will impress any opponent, even if the actual effectiveness is limited. But if we cause fear and surprise, that's at least as good as a few well-placed explosions."

Inugami's voice was lost, as he stared thoughtfully into the distance, deep in thought. Aritomo had heard him well and could not help agreeing with Inugami's plans. If the ammunition of the rifles and the cannon was used up – apart from the fact that it would be very difficult to dismantle the latter and put it on a gun carriage to make it mobile –, then they would have to have other weapons with which they could scare their enemies. Their superiority had to be made visible, even in symbolic gestures that might not have had a rash in a battle for purely material reasons, but whose psychological impact was not to be underestimated.

Inugami had a considerable amount of empathy. What a pity, Aritomo thought, that he used it all for the question of how he managed to control his allies and destroy his enemies.

"I'll sit with them," Aritomo said again, lest Inugami hear his doubts and concerns. The captain seemed content, took another sip of water and glanced at his watch.

"Another hour of endurance training," he explained. "Then we take a break for a quick meal. This afternoon we will start with drill exercises. Marching, correct placement, basic commands. We have to make them a coherent unit, and nothing helps more than a proper march formation, a few clear drill-maneuvers, and ..."

He paused.

"A song."

He looked at Aritomo.

"We need a song, Second Lieutenant. Our song. Ours alone, the song of the Imperial-Japanese army on Mayan soil, one we will all sing when we go into battle, a song which will carry fear into the hearts of our enemies."

Inugami's flow of ideas really didn't end, and this particular one proved that he was aware of the psychological component of his plans. The idea was absolutely obvious. The Maya knew many songs – he had already heard a few –, but a loud, harmoniously war song, supported by ...

"Drums," Aritomo said almost against his will. "The Maya have something similar, they call it *tukul*. It consists of a hollow tree that is struck with a kind of rod."

"That's not enough. Real drums. A hard, penetrating tone, with eight or ten of them, perfectly tuned, a rousing rhythm." Inugami looked piercingly at Aritomo. "Drums, Second Lieutenant. And a song. Take care of that."

Aritomo bowed his head.

Inugami was on the right track. He created a devoted army that would be more disciplined and scary than any previous Mayan force. And he would use it. He would let it grow up in battle, shared experiences. He would equip and cherish them and praise them, and their reputation would rise, and only to him would they obey and do whatever he commanded.

Inugami was on the right path, and he thought of everything.

But where would this path lead to ...

184

It was time. Inugami got up, shouting something. There was movement in the crowd, swift, obedient, without any delay. Nobody wanted to be chastised.

The men rose. One hour of endurance training.

Aritomo was grateful for that.

26

Lengsley left the palace and involuntarily stood under the opened canopy of the side entrance. An ominous thunder greeted him. The sky had darkened, like a leaden wall that seemed to swallow the light of the sun. The Briton watched as Mayan women, with children in their arms, quickened their pace. He saw how the windows on buildings were covered with mats. There was a bustle everywhere, despite the sweltering heat of midday. Normally, every activity stalled at lunchtime, and Lengsley couldn't blame anyone. It was sultry-hot, and every movement seemed to lead immediately to violent outbreaks of sweat. Breathing was sometimes difficult and every movement was agony. Even in Japan there were warm summers with almost tropical temperatures, but the climate here tested the Briton's endurance.

The Maya had grown up in this environment, but they too were just humans. At midday one sought the shade, tried to rest, did only the most important business. There was a nap inside the buildings or under one of the wide-spreading trees that were planted all over the city – and for good reason, as Lengsley now realized. Even the animals looked sluggish and slack, now that the sun was highest. A serene calm covered the metropolis at these times.

Today it was different, and the cause was the violent weather that was ringing in the sky. A tropical storm would soon come down on them and have both positive and negative effects. It would purify the air and lower the temperatures a bit, it would bring air movement, and thus cooling within the houses. And it could be potentially destructive if the masses of water hit with pristine force like a wall that hit the roofs with sudden gusts of wind, a real force of nature. The city had been cleverly built, all the major boulevards and squares were either slightly sloping or had drainage channels, so there was usually no stagnant water to worry about. The large reservoirs had drain valves that were opened to release any surplus. But out in the suburbs, where the fields were planted, the situation was more difficult. The terraces were able to soften and sink, precious earth could be washed away. And the simple clay buildings of the farmers, not as magnificent, elaborate and stable as the buildings of the city center, threatened to be destroyed as well.

Lengsley was no expert, but the dark blue wall of cloud that swept all over the sky and came steadily closer, sending off the first gust of wind, which blew through his hair and caused the tarpaulin shading at the entrance to the palace to chatter, suggested a particularly intense event. He looked down the street in the direction of the submarine and wondered if he would make the path to it with his feet still dry. No sooner had he formulated this thought than a thick drop of water fell on the floor right in front of him and splashed dust away.

That was probably the answer to the question.

It took less than ten seconds for a wall of water to break down the tarpaulin. He felt a hand on his arm, which pulled him back a step, and then one of the wooden supports collapsed, the tarp slid down and poured an extra barrage of water on the floor of mashed soil, which in a few moments turned into a mud bed.

Lengsley glanced around and saw a young woman, dressed in the robes of a high-ranking lady, nod her head and then gesticulate. Lengsley looked at her hands, which were surprisingly long and delicate, not just the hands of a lady who had never seriously worked with them. Lengsley was a man who trusted his hands and had to rely on their skills over and over again. The hands of this woman had never skinned animals, never washed clothes, never mashed corn, never cut hard with the obsidian knife. But they had the powerful grace of a movement that pointed out that they ...

Lengsley bowed, rummaged for the chunks of Maya in his head – now, after all the weeks of daily, several-hour study in the class of the Sawada, maybe a little more than just chunks – and then said hopefully, "Thank you, noble lady. You saved me from a great misfortune."

He must have been reasonably correct, for the young woman smiled and waved him back inside the palace. "Follow me, messenger. It will take a while."

Lengsley glanced outside and found that the sky was now dark, and the tropical storm began to affect the city badly. No one who was reasonably sane remained in the open air.

For lack of a reasonable alternative, he followed his savior. They didn't walk for long but soon ended in a larger room that looked like a workshop. The Briton now recognized where the impression of power and experience that the young woman's hands had given him came from. She sat here amidst feathers, fabrics, and other utensils, and seemed to be busy making headscarves that Mayan noblemen liked to wear on special occasions, and whose artistry and splendor gave a more accurate account of their respective social status than Lengsley was able to gauge so far.

"Sit down," she said, pointing to a stool on the wall.

The Briton obeyed. The young woman, too, squatted down, looked at her manual work for a moment, then picked up one of the head plasters and arranged feathers. She said nothing, was engrossed in her work, and Lengsley was able to familiarize himself with the movements of her hands, which radiated the certainty of years of practice, showed a remarkable speed, and seemed to work almost without the conscious intervention of her mistress. Then his eyes fell on the concentrated face of the woman; he admired the flawlessness of the light brown skin, the large, dark eyes that were constantly fixed on the headdress, the deep black hair tied back. Her face was quite narrow, which Lengsley's impression was unusual for the Mayan women, and he had already noticed at their brief meeting that her otherwise beautiful teeth lacked the upper right incisor.

The rain drummed on the palace, and thunder repeatedly swallowed every other sound. Even if Lengsley had known the words he would use to start a conversation, it would've been difficult to communicate clearly. There was nothing left for him but to wait for the end of the storm.

His attention was distracted by a suddenly appearing maid who gave Lengsley a questioning sidelong glance but otherwise just

188

dropped to her knees beside the working woman and whispered something in her ear, answered by a nod. Then she whispered back a bit, and the servant hurried out of the room, only to return a short time later with a wooden tray and some food, including the usual stuffed corn cakes, and silently put it in front of him. Lengsley was indeed hungry, but he shied away from eating for fear of being considered rude. Only when the woman with the headdress looked up and made an encouraging gesture in his direction, he decided to accept the offer.

The rain continued.

Lengsley's regret over this fact was limited. He was sitting in the dry, with a full stomach and a very agreeable company, who gave him a very charming smile at regular intervals, which somehow got a particularly cheerful feeling resulting from the gap in her teeth, though that was surely only an interpretation by himself. He always tried to return the smile and to avoid any impression that he felt bored in her presence. Eventually, however, his knees hurt from sitting on the quite low stool, and he got up cautiously, took a few steps to start the blood circulation in his legs again, and looked around a bit, although he had already thoroughly inspected the room with his eyes.

"I'm Une Balam, a sister of the king," the woman suddenly said.

The Briton was a little embarrassed at once – it would probably have been necessary by etiquette if he had first introduced himself, and he hadn't even tried, because he was extremely uncertain of his language skills. He hurried to introduce himself, and he liked how the woman – a royal princess, not less! –, rolled his name around in her mouth until she got the pronunciation amazingly perfect.

"Do people in your country carry such a thing?" she asked slowly, pointing to her handiwork.

"No. There are many ways to cover one's head, but not such a way. Our rulers wear a metal crown. It is very heavy."

Une Balam smiled. "This is heavy, too, once I'm done with it."

"I believe that."

"It is as hot in your country and it is raining as intensive?"

"That's possible, but much rarer than here. It's usually colder, and the rain is weaker, but it lasts longer." Lengsley sighed as his memory of the rainy British weekends came to life. "Much longer."

"You miss it?"

"I'm not feeling at home yet, if that's the question. It's all very strange."

"You are afraid of many things."

"Many things and the future."

"Ah, but that's stupid."

Une Balam made a reprimanding gesture. Lengsley didn't feel offended, though the woman spoke to him as if he were a naughty child. He found it a welcome relief to the conversations of recent weeks, which had always been about planning war or defenses, with a silent threat that had laid above every word.

"The gods finally determine everything. It will happen as it should. We can ask for mercy, but ultimately we are at the mercy of higher powers. Do we know exactly when we enrage the gods and when our behavior is pleasing to them? The priests claim to understand it, but with all their wisdom I can hardly believe it."

She paused, as if to make sure Lengsley understood everything well. She spoke slowly and emphatically, and once she used an English word, so she had come to enjoy one or more language lessons at some detour. Itzanami, the docile priest, was probably a very, very hardworking man during this time, and taught his throat to hoarseness, without the crew of the submarine learning too much about it.

"So what are you afraid of? Everything happens as it should. Just look. Outside, a rainstorm is raging. Suddenly the roof can break in and kill me. I can take a step outside, and lightning strikes me down. Floods swell and carry me along. Why the worry? I sit here and do my work, enjoy this beautiful piece. That's far better than thinking about what might be."

Lengsley was not sure which devil rode him when he formulated his answer. "When the floods come and carry you away, I will do my best to save you, Princess. That is the least with which I can repay your hospitality."

190

Une Balam smiled mischievously then set aside her handiwork and looked Lengsley straight in the eye.

"So, you see, I don't have to be scared. Why are you? Didn't I save you from the rain, messenger? And from hunger? And from boredom? Three times you have already escaped a desperate fate today. From this you should learn a valuable lesson."

The Briton indicated a bow. "I appreciate your wisdom, princess."

"I hope you find something else worthy of me. Otherwise, you would hardly want to plunge into the floods for my rescue."

"You are a princess. It would be my duty."

"Ah, duty." Une Balam smiled back through her tooth gap and shook her head. "How convenient that you can always go back to that one word."

Lengsley didn't quite understand what she meant – or he lacked the vocabulary –, so he decided to give up on an answer and remained silent. The rain outside seemed to relax a little, if one trusted the sounds. His stay here came to an end, and he was surprised to find that the prospect was not pleasant.

He remained a little hesitant. How did he say goodbye in a way that was not considered rude and made a bad impression? The princess didn't seem to attach much importance to a certain etiquette, but above all he didn't want to appear ungrateful and not too brusque …

He had an idea.

"I'd like to reciprocate your hospitality," he said several times, until he was reasonably sure the lady had understood his intent. "Assuming the captain of our vessel agrees, I'll invite you on board and show you the inside."

In fact, Inugami regularly agreed to such sightseeing tours because he was keen to impress the Maya. As the cramped interior of the boat also provoked near-claustrophobic reactions in many of the visitors, adding to the fear of the strange apparition – and those who "mastered" it –, this was definitely a welcome effect.

Lengsley's intention wasn't to scare the young lady. But if she was curious, he wanted to give her the opportunity to satisfy her interest.

Une Balam didn't seem to want to ponder the offer for too long. She seemed to be quite pleased. An expectant glint was in her eyes, and her approval came immediately.

"I would be very happy if that was possible. So far I've only had to listen to the men's descriptions." She paused. "It also seems that the messengers don't carry women with them. Are there so few of us in the country you came from?"

"Not at all," Lengsley hurried to say. "But we do not usually take them on dangerous trips."

Une Balam nodded; this practice may have been known to her as well. It was rather uncommon for women to go on military campaigns, though not impossible – the Maya also knew female rulers, who often went to war with the same fighting spirit and determination as their husbands, and were not very apprehensive when it came to exterminate their rivals.

Rightly, Une Balam's interest in visiting the boat could also be related to the fact that, according to Lengsley's memory, not a single woman had ever been inside the vehicle. Sure, there were women who climbed the pyramid, usually heavily laden with food, which they brought to the messengers for their daily provisions. But this was then deposited on one of the pyramidal steps, or at best on the foredeck, and brought inside by the men. A woman ... no, the Briton didn't indeed remember that a woman had ever entered the interior of the boat. If the princess could claim to have been the first, perhaps this had an impact on her reputation among her mates? Lengsley could only assume that, he had no knowledge of the relationships of women in the upper class of Mutal to each other to be able to evaluate this conclusively. But Une Balam's zeal would be explained by this.

It was, in any case, only proper.

His offer had also been the ideal prelude to his farewell. The rain had stopped. As he stepped outside with the Princess, they both took a deep breath. The pleasant smell of the refreshing cool air wouldn't last long, but for a moment it was a treat. Lengsley said goodbye once more and was dismissed by Une Balam with a gracious wave of her hand.

As the Briton marched across the damp and slightly muddy ground and headed for the boat, his thoughts kept wandering back and forth about his recent meeting with the young woman. In his mind's eye, what a weird combination, the smile with a tooth gap mingled with skilled, quick fingers.

He was looking forward to her visit and decided to ask Inugami for the small tour soon enough.

When Lengsley reached the boat, he came to the surprising conclusion that he was in a really good mood for the first time since his arrival in this strange world.

27

It was late evening when Balkun curled up on his mat and closed his eyes. He felt every one of his bones, and no matter how he lay down, something tweaked and ached in his body. During the long day of training they had been scrutinized by the messengers and been given sufficient food and drink. After the exercises the order was given to retire immediately. They were all slaves and did as they were told. Balkun was no exception. He wasn't willing to provide beatings or other punishments by mere stubbornness, and he was indeed terribly exhausted. Obedient he had laid down, judging his fate to consist of the seemingly endless row of exercises and lectures. But whether it was the heavy cornbread in his stomach or the ubiquitous pains that run through every fiber of his body, or the thoughts, the memory of his life before the great defeat, in any case, he just couldn't find sleep. He struggled with himself for a while. His mind was busy and restless like never before in his life, not even like when he had begun the campaign of conquest under the command of the King of Yaxchilan, which had ended so disastrously for all of them.

Well, Tatb'u's had turned out to be a lot more catastrophic than his own. Balkun had emerged from the battles only slightly injured – he had to admit that he'd never been a particularly eager soldier and had always preferred domestic farm work to warcraft. Every time the King called for a campaign, Balkun had followed the call with mixed feelings. He had the impression that fame, honor and loot were in the aftermath of the greatest victory always a little ... unevenly distributed. Well, a clever man with alert eyes, of course, always found an opportunity to load his back with valuable goods, and Balkun didn't want to be unfair. He had a strong back that held up a weight, and one time or another, he had returned to his wife adequately laden, which she had noted with benevolence.

194

Balkun seized upon the thought of his wife and three children. Two sons and a daughter, who now had to tend to the fields alone and in uncertainty about the fate of their father. Balkun prayed for their and his strength in order to return to them, though he didn't expect to see his family so soon. He lived and reminded himself of that fact again and again. As long as he lived, there was hope, and that feeling sustained him. Others were less comfortable with it, struggling with their fate, and wondering again and again how a campaign that had begun under such wonderful signs could have ended so horribly. The doubts tormenting them were both of a military and spiritual nature, along with fear about their individual fate.

After all, they were taken care of, and almost none of them felt had the sacrificial knife. This was unusual, but the strange teachings and behaviors of the messengers fitted well with this fact.

Balkun knew that death came faster than expected. The messengers forged a military force out of the prisoners, one, as there has never been one before had never in the land of the corn people. Balkun was already a better fighter than when he attacked Mutal, and he had been a veteran of three campaigns. He became a real warrior, and the farmer in himself felt like a flower without water. The thought didn't suit him. A warrior only made sense if used. And it was an assignment that entailed the danger of dying. But Balkun wanted only one thing: to return and have a peaceful life on his land. Should kings and messengers fight their wars themselves. They could sacrifice their blood to the gods as they pleased.

Why did they have to involve him in the matter?

Balkun was highly dissatisfied with his situation, although he had to admit that the messengers tended their slaves properly. They were not hungry, and nobody had to sleep outdoors. Only the very stupid or very independent minded were beaten, but even there nobody was crippled or even killed. And they promised them a return to their three cities, as conquerors and then as an army of the messengers, who preserved law and order for the newly appointed rulers. If all went well, Balkun would become a man of some standing who deserved respect, whether slave or not, a perspective that made some happy. But the good treatment gave the opportunity to brood, and that didn't suit everyone.

Balkun didn't trust his luck. It had proven to be quite unreliable at last. Moreover, he didn't look for respect outside his family. It was this addiction to reputation and false immortality that had led to the death of Yaxchilan's king and the defeat of his army. Balkun was anything but stupid. He drew his own conclusions.

Maybe he should draw fewer conclusions, he thought, think less. There were fewer problems if he did so. Then he might also find sleep. The messengers had announced something for tomorrow, which they called a "very strenuous march", and that consisted of circumnavigating Mutal's city limits, divided into small units, within a certain time and under careful supervision. They would all be heavily packed. The victorious unit, according to Inugami, their new general, would receive chi and one day off duty. Balkun found this prospect quite auspicious, but was by no means certain that it justified the effort involved.

He closed his eyes. The loud snoring of his comrades didn't help him find the desired peace. And when he listened in, the images of his children rose in his mind's eye immediately and absolutely uncontrollably, and the pain involved was stronger than any need for sleep. He cursed himself. He cursed the King of Yaxchilan for his arrogance, and he cursed Mutal's new masters for not letting the prisoners go home, as had been the case on previous occasions, after making an example of the nobles and leaders. But there was no doubt about his status. He remembered what had happened to the two men who had tried to escape at night. Their corpses had been presented to the assembled crew the next morning, without much comment. The grim glances of Mutal's soldiers, who had picked up the deserters, spoke for themselves.

Balkun sensed that he simply had to survive. He had to trust the promises of the messengers. If he served well, he would be reunited with his family. He would live a good life, far from anything else imagined as slavery. He had to believe it, so as not to go completely crazy.

196

Balkun heard a noise. It sounded different from the usual sounds of the night, and that caught his attention. He rose to his elbows, listening to the darkness. There, again. It sounded like the night when the two deserters had gone, a paw of footsteps, a suppressed whisper. Balkun looked around. There was no one among the warriors who stirred. They all slept enviably. And the guards kept away from the slaves' camp, patrolling the surrounding streets, the edge of the woods, all the escape routes that one could imagine, though there were certainly others.

Balkun straightened up completely.

He turned his head in the direction of the sounds.

Then he got up. He climbed over his neighbor's body, stepped out from under the roof of the large balustrade that formed the camp with others like it, until the buildings were finished, which were called "barracks" and would be equal in size and extent to a temple.

The night was bright, a clear sky from which a three-quarter moon and the stars were shining. Out of the darkness, two figures peered in crouched attitudes, their eyes fixed on the torches of the guardhouse. There, four of the slaves pushed the night watch, and as Balkun knew from experience, they were not half as attentive as one would expect. If these two figures were unannounced visitors or deserters, the guards would be in for a lot of trouble. The lord of the messengers wouldn't hesitate to publicly chastise the men. He seemed to take a certain pleasure in it, though he was careful to beat only those who had actually been deserving because of their gross misconduct.

Balkun's eyes narrowed. The way the two moved was clearly aimed at moving undiscovered, and no one had noticed their presence except for the sleepless Yaxchilan man. Balkun thought for a moment to just lie back down and pretend that nothing had happened. The two men might be up to no good, but surely the slaves wouldn't be the target of their intentions. But then he thought of his fellow sufferers in the guardhouse and the torments they would expect if the two intruders not only went undetected, but seriously ... did something. Whatever they were going to do.

Balkun made a decision, even if it wasn't easy. He stepped out into the dim darkness of the night and followed both figures. He knew his way around here by now. In the surrounding fields he had come to know the earth more closely and intensely than he ever thought possible, sometimes with his face pressed into the dirt, the heel of a trainer in the neck, the ultimate submission, and an intense, harsh lesson in that what Inugami demanded of them when a supervisor shouted loudly "Cover!"

Balkun felt at an advantage, and he wanted to use it. Maybe something came out o fit for him in the end. It wasn't the loyalty to his new masters that drove him. It was the thought of his children and the yearning for them that inspired him to do this. Perhaps ...

The two figures moved.

Balkun followed.

He kept proper distance. If anyone should become aware of the two strangers, he did not want to be associated with them. How soon could you turn from an attentive warrior to a co-conspirator, no matter what the two were up to?

The road led away from the slave warrior's quarters, into the city. Several times they encountered the nocturnal patrols roaming the broad streets of the center of Mutal, big torches in their fists, spreading their wisp of light over the sleeping city. Balkun knew that now he himself began to do something very wrong, because he wasn't allowed to leave the well-defined area that served them for accommodation and training.

But he couldn't go back. He not only needed to know what was happening here, he also had to make sure that his entrance was favorably staged.

The two men didn't seem to be lost at all. They knew where they could stop and wait for the guards to pass by. Balkun also felt that the guards were less numerous tonight than usual. Perhaps Inugami began to put some confidence in the discipline of his men.

The strangers approached the king's palace with a certain determination. Here, the number of guards would increase significantly. Balkun hesitated again. Shouldn't he return? It was almost impossible to invade the palace unrecognized. There were sentinels at every entrance. And they were known to take their job very seriously. When they were found asleep, the next day they hung eviscerated by a tree trunk, a fate that wasn't very pleasant to anyone.

Balkun overcame his hesitation.

This was also because the two strangers didn't want to go to the palace at all but apparently expected someone to come out. In the dim light, he was only able to recognize that they were probably men. The third person had easily stepped out of the side entrance of the mighty structure and then quickly disappeared into the shady darkness where the two arrivals had been waiting.

Balkun sneaked closer. He couldn't see much but maybe could listen.

He had good ears. Those who had children running around in the fields with youthful recklessness had to have good ears.

He moved in, careful to make as little noise as possible. Scraps of voice came to him, and he closed his eyes to concentrate. There, now he could grasp what was being discussed.

"That's all?"

"The paste is very suitable. The fire will spread quickly. We milked the tree for hours, three long nights. You just have to smear it evenly."

"I don't want to burn myself."

"You escape in time. Not too early. The fire must be big enough."

"I know a way."

"Well."

"And you keep your promise?"

"As agreed. Your daughter marries my son, you yourself become high priest."

"The House."

"And the house. It's yours."

"And not a word."

"The winners write history. When everything is done, you will be honored. Not a word before, as it has been agreed."

Balkun came more and more to the conclusion that the two strangers were no strangers at all. The fact that they were sneaking through the city at night was more likely to be due to the fact that they generally didn't want to be seen. Maybe they had done something at the edge of the forest near the training grounds. Balkun knew what kind of paste the unknown man was talking about. There was a resin that, when scratched from the tree, formed an excellent foundation for kindling a fire, much better than wood or straw. A small spark was enough, and a big campfire, covered with resin, exploded in seconds. Most housewives didn't use it because it was barely controllable. It was usually kept very carefully in neatly closing clay jugs, outside the house, far away from every fire pit. If you ever used it. In any case, this paste didn't exist in Balkun's house. It was a bit more cumbersome to use only wood or straw, but also more economical – the paste was never made in large quantities – and safer.

Balkun blinked. The yield of days and hours of resin extraction had to fill a decent clay jug. Igniting this paste at a central location in the palace, the mighty building would soon turn into a burning inferno.

An attack on the King!

His heart beat faster than he realized it.

Balkun should be happy about that.

Chitam was actually his enemy.

But he followed his spontaneous impulse again. He didn't run back to his sleeping place, he stayed and watched what happened. When the two men handed the pitcher to the figure from the palace, they stood for a moment in the faint moonlight. Balkun didn't know any of these men, and he didn't even know if he would recognize their faces beyond doubt in daylight.

But he understood determination when he saw her, and these three conspirators were determined.

"Tonight, then," said the traitor from the palace.

"Start right away."

Balkun suppressed a loud breather.

They wanted to take action immediately! This wasn't the preparation, this was the conclusion of their plans! Fear crawled up in his throat, feeling his knees soften momentarily. He clung to the wall of the house, in whose shadow he had remained. His thoughts were racing. He had to do something. Act. React. But what – how? For whom?

And what risk would he take?

The three men before him were not plagued by these doubts. No horror paralyzed them. The pitcher changed hands, some brief words were exchanged, and then the man from the palace broke away from the group, struggling back to unleash the great disaster he had conspired to do.

The other two men disappeared in the darkness.

Whom to follow?

Whom now?

Balkun stood there frozen, lost valuable seconds, but then he finally made a decision and went determinedly behind the traitor. Toward the palace. That might mean his end. But now there was no way back for him.

He heard a suppressed cry. He quickened his pace, almost stumbling as he saw the corpse of a warrior lying in front of him, in the area of a side access door to the palace, in the midst of a steadily growing pool of blood slowly drifting off the dusty ground. Naturally! Intruders from outside have set the fire, to this simple conclusion any investigation would come. Much better than having to deal with the unpleasant and painful realization of a betrayal.

Balkun stepped cautiously over the body of the dead man, murdered by another whom he must have recognized as his equal, for there was no sign of resistance. Treachery of the worst sort, and Balkun felt bitter bile rising in him. Tatb'u may have been a megalomaniac king and had led his army blindly to destruction – but he had faced the enemy openly on the battlefield. He deserved respect for that.

This traitor, however, deserved nothing else but contempt.

Balkun hurried into the darkness of the barely lit corridors. He didn't know his way around here. He had never entered the palace of Yaxchilan, a bit smaller than this building with its meandering suites and narrow doors. He had been a warrior and a peasant; the only buildings of value to him were the hut of his family and the temples to which he had hurried to pray to the gods. Palaces had always been very far away for him, and he had never developed a particular ambition to change that.

But it was wonderfully quiet.

He heard footsteps and a thud. The sound of someone putting on a clay jug that was well filled. Balkun stopped, listened, oriented himself, took a few steps in the hopefully correct direction. He cursed softly as he bumped his knee against a low dresser he hadn't noticed, pausing again, hoping no one had heard him.

It would be bad to be arrested as an assassin now, while the true threat could accomplish his work undisturbed. That would fit well. A revenge from a slave. He would play into the hands of the conspirators.

He took a few more steps, stood by a door frame, heard a characteristic crackle, then a hissing sound, and felt a heat wave strike him.

He started screaming. He screamed with all his fervor. "K'aak!"

The warning spread. People awoke.

Balkun went on, saw someone rush past him, ignoring him, a person who also invoked the loud "K'aak!" shouts, and yet, it must have been the traitor.

Another scream, this time no warning but a cry of horror. Balkun rushed forward, his arms jerking as he stared into the conflagration, which was spreading rapidly, eagerly eating the walls and carpets, and furniture, fueled by the resin of the tree, giving the heat a frenzied, insatiable power.

He backed away, feeling his hair smolder. There, another door, not yet attacked by the fire. Through the smoke, he recognized the helpless figure of a child staring at the deadly force, crying, paralyzed. A girl about the same age as ...

Balkun didn't think.

He jumped forward, hopping lightly over a burning carpet, standing in the doorway, yanked the girl, who didn't resist, already half unconscious through the pungent smoke. Balkun felt the flames lick his skin, felt the burning pain of searing flesh on his ankles, jumped again, wide, with all his strength, suddenly grateful for the hard training in the army of the messengers.

202

He felt the heat under him as he propelled himself over the flames, and he struggled for balance as his feet touched the ground again.

No time to hesitate. Balkun ran into the chaos of the palace, where now everyone had awakened and warriors had begun to evacuate the rooms, to tear the sleepers out of their slumber. He saw servants rushing up with water jugs and blankets, and he saw them shrink back in fear from the brutal intensity of the heat coming from the fire. He dragged the girl out, away from the smoke, gasping and coughing, filling his lungs with fresh air, then staggering to his knees and feeling the child's release from his arms. A sudden weakness spread in his body.

He heard shouts and cries from men who gave orders and tried to bring order to chaos.

He looked around, regained his strength. Everywhere people ran around. Then he beheld the figure of the King, who wore no more than a loincloth but was obviously safe. He saw the Queen, who stood there, weeping and crying, looking around, pleading with her husband for something. The serious face of Chitam spoke volumes as he took the Lady Tzutz in his arms and reassured her. Then the King looked up, his eyes piercing the chaos, and he fell directly into Balkun's eyes … no … something to the side.

The girl!

Moments later, Tzutz stormed in and embraced the crying child, then listened to the excited narrative, a waterfall of words that could have extinguished the raging fire alone, it was made of moisture. Balkun felt uplifted by the strong arm of Chitam, and he heard words that he understood slowly, full of gratitude and praise and …

That was the King's daughter, Balkun realized, and he managed a faint grin. He looked down at the violently reddened skin on his legs, which burned and stretched uncomfortably over the flesh. He knew what burns were like, and he knew it was not quite as bad as it looked. And apart from the lower legs, a little at the ankles, the fire had spared him.

Someone handed him a big cloth, damp with cool water, and Balkun squatted, wrapped the wounds in the fabric, enjoyed the pleasant feeling of relief, and found the power to smile. He took the cup of water, which was served to him at the behest of the King, drank greedily, coughed, drank again, and the invigorating power of the liquid filled him.

"What's your name?" the King asked.

"Balkun, sir. I belong ... I am a ..."

"Your clothes tell me. You are one of the slaves of the messenger's army."

Balkun bowed his head.

"What are you doing outside your camp during the night?"

The man from Yaxchilan began, first hesitantly, then increasingly fluent, to report on his experiences that night. Chitam listened to him as attentively as Queen Tzutz, who still clutched her daughter after she had been well supplied with water. Around them, the turmoil of the rescue continued. Human chains were formed from the nearby reservoir, bringing in water. The extinguishing work was in full swing, but it was already apparent that it was more about protecting adjacent buildings. The palace was beyond salvation and would probably have to be rebuilt from scratch.

When Balkun had finished his description, Chitam nodded thoughtfully. "You have done well, Balkun. I'll talk to the Lord of the Gods. You should be freed. You shall receive honors and return to your homeland."

Balkun suppressed his joy. While Chitam might approve of this, Balkun had the feeling that the power in Mutal was not quite as clearly distributed as the King hoped. And he had a good reason to have legitimate doubts about his imminent release.

"Can you describe the man who was responsible for all this?"

Balkun's vague portrayal was frowned at by Chitam, and the slave didn't mind the King's reaction. He had only briefly seen the man. If he faced him, he might recognize him. Or not. It would prove fatal if he accused the wrong guy.

Fatal especially for Balkun, when his mistake became known.

Before the King could ask any more questions, one of his men approached him. "Lord, we have been able to save almost all people from the palace in time. The early warning helped. Two servants inhaled too much smoke and are struggling to catch their breath.

204

There are burns, and there will be scars." The man looked down at the still standing Balkun and nodded to him. "This man saved many lives tonight, my King."

"He did," Chitam replied, giving Lady Tzutz and her daughter a long, warm look. He looked at Balkun and added, "We'll talk later. You remain at my disposal."

Balkun just bowed, coughed and nodded.

While the King returned to the firefighting operation, Balkun crouched and sank into deep brooding. He recalled the events of the night and followed his own steps and observations until then.

He knew why he feared that Inugami would not be pleased with the exploits of his runaway slave. Of course, Balkun couldn't be sure. Maybe there was a dispute among the messengers, or someone wanted to take matters into their own hands. Anyway, Balkun was determined to keep one important fact to himself until further notice.

Namely, that one of the two men who had given the assassin the pitcher with the tree resin – and for that Balkun took every oath! – had been a messenger of the gods.

28

Sarukazaki held a list that both Inugami and Aritomo regarded with a sorrowful expression. They were all exhausted, for the palace fire had also necessitated the help of the submarine's crew. At first, Inugami had refused to provide the boat's medical supplies for the treatment of the wounded, but then there'd been burns that turned out to be very painful, with many a child and many a woman affected. A pitiful sight and none that could leave one cold. After all, Inugami had finally softened, especially since the supplies of burn ointment were sufficient and they wouldn't last forever anyway. On board the boat were two men with paramedics training, and both set to work on orders. Aritomo had also given them an extra instruction – they should also look closely at the treatment methods of the Mayan healers and try to identify those medicinal plants they used to care for their patients. Even the crew of the submarine would need such treatment before long, and it was only proper to prepare for the day it became necessary.

Otherwise, they had helped with the cleanup, where it was possible. This help, as Inugami had finally admitted, was a good idea, because it showed the commitment of the messenger even in mundane things. The Maya were shaken by the fire and agitated, a similar attack had never occurred in the history of the city. Rumors flew around, and the center of attention was a man from Inugami's Janissary Army, who had distinguished himself by his timely warning and courageous intervention. Although Inugami had been very angry that the soldier had left his camp without permission, he knew he needed to put a nice face on the issue right now. He had publicly praised the man named Balkun eloquently. More hadn't happened so far.

But today it was about Sarukazaki's list. The fact that the engineer had also been joined Sawada and Lengsley suggested that they were facing a very exhausting meeting, the contents of which would not give them much pleasure.

At least, Aritomo took that from the engineer's expression as he sat down with a bow following the captain's invitation. It was, as always, very hot, and they had set up a table and chairs on the foredeck of the boat, shaded by a stretched tarpaulin that fortunately had been part of the boat's equipment. The shade protected them from direct sunlight, but today's almost immobile air, with its heavy moisture, made breathing very strenuous. Not far from here, smoke rose from the ruins of the palace. Aritomo's gaze kept falling on the smoldering ruin. It was a depressing symbol that they were vulnerable here, in the middle of Mutal. He had doubled the guards and wanted to talk to the warrior slave who had saved the lives of the palace, but so far Chitam had denied him access.

And Inugami hadn't made it a big affair yet. A restraint that was almost uncharacteristic.

"Captain, we've been here for a few weeks now, and the problems are starting, just as we expected." The technician nodded to Lengsley to show who he meant exactly "we." Inugami made a gesture of agreement.

"For one thing, we're going to run out of diesel shortly. We have the engines running again and again to recharge the batteries. Without electricity, we can't illuminate the boat and stay in it, we can also perform no maintenance. It was our effort to handle the diesel as carefully as possible, and we saved where we could, but even with the strictest rationing, we might have two weeks left." Sarukazaki paused, frowning. "Unfortunately, that has some very unpleasant consequences. For one, we can't orient ourselves properly inside the boat. If the batteries are not charged regularly and if we can no longer operate the electric motors, there is a risk that they will lose their functionality. The batteries are especially a big concern for me. Sooner or later it will not matter if we get the boat off the top of the temple or not, it will simply not be functional anymore. So we have to make several decisions about that."

Sarukazaki looked up, gazing at Lengsley, who apparently had nothing to add.

"There's more to the list," Aritomo said. "We want to hear everything."

The man nodded. "Yes, sir." He lifted the paper and continued talking. "Things are looking better with the cannon and the weapons. We used up a bit of ammo when we fended off the attack on Mutal, but supplies are still sufficient, especially as we don't have to waste cartridges for hunting or anything like that. The cannon is in good condition. If we take care of it, it should continue to serve us for a while. The problem lies elsewhere: Despite all our measures to support the boat, the battle has negatively affected the static position. If we walk around on it, it's not so bad, but I specifically want to warn against firing the cannon again until we find a permanent solution. Lengsley?"

The Briton stretched. Apparently, that was his part now. "We have two options – actually three. We can rebuild the base of the boat, but serious construction work is needed. More or less it would be necessary to rebuild the building under the boat and deliberately plan its architecture to serve as a permanent platform for the boat and thus for the cannon. That is possible, and I think the Maya are well-qualified to do this quickly and effectively. The other option is to dismantle the cannon and place it on a stand-alone platform, which should also be deliberately designed only for this purpose. We could position it centrally so we could make the most of our reach, which would be a significant asset to the city's defense capability."

"The third option?" Aritomo asked.

Lengsley shrugged. "The boat has to go back into the water. The question is: Do we need a boat in the water and do we deprive ourselves of an important weapon, especially in defense of the city? This is a strategic rather than a tactical decision. It has to be clear what the boat means for us in the future and what we want to use it for. Whereby, as Sarukazaki said, a submarine without fuel is illusory anyway. We need diesel."

"Or something equivalent," the technician interjected.

"What do you mean?" Inugami asked.

"The machines are sturdy. We can operate it with poil. There are some minor modifications necessary, but we should get that done. The engines will then run with less power, but it should work."

"Poil?"

"Vegetable oil."

Inugami nodded slowly. He had a good enough understanding of the technology to follow the argument. An officer on a submarine was in many ways an all-rounder.

"What do we need for that?"

"First of all, suitable oil plants. I want to discuss the matter with some of the Maya. And on that basis I want to equip a small expedition and go on the search. I'm confident that we will quickly find suitable plants. Then I have to build a suitable apparatus for creating the distillate. The principle is not too complicated, and we have much of the necessary equipment on board, or we can make it with local resources. Once we have created the suitable formula, I can rebuild the machines and keep the engines running. Of course, this does not solve our long-term problem – spare parts, lubricants, everything. But we can't extend the life of diesel and electric motors if we can't operate them. I would therefore ask you, Captain, to give this project a high priority."

Inugami nodded. "I concur. Do what is necessary. If there is a problem, ask Second Lieutenant Aritomo. I want you to succeed."

"Yes, sir."

"The difficulty remains that we have to make a decision regarding the fate of our boat," Aritomo reminded them.

"It's related to other military decisions," Inugami replied. "Soon we will attack the two neighboring cities that joined the alliance with Yaxchilan against Mutal. I intend to conquer them permanently. This gives us direct access to a large lake, I have learned. It would be possible to position the boat there, which would not only give us a chance to travel quickly in a certain area, but also to find a good position for the cannon. Of course, this is just the first step. We also need to reach the shores in our expansion efforts. Only there we can make use of the submarine to its fullest extent. In any case, my decision is first: The boat must be moved. It has to go back to the water. We will not have to defend Mutal again soon." Inugami smiled bleakly. "We're going on the offensive."

Everywhere, Aritomo saw a confirming nod, even a look of anticipation – including Sawada and Sarukazaki. The prospect of a campaign, an empire didn't seem to deter them. Only Lengsley shared the first officer's doubts. Aritomo clenched his teeth. To address the topic here was meaningless. He exchanged a silent look with the Brit, who nodded imperceptibly. Lengsley was in an even weaker position here. He would be careful not to speak too boldly to Inugami. It was getting harder and harder – Inugami quickly learned and started to treat the Maya with arrogance, but ... more deliberately. Whether he would eventually show respect for the locals or whether this was only a charade for everyone to become loyal to him, remained to be seen.

"Then there's the point of technological development of the natives," Inugami said. Aritomo realized that he now rarely used the word "savage," another indication to the thought he had just cherished. "Sarukazaki's remarks point to a central problem: We will have to leave the submarine sometime. The machines will not work forever. The ammunition will be used up. Until then, we must, at least, have upgraded Mutal's warriors – and our own army, first of all – to a higher technical standard. We have to achieve some degree of superiority so that no other Mayan state can effectively put up meaningful resistance. That's why I need ideas."

Again, all eyes turned to the two professionals. This time it was Lengsley who spoke.

"The problem is metal. Give me metal. All right, for a start only copper. But we need more than just obsidian. The stone replaces the metal in many ways, but is less malleable and breaks more easy. We can't build an obsidian cannon. We can't build any claimable machines with small parts without metal. The Maya don't have a lot of metallurgy because they lack access to the most important resources. Give me metal, and I'll start making suggestions."

Inugami nodded. "You're right, Lengsley. And we have to search for it. Another expedition perhaps, as Sarukazaki has suggested.

But we can't rely on a quick fix. I need improvements right now. And if we only have obsidian, it's just that."

Inugami moved impatiently. At first nobody said anything, but then Sarukazaki hesitantly raised his hand.

"Speak!"

"I talked with Sawada about it … he's much better at history than I am. We discussed some ideas, not very much in detail. But we came up with some ideas that could be implemented if we got the necessary resources."

Inugami waved. "Suppose that we get everything we need in terms of existing materials and labor. What are your ideas?"

"Catapults and onagers, Captain. They are feasible with local resources. I would like to fire not so much obsidian missiles but rather bags with splinters that fly in all directions on impact. Very effective against massive attacks by warriors in close formation. Other projectiles would be good at fortifications, but so far we haven't noticed many of them. Most cities are not walled or even gated."

"That may change if the Maya get wind of these weapons," Lengsley said, and Inugami nodded to him.

Sarukazaki looked up from his notes. "By the way, that's something we can change with Mutal once the cannon is no longer available to us. A decent city wall, best with ditch and thick gates. The Maya do not seem to have developed a sophisticated siege tactic at the moment."

"We're going to go on the offensive," Inugami reminded him with a little indignation in his voice.

"Captain, with respect: Such a fortification is entirely within the abilities of the Mayan craftsmen and requires no additional inventions. If we go on the offensive …"

Aritomo helped the technician, who apparently had a problem teaching his captain. "Captain, if we conquer other cities and are perceived by them as a threat … collectively, I mean … there are two consequences: Some will submit to us because they are afraid, and others, especially the larger cities, will eventually form an alliance and try to attack us. And depending on how such a campaign proceeds, they may also approach Mutal. It is a logical first goal. We should prepare for such an eventuality. An offensive, as good as it works, has always included a strategic defensive. Everything else would be very unwise. And we can't assume that all these innovations will be a lasting advantage. The Maya are not stupid. They will look at the new weapons and then possibly copy them. Once that's the case, we'll need walls even more urgently. Sarukazaki is absolutely right."

Inugami looked at Aritomo. His eyes were pinched and he didn't reply at first, then came a slow nod.

"Well. I accept that," he said then addressed Sarukazaki. "Catapults and onagers. I'm not familiar enough with that. You will make drawings for me to understand what you intend to do. And we talk about the walls with the Mayan architects."

"Yes, sir." Sarukazaki gave Aritomo a grateful look.

Inugami looked around.

"Further points?"

Sawada raised his hand.

"Yes?"

"There are medical issues to discuss."

Inugami leaned forward.

"I think I know what you're aiming at."

Sawada cleared his throat. "I'm not talking about our medical supplies, which of course are running low as well. The point is that we have diseases that the Mayans are unaware of, and they have very specific problems that are completely new to us. I remember reports of what happened after the Spanish conquerors fought and overcome the natives. There was something similar to an extinction – and the causes were diseases such as the flu. Or measles. The same thing can happen here." Sawada sighed loudly. "I even fear it will be inevitable."

"People in Japan are dying from the flu, too."

"Yes of course. But many survive, and those who survive manage the next infection better. Our doctors have no cure, but they know the disease and can recognize it early and treat the symptoms. This alone increases the chances of survival already quite much. But we,

Captain, are the only ones, and the natives here ... they may be confronted with a disease that their bodies can't tolerate because they have never been exposed to it. I must urgently warn, this is the potential of disaster."

Inugami frowned. It was clear that he hadn't thought much about it so far.

"And the reverse is true as well. I can only speculate about that. I don't know about tropical diseases, but ... the malaria maybe? We don't have quinine," Sawada added.

"What do you suggest?"

"We have to pay attention to our health. If someone is sick – fever, runny nose, general weakness –, we need to isolate this person immediately. In addition, we have to think about hygiene – and about a hospital."

"A hospital?"

Sawada nodded seriously.

"With an isolation ward."

Inugami sighed.

"We need to improve our medical knowledge," Sawada went on, unimpressed. "Medicinal plants. Diseases and their symptoms. There are healers here. We must continue talking to the Maya, including about the treatment of the wounds after the palace disaster. We have to catalog knowledge. Write down therapies. It increases our life expectancy. We can't prepare properly because we don't know what to expect – but we should create structures that handle the unexpected better than it is now possible. In addition, you spoke of an offensive, Captain. Your vision is well-known to me. We will deal with injured people, not just the Maya. Let's be honest. Our men will sooner or later get into risky situations and possibly suffer injuries. It is therefore in our own interest that we can treat them as best we can. We are so few, Captain. And every dead person is a big loss. We must do everything we can to protect our health."

Aritomo saw that this last argument had drawn in Inugami. His critical thoughtfulness had turned into agreement. And Aritomo supported Sawada in his words. The teacher had addressed a fundamental and very important problem. And the list of things they still needed to do and organize was getting longer and longer.

That in turn meant …

Inugami looked at him. "Hara, you'll deal with Sawada and the Maya."

Aritomo bowed his head in silent agreement.

Exactly.

That's exactly what it meant.

What had become of clear priorities? They had so many pressing issues, it was almost impossible to establish a firm hierarchy to work through. And they were so few …

The rest of the conversation revolved around many more details, and both Lengsley and Sarukazaki proposed a lot of interesting suggestions, but their practicality was not always beyond doubt, at least for Aritomo. It wasn't just a matter of resources but also a challenge of having the right tools. In Aritomo's view, they lacked tools to build the tools needed for further development. It was such a complex problem that Aritomo didn't even know how big it actually was. He was glad that they had experts who dealt with these challenges.

When the meeting was over, Inugami waved, motioning him to stay a little longer. He grabbed his arm, and they began a walk that led them almost inevitably to the training area for the captain's private army. The men were all assigned to take part in the clean-up after the fire in the palace.

And that was evidently also the topic of the conversation that the captain wanted to have with him.

"Is there any indication of who is behind this attack?" Inugami asked, sounding not half as curious and interested as his first officer would've expected.

"There have been several conversations with this Balkun, one of our people."

Aritomo used the term "our people" almost automatically, and it didn't seem so wrong as it did at the beginning. Inugami seemed to have bigger problems with this term. They were not "ours," they were "his" people. And it was probably not even "people" for him but not much more than human material of specific use.

"I want to talk to the man too. He probably ... prevented the worst."

"He saved the king's daughter from the flames. Chitam is very thankful. He wishes the man to be freed."

Inugami shook his head. "That's a point that's not debatable to me. This Balkun belongs to me. He will of course be praised and receive honors. We can give him rank. But he will have to fight in my army and earn his freedom with blood. If he distinguishes himself, he will become an officer, and all officers will be free men."

Aritomo raised his eyebrows. That was news the Captain hadn't told him yet, and the idea was surprisingly ... liberal. Inugami actually began not only to intensively worry about some things, but also to adapt to the circumstances. Of course, only if they served his overarching purpose, there was no doubt about that.

"Balkun stays close to the king. Chitam hasn't yet allowed him to return to the camp."

"I will give the order. I don't really want to get into a contest of power with Chitam yet, but I can't accept him doing whatever he pleases. My authority mustn't be called into question by a native chief."

Aritomo fell silent. Chitam wasn't a chieftain or something like that. He was the king of one of the most powerful cities in Central America and came from a family that had been established by the local superpower three generations ago. A superpower, he remembered, whose existence he had not even discussed with Inugami. Only a brief conversation with Sawada had led to this topic.

But Inugami would need to confront that particular issue by himself.

Aritomo saw the clouds darken on the horizon – and that even though it was a day with a bright blue sky.

"What will Chitam do to find those responsible for the attack?" Inugami returned to the topic. The question seemed to upset him a bit.

"I don't know. His people walk around asking questions. If they can figure something out ... I can't guess."

"Will we learn about the results of his inquiry?"

"I'm sure we'll be informed if we ask."

"What are the current assumptions?"

"I understand that the prevailing opinion is that we missed some fleeing warriors – and nobles – from Yaxchilan who secretly sought revenge and somehow organized the attack – with certain promises, if we want to believe Balkun."

Inugami nodded. "Very well. I think we should support this possible explanation. It offers an excellent opportunity to justify the planned campaign. We're creating additional legitimacy." Inugami paused, looked thoughtful and a little sad. "Of course that would have been easier if there had been some spectacular deaths, preferably from the royal family. But we have to work with what fate has granted us."

Aritomo thought of the king's little daughter, who was still wincing and crying at every open flame, as Dame Tzutz had told him at their last meeting.

He thought it better to keep to himself the retort that forced itself on his tongue.

"I want you to keep me informed of the progress of the ... investigations."

"Yes."

Inugami pursed his lips and nodded.

"And bring me this Balkun. He showed ... initiative. I'm not sure that's such a good thing, but if he's somebody to make proper use of, then I want to talk to him."

"Yes."

Inugami nodded and gestured. Aritomo was dismissed, he saluted and turned away. He suddenly felt the need to bring as much distance between himself and the Captain as possible.

He wandered over the training field and noticed that his feet were carrying him to the palace ruins. He didn't mind. It was a good place to get an idea of the course of events and obtain the information Inugami expected of him.

216

When he got there, he realized to his surprise that the Maya didn't want to endure the shame of a smoldering ruin in the middle of their city any day longer than necessary. Long chains of workers had formed and carried off what their comrades in the ruins broke into pieces. All the remains were systematically removed and leveled with an impressive speed. Hundreds of men were at work here, many of them Inugami's soldiers, and they operated under the guidance of experienced builders who had a good grip on the entire construction site.

On the square, in turn, building materials were piled up by other construction crews, most notably bricks from the nearby fractures but also wooden beams, tools, other materials, all carefully layered and thus ready to start with immediately after the demolition had ceased. What proved to be recyclable from the ruin of the palace was also placed here.

The fire had not affected the foundations of the mighty building, so it could be built upon. This would significantly reduce the time for reconstruction. If Aritomo overlooked it correctly, the Mayan builders used their workforce in a very effective way. Since this project had the highest priority, everything would be done very, very fast.

That was a problem, because it endangered the construction plans of Inugami. Proper barracks for his army? Sarukazaki's city walls? Aritomo had some guesses on additional plans. Improved tools and materials would be used, sure. But above all, there would be a need for many additional workers, which in turn meant that the Maya would increasingly turn into a slave-holding society – if Inugami didn't come up with yet another idea to increase the population.

The Maya knew slavery. Enslavement was the preferred punishment for serious offenses such as murder, burglary or adultery, although the application of this penalty varied depending on the social status of the person to be punished. He who was born into slavery remained a slave. Those who raised enough wealth to buy their freedom or served their master well could be released. All in all, there wasn't an endless amount of slaves in Mutal, and most of the work of lower nature was done by free citizens of the city. What would happen if the proportion of slaves increased significantly, if they were collected by Inugami's campaigns and if their only hope for freedom was to find favor in the captain's eyes?

Aritomo knew where these thoughts led to.

Chitam, if he was wise, would have the same reservations.

He stood there for a while watching the well-organized activity and imagined what it would look like once Inugami realized his imperial fantasies. Would there be another palace, completely cut off from the city, with its own life, a place to which only selected people had access, and nobody knew what was actually going on behind it – much as it had been the case in Meiji-times in Japan? To assume that the young prince would be more than just a doll in the hands of a shogun Inugami would be absurd. The boy himself already guessed what was in store for him, and each day he seemed more introspective and reserved. Sawada took great care of him, but he had many other duties and, as an old man, needed rest too. Aritomo wanted to suggest allowing the prince access to peers, perhaps by establishing a common English class. Sawada would have endorsed this idea, but Aritomo already knew that the Captain would oppose it. Officially, of course, in order not to pollute the exalted and sanctified status of the prince with the presence of filthy savages – in reality, to keep the young man as isolated as possible to prevent him from developing other, uncontrollable loyalties, even friendships and, thus, influences that might detract from the right path.

A "right path" whose direction only Inugami sought to determine.

Aritomo decided to start another conversation with the prince at the next opportunity, if only to give him some comfort. His situation was far from enviable.

The officer sighed.

It was not his major concern either.

But unlike the prince, he had the means in his hands to initiate change.

He saw Lengsley heading for the construction site. He would surely meet some of the Mayan artisans to discuss with them the things the Captain had told them to do. The Maya showed quite a desire for learning, even though there were still major problems with understanding. In men like Lengsley and Sarukazaki, however, they recognized practical craftsmen who seemed able to create something grand from nothing. Beyond the spoken word, they shared a common language on a very different human level and a desire to mold nature to their own will and do it a little better each time than before.

Aritomo gave himself a jerk and followed the Briton.

29

Inocoyotl looked down from the hill at the small settlement and wondered how much wretchedness he would have to endure on his journey. His expression must have betrayed his feelings, for Queca, the officer of the thirty soldiers who accompanied him along with his own servants to protect the expedition, shook his head.

"Besides Teotihuacán, all towns are villages, and all villages are dirt holes," the imperial officer said with a mixture of satisfaction and contempt. "The Maya will forever be in our shadow, ambassador."

Inocoyotl nodded. "Yet they are not to be underestimated, my friend. Some of their cities are not without majesty. Have you been often so far south?"

"No further than here. I'm a border guard."

"Then arm yourself. Although no city resembles our capital, you will see that this," he gestured toward the village," is by no means the standard we can expect in the future. In fact, if the Maya agreed and all of them would follow a single ruler who has both courage and energy, I would seriously fear for the good of our kingdom."

In Queca's face, there was the conflict between the respect for the honorable envoy, who had personally received a seal from the Divine King, and his doubt about the man's testimony. A challenge for the great Teotihuacán? Who on this earth should have that much power?

Inocoyotl didn't mind him. He knew this attitude from all those who, blinded by the greatness of Teotihuacán, often didn't want to realize that the world beyond their own borders was not as run-down and inferior as they commonly thought. Queca would learn a little more with each day of their trip, and possibly bring a different picture back with him on his return.

As a border guard, he was already someone who was ready to make certain concessions, but as the big Mayan cities were still further inland and they had just crossed the uncertainly defined border, he was relatively inexperienced as his busy neighbors were concerned.

And they were busy. Inocoyotl had spent the last day before entering Maya territory meeting with all kinds of traders who were delivering obsidian to Teotihuacán. They brought news of thriving cities and powerful rulers and rumors of gods that had plagued the Maya and ushered in a new epoch in the history of their people – a perspective that was greeted with more anxiety rather than anticipation by its interlocutors.

Queca thought that was sloppy talk, just showing off. He had joked, luckily not in the presence of the traders but afterwards and a lot. His men had laughed. Inocoyotl hadn't.

He had learned that no one in his presence, in front of the Eye and Ear of the Divine Ruler, seriously thought of stories that didn't carry a small kernel of truth. To find this kernel and thus to explore the situation to the fullest, he was about to do.

The Divine King expected him to do his best.

Inocoyotl expected no less of himself.

"We will not stay over there for long. But we can't help but to pay a salute to the head of the village. He will then broadcast the news of our arrival to the neighboring larger cities, so we will be received appropriately there. We don't want to embarrass anyone by our surprising appearance."

Queca bowed. "I will send soldiers in advance. I don't want to risk anything."

Inocoyotl wanted to stop him for a moment, then decided against it. It didn't make sense to manage the officer too much. He would have to work with him for many months, and a good personal relationship was crucial. And he found it worth noting that the man was worried about their safety, though no serious danger was to be expected.

"A wise decision. But they shouldn't be too bossy and not scare ordinary people. We don't come as enemies. We want to talk to them, exchange information, affirm friendly ties. Let us behave that way."

Queca made a contemptuous snapping sound before he turned away to give his orders. Inocoyotl didn't mind him again. Queca was full of arrogance, but he followed orders, and with great discipline. A successful expedition and a benevolent report at court would improve his own position. The ambassador wasn't afraid of real insubordination.

Shortly thereafter a small group of soldiers trotted off, carefully briefed. Inocoyotl's eyes followed as they ran down the path, open and visible to anyone, their shields tied behind their backs. Queca had faithfully followed his suggestion, and that was a good thing.

An hour later the rest of the column followed, at a more leisurely pace. In addition to the soldiers, Inocoyotl had brought twenty porters from his household to transport the supplies and tents, gifts for the Mayan rulers they'd meet, and their gifts on the way back. In addition, he was accompanied by two Maya from the Teotihuacán alien quarter, who would serve as translators and mediators. They were reliable people, chosen by the palace itself, beyond any doubt. Inocoyotl himself spoke Maya, but he was well aware of the variety of dialects, which differed significantly from each other. And he hadn't been here for a long time, so there was a danger that his language skills were a little rusty.

When they reached the village, they were already greeted by those who were leaders in this small estate. The village chief was the highest man of the local nobility and thus for someone from the big cities only little more than a glorified farmer. The ambassador's attendance noticeably embarrassed the elderly man. He looked nervous and wasn't alone in this feeling. Surely, many were scared here too.

Inocoyotl decided to continue to be gracious and show consideration.

He smiled with warmth.

The man stared at the envoy, looked at his gorgeous clothes, and decided to show the only correct reaction that couldn't be mistaken. He threw himself flat on the ground, pressed his forehead to the ground, and said, "Greetings, lord. Me and mine are at your disposal."

Inocoyotl was pleased to see that the man's few companions also followed suit. Even Queca, who had a look of disdain on his face all the time, seemed content.

"Get up!" Inocoyotl said to Maya. In fact, it could be assumed that he would have been understood in his own language, because here in the border region a good relationship with the powerful neighbor was of particular importance for the Maya.

The Maya followed the order, their expressions still insecure. The headman crouched on his knees and looked respectfully at Inocoyotl.

"Sir?"

"Do not worry. We come in peace."

The old man didn't look reassured, and Inocoyotl knew why. It wasn't so much the fear of a military attack – a quick capitulation would immediately solve this problem – but the fear of a prolonged stay of the guests which was in his mind. Those many visitors consisted of many mouths that would stretch the barren supplies of the village, if they were to stay longer.

Fortunately, they had no intention.

Inocoyotl smiled reassuringly.

"We will not stay and bother you too much. Tomorrow we want to continue traveling. We only remain for one night. Please show us where we can set up tents."

The village chief bowed. "You, my lord, are welcome in my house."

The relief in his voice was audible – and the invitation was honest. A gluttonous nobleman for one night, that was to be mastered. Inocoyotl would eat more out of courtesy; he didn't like feasting, as it interfered with his clear mind.

The village head got to his feet. "Lord, you're certainly on your way to the summit."

Inocoyotl hesitated. He didn't know of any such meeting, but it was highly inappropriate, even in his position, to admit lack of knowledge. He turned his face into the usual mask of jovial arrogance he could put on anytime to hide his feelings and said, "It's a very important meeting."

The village head nodded eagerly. "The King of B'aakal has invited Popo and the lesser rulers of the surrounding area."

"Not you too?"

"My village recognizes the rule of King Chaa'j, and we are more than worthy of him. I'm not important."

In Queca's face was to be seen that he shared the sentiment. Before the officer could say anything wrong, the ambassador ordered him to prepare the campground and to gather the men there. He obeyed.

Inocoyotl turned back to the village chief. "Join me."

The man obeyed hesitantly. Inocoyotl waved to his companions, who immediately understood and made their way with bows. The envoy placed a hand on the old man's shoulder in a confidential gesture, which he acknowledged with a look of severe discomfort. Inocoyotl smiled reassuringly at him.

"If you are represented by the king of B'aakal, then you will surely have an opinion on the subject of the meeting. I'm eager to find out."

The village chief hurried to draw a gesture of denial in the air. "I'm unworthy of talking about these things. War and peace are decided at the highest level. If there is a war, I send my men. If there is peace, we tend to our fields. We do as we are told."

"That's very commendable," Inocoyotl said approvingly. "But let's talk about far-reaching decisions that you, too, have to explain to your village. That alone requires a certain standpoint."

"You flatter me and place me in a status I don't deserve."

"Your modesty honors you. So, in the light of this restraint, indicate how you see the situation."

Inocoyotl was tired of this kind of verbal dancing, but was not allowed to show his growing impatience. He wanted to know something without revealing that he himself had no idea what was going on, and that required a certain amount of intuition.

The village elder finally gathered some courage.

"Well, sir, if you insist, I may say that I'm worried. If it is true, as the rumors say, and Mutal has received direct help from the gods in a hitherto unprecedented manner, a manifestation ... an apparition ... then I am greatly afraid that any alliance against this enemy without its own ... assurance made by the gods is doomed to failure."

"Sure, sure, that's well considered," Inocoyotl muttered, trying not to sound too absent-minded. Mutal? The city that was once, more than a hundred years ago, blessed by men from Teotihuacán with a new dynasty, a noble family of the highest birth, and thus formally subordinate to the Divine ruler of Teotihuacán, at least as a formality?

Had his master known or at least suspected it? Had he also heard rumors?

Was this the true background of his journey and had all this been withheld from him to give him an unbiased impression?

No, he couldn't imagine that. It had to be a more recent development, unpredictable, and fate was asking the envoy to handle it. He spoke for his city. But getting involved in a war that went against Mutal ...

Inocoyotl almost ordered his men to return.

But he suppressed the motion. The first, the spontaneous impulse wasn't always the right one.

His king wouldn't be happy if he came back so early only with rumors and vague clues. And it was Inocoyotl's highest aspiration to make his king happy. It would be very beneficial to his life expectancy – and that of his family.

"Have other rulers been summoned? I was traveling and may not be up to date."

The chief frowned. "Lord, who am I to learn such a thing? I know that my King has taken great care to invite as many rulers of importance and rank as possible, but he hasn't shared the names with me and certainly hasn't told me who has promised to attend and who has not." He glanced at Inocoyotl anxiously. "Please forgive my ignorance, sir."

"It's not your fault," he reassured the old man. "I'll find out soon enough. I thank you for your help. It will be all the more necessary to leave early tomorrow to complete the journey very soon."

Inocoyotl noted that the old man masterfully concealed his relief and even managed to show polite regret. It was clear that the man was clever at dealing with high-ranking personalities who could potentially cause him much trouble. Inocoyotl felt a sudden kinship with him, perhaps on a slightly different level but nonetheless as a victim of the same unpredictable hierarchy he had to deal with.

The ambassador of Teotihuacán turned away and joined his people, who had meanwhile built a tent for him, in which he would spend the night if he considered the house of the village head to be inappropriate. Inocoyotl had already slept in very strange places and in difficult, even dangerous circumstances and therefore didn't assume that he would insult his host by calling his house inadequate. He would have a roof and a sleeping mat, would politely refuse the services of one of the host's younger daughters to keep him company at night, and, as he was sure, there would be a suitable place near his bedchamber, where he could do his business – without anything biting his more valuable body parts during the process. He was already quite satisfied. Queca would use his tent.

The officer turned to his master and bowed.

"Lord, I hear that things are developing. Shall I send a messenger with a summary for our king to receive this new information?"

The officer had probably listened, too, a sensible precautionary measure. The man wasn't without intelligence, and Inocoyotl respected that.

"I will write such a message," he replied thoughtfully. "We don't know much yet and have to promise more information. I'm not sure what's behind it all, but it seems our Divine Ruler has dispatched this expedition at exactly the right time."

"The gods must have guided him," said Queca, returning to his work to secure the small camp.

Inocoyotl was not sure if the gods were responsible for it or if this was simply the instinct of a good ruler who reacted when impending danger lingered on the horizon to be prepared for. The envoy felt restless and unbalanced. Events happened that he hadn't expected, and he felt a little overwhelmed. He knew that his King saw things

226

differently. He had sent Inocoyotl because his ambassador was ready and able to use his own head.

And if he didn't like the way he used his head, he would have it cut off.

Inocoyotl sighed.

It was so easy to be a king.

30

And so Balkun was rewarded, and then again he wasn't.

Inugami, his lord and god, spoke to him for a long time, assisted by an ancient messenger of the gods who helped with the translation. He had again to describe what he had seen, and again he had kept the most important information to himself, since he couldn't guess whether the god's messenger he had observed acted on behalf or against the will of Inugami. To continue being careful seemed wise.

Since Balkun had been treated very honorably and warmly by Chitam and his family, the slave found that his personal loyalties were more to the King of Mutal than to those who wanted to harm his family, and that he didn't want to risk being over-zealous, as accidental disclosure of information in the wrong place would certainly call for ... irritations.

He felt how this information put pressure on his soul and everything in him was longing for someone who could help him to carry the burden of this knowledge. So far he hadn't wanted to confide in Chitam. He didn't know how his relationship to Inugami developed, and he didn't know what would happen to him if the holy messenger found out that he'd shared that kind of information with the King.

He wasn't sure if his master and owner condoned his actions or not. He wasn't punished for his impudence in leaving the camp, which was already a positive sign. He was promoted to one of the 25 officers who had been chosen from the midst of the warrior-slaves, and he got his own sleeping place, better food, and the freedom to leave the camp after previous logoff. Balkun should be thankful for that, and in fact he enjoyed the privileges. But his quiet hope that his heroism would give him the most precious thing that filled his heart with great yearning hadn't been fulfilled: no real freedom, no return to his family, no end to his humiliating status as a slave.

But he hadn't expected it anyway.

He had no choice but to keep that hope deep inside, a small flame that never went out.

Balkun now felt disappointment and pain at the point where he had fed the flame, and he had to make sure that these emotions didn't overwhelm him. There would be another chance, he kept telling himself. He just had to believe it. And it clearly showed him where and how the power was distributed in Mutal. Chitam had promised him freedom in his gratitude. Balkun didn't believe that the King didn't want to fulfill his promise. He rather assumed that he hadn't been able to prevail over Inugami.

Balkun didn't need to know more.

He plunged into his new duties, and his newly elevated position had given him plenty of such. He now commanded a force of about 100 soldiers, and he was directly responsible for a number of organizational issues that had previously been in the authority of the messengers themselves. Incidentally, he was also responsible for discipline and training, based on instructions he received from his masters. Many things were new to him. If he could find anything positive in relation to his status as a warrior slave, it was the fact that he'd never learned so many new things in his life as he did in those weeks and months. And this wasn't just about how to discipline and how to effectively kill any adversary. He learned about medicine and hygiene, he learned a lot about commanding and leading, and he learned that a nobleman was not necessarily a good leader. Warrior slaves were all alike and could only rise out of the crowd if they rendered special services, and so Balkun held a position that would have been granted only to a clan chief in his city – regardless of whether this person knew what he was doing or not.

Balkun tried to reconcile with his fate.

He also didn't have much opportunity to think about it too much. When he was called, together with his comrades, to be informed of new commands by the Lord of the messengers, he hadn't thought much of it at first. Perhaps a more intensive training program – or an acceleration in barracks construction that had been interrupted due to the repairs to the palace and lagged behind schedule? When

Balkun took his place among the twenty-five officers, he expected, above all, the instruction to work even harder and to endure even more torn hands and injuries through intensified efforts.

But Inugami, who set up in front of them, accompanied by some of the other messengers, had something else to announce, and Balkun's joy was very limited. In fact, he would have accepted every additional construction project with great enthusiasm, if only ...

"Men!" Inugami said loudly. He read from a parchment on which he had written down the exact text of his speech. The Lord of the messengers was not half as eager to learn the Mayan language as Balkun had expected. And while the English lessons of the warrior slaves had made good progress, most of them didn't know more than simple commands and had some understanding of verbal abuse and discipline.

"It's a decisive time to live in. The provocations of our adversaries are not diminishing. Therefore, I have decided to reduce the number of our enemies and show everyone that Mutal's power has grown and a new epoch has begun that will change the face of the land. I gave the order today to begin preparations for a military campaign immediately. This fight will be your baptism of fire, and everyone who proves himself will be rewarded and promoted. It is the start of a glorious time when great men can prove themselves, a time that demands heroic deeds as well as sacrifices."

Inugami paused. Balkun had the impression that, above all, he expected a lot of sacrifice from his warrior slaves, and at least in that he was just like any king or a clan chief. Some things didn't change.

"Our destination is Saclemacal, the capital of Kowoj. An old, a venerable, city with a long history, I was told. A first and worthy contribution to the new kingdom of Mutal, to the land of the new god-emperor, to the empire of the Maya and the messengers of the gods."

Balkun looked up. Inugami had raised his voice, his words held a triumphant tone.

New god emperor? Empire? The latter term, the underlying concept, was not immediately understandable. It was probably

230

about great power, a large territory, great influence, permanent ownership. Balkun considered these terms for a first time. So far, the Lord of the messengers had hidden the details of his plans from them, but now he had ... announced a program, a vision, and it was bigger than Balkun had expected and showed that now it was about much more than to remind an unruly neighbor that Mutal knew exactly who was to be considered as friend or foe.

What followed after Saclemacal? Surely Tayasal, the next ally of Tatb'u's on the way to Yaxchilan. And then Balkun's homeland itself. And after Mutal dominated the big lake and ...

Balkun closed his eyes.

From there, every option was possible. Calakmul, the old rival of Mutal. Or Caracol in the east. The smaller cities in between. Balkun had no doubt that it would go in that direction. And Inugami would someday have an army – a combined army, organized according to the new principles, with a corps of warrior slaves in its center, with clearly defined units and branches of arms – against which no Mayan city would be able to assert itself. The small force in which Balkun served was a replica of this future force, strictly organized into spearmen, the artillery that fought exclusively with the atlatl, and a unit of especially well-protected soldiers, armored like ballplayers carrying obsidian axes instead of spears and covered by big shields, soldiers designated by Inugami in English as "shock troops," where only the strongest and largest men served. Balkun looked down. He himself was one of the spearmen because he was quite strong but rather short and considered a fast runner. Spearmen were agile. The artillery softened the enemy's resolve and offered protection. The shock troops crushed the enemy in rigid, armored discipline.

Inugami's opponents would not know what happened to them.

"We're leaving in a week as soon as the priests have completed the necessary rituals," Inugami said. "Mutal's soldiers fight by our side. Together we will carry the war to our enemies and teach them a lesson. I know that this will be a glorious hour for all of us. Prepare everything! I expect you all to be ready when the day comes!"

Certainly not an inspirational speech, woodenly expressed, like being read, and unaccented. No one moved, but there were astonished glances, too, fear, suppressed murmurs, the scratching of feet. No one had expected them to practice and train for fun, but no one thought that the first mission would come so quickly.

The generated uncertainty. And that couldn't be covered with sound talk of glory and probation.

Inugami stepped aside. Other messengers began to give a list of commands that Balkun only half listened to. He knew that many of the messengers thought they were a bit stupid. Each order was repeated two or three times anyway as if they were talking to children or very old people, and many of his comrades still felt offended by this type of communication. Balkun had decided not to have time to be offended. Moreover, not all of them acted that way. A few seemed to see equivalent human beings in them. That gave him hope.

When the gathering was dissolved, everyone immediately fell into hectic activity. Balkun, on the other hand, remained calm. One week's time was more than enough. He was much more interested in how Inugami had managed to give such a far-reaching command to the King of Mutal. Because actually there was only one person in a city of the Maya who could really give the order for a military campaign: the king. Sure, it was the priests who told the king when the signs were favorable and when they weren't, and depending on how strong the monarch was, they might even decide when to launch an attack. But Chitam was no tool of his priests – at least Balkun had not gained this impression so far.

Something must have happened, which had already become apparent in relation to the fate of his own person. Within Chitam's court, forces had grown ready to submit to the messengers. The defense against the attack of their enemies had contributed to this. Should Saclemacal fall quickly – and Balkun had no doubt about that given the superiority and quality of the troops –, this would further strengthen the prestige of Inugami. It was only a matter of time ...

Balkun frowned.

Until what happened?

Would the Lord of the messengers get rid of Chitam? Twice the warrior-slaves had been brought before a young man, Balkun,

232

without being able to remember his name, who had been introduced as the true divine king, as ruler of that distant land from which the vessel of the messengers came. He had made no particular impression on Balkun and his men, a thin young man who had stood there with his face without expression, saying no word and presenting himself as no more than ... a shadow behind Inugami's back.

What kind of king should that be?

One who finally did only what Inugami wanted, Balkun completed his train of thought. One who didn't, like Chitam, tried to develop his own ideas, even if he didn't succeed in implementation right now.

A puppet.

Balkun nodded. He saw Inugami's way clearly before him. Everything fell in place wonderfully. And he began to fear for the life of the King of Mutal, who was once his enemy and who now threatened to be a victim of the victory which the messengers had bestowed upon him.

Balkun paused. He looked around. Everyone was busy. Everyone went his way.

Nobody would bother him. There was nothing unusual happening on the way to the construction site of the new palace. Some of the warrior slaves were still working on the restoration of the building. And Chitam lived in the great mansion of a noble nearby until his own lodgings were finished.

Balkun felt driven. It was worry that disturbed him and a strange sense of responsibility that had filled him since the night he'd saved the life of Chitam's daughter – and probably many other residents of the burning palace. Balkun took this feeling seriously.

Although, he was pretty sure it would cause him great trouble.

31

"That's a real bow!"

Lengsley pointed to the stones he had put together. The clay was not yet dry, and the construction was very shaky, but since each of the stones, broken from the remains of the palace rubble, was no more than five inches wide and only two inches thick, it didn't matter. Beside him sat five builders from the city of Mutal, older men, not noblemen, but of high esteem and rightly proud of their achievements and abilities. Lengsley had tried to teach them the improvements as gently and respectfully as possible – and quickly realized that his worries had been completely unfounded. Not only did the five men know exactly what he was talking about, they had not the slightest problem with being taught by the messenger.

Lengsley endeavored to dissuade them from the practice of constructing the entrance arches of their buildings as false arches or cantilevered arches. Although these were easier to do by hand, they produced both compressive and tensile forces and were therefore less stable than a genuine bow that could withstand only compressive forces. A false arch, in which the capstone was not clamped between the other stones of the arch but put on it without any tension, made it inevitable that the archways had to be build narrow and tall. The advantage of their design was that they could be built without a scaffold and therefore be finished faster. But ultimately it required more building material due to the required massiveness and made the access to important buildings unnecessarily narrow.

Lengsley had always been a bit interested in architecture. When he realized what the builders were doing to rebuild the palace, he had noticed immediately that they were content with the historic precursor of what Lengsley knew from his time. He had then broken up a few smaller stones and cut them into uniform blocks to demonstrate the difference between the construction methods. His hands had been the scaffolding, and a small loan of clay was the connecting element that gave the necessary strength to the demonstration after a few minutes in the sun.

Lengsley couldn't explain every details to the craftsmen – he still lacked the necessary vocabulary –, but his way of explaining the principle using the practical example proved to be perfectly adequate. The audience consisted of professionals, under their leadership mighty pyramids had been build. They didn't have to be introduced to the basics of statics and materials science that Lengsley couldn't provide anyway. On the basis of their many years of experience, they understood what the Brit wanted to show them and how he did it. And they learned.

They learned damn fast.

One of the men turned to the remaining stones and began copying the demonstration. With encouraging words from his colleagues and with occasional helpful hints, at first somewhat uncertain, but then with confident assurance and great skill, he copied the small, true bow that Lengsley had built for them. When he was done, the clay still moist and shiny and using the hands of his colleagues as a scaffold, he looked inquiringly at Lengsley.

He nodded and smiled. "An excellent job. You learned it!"

The man smiled back delightedly, bowing his head gratefully. "A valuable lesson. We thank you for the opportunity to learn."

Even more thanks poured from the mouths of everyone. And before Lengsley could reply to that, one of the men brought more stones, and they all began with utmost concentration and mutual help to construct a true bow a third time, and this time the model was a little bigger and thus more difficult to construct. Lengsley didn't understand everything they said, but it was as if they were already discussing the type and scope of the scaffolding that would be necessary to build a portal for the new palace that could only be described as royal.

Lengsley listened for a while, watched the progress of the third arc, not recognizing any need for further advice, and got up. He was politely greeted by all his students, and the Briton gratefully accepted their words, telling them to just keep going and not to worry about him.

His attention was focused on another person approaching, whose presence filled him with a whirlwind of his own kind. Accompanied by two servants, Princess Une Balam steered into his direction, looked at the eager craftsmen and their new toys, smiled delightedly, and nodded to them as they started to rise and greet her.

"I'm not here," she said simply, waving to them. The men still bowed before returning to their discussion.

Une Balam looked at Lengsley. Her brown eyes were searching, her delicately drawn mouth gently shaped into a smile that immediately captivated him. Again, the gap in her teeth caught his attention, as it gleamed between her lips. For a moment he wondered if he was expected to bow, but the young woman placed a confident hand on his forearm.

"Come with me, Lengsley. You look tired."

Lengsley *was* tired. He got up early and had worked hard for the past eight hours, sweating a lot and pausing only for a quick meal. As if the words of the princess had reminded him of this, he now felt the leaden exhaustion in his limbs – and was suddenly aware of his body odor, a mixture of sweat and dust, and clay, which surely offended the fine royal nose.

If so, then the owner of said nose didn't show.

Lengsley first noticed that he followed the princess' invitation like a sheep that had no will of its own when they almost reached the building. Since the palace had served many people as a home, some of the surrounding houses had been requisitioned by Chitam, and this seemed to be the temporary residence of the king's youngest sister. As she had a number of servants, the relatively small house was nearly full, and the hustle and bustle therein showed that it was not actually designed for such a number of residents. Where the original owners of this property – certainly important nobles – had disappeared, Lengsley couldn't guess. He suspected that the displacement of the social hierarchy had continued downward: The inhabitants of this house had snatched up one of their clan's people, who were a little less important, and they had continued to do so until somewhere out there at the outskirts of the metropolis, a simple peasant squatted with neighbors or immediately built a new hut, since nothing else remained for him to do.

Une Balam had the privilege of having a beautiful, spacious room for herself, and once the servant, who had just started sweeping with a brush, had been dragged out, she herself adjusted the two heavy curtains that replaced a door to cover access to this room.

"Sit down, Lengsley."

Her tone didn't allow for any objections, and Lengsley saw no reason to resist unnecessarily.

The Briton was pleased to learn that a simple meal had been prepared, consisting of baked corn patties, often stuffed with vegetables or meat, which were the staple food of the Maya, and whose variations Lengsley now knew in detail. He had found taste in this food, which, despite its consistent appearance, had a remarkable variety of ingredients. But he had no illusions that this variety and the care of preparation were a privilege of the upper classes. He had to assume that the lower social ranks had to settle for less. On the other hand, he had not seen any signs of malnutrition or massive deficiency symptoms. No matter how big the differences were, no one was starving here, at least in good times.

"What do you want to drink?"

Lengsley struggled with himself, but then decided to play it safe. "Only water, noble princess. Please, I'll take it myself ..."

"Not at all."

The tone of Une Balam had again been decidedly crisp, and Lengsley was trained to discern authority, not least because of his extensive experience with the military. In this situation, he felt it was better to obey, and the tiredness in his limbs made that easy for him. Why not enjoy a moment of calm and caring? It wasn't like he didn't deserve this. When was the last time someone cared for him? He tried to remember, but soon lost his thoughts. It was as if the time before his arrival in Mutal was increasingly hidden behind a veil.

The water was clear and fresh and Lengsley drank it with gratitude. Une Balam settled down next to him. A considerable portion of her well-formed, cream-colored legs became visible as she sat sideways on a pillow, lifting her robe. Lengsley tried not to stare too openly, but the princess's slightly mocking, but in no way reprimanding glance hinted that she was well aware of the British's unilateral attention.

"The palace is making good progress," the engineer said in an attempt to start something like a conversation.

"As I saw, your contribution is important," said Une Balam, who picked up a cup of water and took a tiny sip. "This archway thing ... the builders were thrilled. They learned a lot today."

"I just wanted to help."

"Not all messengers want that, I have the impression."

Lengsley was silent. He guessed what the princess was alluding to, especially the campaign that caused the city to break into hectic bustle. It was a feeling of great expectation and enthusiasm, and Chitam made a good face, hiding his feelings. But it was clear that this was the war of the messengers and that the king only played the role of a spectator, even though he formally gave the orders to the city's soldiers.

"I can't speak for others," he said finally. "I'm not commanding. I am a servant."

"A servant?"

"I have no authority on the vessel. The boat."

"Ah, yes, you call it the boat. It's so much more for us."

"That's going to change. Maybe someday, when everyone sees it for what it is. A big iron boat."

Maybe someday it would be like that, especially now as they had proved that Inugami's orders to bring the boat back into the water as soon as possible couldn't be carried out. Inugami hadn't been pleased about it, but had ultimately been unable to ignore the facts. Now Lengsley considered how to turn the pyramid into a permanent seat for the boat, a symbol of Mutal's new power, and at the same time a gun platform – and defense in case of emergencies.

Une Balam set down the cup. "Until then, the Lord of the messengers will have replaced the reverence for the Sacred Vehicle with another form of fear and respect."

238

Lengsley bowed his head. This woman had a sharp mind and knew exactly what Inugami wanted. But what use was this knowledge, if not even the first officer of the Japanese, whom Lengsley considered a reasonable and thoughtful man, could do something about it?

"That's true," he said, trying not to look too worried.

The princess frowned with her shapely forehead. "I have come to the conclusion, Lengsley, that not all of the messengers take advantage of our girls to the same extent, though there is no shortage of opportunity."

Lengsley blinked at this change of topic. "It's like that," he began cautiously. "Inugami has given orders to exercise restraint, which is not something everyone is equally aware of."

"I have heard of that."

Lengsley thought that had been one of the captain's more meaningful instructions. They'd had to find out quickly that there was a difference between the King turning a blind eye to a banquet for some amusement or a normal Mayan lady in everyday life. The morality of this people was relatively rigid. For example, adultery was punished by slavery or even capital punishment. Marriage was a serious matter, often arranged, which was by no means dissimilar to Japan. Inugami had quickly realized that this was an area in which it was better not to provoke anybody. On the other hand, the adventurous crew members – and curious Mayan girls – caused the commencement of the natural course of things. But the attitude that all women were fair game for the Japanese was something the captain had quickly expelled from their thoughts, although some in their arrogance – or naivety – had assumed exactly that. At some point, things would develop as expected, and the Maya would find that the messengers were just as good or as bad men as their own. Lengsley believed that, despite the captain's resistance, this normalization would eventually lead to lasting partnerships. It was absolutely inevitable.

"I see a good development in that," the princess said. "Men must be kept under control."

Lengsley didn't know what to say, mostly because he wasn't sure what the lady meant – or if he misunderstood it because of his lack in language skills.

"You yourself, I hear, are also very cautious, though you look different from the rest of the messengers and … there was certainly interest. You are the stranger among strangers. That makes you interesting. There must have been offers."

Une Balam smiled gently. "Am I right?"

The Briton cleared his throat. "There was … yes." Meaningless to deny it.

"And?"

"I have been very busy. There is much to do."

"That didn't stop others."

"I try to be as polite and restrained as possible with my hosts."

"We are your hosts? Not everyone sees it that way."

"I can only speak for myself."

"This is true."

Une Balam paused for a moment, her lovely forehead still in thoughtful folds. She took a deep breath and leaned forward to reach for the plate on the low table. Lengsley couldn't help but notice that the cleavage of her dress was cut slightly wider than usual, so that he could take a look at the pleasant curve of tapering breasts.

Une Balam acted as if she hadn't noticed, and Lengsley came to the conclusion that he was the victim of a carefully orchestrated drama, a play of which the script he hadn't read, and which was directed by a mistress who had a very clear idea of the last act. The Briton wondered if he was really that easy to influence and if that was what she meant by "keeping things under control." He came to the conclusion that the answer to both questions was "Yes!" … and that he didn't care.

Une Balam was a woman of intelligence and culture, and she was used to the fact that others were considerate of her wishes. Otherwise, Lengsley recalled, her father would've married her to a nobleman or the King of a neighboring town a long time ago. Dynastic marriages were as common among the Maya as in Europe, there was actually little difference.

240

Anyway, why bother? If she wanted to manipulate him, he was quite ready for it.

"We Mayan women may be ugly to your eyes," she said quietly.

"Not at all," Lengsley hurried to say. "Not at all."

"I hope that includes me."

Lengsley felt his throat go dry, and he took a sip of water.

"Indeed ... I have seen few women of your people who were more charming." The words sounded awkward and stilted, but it was apparently an acceptable answer, for Une smiled contentedly and straightened up.

"Now I have another question, Lengsley."

"I'm happy to answer."

"You are the tallest man I have ever seen in my life."

Lengsley lowered his head, feeling a little bit embarrassed. He couldn't help it. For one thing, Europeans generally seemed to be bigger than Japanese and Maya, at least according to his impression. He didn't make the mistake of deriving any kind of superiority from this fact; actually, he felt quite clumsy sometimes. It was simply a plain observation of facts, and it caused trouble for him – especially in tight spaces like on a submarine, which were particularly limiting for him. On top of that, he was also regarded as tall for his British compatriots. Une's head reached up to his shoulder. Chitam, like other men, could look him in the nose from below. The same was true for the Japanese although they had never shown him that they were annoyed about it. His size and his somewhat coarser limbs were considered by many rather haughty Asians as an indication that he came from an inferior race and were therefore a cause for amusement and ridicule, also something that Lengsley had learned to endure. Anyone who was very tall, his father once told him, learns to be more humble or at least pretend to be so.

"I'm quite tall," he said, nodding. "It is not easy. It's often a hindrance."

"That's it. Now tell me, your manliness ... is it as tall, too?"

Lengsley's eyes widened and stared at the princess, dumbfounded. He hadn't really expected that question, and ... he was by no means sure how to react to it. The adolescent years, in which something like a comparison still had a meaning, had long been behind him, and he had always been of the opinion, whether true or not, that size didn't matter in sex, but the question posed by this woman next to him, who looked at him with expectantly gleaming eyes and seemingly filled with serious curiosity, suddenly put his certainty in question.

God, what did he answer? He felt like an animal in the zoo, the visitor staring bashfully at the thing. And that, though Une Balam's eyes were fixed on his face alone.

"I ... I think ..."

"You don't have the comparison."

Lengsley nodded hastily. "That's true."

"I have."

Lengsley opened his mouth, but before he could speak, he felt her on his lips, swallowing every word in a hungry, searching kiss. The Briton closed his eyes and enjoyed the fresh taste of her touch, inhaling the smell of her skin, a mixture of sweat, the colors she had applied to her face, and an earthy odor that he found very pleasant.

More than that. She aroused him. He felt the object of her interest begin to harden. And as her slender hand pressed itself urgently between his legs, slipped under his waistband and closed around his growing member with amazing power, it no longer elicited confusion and surprise but a hot wave of desire. His searching hands found her breasts, the large, pointed nipples that stretched out expectantly. The woman huddled against him, massaging his penis, trying to escape the tightness of his pants, and then they both lay on the mats on the floor, clothes brushed away, and Lengsley's gaze on the pale brown skin, the flawless body, the gentle sweep her thighs, which opened up attractively ...

"He's taller!" Une Balam said. "By all the gods, will I be able to receive it?"

Lengsley kissed her between her breasts, tasting her sweat.

She pulled him to her.

"We'll find out soon enough," she muttered hoarsely, guiding him knowledgeably. "We'll probably find out very soon indeed."

The experiment became a huge success.

242

32

Chitam looked at the assembled force and told himself that it should actually make him proud. Was not all this quite in keeping with his wish, had not he urged his father, more than once, to make Mutal's foreign policy a bit … more expansive? Had he not promised himself, if he would once sit on the throne, to summon the men and … do things like this?

Saclemacal was an old friend and an old enemy. One did not always exclude the other. Now it was the enemy and Chitam couldn't contradict Inugami in this. An enemy who had joined an even greater adversary to attack Mutal with a superior force, a plan that would have been successful if not for the timely and effective intervention by the messengers.

All right. Saclemacal didn't deserve anything but retribution.

But not like this.

Chitam looked at the men, stood on the steps of the temple, and felt the expectant eyes focusing on him. All necessary rituals had been completed, all preparations made. The King was now expected to have confidence and determination to fight, to display courage and energy. Chitam didn't lack courage, and he was also confident that this campaign would produce the desired result. But he lacked the will to fight and the energy, for he was increasingly sure that victory, the inevitable triumph, wouldn't be his.

It would be the victory of the messengers, Inugami's victory, as he led his own army alongside Mutal's men, smaller and unlike any force ever commanded by a Mayan city, organized differently, with new tactics and, how Chitam was surprised to discover, with new weapons. Under the guidance of the messengers, the artisans had developed mechanical monsters that had to be served by two men. "Onager" they called these weapons, and they fired bundles of arrows, not unlike the atlatl projectiles, or mighty single projectiles that could pierce several men simultaneously. The range and penetration exceeded that of the traditional spear-throwers, but the devices were harder to use and reload. The messengers had placed them on the newly constructed carts, which were drawn by the soldiers in the absence of suitable animals. More carts served the transport of supplies and ammunition, spare weapons, and all sorts of other materials, which no longer rested on the shoulders of the soldiers – who would, therefore, arrive less exhausted at their destination, since the vehicles were pulled by a separate unit, which was solely responsible for replenishment and supply.

Chitam felt some envy. He knew that these innovations would soon be transferred to his own army – but for this campaign, Inugami's warrior slaves would be the ones to try the new tactics and weapons.

Inugami was no coward. His troops would be at the front line. Ten of the messengers would accompany the expedition, led by their Lord himself. The others would be left behind and remain, as Aritomo had said, "diligent."

Why did Chitam see this statement as a subliminal threat? Did he have reason for his ever deeper mistrust, yes, his fear, the growing unwillingness?

He was pretty sure there was every reason for it.

But he did what was expected of him. Wherever he lacked energy and the will to fight, his priests and clan leaders lacked neither one nor the other. They were enthusiastic about Inugami's vision, pleased with the possibility of revenge on Saclemacal, and basked in the feeling of witnessing truly historic events. This battle would be immortalized on the great temple walls in full detail, detailing all the incidents beginning with the Battle of Mutal. Events would find their way onto the stelae and more walls, to inform posterity of their glory ...

Yes, Chitam confessed.

To show the glory of the messengers. Not his, although his name was certainly duly mentioned somewhere. It was about the strangers, about Inugami, about his vision. And the goals of Chitam were heard only as long as they met the goals of the Lord of the messengers.

244

That, the King realized, was the real problem.

He was the problem. He called himself King – an office he had never aspired with great desire, rather the opposite –, and actually he became a lesser ruler every day. Sure, he still made decisions. Inugami was only marginally interested in the administration of the city, in lawmaking, law enforcement, and public policy – all of which he gladly left to Chitam. He also ignored the religious obligations, the necessary rituals and festivals, the sacrifices for the gods. He was only interested in public buildings if they had military character or prepared to transform his holy vessel on a grandiose structure into the new landmark of the city. Everything else, the necessary sacred buildings, the planning of the agricultural areas, the maintenance – all this was still the task of the King and his servants.

And so Chitam fulfilled a role that didn't fit the title he carried, at least less and less. This King observed how more and more of his nobles referred important decisions to Inugami, he observed those who wanted to leave everything military entirely to the Lord of the messengers, who put all their hope of grandeur and triumph in the way Inugami did prepare war.

They were quite right, as Chitam had to admit. There was no doubt that the messengers would lead them to victory. They would realize their vision of "empire." They would push the gods more and more into the background, which also led to the fact that in the long run, they would be less and less regarded as their emissaries, a point which in Chitam's view would have unpredictable consequences. At some point, the king of Mutal would at best be a governor who continued to oversee public buildings and was allowed to preside over festivities.

Chitam looked at his men, who were not his men after all.

Was this perspective so bad?

The King wasn't sure. He sensed, however, that Inugami's vision went far beyond anything that had ever been done and would cost many more lives than any campaign in Mayan history, including the capture of Mutal by Teotihuacán two generations ago.

Years of blood and tears lay before them.

Or it all turned out quite differently, and the cities, overwhelmed by Inugami's power, eventually submitted voluntarily.

Chitam took a deep breath. He didn't know what he wanted, but he sensed that his ability to implement his own will waned with each passing day. Once Saclemacal fell, it was clear that Inugami was the actual, if not yet official ruler of Mutal. And if the messengers governed two cities, they would make their young man, the son of their own king from their own time, the greatest of all kings, king of kings, something they called Tenno, and every lord of every city would owe loyalty to him alone.

Yes, that was exactly Chitam's problem. He wouldn't become king of kings, but someone else – a stranger who truly didn't deserve it, puppet in the hands of Inugami.

By the gods, how much he hated this thought!

Chitam raised his hands and blessed his soldiers as was his duty. The gesture seemed hollow and empty, though it seemed to fit the men's expectations. He did as he had to do though it didn't fill him with passion.

When he had finished and retired, going down the steps, measured, dignified, with a stony face, he finally disappeared into the group of his servants and priests and hurried to the construction site of the palace. Nearby he had commandeered the magnificent house of a clan-chief, but he didn't feel comfortable there, more like an intruder, reminded of the fact that someone had dared to take his home from him – and that he had been unable to prevent this, another symbol of his increasing powerlessness.

A servant approached him. He bowed submissively. In his closest retinue, he was still the King, and Chitam sometimes felt as though he was cheating on his followers, who saw in him more than he remained to be.

He sighed. These thoughts darkened his mind, obscured the clarity of his thoughts. They led to mistakes, wrong assessments, and they would make him a grim, sad, unjust and ultimately unbearable man. His father had sought death because he believed that his son Chitam would be better able to cope with the new and unfamiliar situation. That thought alone should set him up. He owed it to his father not to let himself be dragged down by the maelstrom of gloom in his mind, falling into an abyss from which he might not be able to ascend back up again.

The servant, an old man who had served his family for a long time, approached and asked to speak close the ear of the King. Chitam's retinue kept a respectful distance at once. It had to be a confidential matter.

Chitam bowed his head and felt the breath of the man in his right ear, as he began to whisper softly.

"Lord, you have visitors. The guest wished ... to meet you secretly. I put him in a room where he is waiting for you. If you want to see him ..."

Chitam frowned, grateful for the distraction. He always felt better when he was able to devote himself to tangible problems.

"Who is it?"

"One of the warrior-slaves. The one who saved your daughter's life."

"Balkun? He is always welcome. But secretly?"

"Only I know of his arrival."

"It is good. Where?"

Chitam straightened, made a gesture, and dismissed his retinue. He removed his magnificent but very impractical headdress and handed it to one of the servants. There was still some time left before the army would march off. He could still take care of this. Something told him that it was well-invested time.

Balkun was waiting for him in the small room, and when Chitam entered, he threw himself on the floor in front of the King.

Chitam closed the heavy curtains behind him.

"Get up, Balkun. I'm in your debt. You don't have to humiliate yourself before me."

The addressed man rose hesitantly and nodded. Chitam immediately realized that a problem was bothering the warrior. It was very unfortunate that Inugami had failed to fulfill his request to release him from slavery. It was very, very unfortunate that the King of Mutal could only ask the Lord of the messengers and that he had had to accept the man's dismissive decision.

"What are you up to, Balkun? Here, we sit."

The warrior took his place, as did Chitam. He needed a moment, then words gushed out of Balkun.

"Lord, I have something to tell you – a memory from the night your palace was set ablaze. I ... I have kept it to myself so far. But now we are facing a campaign, and I fight on the front line. However superior we may be, it may well happen that I won't survive this fight. The gods are unfathomable in their counsel. But if I die, my knowledge is lost. That mustn't be, at least, I think so." Balkun hesitated. "Sometimes it's better to take things to the grave. But in that case, my conscience urges me to reveal something to you, though I can not foresee where it leads to."

Chitam was attentive, curious. He raised his hands. "Speak, Balkun, and if it is your will, I won't tell anybody what you reveal to me."

"I gladly accept your promise, but I'm not sure you'll be able to keep it."

"You doubt my word?" Chitam's question sounded not aggressive but genuinely interested.

Balkun hastily made a negative gesture. "There are situations in which it will become clear who you must have received this information from. But I'm aware of this risk. Speaking to you gives me a feeling of liberation. The danger is very present, and you can hardly protect me. Seen that way ..." Balkun sighed briefly. "It wouldn't be bad if I found my end in Saclemacal."

Chitam shook his head. "We don't want to talk like that, Balkun. So speak, what is on your mind regarding the events of that night?"

"For a brief moment, I saw the people who talked to the arsonist, gave him the material for his crime, and so I regard them as his employers or supporters."

Chitam's eyes narrowed. "Someone I know?"

"Nobody I know in person, so I can't tell."

"So what's your secret?"

Balkun stretched, his face strained, as if he had to squeeze out the next words with willpower.

"One of these men was undoubtedly a messenger of the gods, my lord."

Chitam stared at Balkun, as if he couldn't quite grasp the meaning of these words, but then he nodded slowly, very slowly, as if this would help to classify the statement correctly and give a fitting answer.

"I should ask," he said slowly, "if you are sure, Balkun."

"I am indeed."

Chitam saw no hesitation and no doubt in the face of the Yaxchilan man, and so he believed him. The King closed his eyes for a moment. He wasn't that surprised. It was wonderfully befitting. Just as he was thinking of what role he played in the great plans of the messengers, they did their own considerations. And someone – probably Inugami himself – had come to the conclusion that the best solution would be to eliminate the stubborn king and then either choose a new candidate of his own or immediately overthrow the old system altogether.

What did that mean?

Well, since this attempt failed, there would undoubtedly be more.

Chitam felt cold, although the morning already began to develop the familiar, oppressive sultriness. It was by no means the rule that Mayan kings fell through internal revolts or assassinations. It happened, certainly, as there were sometimes extreme situations, such as particularly hated or incompetent rulers, injured vanities, or the helping hand of a foreign rival. But if a Mayan king died violently, it was usually directly at the hands of the enemy, either in combat or subsequently as a prominent sacrifice in a ceremony for the gods of the victor.

What should he do? How to protect his family?

Balkun didn't say anything, and Chitam sensed how he was being watched by him, not without pity, but above all relieved to be rid of the information that had been in his heart. Chitam could imagine that this knowledge must've been a burden, and he knew it because he now felt the weight on his own shoulders.

"Thank you, Balkun," he said finally.

"What will you do?"

Chitam looked searchingly at the man. Was he honest and trust-worthy enough to talk to him about these things? Didn't he have to be someone who in the end was more loyal to his master than to him? It was difficult to assess Balkun because Chitam was convinced that the man wanted one thing above all else: to return home to his family and there, more or less, to be left alone.

What would he be willing to do if he had the serious prospect of fulfilling his wish?

"I have to think about it," the King said.

"If I ..."

"No fear. No one will know it from me."

Balkun hesitated but left it at that. Chitam didn't mind his doubts. Who would trust a king who owed no account to anyone but the gods? And these, in turn, were apparently not very happy about Chitam of Mutal when they sent messengers who tried to burn him alive.

Chitam was certain that the gods had little to do with all this, and that the strangers, mysterious as they were, pursued goals and intentions that a priest would only be able to explain if he was an expert in power-politics.

Balkun got up. "If I may leave you now, my lord? If I'm absent for too long, it raises questions."

Chitam waved. "Go. I wish you a successful fight, a victory, and your survival." He meant that honestly.

"Thank you, my lord." Balkun bowed before pushing aside the heavy curtains in front of the doorway and leaving behind a very thoughtful and increasingly depressed King of Mutal.

Chitam just sat there for a while. He failed to make a clear decision. He was scared of so many things: his life and that of his family, the traditions of his city, the future that now seemed so unpredictable. In the past, the prophecies and invocations of the priests had been something that gave a sense of direction and confidence, but today all this seemed stale and empty. The messengers turned everything upside down and robbed him of all the confidence he had. He could no longer even trust his own people, the closest advisers and servants, for it was difficult to gauge how many of them were already infected by the grandiose vision of Inugami and, in case of doubt, would also decide against their King.

Chitam had always known that the office of the ruler of Mutal was a lonely one, one reason why he had wished his father a long, healthy life. He hadn't expected, however, that this loneliness would manifest in this brutal way. It was very depressing.

Chitam suppressed his desire for large quantities of chi. That would be the easy way, combined with the wonderful excuse of getting intoxicated to gain a vision of the gods who should give him direction. But Chitam found that the gods had intervened enough and had little to say to him, if he had attracted their displeasure. Inugami may not be a messenger of the gods, but his mere arrival and existence was tolerated by the heavenly powers. And if they gave him the victory over Saclemacal, it was clear that Chitam's fate unfortunately played only a very minor role for these higher beings.

So what was there to do?

Chitam got up. Soon he would leave and fight. If he was lucky, fate would solve the problem for him. A spear, a blow from a mighty warrior, no matter, a quick end that would relieve him of all melancholy. A clean solution that ended all worries.

He felt that even this hope wouldn't be fulfilled. But the upcoming fight helped him concentrate. He was supposed to solve a task. After that, he would continue watching.

But he already made a decision.

Two hours later, when he was on his way to Saclemacal on foot, to prove his friendly ways with the warriors and because the exercise helped to occupy his mind, he was almost in a good mood. His wife and two daughters were also traveling. They would get shelter with their clan, fake fatigue and fear of another attack on the palace, move into a beautiful villa on the outskirts, out of focus, then head off to one of the smaller vassal villages once the soldiers were even further away from any public attention and thus, Chitam hoped, far from any further danger.

He didn't know if that would be enough. But it helped him to regain some inner peace.

33

"It's not quite what I expected."

Dame Tzutz Nik, Queen of Mutal, looked anxiously at Une Balam. There was cause for concern in many ways. Her husband had sent her and her daughters away, and that had made her more unbalanced than she wanted to admit. She understood Chitam's motivations, knew about his fears and the consequent helplessness. That didn't mean that she agreed to be taken out of the line of fire by her husband. She hadn't wanted to cause him any additional trouble and accepted his decision without complaint. But the words had been on her tongue.

This made her current situation even more difficult because she had to encourage Une Balam to something she didn't want to do herself. Therefore, her words lacked convincing power. And Queen or not, her husband's youngest sister always had been remarkably stubborn. This stubbornness became visible down especially when it came to someone else pretending to make decisions for her. Even if she actually agreed to this decision ...

Which was not the case this time and made the discussion even more difficult.

"I'm sorry I didn't meet your expectations, sister-in-law," Une replied, not at all snappy. That made it difficult for Tzutz to be really angry with her.

"Your brother is worried."

"He is the King. That's what he's supposed to be."

"You should really accompany us. It is for your benefit."

"My well-being is in good hands."

"Une ..."

"Did my brother say my name?"

Tzutz sighed. "He said the closest family."

"He didn't call my name?"

"Don't you belong to the closest family?"

Her husband's sister grimaced. "Sometimes this family is like a curse on me. I wish father was still alive."

"That's because he always fulfilled all your wishes."

"I don't deny that. My sister-in-law, I certainly appreciate my brother's concern. And I even believe you, that he has considered me in his directive. Under other circumstances, I would obey this request."

"What's stopping you from doing it now?"

Une said nothing, looked down, and seemed to think carefully of her answer. "There are many reasons, sister-in-law. I'm by no means as in danger as you are. I'm an unmarried relative, not a woman of power. I have the impression that the messengers regard women even less as influential as our own men."

"That is possible. But the danger is only a bit smaller for you. You shouldn't feel too safe, that could be deceiving."

"There is someone among the strangers who will most probably protect me any time."

Tzutz's eyes widened. "Une! What are you telling me?"

The Princess laughed. "You are not so naive, are you? My brother himself has repeatedly emphasized to others that he wouldn't mind if I looked at the representative of Inugami, the man named Aritomo Hara. He thinks he is more accessible than his master."

Tzutz shared her husband's assessment. "You tell me that you succeeded?"

"Absolutely not. I have never exchanged more than a few words with him."

"I beg your pardon?"

"He surely is nice. I take him as being quite closed up. Too much work for me, with little chance of a quick success."

"Une!"

The Princess shrugged. "I took the man whom the other messengers call the Gaijin. Lengsley. A smart man but not too smart." She hesitated, smiling thoughtfully. "He has other advantages."

Tzutz decided not to press for details now. Maybe later, but now other topics were more urgent.

"Does Chitam know about it?"

"I haven't told him yet. But it's not a big secret either. Lengsley has been my guest once or twice, and we have not only dined or improved our language skills. I have no great faith in the ability of the palace servants to maintain discretion. I think Chitam or you could have known about it if you were really interested in my whereabouts."

No reproach in her voice, a simple statement.

"Good," Tzutz said. "Or not so much. Lengsley seems to me to be somewhat isolated among the messengers. He looks different. He speaks differently. He doesn't seem to have many friends. I often see him in the company of Aritomo Hara. Maybe your preferences are not so far away from your brother's wishes."

Une smiled. "That wasn't my main motivation."

"Of course not."

"Can he protect me? I think so. His work is appreciated. He has a lot of knowledge. I was allowed to convince myself of that."

"Une!"

"Your imagination is your problem."

Both women shook their heads, albeit for different reasons.

"It's too dangerous," Tzutz muttered.

"Tell Chitam, if he should ask, who is better at getting secrets from an important man than a beautiful woman holding his balls in her hand?"

"Une!"

"Why was I supposed to give Aritomo advances at Chitam's behest?"

"Une!"

"My brother will understand what I mean."

Tzutz looked outraged at her sister-in-law. "Une, let me remind you that my husband has no secrets from me!"

The sister-in-law looked appraisingly at her, her eyes finally fixed on her hands. "You have strong fingers."

"Une!"

254

Tzutz realized that they wouldn't come to any conclusion in this. She got up. Time was pressing. Her own departure approached. She couldn't try to persuade her stubborn sister-in-law forever. In the end, Une would always do what she thought was right. The women hugged each other, short but firm and tight. They might not agree on everything, but, no matter how annoying it sometimes could be, they were family. And a special family too.

"All the best and a good trip," said Une Balam in a husky voice. "Watch my nieces above all else."

"And a safe stay," the Queen replied. "Look after yourself and disappear if Chitam's fears prove true. Don't say that these are only doom shots. I'm convinced that there is a real danger."

Tzutz had withheld from her sister-in-law one piece of information about the history of the arson attack on the palace. Chitam didn't want that to go round. Tzutz had had to use her strong fingers with great skill to get that fact out of him last night.

Of course, although she had played the indignant, she knew exactly what her sister-in-law was talking about.

They finally parted.

Tzutz left the building where her sister-in-law was housed, accompanied only by two servants. There were still a few things to pack for her although she would only move to the outskirts of the city. She was in thought, planning and brooding, and when she arrived at the house she currently occupied after the fire, she immediately gave her instructions. Satisfied, she realized that everything had already been well-prepared. There was not much work for them anymore, which was a stark contrast to the hectic activity of the last few hours. She could actually rest until she left, but she found no relief, walked around, monitored, commented, and, in short, annoyed everyone except that no one dared to tell her.

Her activity, however aimless, hindered everyone not only through the fact that her involvement disturbed more than helped but also led her servants to overlook another important detail: that one of them disappeared for a moment, crossed the street, and gesticulated to a man. He wore the clothes of a peasant, with a hat drawn low in his face. But on closer inspection, one might have noticed that this man had a striking resemblance to one of the two bodyguards of the young prince the messengers carried along.

This knowledge would've given her a lot to consider.

34

Inugami looked through the binoculars and took his time. Regardless of his well-groomed confidence in showing everyone that he had everything under control, that he always knew the right answer to all questions, and that the situation always developed as he saw fit, he didn't fool himself: He wasn't an infantryman. Like all Japanese naval officers, he had enjoyed a general basic training that hadn't been restricted to maritime aspects. But then he had specialized quite quickly, and when it became clear that the submarine fleet would be his area of responsibility, this specialization had taken on even greater proportions. Inugami knew, theoretically, how to wage war in the countryside. But it was just a theory. To be honest with himself – and he did that more often than others sometimes trusted him to do –, he also knew maritime warfare only from theory. The submarines on which he had served had never been sent to battle, apart from a brief engagement in the Russo-Japanese War, which hadn't contributed much to the glory of this part of the navy. And here weren't even the weapons at his disposal whose use and installation he had once learned. And the soldiers he commanded here neither spoke his language nor were they …

Inugami searched for words.

What he lacked and what made it so terribly difficult to understand in these Maya was hard for him to express. They were in some ways incomplete people. Yes, they had an impressive architecture, and their absurdly stupid religion had a certain complexity. But they ruled only cities and their surroundings, their language sounded strange and inaccessible to Inugami's ears – although he forced himself to learn it –, and their whole culture, their food … everything was unbearably different.

And so he thought to change, to educate, to civilize these savages.

He wanted to make *real* people out of them.

To do that, he had to make them forget everything that had previously kept them from true civilization, and he had to teach them what it meant to be a refined person. The prerequisites for this lesson were obedience and submission to a superior will.

His will.

However, to gain ensure their loyalty, a victory was required, and many other victories to follow.

That was Inugami's big challenge.

He didn't understand the Maya. He didn't *want* to understand them. That was meaningless to him. He wanted to control them and mold them to his will. It was a big project, and maybe he wouldn't finish it in his lifetime. But as a descendant of an ancient culture with a strong sense of history, the officer was able to think in epochs. He started a new era. That was his mission and his vision. What he lacked in understanding, he had to make up for through dynamism, through brilliant example, through fame, and rapid wealth. The Maya understood the basic concepts of power and influence very well. They linked them to strange and obscure religious beliefs whose purpose Inugami was alien to – in fact, he was absolutely sure that they basically didn't contain any.

He had to take all this and smash it in order to reshape it. Just as he had taken the prisoners of war, smashed their origins and their old loyalties, and reshaped them as a unit. They represented the prototype of the empire he intended to found, and they were also the instrument he was planning to use for that purpose.

And this fight against the city of Saclemacal had to set the tone, to represent the first step. The victory had to be perfect, the triumph absolutely. Not a bit less than the perfect military attack. After the successful defense of Mutal, Inugami had to prove that he was able to beat an opponent completely without the holy vessel in the background. His superiority had to be so overwhelming that any potential criticism of his ability to win – and thus to establish the empire he had set himself as a goal – became silent.

Not only with the Maya, with troublemakers like Chitam, who apparently still believed in his own grandeur while it had already shrunk significantly. Even among those in his own crew whose enthusiasm he missed or seemed faked. Unfortunately, there were very intelligent and capable men he relied on. Aritomo Hara was at the top of the list, and he worried Inugami. Lengsley, the Briton, was an unsure companion by its very nature alone. Sawada was old and prone to over-indulgence, which was far from appropriate in such a situation. One or the other name came to Inugami. What worried him greatly was that the young Prince was evidently not overly excited about becoming an emperor, as Inugami had intended for him. The Prince was, Inugami dared to formulate this thought, so far a veritable disappointment. Here the officer was in a deep dilemma. His great reverence for the imperial family, trained in his earliest years, was in clear, irresolvable contradiction to his estimation of the Prince's potential. How was he supposed to deal with this question?

Inugami tried to concentrate on the task at hand. From the hill, he had an excellent overview of Saclemacal. The city lay peacefully at dawn. Of course, the deployment of troops from Mutal hadn't gone unnoticed. But what should the inhabitants of the city do? Most of their soldiers had been killed or captured in an attack on their neighbors. Some of them now returned as Inugami's soldiers, and they would have to excel in order to dispel any suspicion of lack of loyalty. Everyone who betrayed him was dead. That had been unmistakably communicated to the troops.

The Lord of Saclemacal might have a reserve force, and some of his warriors had escaped from the turmoil of the Battle of Mutal and returned home. But that could never be enough to effectively defend the city. But had other cities left men in Saclemacal because they expected exactly what Inugami intended to do? Did the alliance of the three cities go so far as to be mutually supportive in defense?

The march directly southward hadn't taken too long. They had reached not only the city but also the great lake in its vicinity – Saclemacal was of interest to Inugami mainly because it was a port city. This made it a potential access point to open up new transport routes. From here, the road to the west was also under control, to Holtun, from where the traveler easily reached a western group of Mayan cities – Topoxte, Yaxha, both located on a smaller lake, and the larger metropolises Nakum and Maxam. The latter city was of particular interest to Inugami, as it was regarded as quite powerful and a direct competitor to the rulers of Mutal, more suitable opponents than the small Saclemacal, which could hardly defend itself.

But one after the other.

Inugami lowered the binoculars and turned around. Ahk sat next to him. The man was a good ten years older than Inugami and had been proposed to him by Chitam as a kind of general. Although the King was among them and formally had supreme command, he left the subtleties of tactics and organization of the troops to the nobleman, who had already served his father as warlord. The man with the weather-beaten face, who had used the binoculars without further hesitation and who seemed to be particularly pleased with the prospect of fighting against the traitors of Saclemacal, had proved to be uncomplicated. He seemed to be able to submit to the leadership of Inugami without any problems and was also ready to deploy the official army of the city in close coordination with Inugami's janissaries. He also knew the area well – much better than the Japanese – and shared his knowledge generously.

Inugami coped well with such people. They were almost real people for him.

He looked at him encouragingly.

"I have seen no one," said Ahk, appearing so relaxed in the presence of the messenger as though he had never done anything but talk to a celestial minister about military issues. "I don't think there are more than a handful of ready-to-fight men there. I also assume that we won't fight a battle and we'll shed no blood. We should march open and force the king of the city to surrender. It would be helpful. We save men for the really important opponents."

Both agreed that at the latest Yaxchilan would prove to be a much tougher nut. Inugami was on a fast campaign. He didn't want to leave Mutal in Aritomo's hand for too long. He had to keep an eye on things himself. The question therefore was: continue to Tayasal and attack the next city, or return and enjoy the triumph and use it politically?

260

The captain was still undecided. A quick win without a fight would, of course, suggest an immediate continuation of the campaign. It would be expected of him, it was a matter of credibility. Inugami acknowledged that, despite his power, he began to be guided by external expectations and influences. That was probably called politics. He would have to get used to it, for as much as he looked down on the Maya and their primitiveness, he needed the appropriate human material to make his plans come true.

Plans.

Which brought him back to the task at hand.

"Work is being done in the fields. I hardly see any warriors," Inugami said.

"There will be scouts who have been hidden from us," the general replied.

"What can they do more than watch the approaching disaster?"

"Nothing."

"Can we expect a desperate act? A big mass suicide?"

Ahk looked at the Japanese strangely. The question was not completely absurd. There were situations in which suicide was acceptable even among the Maya, a kind of honorable way out of a lost situation. But this was by no means common and usually affected only individuals.

"Hardly," the nobleman said finally. "If someone kills himself before our attack, then it'll be the hapless king, to save himself the shame of submission. His son will expect us to confirm him in office, demand a tribute, acknowledge the formal supremacy of Mutal, and return home afterwards."

Inugami nodded. Lasting conquests certainly occurred in the history of this people, but were by no means the rule. In a successful campaign, the opponent submitted, if he got the opportunity to do so. Kings continued to rule or were replaced by a new dynasty that swore allegiance to the victors – which didn't always last too long because at the latest the sons were often no longer bound by the promises of their fathers. It rarely happened that governors were deployed and soldiers were stationed. Each warrior was always a farmer who was needed at harvest and sowing season and therefore had to return home after the end of an attack to tend to the fields. Only the nobility and priests could afford to be permanently involved in the task of government or spiritual considerations. But that was not enough to govern a once conquered city permanently and directly.

Inugami thought to change that.

He just didn't know exactly how.

It all depended on how they would be received in Saclemacal.

"We take the risk," he said finally in English, the language Ahk had learned with great zeal and in which he was better than the Japanese in the Mayan idiom, which was still causing him considerable problems.

They rose and went back to the waiting army. An officer of the warrior-slaves saluted and reported in front of him like a Japanese soldier, and Inugami was glad that the familiar gesture had become such a flair for the men. There was nothing like a proper drill, he thought.

Nothing had happened. No contact. No attacks. Was that a good or a bad sign?

Inugami decided to find out. "We start marching. The arranged formation."

Orders were issued. Activity broke out. Inugami watched as Chitam gave instructions. He allowed himself a smile. Soon the King of Mutal wouldn't bother him anymore. Soon this problem would be a thing of the past. And the King would take care of it himself. He just didn't know it yet.

Inugami took his position in the formation.

Nobody could accuse him of cowardice. He may have other uncharacteristic traits, in many ways he was too arrogant, too harsh, inconsiderate, no doubt a racist, convinced of his holy mission, perhaps a little megalomaniac.

But he was not cowardly.

He checked his pistol and found everything in perfect order. He saw the onager they had carried on the cart into position. For them, there were good positions from which they could target the city. Militarily irrelevant, psychologically important.

262

The Japanese man stood at the head of his warrior-slaves, surrounded by their officers, and thus a target for a daring, rapid attack that could lead to the death of the messenger with luck.

Inugami also took that risk. If he wasn't ready to endanger his imperial dreams, he was not worth those dreams. He would prove himself worthy of destiny, and destiny was worthy only of those who could justifiably claim the triumph on the front line. Inugami was aware that he needed to be a role model in these matters. He needed loyalty, and he instilled it by living up to what he asked of his subordinates.

An important step. A central task.

"Forward! As ordered!" The Japanese bellowed, and a polyphonic answer, that had to be audible in Saclemacal, was the answer. No reason for secrecy.

They should hear it.

Inugami took the first step to fulfill his destiny.

35

Ixchel watched her mother and learned that she was sad and worried. She didn't always know her mother to be cheerful and boisterous, especially since she had become Queen of Mutal, but Tzutz was not a woman who was constantly downcast by fears. Ixchel, the eldest daughter of the royal couple at the age of thirteen, had also learned this from Tzutz, and that was fine. The nightly arson attack on the palace had frightened her greatly, but the courageous intervention of Balkun had saved not only her younger sister Nicte's life but also her own, since she had been warned in time and escaped the inferno unscathed.

Now they left.

Their stay on the outskirts of Mutal had not lasted long. Tzutz had been seized by a great deal of restlessness, transmitted to her companions and her two daughters. They had barely unpacked the numerous things they had taken along on their way through the city. Tzutz had immediately brought the onward journey across the narrower city limits in a neighboring village into conversation, as if she wanted to put a long distance between themselves and ... yes, probably the messenger as soon as possible.

Ixchel tried to understand her mother. The arrival of the messengers had been a fascinating and frightening event, there was not the slightest doubt about that. But it was also exciting, with the promise of something new, a change that envisioned great things.

Ixchel had never talked to one of the messengers, only occasionally watched them, and had come to the conclusion that the threat her mother had perceived had escaped her observation. But as things had got worse and worse after the palace's fire, the smart thirteen-year-old had begun to draw certain conclusions she had never shared

264

with anyone. The central conclusion was the assumption that the messengers had something to do with the fire. That would most likely explain her mother's behavior. So that was the basis of their thinking.

But why should the messengers do such a thing?

Ixchel couldn't talk to her mother about it because she was constantly busy with all sorts of things, as if her attention alone would ensure that everything was in order. Her friends, mostly daughters of other high nobles, stayed behind in Mutal. Her younger sister understood these things even less than she did. Then there were still servants – who didn't take part in this kind of conversation – and the numerous guards, fierce-looking warriors, who felt the same discomfort that was affecting their mother – probably a major reason why they had been selected for their watch.

Ixchel felt left alone. Sure, she was cared for and served, and everything ... but that was about it. After all, she had resumed the lessons her father had once forbidden, now tolerated, almost encouraged by Tzutz, who suddenly enjoyed watching her daughter learn something normally reserved for men: dealing with the atlatl. Her teacher, both then and now, was Aktul, one of the king's bodyguards, a man of advanced age and slow-limbed, who was still in their service only because both Chitam's father and Chitam himself were connected in friendship and gratitude to the old man. But as old as the bones of Aktul were, once he held the spear-thrower in his hands it seemed to enliven him, and he was still difficult to beat in marksmanship.

There was a worse pastime than practicing with the old man. She was pleased with his praise and steadily improving targeting skills, the strength of her arms, and the force with which she sank the ejected spear into the designated targets. She liked to feel the power of her body, the soreness the next day, and the amazement in the maidservant's eyes, when she ate with a craving that could be traced back to the physical effort.

As her mother allowed her to do this, she must have had the greatest fears for her daughter's safety. That was Ixchel's conclusion, and it scared her. But Tzutz didn't talk about it, just drove the workers, and when they were ready to leave one morning, there was a mixture of relief and constant worry in their mother's face, and Ixchel grabbed the spear-thrower and a few projectiles in her private luggage, which she refused to be taken by anyone.

The porters set off. Tzutz and her daughters were carried in litters. The road was clear and led past fields passing a small piece of forest to the east. Everyone expected no more than a two days' journey, and Ixchel was eager to get out of the swinging litter and use her own legs as quickly as possible, even if it was considered unseemly at the moment.

But the atlatl, she kept close.

Adults were, Ixchel knew that for a long time, rarely consistent.

They had traversed the outer fields around Mutal at noon, and although Ixchel was not feeling well in the litter, she had become a bit sleepy. Under the small canopy, it was stiflingly hot; its only real advantage was that it protected from somewhat annoying insects. But she would have given a lot now ...

She began to doze, her mind wandering around. She didn't sleep, but she was no longer awake. Soon she could no longer distinguish between real perception and dream. The sounds of the environment faded into the background. The swaying of the litter seemed almost pleasant. She curled up and gave herself up to the feeling. Sleep was much better than endless hours ...

Then her head went up.

Someone screamed.

It was not an oppressed cry, like when a sharp stone entered your the sandal or an unfortunate tripping, it was the scream of a man who was just realizing that he was dying.

Ixchel knew this sound.

Fighting!

The litter jerked, Tzutz held her daughters, slid sideways, then slumped to the floor, crying, and then someone tore off the cloths.

It was Aktul.

He was bleeding. Ixchel stared at the red liquid as if she didn't want to realize what she saw there.

266

"Run!" he shouted. "Get away from here. A betrayal, mistress!"
Fighting indeed.

Screams. Weapons. Death.

The impressions pounded in on the girl, and only slowly did reality enter her consciousness, trigger fear, make her body tremble.

Ixchel looked with wide eyes as one of the men was impaled by her bodyguard; the spearhead came out of his body at the back, with such force the attacker had driven the weapon into him. A gurgle was all that was audible from the victim, and when the attacker let go of the useless weapon, he sank to the ground. He looked around as he fell, staring straight into Ixchel's eyes, with pain, despair, and a plea for forgiveness.

"Down there!" Aktul shouted, pointing to the edge of the woods. Enemies came rushing, all with covered faces, hoods hiding their identity. Aktul's spear described a wide arc, guided by a practiced hand, old, but with all the strength yet to be mobilized. The sharp obsidian blade went through the throat of a man. Blood spattered, the victim pressed his hands at his open neck, staggered backwards, his scream drowned in the liquid spewing out. Someone screamed, loud, sounding alarmed.

Ixchel looked around, expecting that it had been Nicte, and then realized that her own mouth was open and she had uttered the cry.

Her mother took her hand, pulling the smaller sister with her, stumbling in the direction that had been directed by Aktul. The old man showed great energy in the face of danger, and the attackers paid tribute to him by pressing on with vigor.

Ixchel was pulled into the undergrowth.

As if suddenly grown from the ground, a man appeared in front of her. He stood ten feet away in the woods, like a ghost appearing out of nowhere. She opened her eyes wide, and there was another cry, this time from her mother's mouth, pushing her children behind her. The man was not a Mayan warrior but one of the two bodyguards of the prince of the messengers, one of whom who never left the side of the strange boy.

Her mother was right, it shot through Ixchel's mind. She was right in everything!

The man didn't say a word, his face a motionless mask. He raised a thing, one of the thunderous metal pipes, and without hesitation he squeezed it.

Ixchel heard the bang and saw the fire from the mouth of the pipe.

Then nothing happened. She was unhurt.

"Mother?"

Tzutz stood and looked down at herself. Her dress was of a radiant, damp red that her daughters had never seen before. She groaned, only very softly and very briefly. She looked at Ixchel, and her eyes were filled with fear for the well-being of her daughters. Her pupils veiled, and all her strength left her. Then she collapsed, silent forever.

Ixchel took a step back, looked at her mother's body, understanding what she saw there. Her little sister cried and came toward her, but Ixchel could only grab her and clasp her tightly. There was no grief in her, no horror, though both would surely come later. There was a strange feeling in her that she had rarely felt in her life and whose power filled her to the last fiber of her slender body. She watched herself extracting the atlatl, then pushing Nicte away, ignoring the sister's questioning, tearful face, exploiting the apparent indecision of the assassin, who looked at the girls as if he didn't know what to do with them.

A whirring sound, then the man woke up and moved quickly.

Not quick enough.

The spear-thrower released its projectile and scraped deeply through the skin on the shoulder of the messenger, who screamed, backed away, stumbled backward, and fell to the ground into the undergrowth. His weapon escaped him, and with a quick, flowing movement Ixchel picked it up.

It was warm.

A noise made her whirl around. It wasn't her sister, who had sunk to the ground, sobbing beside her mother's lifeless body, but Aktul, covered in blood, though in possession of all his limbs, looking with deep pain in his eyes at the Queen's corpse. Then he saw the two children alive and replaced the pain with sudden, wild determination.

"We must go!" he said softly, insistently, through the tears and cold rage with the strength of his voice.

"Where to, Aktul?" Ixchel asked, still clinging to the strange weapon.

"Just away. First of all, just away, before they find us. Whoever wishes your mother to die will not shy away from you and Nicte."

Ixchel wasn't so sure if that was true. The messenger had hesitated too long for that. His reaction had come only after she reached for the weapon. Maybe the assignment had been different. Perhaps ...

"Away," she said, nodding, grabbing her sister's arm, who let itself be pulled. "Get away from here."

Aktul pointed into the forest, deeper into the undergrowth, and Ixchel merely nodded. The old man raised his obsidian blade and marched off.

The two girls followed him, softly, but now and then a wail arose the younger daughter and Ixchel clutched her arm tightly, transmitting her strength and determination, enough for two, enough for her dead mother and her ignorant father, who would no doubt return from Saclemacal to meet his ruin and Ixchel, of which she was suddenly very sure, would never see him again in her life.

They ran.

They just ran.

Aktul pointed the way, but Ixchel knew that there could be only one direction at this time: deeper and deeper into the forest, farther into the woods, away from the road and the assassins still fighting the surviving bodyguards.

But the sounds became quieter, and Aktul slowed down. He made gestures, and Ixchel understood. The old man grabbed her sister and picked her up, the girl let it happen. He knew Aktul, he was an uncle, a familiar face and no danger.

"Quiet now," the warrior whispered. "We're sneaking, we're not leaving a trail, we're not scaring any more animals. We walk through the forest like shadows. Shadows are still, quieter than the whispering wind. Can you be like the shadows?"

The girl in his arms nodded and rested his head on his shoulder, closed her eyes, remained motionless, and Aktul stroked his hair.

He looked at Ixchel. She had been in the woods many times, too often, as Tzutz complained, and too often without proper escort or with children of commoners who were no adequate companionship for her. She had injured herself, met animals, had fallen and stumbled, but with each visit a little less.

"Like a shadow," she whispered.

Aktul grinned encouragingly, turned around, lifted his foot, searched for the right step, strode forward. Slowly, quietly. No branch was moved. No bird fluttered. Ixchel slid across the floor behind him, her steps even lighter, her slender body hovering over the fouling, her eyes constantly searching for something that might accidentally make a noise and therefore be avoided.

They disappeared in the forest, leaving behind death and betrayal.

Ixchel knew that one day she would return here. This was the road to Mutal, her home, and there now ruled those who sought to destroy her family, who had murdered her mother and betrayed her father.

Oh yes, she would come back here, someday.

Like a shadow.

Epilogue

Marcus Vicinius Langenhagen took a deep breath and inhaled the fresh sea air. He stood at the far end of the pier, which stretched a good two hundred meters into the Atlantic Ocean, and when he directed his gaze in a certain angle, he could almost forget the existence of the expedition vessels that were being equipped behind him as they disappeared out of his sight. Of course, this was just an illusion that lasted for a moment. The sounds of the hustle and bustle were barely fading. The supplies were brought aboard the steamboats, food, hard coal, water, medicines, other essential items. In three days the preparations should finally be completed, then the Emperor intended personally come to Burdigala and attend the farewell ceremony. Langenhagen didn't know if he should be pleased about this prospect. On the one hand, this date would mean the longed-for end of the lengthy preparation period, on the other hand everyone was aware that Emperor Haraldus, son of Thomasius, and with all his privileges in now a quite advanced age, was a thoroughly angry man and had not been particularly enthusiastic to give the post of expedition's commander to Langenhagen. Admiral Marcellus had finally convinced Haraldus with his arguments, but only with great difficulty. This put considerable pressure on Langenhagen: first of all the Admiral's expectations that his appointment, which had cost him political capital, was not a wrong decision; then that of the Emperor, who had had to get through and had to prove to the young officer, grandson of one of the legendary time-travelers, that he was not a creature of political intrigues and cliques but simply an excellent naval officer and cartographer, one who knew exactly what he had to do.

He turned around, destroying the brief illusion. Three frigates, all Dahms-class frigates, were an uplifting sight. They were three-masters, their slender hull no longer reminiscent of the lumbering first- and second-generation steamers. They could maneuver in any weather, both under steam and under sail. Each of the three frigates was about eighty feet long, each carrying twenty-two cannons in its iron-studded wooden hull. They were warships, but with fewer soldiers for this expedition, in order to carry scholars and, unfortunately, politicians – diplomats, as the Emperor called them, especially the young Senator Adrianus – who wanted to make a name for himself and at least had the courage to participate in such an expedition.

Probably to build reputation at the expense of the commander, Langenhagen thought again and again. So far, however, the senator had behaved perfectly impeccably, one had to grant him that. Hopefully it would stay that way.

The sight of the three ships under his command filled the officer with pride. The *Gratianus* was the flagship of the expedition, with a pedigree back to the very first steamboats built more than 70 years ago. The two other frigates were called *Rheinberg* and *Saravica*, also both names which had a deep historical significance in the Roman fleet. The actual ship of the name *Saravica* had been in a large dry dock near Ravenna for years, carefully preserved as far as possible, since it had been finally cleared out of the water ten years ago and turned into a museum. The Academy had previously been assigned all the important machinery and tools to guarantee the officer training, whose product Langenhagen also was.

A fourth ship was now also visible, slightly larger and slightly more bulbous than the three frigates and barely armed. The transport ship was called *Ravenna* and would carry with it many important supplies that were urgently needed for the success of the mission.

Langenhagen marched slowly toward his flagship. The closer he got to the hustle and bustle, the more his presence was noticed, he had to reciprocate greetings and generally make an attentive and interested impression. No one here needed to be overseen by him – the officers of the three ships had the process under control –, and he didn't want to give the impression that he thought it necessary. So he didn't look so closely, perhaps seemed a little lost in thought, and reached the

Gratianus without really having absorbed the events around him in detail. At the railing the ship's second officer stood, Helmut Köhler, the youngest son of the famous crewman of the time travelers, who had brought the curse of brandy and, at least to a great extent, the blessing of coffee to the Empire. Meanwhile almost a folk figure, even years after his death, growing up in the shadow of his father had not been easy for the younger Köhler. Nevertheless, he had completed his career without special protection or promotion and had been selected for this expedition simply because Langenhagen considered him a good man.

Köhler wanted to open his mouth to report, but the Navarch – this rank had been given to him only a few days ago to underline the importance of this expedition – raised a hand and shook his head. He climbed up the gangway and looked around. Everything looked perfect, as one would expect, and the smell of fresh color rose into his nose. The *Gratianus* was not a year old and had already proven itself in many a storm. It was a good ship. The whole class it belonged to was the backbone of the ever-expanding fleet. Three months ago, the other two expeditions had been sent to reconcile the maps they had brought from the future with the facts – and only the senior officers of the fleet knew that another aim of these expeditions was to find out if there were any other time-wanderers besides the British merchants who had fallen into the hands of the Huns and the men of the *Saravica*.

Especially ones that might pose a threat.

An expedition was on its way around the African continent. Since the great canal in Egypt had been rebuilt and renewed, it was a trip that was in itself unnecessary if one wanted to go further east, but it was necessary to keep an eye on developments in Africa. The last third expedition had used the channel and were on their way to India and China.

But he, Langenhagen, would lead the way across the Atlantic toward America, and that was a special task for the Roman in many respects. Everyone knew that Africa and India existed. There were even sporadic trade contacts with China. These lands were far away but understandable, they were among the geographic certainties

273

that the Romans had known before the time-travelers had presented their detailed maps.

But America. The existence of America, that you had to simply believe the time-travelers. That wasn't too difficult for most people. The time travelers didn't invent with these things. But it was quite another issue to venture into a region whose existence you knew only from this one source than to travel where you were reasonably sure to find something.

Langenhagen strove for this security. But the excitement about the new, the unexpected, and the very faintest doubt as to whether one might not ... find *nothing* (or something entirely unexpected) never completely receded.

He went to the quarterdeck, directly to the roofed position where the helmsman stood, sheltered by a wide and thick panel made in the great new glass factory near Rome, made of this precious material once only available to the wealthy but now mass-produced. The room was empty, the big wheel was lashed tight, and Langenhagen leaned over the small card table in the corner, behind which, in a compartment, rolled up, were the carefully copied American maps of the time-wanderers, which he had to correct and falsify. In the future, the coastlines were often different as they had already been able to determine in their comparisons on the Mediterranean. After all, the nature of the maps and the cartographic teaching behind them had led to the updates and re-surveys being made to a very high standard. On each of the three ships resided a trained cartographer, and the only task of these men was to check the maps and create new ones. During the long trip, they also served as assistant cooks, a popular task, as it allowed continuous access to the pantry. Every man on board, except the simple sailors and the soldiers, performed at least two functions. It was a well-trained crew he commanded there.

About 350 men would participate in this expedition. Each of the frigates was crewed with 80 sailors, who were also responsible for the operation of the cannons, whose deployment Langenhagen didn't desire. Fifty men were responsible for the transport ship. In addition, there were sixty marines – they called themselves the "naval legions" – equipped with modern muskets, evenly distributed among the ships. The latest generation of products from the Ravenna gunsmiths had a lot in common with the old assault rifles that had once been brought by the time-travelers. They were no longer loaded from the front like those weapons still used against the Huns, and the powder propellant was carefully packaged in thin paper, better protected against moisture and loss. The muskets could be quickly loaded from behind, into the unfolded tubes, and with their drawn barrels they had a high accuracy of up to 200 meters. That they still carried enough swords and bows – enough to arm the crew – was self-evident. Langenhagen thought of the pistol he kept in his cabin. It was one of seven that still worked, one of the few weapons from the time of Jan Rheinberg that still did its job and for which he possessed three full magazines. The Emperor himself had given him this weapon when he was appointed expedition commander, as well as the navarchs of the other two missions. Langenhagen had received it with great awe and after thorough training had fired three test shots.

He wasn't sure if he was prepared to really view and use this relic, which was still far ahead of the Empire's technology, as a killing tool or as a venerable museum piece to be kept alone. He also hoped he would never have to make that decision, for although an officer of the Roman fleet, the Navarch was a peaceful man deep in his heart and had no ambition to soak his journey with the blood of others. He wanted to draw maps, possibly make contact with those who lived in America – he had some diplomatic authority himself –, and then only make sure that there was no potential threat beyond the ocean.

The small group of eight scientists that the expedition also carried with them was keen to study plants and animals – primarily plants, especially plants that were reported by the time-travelers as medicinal plants, as well as those that promised a potential gain, not least one that bore the name of tobacco and was asked to look for with a special interest. Among the scientists were four women, a fact Langenhagen regarded with some concern. But they were proven experts in their field, and the Navarch trusted in the discipline of his men.

If the conditions permit, they would venture a longer expeditions inland, and for this purpose, the small fleet aboard the Ravenna brought with them a dozen powerful and robust draft horses, whose generous stables had been carefully constructed to give comfort to the stoic animals and to ensure stress-free travels. Three carts with single axles, disassembled into separate parts, were also intended for travel over land.

Langenhagen felt well-prepared. The Empire had spared no expense and effort to equip them for this journey. If he had expressed a wish, it had been fulfilled immediately. The ships were perfectly capable to master high seas and not dependent on the wind, the crew handpicked and motivated. Everyone expected a decent bonus on return, and family members were paid the crewman's pay directly. Those who distinguished themselves here could hope for honors and promotions – and to enjoy attentive listeners and numerous invitations in taverns for the rest of their lives.

Everything was good.

And Langenhagen became more and more nervous every day.

Maybe everything was just too good.

"Navarch!"

The officer looked up.

"We have visitors, Navarch."

Langenhagen frowned angrily. He was fed up with the endless rows of dignitaries, who probably expected an adventurous reputation by being seen here, although they would return to their mansions afterwards, leaving the real adventure to those who were paid for it. He marched to the railing, determined to tell the truth to every person, especially the unheralded one, that they were unwanted. But then he paused when he realized who it was.

There were two visitors. A woman of about 70 years of age, who still resembled the beauty of her youth and who wasn't wearing ornate robes but very practical work clothes, well-known for her appearance throughout the fleet. Her name was Helga Aureliana, she was the daughter of the time-traveling captain Rheinberg and his wife, and unlike what was otherwise expected of Roman ladies, she had devoted herself completely to science, had studied at the

276

Academy of Master Dahms, and now belonged to the best shipwrights of the Empire. She was the model to which the four younger ladies who belonged to the expedition also emulated. The designs of the frigate, which would give Langenhagen and his crews' protection and endurance, went back to her, and although there were still mostly male Romans who considered her profession as unseemly for a woman of Roman nobility, she enjoyed widespread respect. At least from those who had been able to convince themselves that the ships she designed withstand severe storms.

She propped up an old man, who, with very shaky steps, walked down the pier and headed for the flagship. Langenhagen knew him as well. He was over 90 years old, and although he walked upright, he was no longer too steady on his feet. He gripped the handle of a cane with his right hand, his left arm was crossed with the woman's, and so they walked slowly toward Langenhagen. This man too was of general fame in navy circles. He was known to the legionnaires as Magister Sattmann, their teacher at the Academy, not just as a shooting instructor but also as one of the constructors of the modern muskets they would carry with them. Sattmann had actually been retired for many years but was still actively involved in everything that had something to do with his old job. It was no wonder that he showed up here with Helga Aureliana. The few surviving time-wanderers – a small handful of very old men – and their descendants formed a conspiratorial community, connected on many levels with state and business, and sometimes openly, sometimes subtly, exerting influence on the fate of Rome. It helped the Emperor to be part of this group, and at the same time it was his biggest problem. All those Romans who were further away from the prerogatives of power than they thought they should be weren't expected to be too enthusiastic about this close-knit society. Whatever the outsiders had done to good for the Empire, there was no end to courtly intrigues. The great administrative reform of 402, which, among other things, granted the Senate genuine rights to enact laws and granted every Roman landowner the right to vote was still controversial. After all, as a consequence not only old noble families sat in the Senate but also a group of rather pragmatic and well-known upstarts, who knew whom they had to thank for their social advancement. Fortunately, Arianus, their senatorial companion, also belonged to this category.

"I'll help you on board, Magister," Langenhagen called, but the old man waved his hand.

"No need, my friend." Sattmann's voice was still strong and resonant, just as the Navarch had remembered from his training. "I just want to wish you a good trip."

The officer hurried down the gangway and greeted first the woman, then the man with a firm Roman handshake and a kiss.

"I'm hardly happy about visits, but here's an exception," he said with a wistful smile. Helga Aureliana smiled as well and nodded.

"You are now a politician, dear Marcus Vicinius," she said in a confidential tone. They had often met, especially at the preliminary discussions about the equipment of the three expeditions. "You must not pretend that you're just a simple officer who has a difficult task to master."

"I know. And if I encounter something like a state with a government in America, I'm a diplomat as well. But I'm eager to depart. These endless ceremonies and 'informative visits' with all their pomposities are annoying."

"It'll be over soon," Sattmann muttered, his eyes scanning the frigate's lines. His expression showed that he liked what he saw.

"If I were younger, Navarch, I would accompany you," he added. "I've learned to appreciate the sea. I envy you for your task. It may be full of risks, but it is also full of promises, and you are already a historical figure."

Langenhagen raised his hands. "That was never my goal."

"You have no say in these things. You are part of history, whether you want it or not. Believe in an old time-wanderer. I know what I'm talking about."

"The ships are ready," the woman changed the subject. "Can I help somewhere?"

"No," Langenhagen replied honestly, knowing he couldn't insult this woman with the truth. "We are indeed ready. A few supplies are still being loaded. We will receive additional coal. The steam engines are in excellent condition. We even have a refrigerator on

278

board. These ships are the most modern of the fleet. We've done everything possible."

Helga pointed to the long, thin wire stretched on a flexible, thin wooden pole at the frigate's stern. "The shortwave transmitter. You have the latest model?"

"All ships were equipped with it only two weeks ago. We tested everything. The system works perfectly. We hope to stay in touch as long as possible. We also have a complete replacement unit and a portable unit that runs on batteries. Morse signals should be unquestionably received."

"Excellent. What was agreed in regard to reports?"

"I am currently assuming a daily short status report as well as a longer weekly message. If there's anything else to say, fleet command will surely let me know."

"I'll squat on the other end of the line every week," Helga Aureliana promised. "Like the Magister here, I very much wish I could go too."

"If you had requested it, no one would have been able to deny the wish."

She laughed and shook her head. "That's true. But other commitments are more urgent. The draft for the new class of ships is on the agenda. We want to put the first real ironclad on keel already this year. It's supposed to be available in 450 for the big celebration, which means we have about two more years to build it. I would really love to see the ship in my lifetime."

She grinned like a girl. "And besides, I'm really too old for such a long journey, Langenhagen. You just want to flatter me. But I don't fall for that."

Sattmann laughed and chuckled, shaking his head. "Navarch, I'll be dead when you return." Langenhagen returned the old man's gaze and felt a sudden sadness rising at these words. Hardly any time-wanderers were still alive. The youngest of them was in his late 70s, a former oil monkey, no more than a boy when he was taken his voyage. It was quite possible that none of them would be alive when he returned home. The duration of the expedition was officially set to only a maximum of 18 months, but one never knew what was about to happen.

"I want to hurry my mission," he said in a slightly husky voice. "I promised to bring tobacco."

Sattmann made a defensive gesture. "I was never a big smoker. It was good that I got rid of the stuff. I probably wouldn't feel well. I've become so old by renouncing the vice, I suppose."

He nodded, more to himself and then stretched. "Helga, my dear, I'm tired. We only stop the Navarch from important tasks."

"Never!" Langenhagen asserted.

"Don't be too polite. Save your diplomatic skills for those you may encounter in America."

Sattmann handed the officer his forearm, and they kissed their goodbyes. "I wish you God's blessing and all the best for your journey, Navarch," the old man said solemnly. "I'll listen to your reports every week, right to the end."

"I am honored. And I pray that I will be able to tell you personally about my experiences. I am glad that you will follow my descriptions."

"Rather be not. Feels like I want to supervise you. Maybe I'll take control of the transmitter and send you unsolicited suggestions."

"That too will honor me."

"I see diplomacy is good for you, Navarch. You are already a better politician than you would like to believe."

Helga Aureliana put a hand on Langenhagen's shoulder. "Also best wishes from me. See you again at the official farewell. But my blessing is to accompany the whole expedition from now on."

Langenhagen swallowed the lump in his throat, bowed, and then saw how the two old people carefully turned their steps and walked along the pier to the waiting carriage.

He waited for them to get in, then turned and returned to his ship.

The feeling of having lost something very important – and not just him, all of them – didn't want to fade all day.

List of characters

Ahk: military leader from Mutal

Aktul: warrior from Mutal

Balkun: warrior from Yaxchilan

Aritomo Hara: First Officer of Submarine No. 8

Inocoyotl: envoy from Teotihuacán

Tako Inugami: Captain of Submarine No. 8

Isamu: Prince of Japan

Itzanami: priest from Mutal

Ixchel: daughter of Tzutz and Chitam, sister of Nicte

K'an Chitam: Prince of Mutal

K'inich Tatb'u: King of Yaxchilan

Robert Lengsley: British engineer

Meztli: King of Teotihuacán

Nicte: daughter of Tzutz and Chitam, sister of Ixchel

Pakul: military leader from Yaxchilan

Queca: soldier and officer from Teotihuacán

Yuto Sarukazaki: mechanic of Submarine No. 8

Daiki Sawada: tutor of Prince Isamu

Siyaj Chan K'awiil II: King of Mutal

Tzutz: wife of Chitam, Queen of Mutal

Une Balam: sister of Chitam, daughter of Siyaj, Princess of Mutal

Made in the USA
Middletown, DE
21 September 2020

20299890R00157